Gwendolyn: Idlebury Series Book 1

Be Careful

What You Wish For

JM Hughson

Idlebury Books

Lovingly dedicated to my husband, Jack,
who believed in me and gave me the opportunity to achieve my
dream.
And to my mother and father, Alice and Joseph,
who gave me a lifetime of support and encouragement.

In memory of Joseph Moller — THE BEST FATHER IN THE UNIVERSE

Contents

Introduction

NESTLED ON THE edge of the Slothful Forest, Idlebury Castle lay buried by overgrown vines, weeds, and debris from dead trees. Centuries of neglect blocked the sunlight, leaving a sepia hue that hung over the castle, the kingdom, and its people like a fog, rendering everything and everyone drab. Even in the midst of summer, the castle was cold, dark, and dank. The scent of rotting vegetation and animal waste seeped out of the Slothful Forest, making the air in Idlebury most unpleasant. Oddly, the Idleburians didn't seem to notice.

Some said Idlebury Castle's glorious past had been buried along with the hopes and dreams of its haggard, hopeless, helpless people. Even the Slothful Forest's legendary giant sloth refused to venture from the filthy, wretched forest into the boring, loathsome, lonely kingdom of Idlebury.

After years of laboriously meeting the needs of their idle subjects, King Heroian and Queen Filanthropi held out no hope that their people would learn to care for themselves. So they filled their days with constant quests for food, supplies, and support from other kingdoms throughout the many dimensions of the universe. Their frequent quests, which took them through the Slothful Forest, required meticulous planning, for getting lost in the Slothful Forest could result in

1

an accidental visit to the Field of Wisdom, which was located at the forest's farthest edge.

No living Idleburian, not even the king or queen, had ever ventured into the Field of Wisdom. For according to myth, a radiant light would engulf anyone who entered the field, and while under the light's spell, one's self in all its glory would be revealed. But the Idleburians' fear of self-discovery—learning their strengths, understanding their power, releasing their suppressed love, engaging their dormant courage, and gaining personal wisdom—was utterly overwhelming; therefore, totally avoided. For if they viewed themselves as powerful, capable, creative, and loving, they would bear the unbearable responsibility of taking care of themselves. And as they had believed for millennia, being taken care of was their right. As their ancestors before them, they put their faith and future in the hands of the king and queen who worked tirelessly to meet the needs of their ungrateful people.

Day after day, life went on as usual. The king and queen labored. The Idleburians idled. And everyone's lack of a vision for a better future meant no one foresaw the arrival of the child responsible for the salvation of Idlebury and the survival of the universe. And far away in another dimension, the child who wished for power, fame, and glory—but mostly just wanted to escape her boring life in Idleburg, Pennsylvania—had no idea she needed to be very careful what she wished for.

Chapter One
Birth, Death, Lies, and Half-truths

Queen Filanthropi, in her eighth month of pregnancy with what she hoped would be a girl—the next heir to the throne of Idlebury—tossed and turned on her pillow-laden bed in her sparsely decorated bedchamber as she held her swollen abdomen and tried to stifle excruciating pain. Although the stirrings in her abdomen alerted her to the fact that nature was about to take its course, she dare not tell her husband, King Heroian. She was afraid if he knew their child was to be born at any moment, he would delay his trip to Seedonia where he was to meet with her father, King Harvestor, about providing seeds for the planting season.

The king, dressed in full royal regalia, entered the queen's chamber before his departure. Charged with excitement, he was unaware of what stirred beneath his beloved wife's bedcovers. Oblivious to his wife's pain as well as her perspiration-soaked hair and nightgown, he kissed her on the cheek, bade her farewell, and then strode out of the room with the pomp of the powerful man he was.

When the queen heard the hooves of the king's and his entourage's horses fade into the distance, she let out a howl, causing her servants and chambermaids to run to her aid. As they burst into the room, the queen's favorite and most loyal servant, Morgana, yelled commands.

"Summon da doctor. Get a tub of hot water and plenty of rags. Dis baby's comin' early. Dis baby's comin' now."

The queen screamed and cried as the life within her stirred and fought its way into the world. With one final push, the baby was born. The queen lifted her head to see her newborn child and revel in its first wail.

"It's a girl. It's a beau-ti-ful, little girl. We have an heir ta da throne of Idlebury," Morgana declared.

The other servants and chambermaids quickly hugged each other. Some wept with joy. You see, the law of Idlebury was if a king ruled, only a female child could inherit the throne. Likewise, if a queen ruled, only a male child could inherit the throne. No one was sure as to why, but no one questioned this centuries-old tradition.

Morgana smiled as she held the newborn upside down and spanked it firmly on its buttocks. Everyone held their breath as they waited for the new princess to cry with life. But the thrill of the new princess's birth soon vanished. The baby was blue. Morgana spanked it again. The baby didn't respond. She knew if the infant didn't take its first breath soon, it would be stillborn. She spanked it again. No response.

The queen knew all too well the pain of losing a child, for she had been forced to give up her first child, a daughter, and lost a son at birth before the birth of this, her third child. She reached out her arms and through her tears said, "Give me my child. God has other plans for her. Just let me hold her."

Weary and weak, the queen held the princess and gently

stroked her forehead before giving her back to Morgana, who quickly wrapped the infant in a blanket and handed her to a servant named Fredia. "Please take da princess ta me quarters and wait fer da doctor ta meet us der," she requested with urgency.

"Of course," replied Fredia, who appeared weak and pale.

Morgana noticed Fredia's frail appearance but thought it was due to the shock of witnessing the stillbirth of the princess—an experience that's unsettling for anyone let alone a woman due to give birth herself within the next month.

As Fredia headed toward Morgana's quarters, the bundle moved. She thought it was her overactive imagination. After all, she had given birth the night before to a stillborn daughter, but being overwhelmed with sadness, she couldn't bring it upon herself to tell anyone of her misfortune. So she swallowed her grief and went about her daily chores.

When the blanketed infant jerked, followed by the distinct cry of a newborn baby, Fredia dropped to the floor and gently unwrapped the blanket, revealing the most beautiful baby she'd ever seen. She cuddled the newborn princess and rocked her. "Oh, how I wish ya were mine," she said.

Suddenly, Fredia ran with the baby to her quarters. Weak and out of breath, she strained to open the door. After she entered the simple room, she laid the princess on her cot, then pulled a box from under the cot and slowly removed its lid. She tenderly removed the body of her stillborn daughter and placed her next to the newborn princess. Once she'd carefully removed the sleeping princess from the blanket, she wrapped the blanket around her dead daughter. Fredia then swaddled the newborn princess in a sheet before carefully surrounding her with pillows.

Carrying her dead child, Fredia scurried off to Morgana's

quarters. She entered the room only seconds before Morgana and the aging, pudgy Dr. Flabbagast. Startled by their nearly simultaneous entrance, she almost dropped the dead infant.

Morgana took the lifeless child from Fredia, lovingly laid the infant on her bed, and then gently opened the blanket so the doctor could perform his examination. To her surprise, the child had a tuft of blonde hair. She distinctly remembered the princess had beautiful black hair like her mother, the queen. She looked at Fredia and was about to comment when she decided that due to the day's sad event, she may have seen something that wasn't there.

"When was this child born?" Dr. Flabbagast asked as he gently yet thoroughly examined the deceased newborn.

"Just twenty minutes ago," Morgana replied.

"She appears to have been deceased for several hours," the doctor said as he scratched his bald head. "Must have died before she was born."

Dr. Flabbagast's question about the time of the child's birth filled Fredia with so much anxiety that she broke into insane laughter. Morgana, shocked at Fredia's response, reprimanded her and requested she return to her quarters immediately.

"Please excuse her, doctor. She's due ta deliver a child herself in a few weeks and ya know how dat can affect a woman," Morgana said with embarrassment.

The doctor shook his head in agreement and waved his hand to indicate Morgana needn't be embarrassed by Fredia's behavior.

Fredia ran back to her quarters and locked the door. After a few minutes, she screamed as if she were in the throes of labor. Several servants ran to her room, knocked on the door, and pleaded for her to open up. As she continued to scream and cry, she hoped the princess wouldn't make a peep. When she decided enough time had passed, she fell silent. Despite the noise, the little princess was fast asleep. So Fredia gently shook the baby until she awoke and began to wail.

Upon hearing the cry of the newborn baby, a servant pounded on Fredia's door and screamed for her to open up. The servant's knocks and screams were so loud they drew the attention of Morgana, who rushed to investigate the cause of the ruckus.

"What's goin' on here?" Morgana asked as she pushed her way through the crowd of servants. "Fredia, it's me, Morgana. Let me in."

"I'm too weak ta unlock da door meself," replied Fredia. "Der's a key under da mat. Help me... *please*."

Morgana retrieved the key and quickly opened the door to Fredia's room. She gasped when she saw the frail, pale servant sitting on her cot gently rocking a newborn baby who had a headful of pitch-black hair.

"Where'd ya get dat child?" Morgana demanded.

Fredia pulled the newborn baby closer to her chest to keep Morgana from taking the baby away. "I just gave birth ta her meself. She's mine. She's me beau-ti-ful daughter."

"Yer beau-ti-ful daughter?" exclaimed Morgana. "She looks just like da newborn princess."

Morgana picked up a bloodied sheet and clothing and studied them briefly. Noticing the blood was fresh, she dropped them.

"I'm sorry, Fredia. I have accused ya of a horrendous crime dat obviously ya didn't do. Please fergive me."

Fredia pretended a brief faint.

Morgana rushed to her side.

In a weak voice, Fredia said, "I fergive ya. I know how upset ya are 'bout da stillborn princess. We're all so disappointed."

"What's her name?" Morgana asked as she kissed the newborn child on the forehead.

"I think I'll call her Prudence. It's such a pretty name."

"Prudence?" Morgana exclaimed. "Dat were ta be da name of da new princess, had she lived."

"Was it? I didn't know. I just love da name. It does have a royal flair, now don't it? Prudence it is," Fredia said as she lifted the child high for all to see.

Morgana, still unnerved by the infant's striking resemblance to the queen, excused herself and took her leave. As she walked to her quarters for a much-needed rest, she decided the day's events had played tricks on her mind.

After Morgana's departure, the other servants remained for a few minutes to ooh and aah over Fredia's new baby before returning to their chores.

Once Fredia was alone, she laughed to herself, hardly able to believe she'd pulled off such a deception. She looked at the infant sleeping in her arms and rocked her gently. "Prudence, me princess, I'm ya mother. I'm da mother of a princess," she said. "I won't let anyone, not even da queen, take ya from me. No one, not even you, can ever know who ya are. I'll take da secret ta me grave, I will."

As Fredia kissed the princess and savored the sweet scent of the newborn baby, she realized someone was in the room. Her heart pounded with fear at the thought the person had discovered her secret. To her relief, it was only Morgana's five-year-old son, Thane, who many believed to be deaf because of his indifference to others and his refusal to speak.

"Be off with ya, boy," Fredia said as she gestured for Thane to leave.

When the child left the room, Fredia noticed his likeness to the queen and king. He had the queen's black hair and the king's crystal-clear blue eyes. *Just a coincidence,* she thought.

Fredia closed her eyes and held the baby close as she rocked her to sleep. Suddenly, the room became stuffy, the air so heavy that she gasped for breath. Fear overshadowed her joy when she noticed an immense man in a black cape huddled in the corner of her room. "Whaddya want?" she asked in a feeble manner.

The man slowly stood. He opened his cape to reveal a horrifying scene of human suffering. The image of a crumbling castle frightened Fredia. There was no mistaking it; it was Idlebury Castle. As the man spoke, cold air blasted her.

"If you keep the child, all of Idlebury will be damned to an eternity of misery. She is not yours. She belongs to the people. Their very lives depend on her."

"She don't belong ta da people. She belongs ta me... only me."

"*Liar,*" the caped man roared. "You have sealed the fate of Dimension XIII and the kingdom of Idlebury. As Idlebury goes, so goes the universe. There is only one other who can save the universe. Her name is Gwendolyn, but she is not of this world."

The man swirled his cape around his body and disappeared. Fredia noticed the floor on which the man had stood was cracked as if it had supported an enormous weight. She clutched the infant in fear the caped being would magically reappear and snatch the child from her. Panicked, she looked around the small room to make sure he wasn't lurking in a corner. Convinced she and her child were alone and safe, she relaxed her hold on the infant who remained asleep.

Nonetheless, frightening thoughts raced through Fredia's head. *What if da man told da queen dat da princess survived? Surely she'd take da child away from me. What if I'm punished, or worse, killed fer stealin' the princess? What if da man was tellin' da truth and I'm responsible fer da demise of da entire universe?*

"I won't give up me child. She's mine. I don't care what he says," Fredia cried as she crumpled in a heap on the floor, still clutching the infant as if to protect it from evil forces. "Damn Idlebury. Damn Dimension XIII. Damn da universe. Prudence is *mine!*" Fredia rose, placed the infant on her cot, and then paced as she talked to herself. "But wait, he said der's another called Gwendolyn who's not of dis world. What does dat mean? Is der another princess? Surely da queen must know because da child would have ta have been born of her. Hmm… Da queen has a secret. Dis is very good news."

For several months, Fredia lived in fear of what would happen to her, the child, Idlebury, Dimension XIII, and the universe. She couldn't eat or sleep. She became suspicious of everyone and isolated in her quarters. Dark rings encircled her sunken eyes. With each passing day, she looked and acted increasingly deranged.

One morning, the unbearable anxiety about losing her child and the knowledge the queen was hiding a deeply embarrassing secret drove her to confess. She burst into the queen's chamber, frightening Queen Filanthropi who was alone and at the mercy of this mad woman.

At such a rapid pace that the queen couldn't interrupt, Fredia said, "Yer Majesty, fergive me intrusion, but I have been visited by a mysterious black-caped man who foretells of great disaster ta Idlebury and da universe unless da rightful princess inherits da throne. He claims der's such a princess, but she's not of dis world. Only she can save Idlebury and da universe.

Her name is Gwendolyn."

For an instant, Queen Filanthropi appeared confused. Memories flooded back of the child she'd been forced to give up. Rage surged through her as she yelled, "Be off with you, you impertinent woman. And do not speak of the caped man to anyone... not *ever*."

Fredia curtsied and slowly backed out of the queen's chamber. In a soft voice, she said, "Yes, Yer Majesty. I'll speak of it ta no one. As ya wish."

Once outside the door, the terrified woman raced back to her quarters.

The queen was overwhelmed with mixed emotions. Her first child, her beloved Gwendolyn, was somewhere. Her heart burst with joy because even though Gwendolyn was of another world, there was hope for a mother and child reunion. But her joyful feelings were short-lived. Terror struck as she realized her secret was out. It had been her parents' plan to get the illegitimate child out of Dimension XIII in hopes her secret birth would go undiscovered. The fact the Soul Seeker knew of the child's existence was devastating news. Worse, he was in Idlebury.

Queen Filanthropi paced her chambers, at times stopping in front of the enormous painting of her husband, King Heroian of Idlebury. His journeys to other kingdoms to negotiate for the goods, food, tools, and services for his meek and powerless people had kept him away from his queen and his kingdom for more than six months.

"Heroian, I need you. What am I to do?" she muttered. "Something serious is happening. I must contact you at once."

The queen rushed to her desk, hurriedly wrote a letter, stuffed it in an envelope, lit a stick of sealing wax, let a few drops of hot red wax settle on the flap of the pure white envelope and then pressed her royal seal ring into the warm liquid. Due to the seriousness of the message it contained, she decided not to address the envelope. Besides, she had no idea as to the king's whereabouts.

She pulled the rope that rang the bell that summoned Oof, her most loyal master servant. Oof, a lanky figure of a man, appeared instantly as if he were in the room the whole time.

"Yes, Your Majesty, you rang?"

Startled by the servant's sudden appearance, the queen quickly addressed him in her most regal manner. "Oof, this is a matter of some urgency. The king must be notified at once. Please take this message to him immediately. And Oof, though it will be difficult to spare your service, I do ask that you, yourself, deliver this envelope to the king."

"Yes, ma'am. As you wish," Oof said as he disappeared into thin air.

Queen Filanthropi had misgivings about entrusting Oof with the message. The matter was much too serious to trust anyone, even her most valued servant. In a panic, she grabbed the sides of her modest gown and lifted it as she darted after Oof. She looked down the hall. No Oof. She ran to the railing high above the parlor. No Oof. In a voice that echoed throughout the castle, she screamed, *"Oof, come back immediately. It is urgent!"*

"Yes, Your Majesty."

Startled by the voice behind her, Queen Filanthropi whirled around. "Oh, Oof," she said as she tried to regain her composure. "I have changed my mind. I will take the message to the king myself."

"As you wish, ma'am. I will prepare your carriage."

"No. No carriage. I must go alone and as inconspicuously as

possible. Prepare my horse at once."

Oof, who usually never questioned the queen, expressed concern regarding her request. "But ma'am, I cannot in all good conscience allow you to travel alone on a horse with no one to protect you. I must insist— "

"Are you questioning my judgment?" the queen snapped. "Just do as I say and get my horse."

"As you wish, ma'am." And poof, Oof was gone.

Queen Filanthropi ran to her chambers. She threw open the large, wooden double doors and surprised three chambermaids who were busily arranging her room.

"*Yer Majesty,*" the chambermaids shrieked in unison as they fumbled with freshly laundered sheets and clothing while they tried to curtsy in honor of the queen.

"Please gather my things. I must leave immediately," commanded the queen as she rifled through her wardrobe and drawers and tossed garments at the three dumbfounded chambermaids.

When Queen Filanthropi heard the bay of a horse, she ran to the window and threw open the shutters. To her surprise, Oof had already fully prepared her beloved steed for her trip. "Gee, he's fast," she muttered.

Excited to begin her journey, the Queen of Idlebury scurried out of her chambers, ran down the cavernous hall, and for the first time in her life, slid down the banister of the long, winding staircase. She plopped on the floor, then quickly sprang up, brushed herself off, and straightened her crown before she bolted out the door into the courtyard where Lightening, her trusty steed, awaited her mount. In seconds, she and Lightening were off to find the king.

Oof and the other servants looked on with expressions of

dismay. This frenzied woman was not the queen they knew. They feared something was dreadfully amiss.

As the queen and Lightening disappeared from view, Oof eyed the envelope he held in his hand. It was the very one that contained the message the queen insisted she deliver to the king herself. "What am I to do with this letter?" Oof said in a deliberately loud voice to ensure the others could hear him. "I must guard it with my life, for if anything happens to the queen, I must deliver it to the king myself." He held the envelope high for all to see as he slowly climbed the dilapidated staircase. Once he was out of the servants' view, he magically appeared in the king's chambers.

Chapter Two
The Gathering of the Princess Wannabes

For the tenth day in a row, rain poured over Idleburg, Pennsylvania. News reports from the retro radio on the kitchen island blurted continuous updates of flooded roads and streams, airport delays, traffic backups, and canceled ball games. The news team tried to make light of the lousy weather, but their attempts were pathetic.

Ten-year-old Gwen, outfitted in her favorite medieval princess dress, peered out the kitchen bay window lost in her private fantasy of dragons, knights, queens, kings, mystery, magic, and of course, a princess with great and mighty powers. As she played with her magic coin box, making the coin disappear and reappear over and over, she longed to vanish into a world of enchantment. On rainy days like this, she wished she had a sister or brother to play with, but for the most part, she enjoyed her only-child status.

Gwen's mother, Evaline Fanny, sat at the kitchen table with her nose buried in the latest edition of *Universal Scandals* magazine. Gwen's father, Arston Fanny, an ever-devoted husband, had braved hurricane-force winds and driving rain to buy the magazine for his beloved wife.

"Momma, when is the rain going to stop?" Gwen asked in her best English dialect.

"Don't know princess. Now please be quiet while I read my magazine. You know I like to be informed as to what's going on in the universe and the other dimensions."

Gwen glanced at her mother and noticed for the first time in days, she was decked out in pink sponge rollers and makeup. She wore fuzzy socks over her stocking-covered feet, which were nestled in her faux-animal-skin slippers.

"Are you going somewhere today?" Gwen asked with excitement.

"You never know when the sun will come out. It's always good to be prepared, my dear. After all, the king may want to whisk me away for an enchanting evening," her mother said as she peered over the top of her magazine and winked.

"Oh," Gwen said as she rolled her eyes. Her mother and father's habit of calling each other king and queen nauseated her. But she had to admit she liked her father calling her his little princess. Even better, she liked being treated like a princess. The Fannys barely scraped by, but no expense was spared on spoiling Gwen.

When Gwen turned to look out the window again, the headline on the front of her mother's *Universal Scandals* magazine, Earth Edition, caught her eye: "I GAVE MY BABY PRINCESS TO STRANGERS," QUEEN DECLARES! But the picture of the queen was most intriguing because Gwen's resemblance to her was uncanny.

Gwen jumped from her perch in front of the window and grabbed the newspaper from her mother.

"Gwendolyn, what's come over you?" her mother sniped.

"Momma… look," Gwen pleaded as she pointed at the picture of the queen. *"That's me,"* she screeched, hardly able to contain her excitement.

"This princess stuff has gone to your head. That's not you. That's the Queen of Idlebury."

"But she looks just like me. Read me the story. Please."

"Okay, let me find it." Gwen's mother flipped through the pages as quickly as she could.

If she'd just stop licking her finger before she turned each page, she'd find it much faster, Gwen thought.

"Here it is," Gwen's mother said. "A reliable source has revealed that Queen Filanthropi of Idlebury—Oops, there's the phone dear. I must get it. I'm expecting an important call." Evaline Fanny grabbed the phone. "Mattie. Hi. It's so good to hear from you…" Gwen's mother's voice trailed off as she walked into the living room for a little privacy.

"That stupid phone is more important than me," Gwen lamented. "It's worse than having a bratty, attention-hungry little sister." She grabbed the *Universal Scandals* magazine and started reading.

"A reliable source has revealed that Queen Filanthropi of Idlebury, in Dimension XIII, gave birth to an eight-pound princess a little more than ten years ago. At the time, the queen, who was the Princess of Seedonia, was betrothed to the then Prince of Laborshire, heir to the throne.

"It is well known that the Prince of Laborshire and the Princess of Seedonia had a three-year stormy relationship marked by public disagreements as to the type and extent of government programs. Their relationship disintegrated and eventually led to a broken engagement.

"Two months later, the Princess of Seedonia discovered she was with child. Sources say the princess's parents, the current King and Queen of Seedonia, assumed the Prince of Laborshire sired the child. The Princess of Seedonia swore this accusation was untrue and insisted the child's father was none other than Prince Heroian of Idlebury who she'd declared to be her one and only true love.

"Due to the delicate circumstances and political climate at the time, Princess Filanthropi was discreetly tucked away in Seedonia's Cringley Castle to await the birth of her child. One Earth year after the birth and subsequent adoption of the child, Princess Filanthropi of Seedonia and Prince Heroian of Idlebury were wed and are now the King and Queen of Idlebury. The couple, which had the misfortune of losing two other children at birth, is childless.

"Sources close to the queen say she has anguished over her missing child. 'I was forced to give her to complete strangers, not to mention commoners. It breaks my heart not knowing who is raising my beautiful child. And to think she is the princess of Idlebury; rightful heir to the throne.'

"Sources also confirmed the rumor that the King and Queen of Idlebury have started a multidimensional, universal search for the princess, whose whereabouts are unknown due to the deliberate destruction of all records pertaining to her birth and adoption. One source was quoted as saying, 'There's an unsuspecting and, I must say, lucky couple that has no idea their beautiful, adopted daughter is the Princess of Idlebury.'

"Rumor has it that the adoptive parents of the unknown princess are to be offered a king's ransom for the return of the child to Idlebury. The child could be living in another dimension or anywhere in the universe.

"If you suspect your child is the beloved princess of Idlebury, please write to Her Majesty the Queen, Idlebury Castle, Idlebury Kingdom, W234999&1/2, Dimension XIII. Be sure to include a photo of your *child for physical comparison."*

Gwen stared in disbelief at the live-motion picture of the queen who begged for Princess Gwendolyn's return to Idlebury. "Did she say Princess Gwendolyn? Could it be?" she mumbled. "Could I be the Princess of Idlebury, heir to the throne? I know I'm the princess. I'm ten years old and I'm adopted. And my name is Gwendolyn. I must be the princess. I knew I was special. And look at the resemblance between the queen and me."

Gwen darted into the living room. In an attempt to get her mother's attention she waved the *Universal Scandals* magazine as she yelled, "Momma, Momma, get off the phone. We have to have my picture taken right away. You have to send it to the Queen of Idlebury. I'm the princess. She's looking for me. She's my real mother."

Gwen's mother had just ended her call when she heard her daughter screaming about getting her picture taken and something about the Queen of Idlebury being her real mother.

"Gwen, we've had this discussion before. You have a biological mother and me, your real mother."

Gwen rolled her eyes. "I know. But I'm a princess. I'm the Princess of Idlebury. Look. Read the article."

Gwen's mother tried to quickly scan the article, but the picture of the queen transfixed her. She looked at her daughter, and then looked at the picture, then back to her daughter, and back to the picture.

"Oh... my... God. Go get your father, we must have your picture taken and sent to the Queen of Idlebury immediately. If you're not her child, I don't know who is."

"Daddy, Daddy," Gwen yelled as she tried to locate her father in the Fannys' small house. She opened the garage door to find him fiddling with the engine of an old car he hoped to repair so Gwen's mother would have a car of her own.

"What's the emergency, my princess," Arston said without lifting his head from under the car's hood.

"Look, Daddy," Gwen said, waving the magazine. "I'm the Princess of Idlebury. We have to get my picture taken to send to the queen. She's looking for me."

"Oh, Gwen." Arston came out from under the car's hood, quickly wiped his grease-covered hands on his already stained overalls, and took the *Universal Scandals* magazine from Gwen. He scanned the article. His eyes moved back and forth faster and faster as he read. He looked at the picture of Queen Filanthropi and then looked at Gwen. "I believe you're right. Let's go. But don't get your hopes up, my little princess."

Within a half hour, the entire Fanny family—Gwen, her mother, her father, Nigel their dog, and Snickers their cat—was on its way to Pretty Pictures. Gwen was decked out in her princess outfit, her parents were dressed as a king and queen, the dog was the court jester, and the cat, well, he was a cat, so he went as himself.

The traffic surrounding the shopping mall was a nightmare. Cars, vans, and SUVs backed up for several miles onto neighborhood streets.

Horns blared.

Tempers flared.

People yelled at each other through partially opened windows.

"This traffic is horrible," Arston said. "I guess everyone's looking for something to do on a rainy day. They're probably all going to the movies or out to lunch."

Gwen plastered her face against the car window as she

looked at the commotion. In her hand, she clutched the copy of the *Universal Scandals* magazine. Soon she saw a man directing traffic and holding a sign. "What does the man's sign say, Daddy? Can you read it? Can you read it?"

"No, my princess. He's too far away."

"He's coming toward us, Daddy. He's coming toward us."

"So he is."

The man approached the Fannys' car and motioned for Arston to roll down his window. "Well, I guess I don't have to ask where you're going," the man said as rain dripped off the rim of his hat, causing him to talk as if he'd just come up for air after a swim in the ocean. The man leaned in toward Arston to get a better look at Gwen in the back seat. "I can tell by your costume you're here like everyone else to get your picture taken in hopes of being the long-lost Princess of Idlebury."

"All these people are here to have their pictures taken at Pretty Pictures?" Arston moaned.

"Yep. Just stay in line and follow the signs."

Gwen rolled down her window and yelled, "I'm the Princess of Idlebury. Tell them to go home." She waved the *Universal Scandals* magazine cover at the man and said, "Look how much I look like the queen. I'm the princess, I tell you."

"You and thousands of other princess wannabes. Like I said, follow the signs."

Gwen's heart sank. "But I'm not a princess wannabe. I'm the *real* princess." She stretched across the back seat and pouted.

It was two hours before the Fannys found a parking spot. They fought their way inside the shopping mall only to find long, mazelike lines. Despite the obviously long wait, they took their place in line.

Nigel was hyper.

Snickers couldn't care less.

Gwen couldn't believe her eyes.

There were hundreds and hundreds of little girls dressed as princesses. There were even boys trying to pass themselves off as princesses.

"Daddy, tell them it's no use. I'm the princess. They're wasting their time."

"Gwendolyn, hush. Another word out of you and we'll go home."

Gwen's father's curtness hurt her feelings, but she knew he wasn't going to go home. After all, it would take them another two hours to get out of the parking lot. Nonetheless, she kept her mouth shut.

Gwen scanned the crowd. Something was odd but she couldn't put her finger on it. As she carefully observed the other princess wannabes, she noticed a huge man dressed in a black cape. He appeared to be alone. He hunched his back as if to look inconspicuous. Gwen checked to see if anyone else noticed the man, but it appeared no one had. To her relief, Snickers jumped into her arms. As Gwen petted the cat she whispered in his ear, "See the man over there? He doesn't seem to belong here. I bet if he stood up straight, he'd be ten feet tall. I wonder what he wants." The words were barely out of her mouth when Snickers jumped out of her arms, ran over to the mysterious man and disappeared under his cape. Eyes wide in disbelief, she turned to her father for help only to discover he was engaged in conversation with a woman. So she tugged furiously at the sleeve of her father's costume in an attempt to divert his attention.

"Gwendolyn Beatrice Villroy Hilda Wainwright Morgan Madison Katrina Dimwitty Francine Patrice Fanny, I told you to be quiet or we would go home."

"But Daddy, Snickers—" Her father's chilling stare, with his eyes bulging and his lips pursed, stopped Gwen in midsentence. So she did the unthinkable. She charged the caped man and screamed, "Stop that man. He's stolen my cat. He's stolen Snickers."

The caped man jerked his cumbersome body toward Gwen. When she looked for help, she noticed everyone in the mall, with the exception of the man and her, was in a state of suspended animation. Oddly, she felt calm. She stared into the darkness of what should have been the man's eyes and face and saw nothing, but she heard his thoughts. After a couple of minutes, everything was crystal-clear. She knew for certain she was the princess and this man was here to save her.

The man opened his cape. Gwen felt a force pull her toward him. She tried to break away, but it was useless. He swooped her up in his long, bony arms and wrapped her in his cape before they both disappeared.

Chapter Three
Queen Filanthropi and the Field of Wisdom

A S THE QUEEN rode through the Slothful Forest, her excitement turned to worry. The stench sickened her, and the debris made it impossible to see the tracks of the king's carriage and horses. *Where is Heroian?* she wondered. When she arrived at the border of the Slothful Forest and the Field of Wisdom, she looked out into the vast open field for evidence of her husband's passage. But there were no footprints of men or horses, or marks to indicate the king's carriage had passed this way. To make matters worse, both the queen and Lightening were tiring. So Queen Filanthropi pulled the reins to halt her steed, after which both the queen and the horse rested under a tree. She'd nearly fallen asleep when Lightening bayed and rose on his hind legs.

"What is it Lightening?" the queen asked as she stood and grabbed the horse's reins.

Suddenly, the wind howled. The horse became uncontrollable. He bucked and pulled, knocking the queen to the ground. Once loose, he bolted into the forest and raced back toward Idlebury. Queen Filanthropi yelled for Lightening to return as he ran farther and farther into the darkness. She grabbed a tree and held on with all her might as the wind whipped leaves and debris around her.

"The Soul Seeker is coming," someone said in a sinister voice.

Everything went still. The queen fell to the ground. "No, this cannot be true. Please, not the Soul Seeker."

Queen Filanthropi trembled. She was alone, scared, horseless, unarmed, and the most feared being in the universe was near. Animals scurried farther into the forest as if to escape unforeseen danger. She looked around for a safe place to take refuge. Trees bowed away from her. Bushes shriveled to the ground. There was nowhere to hide. Her only option was to run across the Field of Wisdom, but fear stopped her. She begged for help and guidance. It seemed her cries went unheard. But someone did hear her.

"Run, run," said a man in a whispery, raspy voice. "There is nothing to fear in knowing the truth. There is nothing to fear in knowing the future. Most of all, there is nothing to fear in knowing yourself."

"Who said that? Who would have the insolence to make commands of the Queen of Idlebury? Reveal yourself and bow before me with the deference owed a queen by a mere commoner."

The wind howled around the queen and forced her to the ground.

"How dare you address me with such arrogance? Stand up and bow before me," the man demanded.

"I will do no such thing. I am a queen. I defer to no one."

"And I am who you call the Soul Seeker. Stand up and bow

before me. *Now.*"

The queen trembled as she rose. "How can I bow before you if I cannot see you?"

"You must step into the Field of Wisdom. Then you shall see me."

"No, I will not. No one from Idlebury has ventured into the Field of Wisdom for a thousand years. I simply cannot."

"You must, or Idlebury is doomed."

"Doomed?"

"Do not question me. Time is running out. You must step into the Field of Wisdom now. Then you will know all. Then you will understand."

Queen Filanthropi looked around to make sure no one was watching before she bravely stepped into the blazing light. "I am going to faint," she muttered as she shielded her eyes. Images flashed before her. In an instant, the queen knew and understood all. Emotions raced through her: sadness for the lonely, helpless people of Idlebury; anger at herself, the king, and the generations of royals who ruled before for creating and enabling the laziness of the Idleburians; exhilaration at realizing her own greatness; and marvel at the untapped greatness of her people. The queen was overwhelmed with anguish. "I am a fool. I have ruined everything. I have destroyed Idlebury," she whimpered. Still, she continued to walk toward the center of the field.

As Queen Filanthropi's eyes adjusted to the light, the Soul Seeker appeared. He was slightly elevated so his feet didn't touch the ground, rendering the Field of Wisdom powerless over him. He was enormous, possibly ten feet tall and completely covered by a black cape. The queen froze in place. She could hardly breathe. She tried to run, but her feet felt as if they were weighted down with lead. She knew it was no use to resist. She had no choice but to face her fear. So with newfound courage, she looked at the Soul Seeker. Oddly, her anxiety eased as she realized she wasn't afraid of this mystifying man.

Tales of the Soul Seeker's wrathful and compassionate deeds were pervasive in the folklore of every kingdom in the thirteen dimensions. He was the source of controversy between those who believed him to be evil and those who believed him to be beneficent.

In her younger days, Queen Filanthropi and her siblings begged Oof, who was also a servant of her parents, to entertain them with his lavish enactments of the fables and follies associated with the mysterious caped man. Oof's dramatic tales filled their hearts with terror at the horrors the Soul Seeker had unleashed on the kingdoms. When the children were too scared to hear more, he'd have them weeping with joy at stories of bravery and compassion the Soul Seeker had bestowed on even the most undeserving person. After, Oof would have them roaring with laughter over silly behaviors that revealed the Soul Seeker to be all too human. The confusion over whether to love, hate, or pity this enigmatic being confused many, including the queen.

So here she was, face-to-face with the most feared and admired being in the universe. *Who is this man?* she wondered. *Why does he hide under a cape? What does he want with me?* She scanned his hooded head to connect with his eyes, but she saw only darkness.

"I am standing before you in all my glory. I have risked my life and the lives of my people by revealing myself to you. You could at least do me the courtesy of showing your face," Queen Filanthropi demanded.

"In due time. Right now you must witness what I am about

to show you. Watch and you will understand."

The Soul Seeker stretched out his arms. His likeness to a bird about to take flight unnerved the queen.

"Do not be afraid, for fear depletes my energy and could spell disaster for the future of Idlebury," he said, obviously able to read the queen's thoughts.

Queen Filanthropi's mind went blank as if she were under the control of the Soul Seeker. The huge being opened his cape to reveal a live image of a young girl holding a cat. The girl looked around as if awestruck in a state of pure joy. For a brief moment, the queen's and the girl's eyes met. A bolt of energy and an explosion of light threw the queen back into the Slothful Forest, leaving her to wonder if she had fallen asleep and merely had a terrifying dream.

There was something in her hand. She had read about a device commonly used on Earth in Dimension X capable of capturing a person's likeness without the need to sit for hours for a portrait by an artist. But she had never seen one.

The Queen of Idlebury carefully examined the photo of a young girl dressed in clothing remarkably like those worn by her when she was the Princess of Seedonia. To her astonishment, the girl wore a large necklace adorned with the royal emblem of Idlebury—a man and woman working in the field with an X over the image. In her hand, the girl clutched a small wooden box which the queen instantly recognized as the fabled magic coin box once used by the people of Idlebury to make their money disappear in order to maintain their indigence. The coin boxes were banned nearly five hundred years ago when the then King of Idlebury discovered his people's secret and, in a rage, had the boxes and their money confiscated.

As Queen Filanthropi looked at the image of the child, she

gasped and declared, "It is me. It is an image of me. But she has the eyes of the king. Who is this child?"

"I'm Gwendolyn, the Princess of Idlebury. Why don't you believe me?" the young girl in the photo said,

"Gwendolyn? It is you. I have found you."

The queen turned over the photo in hopes someone had written the name and location of the princess on the back. But the only words read PRETTY PICTURES, IDLEBURG, PENNSYLVANIA, DIMENSION X, EARTH.

Lightening appeared out of nowhere. He reared as if to tell the queen to hurry. She jumped on his back and headed deep into the Slothful Forest as she hurried back to Idlebury Castle.

Chapter Four
The Blank Photo

GWEN TUMBLED AT her father's feet. After she got up off the floor, she noticed she had not moved forward in line. There were still hundreds of princess wannabes in front of her.

Annoyed at what he believed was inappropriate behavior on his daughter's part, Gwen's father angrily said, "Watch it, young lady. It's unbecoming of a princess to be scuffling about."

"But Daddy, I was gone. Didn't you see I was gone? I went to another dimension. The caped man took me to Idlebury. It's an awful place. The people live in poverty. They seem lonely. Worse, they're lazy. They don't do anything for themselves. There was this bright light and I saw the Queen of Idlebury. She looked at me and I looked at her. She was upset about something. So she got on her horse and rode back to the castle. I think she had a picture of me. And when she tucked it in her dress, I suddenly came back here. I'm the Princess of Idlebury. I'm destined to save the entire kingdom, the dimension, even the universe." Gwen rambled so fast that her father's attempts to interrupt were unsuccessful.

"You have a wild imagination, my princess," Arston Fanny

said as his face momentarily contorted into a grotesque, horrific sight.

Gwen's eyes bugged out at the horror she'd witnessed. She could hardly believe she was afraid of her father.

Suddenly, Gwen's father pushed her forward. "Look, it's your turn. Hurry up and get yourself presentable. Evaline, look at Gwen. She's a mess and she's next up for her picture."

Evaline fussed with Gwen's hair and dress and then did the unthinkable. She took out her ruby-red lipstick and quickly applied the gooey red stuff to Gwen's lips, leaving the child no time to protest.

"Mom, I don't need my picture taken. The queen already knows I'm her princess. Besides, there are still hundreds of people in front of me. I have to go. *Now.* I must save Idlebury. Why don't you believe me?"

Evaline Fanny's face became grotesquely distorted as she snarled at Gwen and said, "Don't you ever question me, you ungrateful brat." A second later, Evaline appeared normal, and in her typically sweet manner, she said, "Hurry, my princess. You're next."

Shocked at her mother's terrifying transformation, Gwen was speechless. A force carried Gwen forward. As she floated toward the make-believe throne, everyone appeared to move in slow motion. Parents and children sneered and angrily gestured at her as she approached the front of the line. Some parents tried in vain to grab and stop her. She searched the crowd and noticed a riot had broken out. Police held back the mass of angry princess wannabes and parents.

Finally, Gwen reached the make-believe throne on which Snickers sat. She was happy and relieved to see her cat. But when he looked at her and made an all-too-human smile, she knew something was terribly wrong. Under the influence of the force, Gwen turned and sat on the throne. Snickers jumped off the red padded seat and scurried away. She noticed the cat didn't move in slow motion. Two men dressed as royal guards stood on each side of the throne. There was something strange about the men she didn't like, yet they were familiar.

"I guess I've been in line so long, I feel as if I know you two," Gwen said to the guards. They didn't flinch. But Gwen thought she saw one of the guards eye her magic coin box. She wondered why he might be interested in a child's toy.

"Let's see your pretty smile," the photographer, who was dressed as a court jester and who moved in real time, announced as he made a demented sneer.

Gwen used her sleeve to quickly wipe off the awful red lipstick. She thought it was strange the photographer peered through the lens of what looked like an instant camera. She swore he'd used a different type of camera to take the pictures of the other princesses. She heard the camera click and saw a flash. Suddenly, everything was back in real time. People screamed and yelled as the police continued to hold back the unruly crowd.

The photographer waited for the camera timer to announce the development of the photo. Soon, a ding rang out and echoed throughout the mall, silencing the crowd. The photographer carefully peeled off the back layer of the photo which contained the developing gel. Gwen could see the photo was blank. The photographer looked at the guards, gulped, and then whispered, "It's blank. The photo is blank."

"The queen knows," said one of the guards to the other. "It's too late. We can't stop her now."

The guards stepped in front of Gwen, clicked their heels, and shielded her from the unruly children and their families. Gwen could hear her father demanding to know what was going on.

The guards moved to either side of her to allow the photographer to take another picture. When the camera flashed, Gwen disappeared.

Gwen's mother screamed and fainted. Her father yelled at the photographer to return his child at once. The other parents refused to believe Gwen was the Princess of Idlebury. So they pushed their princess wannabes in front of the photographer. Once again, mayhem prevailed.

Suddenly, Gwen reappeared on the throne.

She looked different.

Changed.

More mature.

Her clothes were no longer a costume, but real. She locked eyes with one of the guards, defiantly opened her magic coin box, and showed him a penny nestled in the slot.

The guard yelled, "She's not indigent. It's against the royal laws of Idlebury. She can't step on Idlebury soil unless she's indigent. She'll ruin everything. Stop her."

Gwen rapidly closed the magic coin box, and then rapidly opened it to reveal an empty coin slot, and in an instant, she disappeared once again.

Gwen found herself rising above Earth. Once out of the planet's atmosphere, she whizzed through the universe, catapulting from dimension to dimension. As she hurled through the dimensions, she began to sense she was not alone. She entered Dimension XII and came to an abrupt stop.

Chapter Five
The Enchantress's Request

Queen Filanthropi and Lightening raced through the Slothful Forest on a mission to return to Idlebury. The queen knew she must alert the king that the princess, rightful heir to the Idlebury throne, was alive and living at Pretty Pictures in Idleburg, Pennsylvania, Dimension X, planet Earth. But she didn't know where to find him. So her best bet was to go home in hopes the king had returned from his journeys.

Lost in thought, the queen didn't notice the bright light up ahead, but Lightening did. The powerful animal abruptly stopped. The queen looked at the huge yellow orb and searched her memory for why it was familiar. "Wilameena?" she whispered, half scared and half thrilled.

Queen Filanthropi dismounted Lightening and stood before the pulsating orb. "Wilameena, my enchantress," she said with delight. "I have not seen you since I was locked away in Cringley Castle many years ago. Can it be you are still alive? I thought I had imagined you. Am I imagining you now?"

"I see you haven't changed. Still doubting your own perceptions of the world," the enchantress replied in a mocking tone as she materialized in the form of a matronly woman.

"And yes, it's me, my friend. But maybe you remember me more like this," Wilameena said as she transformed into a beautiful young woman. "Or maybe like this," she said as she transformed again, but this time into a beggar man.

"That was you?" Queen Filanthropi said with embarrassment as she remembered shunning the beggar a few years back when she was in a hurry.

"'Twas me. And of course, I'm alive. I can't die because there's no such thing as death."

"Why do you come to me now? Where were you when I needed you?" the queen pleaded.

Wilameena chuckled. "Needed me? You're too bullheaded to need me. You didn't call upon me because you no longer believed I could serve you. That was an error in judgment. I don't serve you, you can only serve yourself. Nonetheless, I've watched over you. Now, I can no longer watch you destroy yourself and the people of Idlebury. So I have an adventure for you."

"An adventure?" the queen responded in a cynical manner. "Go on."

"Find Matilda and bring her to me."

"Matilda? She was a make-believe friend—a dragon no less. She is not real and she was never real. I was forbidden by my parents to ever mention her." Queen Filanthropi hesitated as she stared at the enchantress, who smirked at her. "Besides, how would I find her?"

"Use your powers," Wilameena said.

"I cannot. I took an oath to protect the people of Idlebury. I cannot break it."

"And protect them you have. But at what cost?"

"What do you mean, cost? I have been faithful to my people

and my position."

"Your people are helpless, hopeless, ungrateful leeches."

"Helpless? Hopeless? Ungrateful? They are my responsibility. I am their queen. I am destined to protect them."

"Protect them? From what? They're the living dead. No hopes. No dreams. No aspirations. No accomplishments. No joy. No passion. Oh, I'm sorry. I'm describing you. You've projected yourself on your people."

"How dare you talk to me like that? I am the Queen of Idlebury. I demand respect from you as I do from all my subjects."

"Well… I do believe I've hit a nerve," Wilameena said. "The truth hurts, as they say. And just to get our relationship straight, I'm not your subject. I'm no one's subject. Ergo, I'm not at the whim of your commands, demands, tortures, or tantrums. For that, you have the kingdom of Idlebury and its faithful subjects. And while we're at it, the people of Idlebury have you jumping to their every command. Not the other way around."

"Silence," the queen said as her voice quavered. "I have heard enough. I was so happy to see you, and now I wish I had not."

"Pish posh. You need me. That's why I'm here. And despite our contention, I'm here to help you."

"Okay, so help."

"First, find Matilda," Wilameena said before she turned into an orb of light and disappeared.

"It has been years since I have seen her and she still gets on my nerves," Queen Filanthropi muttered as she mounted Lightening. Surprisingly, the horse shook his head in what appeared to be agreement before he and the queen once again set out for Idlebury.

The ride soon became tedious and Queen Filanthropi began to tire. She pulled on Lightening's reins but the horse refused to stop. The harder she pulled, the faster he ran. The queen had no idea why her trusty steed disobeyed her command. He'd never disobeyed her before, just as she'd never disobeyed the commands of her people. *Something is amiss* she thought and shuddered. But she gave in to the feeling and decided to let Lightening take her on a journey.

For nearly fifteen minutes, Lightening galloped toward Idlebury. Queen Filanthropi had just begun to relax when the horse took a sudden westward turn toward uncharted territory.

"Lightening!" Queen Filanthropi screamed. "It is forbidden. Turn back. Go back to Idlebury." She tugged on the horse's reins, but once again, he ignored her commands.

A few minutes later, Lightening slowed his pace. Up ahead, a beam of light extending from the ground to the sky vibrated and hummed. The horse walked up to the beam and reared as if to tell the queen to dismount.

Queen Filanthropi held on tight.

Lightening reared again.

The queen didn't budge.

The steed leaned forward as if to bow before the beam.

The queen remained firmly on the horse's back.

Lightening yelled at the stubborn queen, "Get off."

"What?" Queen Filanthropi asked, astonished to hear Lightening speak.

"I said, get off. *Now.*"

This time, the queen didn't hesitate. She quickly

dismounted. As she set foot on the ground, the beam engulfed her.

It vibrated.

It hummed.

The noise was deafening.

The light was blinding.

Just when Queen Filanthropi thought she could tolerate it no more, she plopped in the middle of the great square of the kingdom of East Wisdomere where individual empowerment, personal responsibility, and accountability were professed. It was the antithesis of Idlebury.

The weather was glorious. Flowers in full bloom adorned the square. Massive trees provided shade for the thousands of people who were obviously out to take advantage of the beautiful day. Vendors sold beautifully decorated cakes, cookies, pies, and breads. The scent of grilled sausages and other meats wafted in the air. Drink machines whirred as they whipped up delectable slushy delights. Well-dressed and well-behaved children played freely; some teamed up for games of all sorts. Groups of perfectly coiffed adults gathered in polite conversation. The women were impeccably dressed; many with doily-collared dresses and gloved hands as well as matching shoes and handbags. Men were clothed as if ready for work that required brain power rather than brawn. Some parents and children were dressed alike as if to announce their familial affiliations and unconditional loyalty to their heritage. Some couples and families laid blankets on the grassy area and enjoyed abundant picnics. Soft music added to the ambience.

Queen Filanthropi looked around in awe. "This is nothing like Idlebury," she whispered. Part of her wished Idlebury was this idyllic, yet in her gut, she knew something was wrong. Everything appeared too perfect. Everyone was the epitome of decorum, even the children. This thought roused her annoyance. Amidst the hive of activity, her arrival had gone unnoticed by the polite, proper East Wisdomerians despite the fact that in her drab garb, she was grossly out of place. "Do they not notice there is a queen in their presence?" she mumbled.

The Queen of Idlebury was about to make her presence known when a beautiful carriage approached. A herald's horn blared, announcing the arrival of King Karful and Queen Prudea. As the King and Queen of East Wisdomere emerged from their carriage, some of their people bowed and curtsied in their honor, some blew kisses, others tossed flowers at the royal couple's feet, and some offered fresh baked goods, hoping for a coveted royal blessing. Still, no one noticed Queen Filanthropi standing ever so majestically in the center of the square.

A wave of indignation washed over her. "How dare they not acknowledge my presence?" she angrily mumbled, unable to believe someone of her social standing would be ignored. "I guess I will have to take matters into my own hands."

With her head held high in an attempt to display her superiority, Queen Filanthropi parted the crowd and walked toward the King and Queen of East Wisdomere. When King Karful spotted her, he stood, and with a wave of his hand, he hushed the crowd. "Well... well. It is Queen Filanthropi of Idlebury," the king said as he disapprovingly glanced at Queen Prudea. "What brings you to our lovely kingdom... unannounced? We are not prepared for a proper welcome. But if you have come begging, well, I guess beggars cannot be choosy."

The people of East Wisdomere roared with laughter at the king's cheekiness.

Queen Filanthropi stood proudly, looked the king in the

eyes, and then said, "Wilameena has sent me."

"Wilameena?" Queen Prudea declared. "She has not been seen here for nearly two hundred years. I thought the old hag was dead."

Again, the crowd broke out in laughter. A few people jeered.

"You are clearly mistaken," Queen Filanthropi replied in a cocky manner. "In fact, she has sent me here on a mission."

"Oh, do tell of this mission. I am all ears," Queen Prudea replied as she placed her hand to her right ear.

"Hear, hear with your ear, ear," the East Wisdomerians disrespectfully shouted.

Queen Filanthropi raised her hand to quiet the crowd. Much to her surprise, they complied. "I am to find Matilda," she announced with confidence.

Queen Prudea's face became ashen. "Matilda?" she muttered.

"You heard me right. Matilda... our dear, long-lost childhood friend."

"But she was not real. She was a figment of our imaginations," Queen Prudea stated in a dismissive manner.

"Evidently not. I am to find her or the kingdom of Idlebury and possibly all the kingdoms in every dimension are in danger. And I do believe East Wisdomere is still part of Dimension XIII. Am I correct?"

The King of East Wisdomere snapped his fingers and ordered his guards to bring the Queen of Idlebury to the castle at once. Immediately, he and Queen Prudea boarded their opulent royal carriage and charged off, stirring up a cloud of dirt. Queen Filanthropi unhappily followed on horseback, protected by the royal guards.

Chapter Six
Gwen Meets Her Other Selves

GWEN'S SUDDEN STOP on her multidimensional journey found her in Dimension XII and the kingdom of Personadonia. She looked around but saw no one. Her only welcome was from a gilded sign hung on a door. The sign read WELCOME TO PERSONADONIA. WHERE EVERYONE FINDS THEMSELVES AND WHERE THEIR SELVES FIND EACH OTHER.

Gwen knocked on the door. When it opened, she received a warm welcome from a rotund, elderly woman with a curiously crooked smile, blue hair piled high on her head, a well-worn housecoat, and spectacles that magnified her eyes at least ten times their natural size.

"Thank goodness you're here," the woman said as she cupped Gwen's hands in hers. "We've been waiting for you. What took you so long to convince your parents you're the Princess of Idlebury? I suspect it's because you spent too much time dreaming about being a princess and not enough time acting like one. But let's make no never mind. All that matters is you're here. By the way, I'm Queen Masklyn of

Personadonia. Come. Your other selves are waiting."

"My other *what* are waiting?" Gwen asked.

"Your other selves. No time to waste. Let's go." Immediately, eleven odd-looking people, one a mere baby, lined up behind Queen Masklyn.

"Who are they?"

"They're my other selves. Now hurry."

Queen Masklyn, with her other selves in tow, floated down a massive corridor. As Gwen followed, the beauty of the building and the courtyards eased her apprehension.

"Here we are," the queen said as she struggled to open a huge old door that was pitted and worn but still bore features of once elegantly carved wood. "This is where your other selves are waiting."

The door creaked opened to reveal a room full of girls and women. There was a crying baby, a defiant teenager, a young beautiful businesswoman, a pregnant mother with a child on each hip, a middle-aged woman decked out in travel gear, on down the line with the last one being a haggard, old woman in a wheelchair, fast asleep.

Queen Masklyn explained to Gwen how her other selves existed throughout the universe in other dimensions, living different lives that represented Gwen's dreams and full potential. But Gwen didn't hear a word the queen said because her attention was fixated on one person who was oddly out of place; a handsome boy just a couple of years older than she. It was love at first sight.

"What's he doing here?" Gwen asked as she pointed at the boy.

"I guess you two haven't met. Let me introduce you. Gwendolyn of Idleburg, Pennsylvania, Dimension X, meet

Kendall of Peasporagehot, Dimension V.

"Pleased to meet you, Kendall," Gwen said like a sheepish schoolgirl as she extended her hand for a polite shake.

"The pleasure's mine," replied Kendall as he winked and kissed Gwen's hand.

Gwen's heart fluttered. She could barely keep herself from fainting. As the old woman guided Gwen away from Kendall, Gwen whispered, "Who *is* he?"

Queen Masklyn grinned from ear to ear, revealing a mouthful of stained, crooked teeth. "My dear child, he's the part of you that you love the most."

Next, the old woman clapped her hands twelve times. With each clap, one of Gwen's selves turned and faced the queen as if under a spell. Only three didn't respond—Gwen, Kendall, and a curiously sloppy, dorky version of Gwen named Aislinn.

"The three of you have fallen into place, as expected. How grand," the old queen said. "Come, you must go. It's time to start your adventure."

"But why is she coming with us?" Gwen asked.

"Aislinn?" Queen Masklyn asked. "Well, she's the part of you that you detest the most."

Gwen was excited to embark on a journey with Kendall. For the first time in her life, she felt like a real princess. And she wanted Kendall for her prince. But she was a little disappointed about Aislinn tagging along.

Gwen, Kendall, and Aislinn boarded a tram driven by a most curious-looking dragon. He was young and pudgy, not to mention an unusual shade of green, and not the least bit intimidating.

"I didn't know dragons were real, let alone so cute," Gwen declared.

"He looks young," Kendall said with an air of conceited confidence. "I'm sure he's harmless."

Aislinn shook her head as if she thought Kendall was a jerk. But Gwen didn't care because she was totally besotted with her Prince Charming.

The tram meandered through the massive building which was dreary and absent of life. After a while, the halls narrowed. Darkness surrounded the trio. Gwen was about to state her concern when she was suddenly blinded by a neon sign that announced their arrival at The Shops of the Dimensions. Gwen, Kendall, and Aislinn rode past shop after shop in which various beings from Dimensions I through XII engaged in all types of commerce: bankers counted and recounted mounds of money; jewelers examined fine gems before carefully setting them in the most exquisitely designed rings, pendants, pins, and earrings; bakers tasted and compared their magnificent cakes, pies, and breads; candlestick makers poured wax into ornate forms; vegetable and fruit vendors carefully arranged their perfect, colorful produce; barbers and hair stylists coiffed Personadonians in styles unique to each person; clothiers fitted people with the most flattering clothes; haberdashers proudly showed their superb sundries to impressed customers; and bookbinders, silversmiths, and others engaged in producing the finest, most unique goods.

Gwen, Kendall, and Aislinn enjoyed the ride until the tram stopped in front of an obviously closed shop. A cobweb-covered sign on the door read NOT FOR THE FAINT OF HEART. ENTER AT YOUR OWN RISK.

"Why are we stopping here?" Aislinn whined.

"I don't know, but it doesn't frighten me. In fact, I think it's a portal to our adventure," Kendall replied as he gently placed his hand on Gwen's arm. "I doubt it's as menacing as it looks."

"Let's find out what's behind the door," Gwen said with excitement.

"Are you nuts?" Aislinn exclaimed. "I'm not going in there."

"Stop your whining. Do you think Queen Masklyn would send us into harm's way? If you don't want to go, Kendall and I will." Gwen shot a smile at Kendall, who winked and smiled back at her.

"Okay, I'll go then," Aislinn said. "But you go first, me second, and Kendall, you take up the rear."

"Deal," Gwen said as she hopped off the tram and ran toward the door.

"Wait," an unfamiliar voice commanded.

Gwen, Kendall, and Aislinn turned and stared at the dragon.

"I think he said something," Aislinn whispered.

"Don't be silly," Gwen replied. "Dragons can't talk."

"Oh, please. Get with the twelfth dimension," the two-hundred-year-old light green dragon said. "My name is Mistofisee. I'm a dragon and I talk. So do as I say and wait."

"A little uppity, aren't you?" Kendall replied.

"You won't think I'm so uppity when you open the door and find out you're not prepared for what's on the other side."

"Really?" Gwen said as she reached for the door handle.

"Wait!" the dragon screamed. Gwen jerked her hand back as the dragon continued, "You have to say the magic words."

"What magic words?" Gwen asked.

"Nothing is real because everything is real. Nothing matters because everything matters," Mistofisee said.

Gwen, Kendall, and Aislinn repeated the magic words but the door didn't open.

"See, it doesn't work. Nothing ever works," Aislinn whined

as she plopped on the doorstep.

"It didn't work because at least one of you doesn't believe in the magic of words," Mistofisee said. "If it's true, the door will never open."

"With all due respect," Kendall said in a most affected manner. "I have no doubt as to the power of even the most ordinary words."

"I'm with him," Gwen declared, still smitten with her new love. "I believe in the words. So the nonbeliever must be you, Aislinn."

Aislinn shot an angry look at Gwen.

With obvious braggadocio, Kendall said, "I doubt we'll be able to change Aislinn anytime soon, but I believe we can minimize the power of her disbelief. So here's what we'll do. Gwen, you take Aislinn's left hand and I'll take her right hand. The power of our belief will cancel her disbelief. Then we'll chant the magic words and I'll guide us to what's behind the door."

"You're a genius, Kendall," Gwen said, starstruck.

"I know," Kendall said. "Are you okay with the plan, Aislinn?"

"I guess so. But I don't know if I'm more afraid of your arrogance or what is behind the door."

"Hurry up," Mistofisee said.

Gwen and Kendall held Aislinn's hands and repeated the magic words, "Nothing is real because everything is real. Nothing matters because everything matters."

Still, nothing happened.

Gwen and Kendall repeated the magic words over and over. "Nothing is real because everything is real. Nothing matters because everything matters. Nothing is real because everything is real. Nothing matters because everything matters—"

Suddenly, the door blasted open, throwing Gwen, Kendall, Aislinn, and Mistofisee to the floor. Kendall quickly stood and extended his hand to Gwen, who gladly took it. Aislinn had to fend for herself.

Gwen looked inside and declared, "It's pitch-black. See, there's nothing to fear because there's nothing there."

"Oh, yes there is. You can't see it because it doesn't want to be seen," Mistofisee said as he brushed himself off. "You're looking at Dimension XIII, the entrance to the dreariest kingdom in the entire universe. Step over the threshold and you'll be sucked into Idlebury, a kingdom of people who are helpless victims of themselves. They think they've fooled generations of kings and queens to cater to their every need. But in reality, they've only fooled themselves into stagnation and boredom."

"Did you say Idlebury?" Gwen asked excitedly. "There isn't a moment to waste. I'm the Princess of Idlebury. My people need me," she said as she grabbed Kendall's hand and leaped over the threshold into the unknown.

As Kendall jerked forward, he grabbed for Aislinn, who grabbed for the dragon. All four landed inside the door, but still, nothing happened.

"Now what do we do, my fearless princess?" Mistofisee asked.

"I don't like this. I don't like this at all," Aislinn said. "I didn't volunteer for this. I shouldn't have to go. I'm going back. You can't stop me. I think you're all a bunch of—" In the middle of Aislinn's whining, the door slammed shut. "Now I can't see anything. I'm scared. I don't like this. I don't—"

"*Shut up!*" Gwen, Kendall, and Mistofisee yelled in unison.

"There's no echo. That means we're inside something solid," Kendall said with authority.

"No, we're not," said Gwen. "We're inside the cape of a big scary man. I know. I've been here before."

"Silence," the Soul Seeker demanded. The inside of his cape lit up, revealing the faces of the souls he sheltered. "You have entered Dimension XIII. And you have made a dreadful mistake by bringing the Innocent with you. His kind is not welcome here. But there is no turning back now. You must come with me. All of you."

"Innocent?" Gwen said.

"Silence," the Soul Seeker said.

"He's talking about me," Mistofisee said, remembering evenings before a crackling fire as he'd hung on every word of Queen Masklyn's intriguing yet scary stories about this baffling being known as the Soul Seeker.

"*Silence,*" the Soul Seeker yelled.

Despite the Soul Seeker's anger, Mistofisee wasn't scared. But when a chill caressed him and his green skin flashed purple, briefly illuminating the darkness, he knew something was terribly wrong, because it meant his mother, Matilda, Queen of Beastonia, had awakened from a two-hundred-year-long Dragon's Sleep. He trembled as recalled the last words she'd spoken before she fell into her long slumber. "Beware, my son. For I won't awaken until the universe is in danger and in dire need of redemption."

CHAPTER SEVEN
QUEEN PRUDEA'S SECRET

QUEEN FILANTHROPI, QUEEN Prudea, and King Karful arrived at East Wisdomere Castle with no fanfare. Two exquisitely dressed servants helped King Karful and Queen Prudea out of their carriage. Despite the offer of a helping hand by the king's stable master, Queen Filanthropi dismounted her horse on her own.

Silence hung heavy in the air as the king and the two queens walked through the castle. King Karful and Queen Prudea were respectfully greeted with bows and curtsies. But Queen Filanthropi was denied this honor. The East Wisdomerians' indifference to the Queen of Idlebury was a statement as to their rigid beliefs of proper behavior and their distaste for the lazy, uncouth Idleburians. Still, Queen Filanthropi maintained a regal air.

A guard greeted the king and the queens as they arrived at Queen Prudea's chambers. He bowed and opened the door as all three entered the richly decorated room. Beautifully designed candles of all shapes and sizes provided a soft light. A blazing fire in the spectacular fireplace provided warmth to the chilly room. Flowers, carefully arranged in a stunning vase

49

and displayed on an ornate table, scented the air. On another table, a plate of delectable cheeses, luscious fruit, and fresh bread accompanied by a pitcher of wine and two glasses completed the ambience.

King Karful dismissed the guard at which point, the tension between the royals vanished and the two queens embraced.

"Filanthropi, my dear friend," Queen Prudea said. "How I have missed you. I have longed to see you, but East Wisdomere law forbids friendship with anyone from Idlebury. I am saddened and regretful you endured such ridicule and indifference from our subjects, but Karful and I struggle to maintain an authoritarian front before our people. It is our burden."

"There is no such thing as lost time between good friends," Queen Filanthropi said. "We have never been apart for you are always in my heart."

The two queens sat before the fire for a serious talk about Wilameena's request.

King Karful poured wine. As he handed a glass to his wife, he said, "Be careful about allowing the enchantress and Matilda, the dragon queen, back in your life, Prudea. Things did not go well before." King Karful excused himself. As he left the room he said, "Pleasure seeing you again, Filanthropi."

For hours, Queen Prudea and Queen Filanthropi reminisced about their childhood adventures with Matilda.

"Oh, how I miss that sassy green dragon," Queen Filanthropi lamented. "Why did we allow our parents to convince us she was not real?"

Queen Prudea took a deep breath and looked down.

"Prudea, what is it? What are you hiding?"

"Well... since my mother is dead, I guess I can speak freely without fear of retribution."

"What is it? Tell me," Queen Filanthropi implored.

"Ten years ago, as my mother lay dying in this very room…" Queen Prudea cleared her throat, rose, and paced.

"Prudea?" Queen Filanthropi said. "What is it you want to say?"

"Well…" The queen of East Wisdomere sat and wrung her hands. "I have harbored a secret for many years; a secret I have told no one, not even Karful." Queen Prudea looked Queen Filanthropi in the eyes and continued, "But since you are one of my most cherished, open-minded, and understanding friends… well, I hope I may confide in you."

"Of course, my dear Prudea," Queen Filanthropi said.

"Well… ten years ago, I sat on the edge of my mother's bed and held her hand. She was so near death that I was not sure if she knew I was at her side. In the late afternoon on what had been a lovely day, the sky turned the most dreadful shade of green. Frightened as to what this meant, the people of East Wisdomere locked themselves in their homes. The servants refused to come out of their quarters. The horses broke loose of their ties and ran for cover in the woods. Thousands of rabbits scurried for the safety of their warrens. Trees bowed toward the ground in an attempt to hide. And insects of all kinds, some never before seen, lined up at the window, and encased the door as if to form a protective barrier between my dying mother and God knows what. Then he appeared. I was never so scared in my life."

"Who? Who appeared?" Queen Filanthropi begged.

"The Soul Seeker." Queen Prudea gulped wine. "When he appeared, my mother regained consciousness, looked right at him, smiled and said, 'I knew it was you.' And guess what?"

51

"What?"

"The Soul Seeker chuckled."

"Chuckled?"

"Yes, he chuckled and said, 'We had such fun. Did we not?' My mother sighed and replied, 'Not as much fun as we would have had with Matilda. Too bad Father banned her.'"

"Too bad Father banned her?" Queen Filanthropi said incredulously. "That would mean your mother and the Soul Seeker were sister and brother."

Queen Prudea rose and whispered, "There is something else you should know."

Queen Filanthropi didn't utter a word, but her eyes pleaded with Queen Prudea to give up her secret.

"Heroian is my mother's brother."

"What are you saying?" Queen Filanthropi sniped. "I know for a fact Heroian was raised as an only child after the tragic death of his older sister."

"Yes, but it is a lie. Mother was the rightful heir to the throne of Idlebury. She was to be crowned queen when she met my father at her precoronation celebration. They fell instantly and madly in love. Because she was the only female heir to the throne of Idlebury, and because of Idlebury's laws of succession, marriage between them was impossible. She begged Father to abdicate the throne of East Wisdomere, marry her, and become King of Idlebury, but he adamantly refused. In her despair, Mother did the only logical thing. She" —Queen Prudea took another swig of wine— "She faked her death."

Queen Filanthropi paced the room. "So how did she marry your father if she was… dead?"

"It was quite simple. Mother changed her identity—a new name, a few extra pounds, and a blond wig—and until this moment, no one ever knew. So this can only mean one thing," Queen Prudea said.

The Queen of Idlebury stopped pacing and stood in front of Queen Prudea. "Go on. Say it. I want to hear the words come out of your mouth," she said.

"I have forgotten how emotional you can be, my dear Filanthropi, so I will get to the point. My mother had only one sibling, a brother, Heroian. Mother's comment implied the Soul Seeker was her brother. Therefore, Heroian is—"

"*Stop!*" Queen Filanthropi shouted. "I cannot bear it." She cried, paced, wrung her hands, and gulped wine as she contemplated the shocking news.

"Oh, Filanthropi, I am afraid it was a mistake to reveal my long-held secret? Maybe I should have kept my mouth shut. But I am relieved to have spoken the truth."

Queen Filanthropi stopped, looked at her friend, and excitedly said, "It all makes sense. Despite the myths, fables, and endless chatter about the adventures and exploits of the Soul Seeker, Heroian never spoke of him. He would walk away when others discussed the powerful, mysterious, and supernatural man. He neither acknowledged, nor denied, nor debated the stories. Heroian is... Heroian is the... Soul Seeker." Queen Filanthropi and her wine goblet crashed to the floor.

Queen Prudea giggled as she rushed to her friend's side. "You silly girl," she whispered as she patted Queen Filanthropi's cheeks in an attempt to arouse her.

A servant who'd heard a thump and the shattering of glass, knocked on the queen's chamber door and asked, "Your Majesty, is everything all right?"

"Just a little too much wine," Queen Prudea said. "Please go away. You are dismissed."

Queen Filanthropi regained consciousness and found herself on the floor in the arms of Queen Prudea.

"What happened?"

"You fainted dead away."

"I cannot believe it," Queen Filanthropi said as she tried to stand, still a little shaky. "Prudea, how kind of you to tell me the truth." She paused and then added, "No one must know."

Suddenly, the fire and candles blew out. The room became dark and cold. The two queens huddled and moved toward the door. Queen Prudea reached for the doorknob. As her fingers touched the brass, a bolt of lightning flashed across the darkened room, revealing the presence of two other beings. They stood in opposite corners as if ready for a fight.

Queen Filanthropi whispered, "Heroian, is that you?"

Maniacal laughter filled the room. In a mocking manner, a woman said, "Heroian is that you? You're pathetic. You've shared a bed with Heroian for years, bore his children, and supported his works and whims, yet you don't know him? It's the Soul Seeker who you address, the one who's feared, loved, respected, and rejected throughout the universe."

"Stop," a man said in a raspy yet booming voice. Light from the window made it possible to see the outline of a dark-robed giant. "Do not mock her."

"Heroian, I need proof it is you to whom I speak. When I met you in the Field of Wisdom, you refused to reveal yourself to me. Now I demand you remove your hood and show your face," Queen Filanthropi said. "Show me who you are."

"I will not," the Soul Seeker responded as he turned away.

"Why not?"

"Because I am hideous."

"You could never be hideous to me, my dear husband."

"I am *not* your dear husband. I am *not* Heroian," the Soul Seeker said as he whipped around to face Queen Filanthropi.

"No!" the other being yelled. "You mustn't reveal the truth."

"But you are my Uncle Heroian. Mother recognized you when you came to her on her deathbed. She called you 'my brother,'" Queen Prudea interjected.

"It is true I came to your mother as she lay dying, but I was not and am not Heroian. I was merely using his soul. It was his soul that I showed her," the Soul Seeker replied.

"Here we go," the other being said in a snide manner.

Queen Filanthropi's legs weaken, but she managed to remain standing. "So the fables are true. You suck the life out of others," she said as she grabbed a chair for balance and tried to catch her breath.

"I do not suck the life out of people. I borrow their souls." The Soul Seeker opened his cape to reveal the lighted faces of the many souls he had taken throughout the years. Some were historical persons from the thirteen dimensions. Others appeared to be ordinary people.

Queen Prudea gasped when she saw her mother's face among the others. Then King Heroian's face appeared large before the room's occupants. He looked Queen Filanthropi squarely in the eyes, but he didn't utter a word. He didn't need to. Queen Filanthropi now knew the Soul Seeker meant no harm, at least not to anyone other than one specific person. She knew in order to survive, the Soul Seeker needed the soul of an innocent yet powerful person. He needed Gwen's soul.

Suddenly, an image of Gwen appeared before them.

"She is the last soul I seek. Her purity and strength will keep me alive for eternity," the Soul Seeker said as he and the image of Gwen vanished.

As the other being stepped out of the shadows, the fire and candles relit, revealing a ten-year-old girl dressed as a princess.

"Gwendolyn," Queen Filanthropi exclaimed as she reached for the child.

Again, maniacal laughter echoed through the room as the child transformed into Wilameena. "Don't let the Soul Seeker take her. The survival of the universe depends on your child. Now go. Find Matilda," the enchantress said and then disappeared.

Exhausted from the emotional toll of the day, Queen Filanthropi meekly asked, "Where do we find Matilda?"

"I do not know," Queen Prudea nonchalantly replied.

Queen Filanthropi continued as if she didn't hear the other queen. "I do not know where to begin. I feel lost and hopeless. I do not know how to save Gwendolyn… my child."

"Well, we have to start somewhere," Queen Prudea said.

Queen Filanthropi stopped crying and said, "I believe we start in Idlebury. I know exactly where Matilda used to live."

With a surge of energy, Queen Filanthropi went to the window and leaned out. Then she whistled for Lightening, but he didn't respond.

"Oh, I forgot. I left Lightening in the Slothful Forest. Come. We must find the beam that will transport us to Lightening and Idlebury."

"No, I cannot," Queen Prudea said.

The Queen of Idlebury took hold of Queen Prudea's hands. "But you must."

"It is forbidden, my dear friend. To travel via the beam would jeopardize my kingdom."

Queen Filanthropi released her hold on her friend's hands

and moved toward the window, her head lowered in contemplation. She remained silent for a few moments, then she scornfully said, "Who makes up these rules we faithfully follow? Rules that go unquestioned. Rules that determine our lives. Why do we give them so much power? Have they no power unless they are believed and followed?"

"It is written. They are eternal rules," the Queen of East Wisdomere said. "I know not who made them up. I only know I am their servant. I vowed as queen to follow the rules and the rules I will follow."

Queen Filanthropi glared at Queen Prudea and sternly said, "Follow the rules if you must. But for me, the rules have diminishing value. I believe it is time to break them."

"At what cost?"

"I do not know. It is a risk with an outcome I cannot predict. But I do know I must find Matilda, our forbidden friend. And to do that, I must break the universal rules of not meddling with the Innocents."

Queen Filanthropi waited for Queen Prudea's response. The Queen of East Wisdomere hesitated as if lost in thought. With a barely noticeable movement of her head, she indicated her answer.

"Very well then, I bid you a fond adieu. And despite your hesitancy, I do believe someday you will change your mind." Before she took her leave, Queen Filanthropi momentarily stared at Queen Prudea.

"Wait," Queen Prudea cried.

A glimmer of hope flashed across Queen Filanthropi's face.

"Let me provide a carriage for you to the edge of the kingdom."

Queen Filanthropi nodded to indicate her approval.

A gilded carriage awaited the Queen of Idlebury's departure from East Wisdomere. Before she entered the carriage, she glanced back at the castle in hopes Queen Prudea had changed her mind, but no one was at the door. Queen Filanthropi looked up and saw what appeared to be her friend standing at a window, crying and waving goodbye. But if she had looked more closely, she would have noticed the woman at the window was too old and too heavyset to be Queen Prudea. And she would have seen her friend running down the castle stairs yelling for her to stop.

Chapter Eight
Queen Matilda Regains Her Power

GWEN, KENDALL, AISLINN, and Mistofisee, still huddled inside the Soul Seeker's cape, remained in the dark for what seemed like an eternity.

Mistofisee mustered the nerve to utter the first word. "Well?"

"Well? What?" Aislinn asked. "Here we are and no one has a clue as to where or why we're here."

"Do so enlighten me," Kendall said in an obnoxious manner.

A roar interrupted the conversation. The earth shook. An acrid smell filled the air. The four new friends choked back their queasiness.

"I will enlighten you, you insolent, arrogant children. You have not seen the power and fury I can inflict on you and the universe. I am all powerful. You are nothing," the Soul Seeker said, and then he broke out in maniacal laughter.

With a snap of his wrists, the Soul Seeker wrapped the foursome in the black fabric of his cape and threw them skyward. Blue skies replaced the darkness. Soon Gwen,

Kendall, and Aislinn plummeted from the sky and landed in a barren, dusty field. Idlebury Castle appeared in the distance. But the trio didn't notice it as they dusted off and checked themselves for injury.

"Where's that silly dragon?" Aislinn asked as she rubbed her knee.

Gwen called for Mistofisee, but he didn't reply.

Gwen and Kendall called and searched for the dragon, but he was nowhere in sight. Finally, Aislinn spotted him perched on a cloud, seemingly oblivious to the other three. He appeared lost in thought.

"How does he do that?" Kendall queried.

"Do what?" Gwen asked.

"Sit on a cloud."

"That's no biggie," said Gwen. "All you have to do is believe and you can do anything."

"Okay then. Let's see you join him up there on the fluffy cloud," Aislinn chimed in.

"Can't," replied Gwen.

"Yeah, right. I didn't think you could," said Kendall. "You're a lot of hot air."

"No, I'm not... but Mistofisee is. He's a dragon. Right? And what do dragons do?"

Gwen stared at Kendall and Aislinn. The looks on their faces make it clear they had no idea what point she was trying to make. "They breathe fire, you idiots," she replied.

"Supposedly," Kendall responded.

"Not supposedly," Gwen said. "They do breathe fire."

"So your point would be?" Kendall mocked her.

"He's full of hot air and that's how he's sitting on top of the cloud."

"And your point would be?"

"Watch."

Gwen reached into her pocket and removed her magic coin box. She opened it and then rapidly closed it. When she opened it again, she disappeared. Aislinn and Kendall looked around to see where she could possibly hide.

"Hello down there."

When Aislinn and Kendall looked up, they saw Gwen sitting next to the dragon on a fluffy white cloud. As they admired Gwen's feat, they noticed something odd.

"What's up with the cloud?" Kendall asked.

"I don't know, but I don't like the looks of it," Aislinn said.

The cloud moved as it became darker and darker until it turned pitch-black.

"That's not a cloud, it's the Soul Seeker," Kendall exclaimed.

Thunder echoed through the sky. Lightning illuminated the dreary Idlebury Castle, giving it an almost majestic look. Insane laughter filled the air. Gwen was gone and the Soul Seeker had her.

Kendall and Aislinn had nowhere to turn for help.

"Look," Aislinn said pointing at Idlebury castle. "I bet someone there can help us."

Kendall nodded in agreement then led the way to Idlebury Castle in hopes of finding Gwen. Despite the noon hour, a sudden veil of darkness revealed the most brilliantly lit night sky, rich with twinkling stars. A shooting star caught Aislinn's and Kendall's attention. They noticed it headed straight at them.

"I don't like this. I don't like this at all," Aislinn whined as usual. "First the sun is gone, then stars appear in the afternoon sky, and now a falling star is about to hit us. Makes no sense to me. I say we make a run for it."

Kendall ignored Aislinn as he watched the shooting star. When he moved his eyes, he noticed the star moved with them. But when he looked at the star again, it stopped. Kendall reveled in his apparent control of the celestial body, tossing the star across the sky at will. Unexpectedly, he crashed it into the ground in front of the castle. He ran to investigate the grounding of the celestial body.

"Don't get too close to it," Aislinn yelled as she tried to catch up with Kendall. "You don't know what it is. I don't like the looks of it. If I were you, I'd wait for help. It could hurt us. It could be alive."

"Quiet, you whiny little pest," Kendall grumbled as he proceeded.

As Kendall and Aislinn approached the crash site, Aislinn's attempts to stop Kendall became more desperate. She tugged on his arm. She pulled his clothes. He appeared unfazed. Up ahead, a gaping hole was visible, adding to Aislinn's angst. Still, Kendall continued forward.

Finally, they reached the enormous opening in the ground. Slimy purple gelatinous goo oozed from it. Kendall bravely peered into the hole. Aislinn squinted as if she were afraid she'd go blind if she looked directly at the goo.

"What is it? Don't get too close. You don't know what it is. Don't touch it," Aislinn said as Kendall bent over to scoop up a handful of purple slime. His fingers nearly touched the mysterious stuff when something pushed him to the ground.

"Don't you dare touch my mother," Mistofisee said.

"Your mother?" Kendall said as he rose. "Your mother is a

pile of purple goo?"

Mistofisee was about to respond when someone interrupted.

"Stop, my son," Matilda demanded. "There's no need to protect me for I'm alive and well."

Kendall and Aislinn stared in disbelief at the gigantic purple and green dragon.

"That's the biggest monster I've ever seen," Kendall declared.

Aislinn was speechless.

The young dragon ran to the giant dragon, jumped on her, and hugged her. "Mother, I'm so happy to see you. But your presence mean"—Mistofisee gulped—"the universe is in dire need of redemption."

"Oh… my… God. The universe is in dire need of redemption. I don't like this. I don't like this at all," Aislinn said as she bit her nails.

"The entire universe is in dire need of redemption?" Kendall bemoaned. "Now isn't that just a *tad* dramatic?"

"You're a naïve, narcissistic schoolboy," Queen Matilda snapped. "The universe doesn't revolve around you. It's much grander and more complex than you can imagine. It's your fault I'm standing before you. You thwarted my purpose. And you," the dragon said as she moved her massive head toward Aislinn, "stop your cowering and whining, it only feeds his arrogance."

Aislinn moved away from Kendall, who smirked at Queen Matilda.

"Do tell, why are you two-toned?" Kendall asked the dragon queen.

"Because she's been ill with Dragon's Sleep," Mistofisee answered as if to defend his mother. "The fact she was able to arouse herself after nearly two hundred years of lethargy and near death is a testament to her will. But it also means we're all in serious trouble."

"Enough," Queen Matilda scorned. "I didn't get off my deathbed to waste my time with this. Now, where is Princess Gwendolyn, the rightful heir to the throne of Idlebury? I have been commanded to find her."

Kendall was about to answer when Mistofisee cut him off, "Shh. Don't say his name. It will upset my mother."

"Where is she?" Queen Matilda roared.

"The Soul Seeker took her," Aislinn courageously replied.

Upon hearing the name of the Soul Seeker, the dragon queen threw back her head and spewed forth a fireball that sent a blinding light over Idlebury. Instantly, she turned completely green. With one flap of her massive wings, she took to the sky.

"See, I told you it would upset her," Mistofisee said as he looked skyward and watched his mother fly away. But when he saw she was completely green, he burst with pride, because regaining her color meant she had reclaimed her incredible power.

Chapter Nine
The Dragon Sighting

Despite the early hour, the appearance of the night sky lured the people of Idlebury to their beds. For the lazy Idleburians, slumber could come none too soon. As usual, their dreams were about what they would get without the burden of labor. Nestled in their beds, they were ignorant of how the event taking place outside their homes was about to change their lives.

Most of the Idleburians didn't notice the flash of light and the rumbling of the earth when Queen Matilda crashed in front of the Idlebury Castle. The few who did notice, only briefly opened their bleary eyes before they returned to a sound sleep. But no one slept through Queen Matilda's roar and the burst of blinding light from the flame she'd spewed.

Gwilym Innaine, Idlebury's Minister of Mindlessness, rushed to the bedroom window as his weary wife trailed behind. As they looked into the night sky, lit by a full moon, they gasped. For they both saw a sight not seen over Idlebury for more than two hundred years—the unmistakable image of a dragon flying across the sky. Worse, the beast headed toward East Wisdomere.

"Dragon! Dragon!" Gwilym screamed as he raced into the village square.

Lights came on in homes across Idlebury as word quickly spread of the dragon sighting. The young and the old emerged from the safety of their homes carrying torches, lanterns, and anything they could find to use as a weapon.

As more and more Idleburians headed for the square, their loud chatter interrupted the tranquility of the midday night. Although some walked hesitantly toward the Minister of Mindlessness, grumbling about the ridiculousness of his claim, others rushed toward him as if to personally challenge him. Gwilym stood on a platform and raised his hand to quiet the crowd.

"Where's ya proof a dragon was seen?" someone yelled.

Others chimed in, "Yeah, where's ya proof?"

"Ya disturbed me beauty sleep," chirped one of Idlebury's less attractive residents, resulting in laughter from the growing crowd.

"Quiet! I know what I saw. And me wife saw it too. 'Twas a dragon. And it was headed straight fer East Wisdomere. Right, me dear?" Gwilym said as he turned to his wife for support.

"A dragon? Maybe. I didn't get a good look. But if me husband said 'twas a dragon, dan a dragon 'twas," Gwilym's wife replied.

As the crowd became rowdy, Gwilym yelled, "Ain't nobody else seen da dragon?"

The crowd became quiet. No one responded.

"Surely somebody seen it," Gwilym pleaded.

"I saw it," someone said with conviction.

"Come here, young man," Gwilym requested.

A dark-haired young boy stepped forward. Comments about the child's beauty rippled through the crowd. He appeared more mature than his years, was dressed in fine clothes, and expressed himself in an educated manner despite his youth. But what was most unusual about the boy was he lacked the dull hue for which the Idleburians were known.

The child confidently walked up to Gwilym and repeated his statement. "I saw it."

"Ya saw what?" Gwilym asked as he bent down and peered into the boy's crystal-clear blue eyes.

"The dragon. I saw the dragon. I believe her name is Matilda."

The crowd gasped. Some fainted upon hearing the dragon queen's name.

"How dare ya speak dat name in dis kingdom, young man?" a woman commented.

The boy pulled himself up on the platform and stood between the Minister of Mindlessness and his nervous wife. "She's not here to harm us," he said. "She's here to save us."

"Save us from what?" Gwilym asked.

"From ourselves," the child replied.

A woman with a keen eye noticed the boy's likeness to the queen and asked, "Who are ya ta know such thin's, me child?"

"I'm Thane. My mother is Morgana, Queen Filanthropi's head servant."

Gwilym eyed the child with suspicion. He wondered why this son of a servant appeared so privileged, particularly when it was against Idlebury law to acquire wealth.

"Where'd ya get dem clothes?" a man said as if he could read Gwilym's mind. "Day ain't da clothes of a servant's child. Day ain't even da clothes of an Idleburian."

"My mother made them with her own hands from scraps. She's an extraordinary seamstress. She designs and sews all of the king's and queen's clothes," Thane boasted.

The crowd appeared to accept his explanation and returned to concerns about their welfare.

"So who's gonna protect us?" screamed a woman from the crowd.

"Yeah, where's da king? We haven't seen da likes of him fer months," screamed another.

"Let's go find da king. We want answers," stated a man.

As they headed en masse for the castle, the Idleburians chanted, "Da king. Da king. Dis is his thing. Not ours. Not ours. Not mine. Not yers."

"Don't tell the king. He need not know. He must not know. *Please*," Thane pleaded. But his pleas went unheeded as the Idleburians ran toward the castle.

As the sun slowly emerged, a young girl fell from the sky into the Slothful Forest. But the Idleburians didn't notice.

Chapter Ten
The Flight of Mistofisee

THE BRILLIANT SUNLIGHT nearly blinded Kendall, Aislinn, and Mistofisee. Nonetheless, a falling object caught their attention.

"Look, it's Gwen," Kendall said as he dashed toward the Slothful Forest.

"I don't like this. I don't like this at all. She's probably dead. No one can fall from the sky and land in one piece. This is dreadful. This could be disgusting," Aislinn said to no one, as Kendall and Mistofisee were already well on their way to where Gwen had landed.

Without warning, a giant snake wrapped itself around Aislinn and attempted to swallow her whole. "*Oh no!* I don't like this. I don't like this at all," Aislinn said as the snake sucked her in, headfirst.

A moment later, the snake regurgitated Aislinn, rose, shook its head in disgust, and rolled on the ground in agony.

Aislinn wiped the snake slobber from her face as her eyes filled with tears. "Nobody likes me. Not even you, you horrible snake," she cried. "I guess it's because I don't even like myself."

"Yes. You might want to work on that as it makes you most

distasteful," the snake said as it gasped and spat. "Besides, Gwen can't save Idlebury if you're sitting around feeling sorry for yourself. Remember, you're one of her selves. As pathetic as you are, she needs you to succeed. Now go."

When Aislinn ran to catch up with Mistofisee and Kendall, the snake changed into a fat, middle-aged woman, who smiled and shook her head as she watched the girl run in the wrong direction.

In the meantime, Kendall and Mistofisee found the lifeless Gwen in a pile of leaves.

Kendall stared in disbelief and said, "She can't be dead."

"Why not?" Mistofisee asked.

"Because I'm not dead and I'm one of her selves."

"You've got a point," the dragon said. "So why does she look dead?"

Kendall scanned the area. "Where's Aislinn?"

"Pardon me," a huge porcupine said in a polite manner. "I do believe the girl in question ran the other way."

"The other way?" Kendall and Mistofisee said in unison.

"Yes. Toward East Wisdomere."

"Where's that?" the dragon asked.

"As the crow flies, it's approximately… well, it's that way." The porcupine pointed to the right of Idlebury Castle.

"Thank you. Let's be off," Kendall said with urgency.

"Excuse me. What about her?" the animal inquired, pointing to Gwen.

"I'll carry her. She's not too heavy for the likes of me," Kendall proudly exclaimed.

"Not to worry. I'll take the two of you to East Wisdomere," Mistofisee said.

"How?" Kendall asked, somewhat agitated.

"You'll see. Tie her to you then grab my tail."

"Tie her to me then grab your tail? Are you daft?"

"Just do it," the porcupine interrupted. "Time is desperately short."

The porcupine scurried around the forest, pointing out the best vines for making rope.

As Kendall gathered the vines and with a little help from the porcupine, tied Gwen on his back, he noticed the dragon appeared to be sick. Consumed with the need to complete his task, Kendall looked away. But the heaving, burping dragon was hard to ignore.

With each burp, smoke rings seeped from Mistofisee's mouth. As he struggled to not let the smoke escape, he looked at Kendall. His eyes screamed, "hurry up." But it was too late. Now full of hot air, Mistofisee rose skyward.

Just in time, Kendall grabbed the dragon's tail and the threesome floated over Idlebury on their way to East Wisdomere.

Kendall caught a glimpse of a fat, older woman standing in the forest, but a horde of Idleburians gathered in front of the Idlebury Castle diverted his attention. When he heard them yelling something about a dragon, he feared they had spotted Mistofisee and would shoot him down. For once, he felt like Aislinn. He didn't like it. He didn't like it at all.

As Mistofisee carried Kendall and Gwen over the Slothful Forest, Kendall spotted Aislinn running in circles. "Nincompoop... nitwit," he mumbled to himself as he yanked on Mistofisee's tail to get his attention.

The dragon, startled by the pull on his tail, opened his mouth to protest. Much to his and Kendall's surprise, hot air escaped, tossing them across the sky like a rapidly deflating balloon. Mistofisee, Kendall, and Gwen tumbled back into the Slothful Forest.

"*You idiot!* Why did you pull my tail?" Mistofisee asked while he tried to get Kendall to release his grip on his tail.

"I wanted you to open your eyes, not your big mouth," Kendall said as he untied Gwen. "If you had, you would've noticed nitwit Aislinn mindlessly running in circles. Now we'll never find… oh, speaking of the devil, here she is."

Aislinn appeared dazed but happy to see the others.

"Where have you been?" Kendall asked.

"Oh, it was terrible. I saw you two run ahead. I tried to run after you but I couldn't because an enormous snake nearly devoured me. My life flashed before my eyes. Fortunately, the horrible snake spit me out. I started to run to catch up with you when I realized I couldn't see the forest for the trees. I kept running, looking for the forest, now I'm here." Aislinn pointed at Gwen. "What's the matter with her?"

"She can't live without you," Mistofisee replied.

Touched by the dragon's statement, Aislinn began to cry. "No one has ever said such a nice thing to me."

"He means she literally can't live without you. You're one of her selves. So we have to stick together for Gwen," Kendall said.

Gwen began to stir. She sat up and said, "I've seen it. I've seen my purpose. I know why I'm here. I'm here to save the universe." Gwen rose to her feet. "Come on. We don't have a moment to spare."

"Maybe we should check her head for bumps," Mistofisee exclaimed.

"I'm fine. I'm the Princess of Idlebury and I will fulfill my prophecy."

Chapter Eleven
The Disappearing Carriage

THE CARRIAGE PROVIDED by Queen Prudea swayed and bounced along a rugged road as it carried Queen Filanthropi to East Wisdomere's border. Inside, the Queen of Idlebury jostled to and fro, but she barely noticed because she was lost in visions of a joyful reunion with her old dragon friend, Matilda, and her daughter, Gwendolyn. Her vision of Gwendolyn's investiture as the Princess of Idlebury filled her with hope for the future of her kingdom. For a change, her heart felt light.

But the queen's newfound joy quickly faded when she realized she'd traveled longer than expected. She pulled back the velvet carriage curtain and discovered she was no longer in East Wisdomere. She peered out the carriage window in an attempt to grab the driver's attention and alert him that this was not the way to the beam. To her horror, there was neither a driver nor horses. Her heart raced. She had no idea where she was and who or what was guiding the carriage. An attempt to open the door was fruitless. Ways to escape raced through her mind. She tried to yell for help, but couldn't. She rocked the carriage in hopes it would tip over. She tried to squeeze out the window which was barely larger than her head. Nonetheless, the carriage continued as if it had a mind of its own.

Suddenly, the interior of the carriage became dark. The air became stuffy. Queen Filanthropi frantically reached for the carriage door again, but all she felt was dead space. The carriage appeared to be gone, yet she was still moving forward.

"This cannot be. This makes no sense. How could the carriage disappear into thin air? It is impossible," she mumbled.

The queen stood then sat. Then she stood again and sat. "What am I sitting on?" she whispered. "I cannot feel anything, yet I am sitting on something."

Her heart pounded. She gasped as she tried to catch her breath. Out of the darkness, a face appeared; then another, and another, and another.

"Oh, my," the queen wheezed. "I am inside the cape of the Soul Seeker."

The words had barely left her lips when she heard the Soul Seeker say, "You, like so many others, are pathetic. Your fear of me leads you to deny my true intentions."

"What are your intentions?" Queen Filanthropi asked.

"I will not tell you because you will not believe me. You and your kind have been brainwashed as to my purpose in the universe. You fear me when I try to show you love."

"*Love?*" Queen Filanthropi declared. "You have sucked the life out of thousands of people for thousands of years and you want to be loved, adored, and worshiped? It is simply scandalous."

"I do not suck the life out of people. I save souls that have gone astray and are off course. I am a savior. You need not understand, but one day you will."

"Why did you steal the soul of my dear husband, Heroian?"

74

"I did not steal his soul. He sought me out. He begged for help. He prayed to the universe to help his people learn to help themselves. I was one answer to his prayers. There were other ways for him to achieve his goal, but he chose to give up his soul for the welfare of his people."

"I do not believe you. Heroian's motto has always been, 'this above all: to thine own self be true.'"

"Quoting Shakespeare? He knew not of what he was writing. He wrote through me. It was me he so eloquently quoted."

Shakespeare appeared before the queen. The old bard paced as he recited some of his most famous quotes. "'In time we hate that which we often fear.' 'Uneasy lies the head that wears a crown.' 'You take my life when you take the means whereby I live.' 'Neither a borrower nor a lender be.' 'There is nothing either good or bad, but thinking makes it so.'"

"You expect me to believe Shakespeare's greatness is due to you?" Queen Filanthropi asked as Shakespeare continued his recitation.

"The man was a tortured soul. He asked for relief from his emotional pain. So I rewarded him with the words to express his torment."

"How did that help him and help the universe?"

"His purpose was to speak universal truths. But the earthly time period in which he was born forbade it. Therefore, through me, he fulfilled his purpose and enriched the psyche of generations of beings throughout the universe."

"So why have you come for me?" Queen Filanthropi said in an angry, disrespectful manner.

"Patience, my dear. You will find out soon enough. You were born to achieve greatness and leave a mark on the universe, but you too have strayed. Your soul is suffering. But remember, I have not come for you. I have come for the soul of your child, Gwendolyn. She is not yet ready."

"Is she not ready… or not willing?"

"You dare to question me? Be off with you," the Soul Seeker shouted as he vanished.

The queen found herself back in East Wisdomere. Before her, the beam vibrated. Without hesitation, she walked into its light and slipped back into Idlebury.

Chapter Twelve
Queen Merry's Innocence

THE SCENERY PULSATED and rippled, but neither Gwen, nor Kendall, nor Aislinn, nor did Mistofisee notice the visual disturbance as they unknowingly wandered through it and into Dimension XII. Gwen appeared unfazed by the crossover as she ranted and raved about her mission to save the universe and her destiny to be crowned Princess of Idlebury. Kendall was groggy as if an invisible force had cast a spell on him. Aislinn appeared to be in a trance. But Mistofisee seemed unaffected as he nonchalantly whistled and strolled behind Gwen as she continued her unrelenting chatter.

Finally, the foursome approached the first kingdom on their quest to find Idlebury and save the universe. A huge, brightly colored sign stopped them. It read WARNING! YOU'RE ABOUT TO ENTER HEDONIA. IF YOU'RE ADVERSE TO MINDLESS PLEASURE, TURN BACK NOW AS WE DON'T WANT YOU.

Gwen smiled and shrugged at Mistofisee as she led her friends to the next sign. It read IF YOU'VE COME THIS FAR, YOU'RE EITHER STUPID OR FUN LOVING. IF YOU'RE THE LATTER, PLEASE CONTINUE. IF YOU'RE THE FORMER, PLEASE PROCEED TO FOOLSVILLE AS YOU'LL FIT IN QUITE WELL THERE.

Gwen and Mistofisee chuckled as they all walked on. But Kendall and Aislinn were unusually quiet. Soon they came upon another brightly colored sign. But it was blank. Gwen walked up to see if the words had faded. With her face nearly touching the sign, she searched for instructions as to what to do next.

"Who goes there?" someone said in a booming, echoing voice as a face pushed its way out of the sign.

Gwen jumped back and said, "'Tis I, Gwendolyn, Princess of Idlebury."

"Oh, geez," the face said as it rolled its eyes and sneered. "Okay, let me try this again. Who goes there?"

Puzzled at how to answer, Gwen stared at the face. Out of nowhere, a phrase popped into her head and she blurted, "I'm Princess Gwendolyn of Idlebury… where everyone goes to do nothing and where no one goes to do something."

"I'm King Funzy of Hedonia… where fun is serious business and where serious business is no fun. Welcome, my fun-loving friends."

The face vanished. Words appeared. WELCOME TO HEDONIA — LAND OF FUN AND FROLIC FOR ONE AND ALL. Next to the words, a picture of King Funzy and Queen Merry grinning appeared.

Soon a vast gate meticulously painted with beautiful scenes of happy people engaged in fun activities opened. As Gwen and her friends entered Hedonia, laughter filled the air. What looked like mayhem was actually people engaged in fun and games.

Children ran and played, nearly knocking over the guests. Mistofisee cringed when he saw several children playing Dragon Slayer with one child costumed as a ferocious version of him.

Adults engaged in a variety activities—playing board games, swimming, surfing, water skiing, snow skiing, skydiving, hot air ballooning, catapulting others across the castle wall, dancing, playing music, acting in plays, painting landscapes and portraits, running three-legged races, reading, crocheting, knitting, and playing of all sorts of familiar and unfamiliar sports.

Gwen was awestruck. But Mistofisee felt grossly out of place and horribly unwelcome because there were no Innocents to be found. From the corner of his eye, he thought he saw a black figure, but when he looked directly at it, nothing was there.

One of the younger Hedonians pulled Gwen into a group of dancers. She quickly learned the steps and danced until she was out of breath.

Kendall and Aislinn appeared like lifeless wax figures, both rendered motionless by Gwen's lack of need for them while she was lost in the magic of dance.

Mistofisee closely observed the Hedonians, hoping to go unseen for fear the children would attack him.

Suddenly, a trumpet blasted. King Funzy and Queen Merry stood before the crowd, desperately trying to get the Hedonians' attention.

"Attention please," King Funzy yelled. The Hedonians didn't heed the king's command. Again, King Funzy yelled, "Attention please." Still, the people didn't respond. Even Gwen continued to dance merrily. Agitated by the insolence of his people, he yelled, *"Stop!"*

Everyone froze in place with the exception of Gwen who continued to dance. When she noticed the others had stopped, she quickly walked over to Mistofisee. "What's up with them?"

she asked, pointing at Kendall and Aislinn.

"Shh," Mistofisee replied, surprised to see a puff of smoke escape from his mouth.

King Funzy addressed the now quiet crowd. "My fellow Hedonians, we are graced today by the presence of Gwendolyn, soon to be known as Princess Gwendolyn of Idlebury, and her friend, Mistofisee of Beastonia, Land of the Innocents."

The young dragon flinched when he heard himself referred to as Innocent friend. "Gee, I was hoping to go unnoticed," he said to Gwen.

"You're a little too gigantic and a little too green to go unnoticed."

King Funzy continued, "Gwendolyn has come to Hedonia with a special request." He paused as if to gauge the response of the crowd, but no one moved or uttered a word. "She requests that Queen Merry and I, as well as the dukes, duchesses, earls, lords, and ladies, join her in Idlebury for the Royal Assembly. Representatives from all of the kingdoms of the thirteen dimensions will attend. We are to leave in a fortnight." The king paused again, but the crowd didn't respond.

"How does he know why I'm here?" Gwen asked Mistofisee. "I didn't talk to him. How would he know?"

"Maybe he's not the king," Mistofisee replied. "This is Hedonia. Maybe he's just having a little fun with you."

"Something is wrong. I don't like this. I don't like this at all," she whispered.

"You're beginning to sound like Aislinn," the dragon remarked.

Upon ending his speech, King Funzy turned and walked

back toward the castle. But Queen Merry didn't move. She remained still with a forced smile on her face. Suddenly, King Funzy turned back as if he'd forgotten something. "It will be great *fun,*" he said.

As he emphasized the word *fun,* the Hedonians came back to life and chanted, "Hail Hedonia, where fun is serious business and where serious business is no fun." They immediately returned to doing what they did best.

Gwen noticed the queen looked dazed. She rushed to talk to Queen Merry, who put out her arms toward Gwen and said, "Come, my child. The Soul Seeker has taken the king, for it was he who spoke and not my dear Funzy."

Queen Merry escorted Gwen and Mistofisee, as well as Kendall and Aislinn, who were still groggy, into the castle.

"Why didn't he take you?" Gwen asked.

"He tried, but as you can see, I'm not fully human. My father is an Innocent," the queen said as she lifted her gown and revealed her hoofed feet. Queen Merry let down her hair and revealed the most beautiful, silky white horse's mane Gwen had ever seen. "As for you, my dear Mistofisee, Innocents are always welcome in Hedonia. So you needn't worry about the game Dragon Slayer. It is mere child's play. You know, humans are quite innocent when they're young."

Mistofisee's heart filled with joy as he nodded his thank-you.

"We must go. Won't you come with us?" Gwen asked Queen Merry.

"I cannot. I have much work here to prepare for the Royal Assembly," the queen replied. "But I will see you soon in Idlebury. I promise."

"Kendall. Aislinn. Let's go," Gwen commanded as her

friends plodded toward her. "What's wrong with them?"

"Who?" Queen Merry asked.

"Kendall and Aislinn. Can't you see them?"

"I see no one."

"But I see them," Mistofisee interjected.

"Pure Innocents can see what others can't. Now go. You must hurry. You have a huge task before you."

"What about King Funzy?" Gwen asked. "Will he be able to come to the Royal Assembly?"

"Don't worry. He's gone off before with the Soul Seeker and he always returns. He'll be back in time for the Royal Assembly," the queen assured Gwen.

Gwen and Mistofisee, with Kendall and Aislinn trudging behind, left Hedonia.

"Now where to?" Mistofisee asked.

"I don't know," Gwen said as she began to cry. "I don't know where the other kingdoms are. I'm hopelessly lost. I feel so helpless, so worthless, and so empty inside."

"Now you're talking like a true Idleburian," Mistofisee mocked her. "I'm hopeless. I'm helpless. I need someone to rescue me."

"Stop it," Kendall said as he regained his full awareness. "She has a right to feel overwhelmed at times. That's why I'm here. When she wants to, she can draw on my strength. After all, I'm the most important part of her."

"Thank you, Kendall," Gwen said as she wiped away her tears.

"What about me? She needs me too," Aislinn whined. "And when you... you bloated baby dragon... make fun of us, well... it makes me feel so small. And I don't like it. I don't like it at all."

"Yeah, we're either in this together or we're not," Kendall stated as Gwen continued to wipe her tears.

"All right, already. I'm sorry," Mistofisee said. "I had no idea you were all so sensitive. Geez, I'll keep my opinions to myself."

"No. If you keep your opinions to yourself, you'd deny your truth," Gwen said. "Sometimes the truth hurts. But it's okay because the truth will set us free. That reminds me, I have a universe to save. So let's go."

"Where?" Mistofisee asked.

"I don't know, but I'm sure we'll find our way," Gwen said with confidence as the foursome set out on their next adventure.

Chapter Thirteen
The Truth About Thane

QUEEN FILANTHROPI ARRIVED in Idlebury to find everything as it was when she left. But for the first time, the overgrowth of vines, bushes, grass, and weeds annoyed her.

When she entered the drab castle, she was met by a crowd chanting, "Da king. Da king. Dis is his thing. Not ours. Not ours. Not mine. Not yers."

Gwilym Innaine, the Minister of Mindlessness rushed over to the queen as she pushed her way through the crowd. "Ah. Der ya be. We have a dreadful situation here. Just dreadful. We need da king at once."

Gwilym spoke to Queen Filanthropi as if she were a commoner. Worse, he didn't bow with the traditional reverence usually afforded royalty. Although this disrespectful behavior had gone unnoticed by the Kings and Queens of Idlebury for centuries, today Gwilym's inappropriate familiarity perturbed Queen Filanthropi.

"Exactly what is so dreadful that you demand the king's presence?" the annoyed queen queried.

The crowd fell silent. The Minister of Mindlessness gulped, then said, "'Tis on good authority dat a... dat a... a dragon was seen flyin' over Idlebury ta day."

"A dragon flying over Idlebury? Is that what you say you saw?" the queen stated in a snide manner.

"Yep. 'Twas a dragon."

"Dragons do not exist!" Queen Filanthropi screamed, causing her face to turn scarlet. "How dare you talk about dragons in Idlebury? It is forbidden. Forbidden, I say."

The crowd gasped because they had never seen a color so bright in all their lives. A few people commented how radiantly beautiful the queen looked.

"I will hear no more," Queen Filanthropi said as she rushed up the staircase to retire to her chambers. When she was nearly to the top of the stairs, the voice of a small child stopped her.

"I saw it."

"Who said that?" the queen demanded as she scanned the crowd for the person who had the audacity to challenge her.

"I did, Your Majesty," Thane said as he bowed respectfully before the queen and then waited politely for her to dismiss him from his bow.

Queen Filanthropi's anger quickly dissipated. She smiled at the child and said, "Approach, young man."

Thane obeyed but maintained his respectful posture.

"You may look at me, my child," said the queen.

Thane stood and looked the queen squarely in the eyes. While the queen marveled at the boy's beauty, she noticed something familiar about him. Her heart skipped a beat. Her visceral reaction to the child struck her as odd. "Who are you? And why are you dressed so extravagantly?" the queen asked. "Are you not from Idlebury?"

"I'm Thane, son of Morgana, your head servant," the boy

replied as he once again bowed before the queen.

"So you are. And who is your father?"

"I don't know. I've never met him, but I hope to one day. I hear he's an extraordinary man."

"Yes, I am sure he is," the queen replied, trying to maintain her composure despite a sudden bout of dizziness.

Her head was spinning. The child had a strange effect on her. She felt as if she would faint. And faint she did. A few minutes later, the queen opened her eyes. Thane looked back at her as he gently patted her cheek. When she looked into his eyes, she had no doubt who he was. He was her child. She cupped the boy's face in her hands and kissed him on the forehead. "Come, my child," Queen Filanthropi said. "We must find the king and address the dragon issue immediately."

Hand in hand, Queen Filanthropi and Thane walked up the staircase. When the queen and Thane reached the top, the queen looked over the banister at her people and said, "Be gone with you. Go back to your homes. There are no such things as dragons, only the wild imagination of a young child."

As the queen and Thane rushed to the king's chambers, Morgana appeared in the hallway. "Thane, come here at once," she commanded. "Yer Majesty, please excuse me son. He's deaf and mute. He knows not proper behavior."

"He is neither deaf nor mute, my dear Morgana. And he is not your son."

"But ma'am, ya know of me son." Morgana gulped. 'Tis him I tell ya."

"It is most curious you never introduced him to me before. Nor spoke of him other than when he was born—at the same time my child, a son, was stillborn."

"Me intention was ta not upset ya, ma'am. After all, ya had

just lost ya own precious child." Morgana tried to steady her shaking hands. "How unkind would it have been of me ta talk about me own child at such a time?"

"Thane is coming with me to see the king. We have a little matter of a flying dragon to discuss." With that, the queen and Thane departed for the king's chamber.

Morgana was terrified. Her secret about Thane was out. So she moseyed back to her quarters to mourn the loss of her son. She was about to enter her room when an image of Fredia's baby popped into her head. She knew she had to get to Fredia before she, too, was forced to forfeit her child, Prudence, to the queen.

Morgana hurried to the long, winding staircase that led downstairs to the kitchen where she knew she would find Fredia preparing a meager yet nutritious meal for the queen and the castle staff. On the way, she remembered stories about a secret passageway that could transport a person anywhere within the castle or the kingdom in an instant. So in the interest of saving precious time, she headed up the staircase to the second floor.

When Morgana reached the landing, she scanned the area to make sure no one was lurking about, particularly not Oof. Confident the coast was clear, she took off running. The sound of her footsteps echoed throughout the castle as she raced down the hall. She came to a sudden stop and examined what appeared to be a blank wall. She gently swept her hand over the wall. Nothing happened. So she swept both hands over the wall. Still, nothing happened. "Open up, ya stupid door," she demanded.

"Who are you calling stupid?" the wall said as huge lips appeared, paint peeled, and pieces of cement crumbled to the floor. "Oh, it is only you... a lowly servant woman," the wall said.

To Morgana's horror, the wall mimicked her voice and verbally regurgitated her story.

"Thane, me love, me child. The queen will never know yer alive. Yer me child now. I love ya with all me heart. Me precious. Me love. Yer a gift from heaven. I'll protect ya forever. Ya'll never know who ya really are. It's a servant's life fer ya. But no matter, I'll give ya da finest clothes. And an education fit for a prince."

"Stop. Why'd ya speak such lies?" Morgana implored.

"Lies? I know not lies," the wall said. "You stood on this very spot more than five years ago. I believe you held a newborn baby; a boy to be exact. A few days later, the queen stood before me weeping about the death of her child. She leaned on me for support as she sobbed, devastated by her loss. She referred to her child as 'my prince.' I put two and two together."

"Who else have ya told?" Morgana asked.

"No one. I do not talk until asked."

"I didn't ask ya ta talk. I asked ya ta open up," Morgana angrily said.

"Oh, my mistake," the wall said. "I misunderstood what you meant by 'open up.' Since I am the Wall of Truth, I naturally assumed you were asking me to speak my truth about your situation. But you called me stupid, which makes my paint peel, so I guess I blurted the truth I have been holding for so long."

"Shut up and open ya secret door. I need ta get downstairs."

"Silly woman, you have the wrong wall. You want the Wall of Passages. One flight up and to the right of the Knight in Shining Armor," the wall said as it grimaced.

Morgana ran back to the staircase and raced up to the next floor. When she reached the top, a towering figure startled her.

"Oh, Oof, ya scared me."

"How so, Morgana," Oof said in his usual snobby manner.

"Oh, nothin.' I'm just in a hurry, dat's all."

"To where, pray tell?"

"The queen needs me ta do somethin.' I must get on with it."

Oof moved aside and let Morgana pass. As he watched the servant head down the hallway, he said, "I do hope your assignment is pertinent to the readiness of the Royal Assembly and the investiture of the Princess of Idlebury."

Morgana looked back toward Oof, intending to respond to his statement, but he was gone as if he had disappeared into thin air.

Morgana huffed and puffed as she ran up the stairs. When she reached the top, she paused to catch her breath. Someone farther down the hall caught her eye. She looked intently and realized it was a knight.

"Over here, my love." The Knight in Shining Armor beckoned. "Come to me. It's our destiny to be together. I'll love and protect you for the rest of time. I'm your warrior, your lover, your friend, and your savior. Please join me so I can serve only you."

Remembering the Wall of Truth said the Wall of Passages was to the right of the Knight in Shining Armor, Morgana raced down the hall. But the knight moved and blocked her way.

"You're my purpose for living. Please be mine. I'll slay your dragons. Dress you in finery. Provide you with a bed of roses on which to rest your pretty head. Your every wish is my desire," said the enamored armored man.

"Move away, please," Morgana requested.

"I can't. Not until I hear you express your love for me," the knight responded.

"Yer a man, are ya not?" Morgana asked.

"I am. With all my heart and soul, I'm the finest of men."

"Den I have no use fer ya."

"But I love you. I've pined for you. I've waited nearly two hundred years for a woman to pass this way. Destiny has brought us together."

"Dat may be, but I have no use fer ya. Let me pass."

"Why? Tell me why you reject me."

"Because a man is a man no matter how shiny his armor."

"Then you know not this man."

"And I don't care ta. Not right now."

"Ah, then there's hope one day you'll change your mind. With hope in my heart, I'll let you pass." The knight moved back into place and allowed Morgana to pass.

The servant woman scanned the wall for a hint of the secret passageway. "Open up. Time is runnin' out," Morgana said as she rubbed her hands against the wall.

A door cracked open. Dust spewed into the air and shrouded Morgana. She sneezed.

"Please excuse my dust, but no one from Idlebury has passed this way in a long time," said a yawning voice. "How may I help you?"

"I need ta get downstairs ta da kitchen and warn Fredia—" Morgana stopped when she realized she was revealing too much.

"Excellent," the weary voice continued. "But for what purpose?"

"Whaddya mean, fer what purpose?" Morgana impatiently

asked. "Are ya not da Wall of Passages?"

"I am."

"Den let me through."

"I will, but first you must choose your path," the Wall of Passages said as its door opened wide. "In other words, you must know your heart's desire for what you are about to do."

A dim light lit the dusty, cobwebbed passage and revealed a labyrinth. Signs, some barely legible, hung over each passageway.

"Remember, choose carefully or you will go down the wrong path and not fulfill your purpose," the Wall of Passages warned as it yawned again.

Morgana quickly read the signs as she looked for the one that would take her to her destination—compassion, love, wonder, curiosity, gratitude, forgiveness, union, peace, joy, serenity, purpose, generosity, empathy, respect, patience, determination, and honesty. "I don't know. All I want ta do is get downstairs."

"Oh, then the fastest path down is the same one that brought you up," the Wall of Passages stated in a bored manner.

"What is it?"

"The stairway, my dear." The Wall of Passages slammed its door and spewed Morgana with more dust.

With no time to waste, Morgana charged toward the stairs nearly knocking over the Knight in Shining Armor as he stepped forward in hopes she had reconsidered her love for him. She scrambled down the long, winding staircase, ran through the castle, and finally burst through the kitchen door, startling the servants.

"Where's Fredia?" Morgana screamed.

"I'm right here," Fredia replied as she stirred a large pot of porridge and balanced Prudence on her hip. "What's wrong?"

"Come with me." Morgana grabbed Fredia and pulled her and Prudence toward the door.

Once outside the kitchen, Morgana whispered rapidly. "The queen has taken me child, me Thane. It's only a matter of time before she finds out 'bout Prudence. You must hide her at once."

"Why'd she take yer child?" Fredia asked. "Why'd she want me Prudence?"

"I knew from da moment I saw yer baby dat she was da princess. I knew what ya done 'cause I done da same. Thane is da child of da king and queen. Me Thane is da Prince of Idlebury."

Fredia feigned a gasp, but Morgana didn't seem to notice.

"Hurry. Take Prudence and go."

"Where? Go where?"

"Ta da cellar. No one will find ya der."

"Da cellar?" Fredia exclaimed. "I won't take me child ta dat disgustin' place."

"She's not yer child. She's the Princess of Idlebury. If ya want ta keep her, go now."

Fredia clutched Prudence and ran to the cellar.

Morgana smiled as she watched Fredia and Prudence disappear from sight. "I wonder if dat old dragon still lives down der," she mumbled to herself. "I guess dat stupid wench will soon find out."

CHAPTER FOURTEEN
THE MERGER

AFTER GWEN, KENDALL, Aislinn, and Mistofisee left Hedonia, they walked for a few hours, but much to their disappointment, they didn't come across another kingdom where they'd hoped for an offer of food and lodging. Now it looked as if they'd have to forage for food and make a bed on the forest floor.

Although all were tiring, Mistofisee was the first to suggest they end the day's journey and find shelter for the night. The other three readily agreed. Within a few minutes, they happened upon a huge hollowed out tree in which Gwen, Kendall, and Aislinn fit perfectly and settled in. Mistofisee, who was much more educated about edible vegetation, scanned the area for fruit and berries. Upon his return, he laid out his surprisingly abundant find. The four friends ate, talked about their adventure, and shared a few laughs. When it was time to sleep, Mistofisee positioned himself in front of the tree to protect his friends from danger. They slept like babies.

At the crack of dawn, they set out again for the next kingdom on their trek to save the universe. Gwen appeared upbeat and energetic. She spoke eloquently about her vision of one big happy universe where all living things existed in harmony. Mistofisee couldn't help but roll his eyes as she ranted about the importance of her mission. Kendall encouraged Gwen and reinforced her dream. But Aislinn was mum. Mistofisee noticed she looked ill.

"What's up with her?" the young dragon asked.

Gwen looked at Aislinn. Their eyes locked. The girls appeared mesmerized by each other. Aislinn became ghostlike and floated toward Gwen. Kendall realized what was happening and tried to stop Aislinn, but his efforts were useless. Once Gwen absorbed Aislinn, she slumped to the ground in tears.

"I can't do this. I must be crazy to think I can save the universe. What have I started? All the kings and queens of all the kingdoms are coming to Idlebury for a Royal Assembly because of me. I've made a huge promise I can't keep. Who do I think I am? I'm just a little girl from Idleburg, Pennsylvania. I've set myself up for failure. The entire universe will think I'm an idiot. I don't like it. I don't like it at all."

"Do something," Mistofisee demanded of Kendall as Gwen continued to sob.

"I can't." Kendall sighed. "She's made her choice. For some reason, she prefers to draw on Aislinn rather than me. I can't change her decision. She has to deal with it."

"Deal with it?" Mistofisee groaned. "She's become Aislinn. Who in their right mind would want to be a whiny, pathetic weakling such as Aislinn?"

"There's something to learn from all aspects of ourselves. Not just our strengths. Sometimes we must face our weaknesses. Gwen's experiencing self-doubt and fear. She'll grow from this experience."

"*Grrreeeaaat!* How long will this take?" the dragon inquired impatiently.

"Don't know. For some people, it takes a lifetime."

"We don't have that long. She needs to snap out of it—now."

What Kendall and Mistofisee didn't know was Gwen's cries echoed throughout the universe and the other dimensions, causing creatures everywhere to pause.

"Silly girl," Queen Garbini of Dresstoria in Dimension VII said while perched on a stool so she could admire herself in a mirror as a seamstress put the final touches on the gown she would wear to the Royal Assembly. "There's nothing wrong with her that a pretty new dress won't cure."

"Yes, ma'am, I'll get right on it, ma'am," the seamstress replied as the queen smiled approvingly at her reflection in the mirror.

Also in Dimension VII, Queen Imelda of Cobblerstonia giggled as she skipped to her closet in which she stored thousands of pairs of shoes, lovingly protected in beautiful gold and silver jeweled boxes. When she opened the door, the shoes pushed off the lids to their boxes, squealed with delight and begged to be the chosen pair.

"Pick me. I'm absolutely the most beautiful pair of shoes in the land," a pair of white satin pumps exclaimed.

"Beauty will take you only so far. I'm the sturdy pair everyone desires for a successful journey," an exquisite yet obviously comfy pair of walking shoes claimed.

"Ridiculous. Feet look most elegant perched on my spiked heels and delicately hugged by my lovely arches and straps," a pair of dramatic dress shoes interjected.

Queen Imelda shushed the chattering shoes as she scanned her extensive collection in search of the perfect pair. "Shoes, glorious shoes. My kingdom for the perfect shoes," she sang as she selected a box tucked away on a top shelf.

The shoes made a collective gasp as they peeped from their boxes to see the chosen pair. The queen slowly lifted the lid and peered with wonder at a petite pair of black velvet shoes adorned with the finest rubies, emeralds, and pearls, and accented with dazzling diamonds. The shoes purred as she delicately lifted them from the box, petted their soft velvet, and then held them up to the light to examine their twinkling gems.

"I do believe you are fit for a princess," Queen Imelda exclaimed.

As the queen skipped out of the closet and slammed the door, the shoes not chosen moaned and cried their disappointment.

In Dimension VI, the King of Chocolatonia admired a fresh batch of chocolate truffles. He popped one in his mouth and said, "I think a little chocolate would go a long way to quieting the Princess of Idlebury."

"Most certainly, Your Majesty. Light or dark?" the confectionary chef asked.

"Surely you tease. It will take some of both to get the child to stop blubbering."

Gwen's cries continued to echo throughout the universe, inciting conversation among many beings in the thirteen dimensions.

"Tell her to shut up before she wakes the dead," a being with a powerful voice said. The comment, followed by crazed laughter, reverberated throughout the universe, creating interdimensional chatter.

"She must be stopped," someone said.

"She must quiet down, right now, or we're all in trouble.

Waking the dead is not to be taken lightly," another being said.

"But only an Innocent can silence her, for only an Innocent can travel freely among all kingdoms in all dimensions and get her the help she needs."

"Yes, but the kingdoms banned the Innocents long ago. Queen Matilda of Beastonia, ruler of the Innocents, has not been seen or heard from in more than two hundred years."

"Someone silence the child. Silence her at once."

Gwen wept so loud that Kendall and Mistofisee couldn't hear the intergalactic chatter. As creatures throughout the universe voiced their concerns, Kendall patiently consoled Gwen while Mistofisee paced and burped smoke rings.

"We must get a move on," the dragon impatiently said.

"We'll go when Gwen is ready," Kendall sniped.

Mistofisee rolled his eyes disapprovingly. Suddenly, a shadow fell over the trio. The young dragon and Kendall looked up to see an enormous, fierce dragon flying toward them.

Kendall positioned himself to protect Gwen.

Mistofisee stared in wonder and said, "Mother. It's my mother."

The huge dragon swooped down, grabbed Kendall and Gwen with her piercing talons and flew off.

"Mother, what about me?" Mistofisee cried. "You forgot me."

Upon hearing her son's whining, Queen Matilda stopped in midair, rose, faced the young dragon, spewed fire, and roared. "Grow up you pudgy, pitiful excuse for a dragon. You're nearly two hundred years old. It's time for you to stop complaining, shed your baby fat, grow wings, and fly."

"But Mother," Mistofisee begged.

"Don't 'but Mother' me. At your age, I ruled a kingdom. A kingdom I gave up to marry your father and give birth to you. I've given up everything for you, you spoiled brat. It's time for you to stand on your hind legs, flap your wings, and fly like a dragon should—unless you want to end up like your father."

The dragon queen took off with Gwen and Kendall. As they disappeared over the horizon Gwen's sobbing got louder.

Mistofisee paced and burped smoke as tears ran down his snout. For the first time in his life, he was furious with his mother.

"Pudgy, pitiful excuse for a dragon, am I? You're a sorry excuse for a mother. You slept all day, my whole life. I took care of you. I took care of myself. Because of your lousy mothering skills, I was sent to Personadonia. Queen Masklyn was more of a mother to me than you were. I taught myself everything about being a dragon... you pompous— "

Mistofisee stopped ranting. Something was happening to him. Wings budded from his shoulders. His body became leaner, his legs more muscular and long. Although he looked awkward, he knew he was transforming into an adult dragon. He flapped his stumpy wings in hopes he could fly, but nothing happened. He tried to blow fire, but still only created smoke.

"Now what?" he grumbled enraged about his new dilemma. "My wings are useless. I can't blow fire. And to boot, I look moronic."

Mistofisee continued to mumble about his anger with his absentee mother. The angrier he got, the more his wings flapped. In fact, they flapped so wildly, they nearly threw him off balance. Then he had an idea.

"If I hold my breath, I bet I can still lift like a balloon," he said with excitement. "And if I flap my wings, I bet I can control my direction and speed."

So he held his breath. Smoke rings escaped from his mouth, preventing him from getting any lift. He released his breath in hopes it would help him relax. As he exhaled, a small burst of fire singed the tip of his snout.

"Fire. I breathed fire!" he exclaimed.

The excitement of his new ability was nearly too much to bear. His wings flapped furiously, nearly knocking him to the ground. He held his breath. Much to his joy, he took to the air. He wanted to scream with delight but thought better of it. He struggled to control his flight and in no time was soaring.

Mistofisee's excitement turned to uncertainty as he realized he didn't know in which direction his mother had flown. Still, he persisted. When he saw something flying up ahead, he increased his speed. As he neared the flying object, he realized it was his mother. His heart pounded. He wanted her to see his achievement.

Queen Matilda stopped, looked at Mistofisee, and smiled. "Follow me, my son."

Mistofisee's heart filled with pride as he joined his mother and together they flew away.

Chapter Fifteen
The Queen's Lack of Purpose

WITH THANE IN tow, Queen Filanthropi burst into the king's bedchamber. She scanned the room for evidence the king had returned from his journey. To her disappointment, everything was exactly as he'd left it several months ago.

A peculiarly positioned envelope on the king's desk grabbed her attention. She picked up the envelope and examined it, noticing it looked like the one she'd given to Oof for safekeeping. *Why would Oof leave something so important just lying about?* she wondered. She turned it over and was shocked to see her royal seal. Worse, the seal was broken. Her hands shook as she carefully removed the note she had written several days ago. When she opened it, a photo fell out. Upon first glance, it looked like the same photo of Gwen the queen had found in her hand upon her awakening in the Slothful Forest after her encounter with the Soul Seeker in the Field of Wisdom. As she stared at it, the image changed into a huge dragon, flying with the princess grasped in its claws. The image grew larger and larger until the face of the dragon filled the picture. Suddenly, an apparition of the dragon swept through the room.

Before the ghostly image exited through a wall, the dragon looked straight into the queen's eyes and said, "Remember me? You were right. I'm as real as you are."

Queen Filanthropi reached for the dragon. "Wait. Matilda, where are you going with my child? Where are you going with the Princess of Idlebury?"

There was no response.

As the queen stared at the photo for a clue as to the whereabouts of her child, something caught her eye. She grabbed the king's magnifying glass and examined the photo. There was no mistaking it. An image of Idlebury Castle was visible in the background. "They are coming here. The princess is on her way home," the queen declared as she clutched the photo to her chest. She tucked it in her bodice, dropped the envelope and note on the king's desk, and then snatched Thane by the hand before she and her son scurried from the room.

"Oof, come at once," Queen Filanthropi yelled as she and Thane raced down the hall.

Oof appeared before them as if he'd expected their arrival.

"Oof, I found the note with which I entrusted you. It was on the king's desk and the seal was broken. I can only assume you've read it. Therefore, you must know Princess Gwendolyn, the rightful heir to the throne of Idlebury, is on her way home. Please make the appropriate preparations."

"At once, Your Majesty," Oof said with a smirk as he bowed before the queen.

The queen didn't seem to notice Oof's respectful gesture or his disrespectful smirk as she wasted no time in getting to her destination. When she and Thane reached the stairs, she instructed the child to return to his quarters. "You must go to your quarters at once. And do not speak a word of what you have heard or seen. I will return for you shortly."

"Yes, Your Majesty," Thane replied as he bowed.

"You need not call me Your Majesty. Call me Mother."

"Yes, Mother," Thane said. "I'll return to my quarters at once. And I'll remain mum about today's events."

As the word *mother* left Thane's lips, fairy dust sparkled throughout his curly black hair. A trail of glitter marked his route as he ran to his quarters. Queen Filanthropi didn't notice the fairy dust because she was well on her way to the dragon queen's old hiding place. But if she had noticed, she would have known Thane was destined for greatness beyond human imagination. Nearly every being in the cosmos knew the legend of the child whose magical powers would one day unite the dimensions and ignite universal peace and prosperity. But Thane didn't know the meaning of the fairy dust. All he knew was he had powers—powers Morgana told him to never use unless his life was in danger. And being ever obedient, he had never done so.

While Queen Filanthropi rushed down the winding staircase, she remembered old stories about secret passageways. She stopped on the stairs to catch her breath and gather her thoughts. If she was right, the fabled Wall of Passages was on the floor above. She ran up the staircase to the next floor's landing and scanned the corridor. When she saw a knight's armor positioned against the wall, she remembered her bedtime stories of how the Knight in Shining Armor protected the Wall of Passages from those who lacked direction and purpose. Countless tales of the horrors suffered by people who dared to make a fast escape via the secret passages rushed through her head. Still, she ran toward the knight in hopes of finding the wall.

"Your Majesty," the knight said as he bowed before the

queen. "Your presence is an honor. How may I serve you?"

"I am desperate to find the Wall of Passages. I must find it at once," the queen replied.

"You've come to the right place, but I must warn you. You must not enter the passage unless you know your purpose."

"My purpose?" the queen said as if she'd been insulted. "My purpose is to get to the cellar."

"I mean no disrespect, ma'am, but that's not a valid purpose."

"Show me to the wall. I will determine *what is* and *is not* a valid purpose."

The knight stood aside and allowed the harried queen to pass.

"Where is it?" the queen impatiently asked as she waved her hands over the wall.

"It's right before you, ma'am. I don't know why it doesn't open for you. It opened for a servant woman earlier today."

"A servant woman?" the queen said. "For what reason would a servant want to elicit the powers of the Wall of Passages?"

"I cannot say for I do not know. She was none other than the one you call Morgana. But she didn't enter the passage."

"Morgana?" the queen muttered. "Why was she here?"

"I do not know, ma'am. She proceeded down the staircase." The knight lowered his head in sadness and said, "I proclaimed my love for her, yet she didn't care. Her only concern was to find a passage to the kitchen."

"Never mind. I will address the issue with her myself. So where is the secret passage?" Queen Filanthropi asked as she scanned the wall with her hands.

"Oh, not again," said a bored voice emanating from the Wall of Passages. "No one has passed this way in more than two hundred years. Now two people in one day ask for passage. What is the universe coming to?"

The Wall of Passages creaked open. Dust filled the air.

"Your Majesty. What brings someone of *your* prominence here?"

"I need to get to the cellar—immediately. I command you to let me pass."

"What? You think you can make demands of me just because you wear a crown?" the wall replied in a snide manner.

"Matter of fact, I do. So open, I say."

"Do you know your purpose? The last woman to request passage did not know hers. So she was forced to take the stairs," the wall said with a chuckle.

"Yes, I know my purpose. And if you know your place, you will let me pass."

"Dear me, I have offended you. I will make amends by allowing you to choose your passage. But choose carefully or you will not fulfill your purpose," the wall said as it opened fully to reveal its labyrinth.

Queen Filanthropi's eyes darted as she scanned the dusty, decayed signs that marked each passage.

"Redemption. Where is redemption?" she asked the wall.

"That passage was closed eons ago. No one from Idlebury has demanded redemption in more than a millennium."

"Well, I am demanding it now, so open it at once."

"Testy, aren't we? Let me see if I can find the old passageway."

The queen watched impatiently as one by one each passage

lit up. Finally, the sign for redemption popped into view.

"Oh yes. There it is," the Wall of Passages declared. "It is at the end of the fork of sacrifice and service. It appears redemption is a destination, not a passage. No wonder it has been closed."

The queen, eager to get to the cellar, began to step into the passageway.

"Stop!" the Wall of Passages demanded. "You are not permitted to cross my threshold."

"I dare say, why not?" the queen asked with her hands on her hips and her nose in the air.

"You needn't take that tone with me," the Wall of Passages exclaimed. "You cannot enter because, I dare say, you are neither innocent enough nor wise enough to venture down the passage to redemption."

The Wall of Passages slammed shut making it quite clear the conversation was over. Dust billowed and covered the queen.

"I command you to let me pass," Queen Filanthropi said as she spat out dust and wiped off her eyelashes.

"Oh, please," the wall replied with a yawn. "Quite the contrary. You are at my command. And I command you to take the stairs. On your left, just past the Knight in Shining Armor."

Queen Filanthropi was enraged at the audacity of the Wall of Passages to dictate to her, but she knew better than to waste another second arguing. So she lifted her skirt and ran toward the stairs, knocking the knight to the floor as he stepped into her path in an attempt to console her.

The queen dashed down the staircase. A few minutes later, she arrived at the cellar door. Suddenly, Queen Filanthropi's courage dissipated and her legs gave way. She slumped to the floor. "What if Matilda is down there and has grown into a fierce monstrosity? Worse, what if I discover she did not exist?" she lamented. "Either way, I am doomed, as is my kingdom. But I will never know if I do not open the door."

Queen Filanthropi's hand trembled as she reached for the door. When her fingers touched the cold brass knob, she fainted.

Chapter Sixteen
Aislinn Pops Out

MATILDA SLOWED HER pace as she, Gwen, and Kendall, with Mistofisee trying desperately to keep up, neared the kingdom of Anhedonia in Dimension XII where she knew the wailing girl could get help and rid herself of whiny Aislinn.

A broad moat that surrounded Anhedonia's castle came into view as the Queen of the Innocents approached the kingdom. According to myth, the moat was formed from the tears of the Anhedonians, a dysthymic group of people believed to be distant relatives of the Idleburians.

Beings throughout the universe identified the Anhedonians by their annoying characteristics of unbearable complaining, unusual sensitivity to real or imagined stress, nightmares, indecisiveness, and narcissistic rage. But their most recognizable feature was their unusually long index fingers which evolved after centuries of pointing at and accusing others of being the source of their problems.

Matilda flung Gwen and Kendall through an opened castle window then flew to the roof to await Gwen's recovery. Mistofisee, unable to stop himself, soared through the window and unintentionally joined his friends.

When Gwen found herself seated on the floor in the middle of a circle of twenty people, she immediately stopped crying. But when she tried to stand and failed, she began to wail again.

"Welcome, my dear. I see we have a new member today," said a skinny, long-faced woman with a sour expression and thin puffy hair that stuck straight up like that of a newborn bird. "I'm Queen Pittipotti and this is King Grimly," she said as she pointed to herself and then pointed to her husband who sat next to her.

"We're the royal duo of Anhedonia, where there's no whine before it's time, and it's always time to whine," Queen Pittipotti and King Grimly said in unison as they smiled.

Gwen seemed oblivious to her surroundings as she continued to wail.

"It appears she's come to the right place, wouldn't you say Grimly, darling?" Queen Pittipotti clasped her hands in front of her face with her long index fingers touching her lips and her thumbs supporting her pointed chin. Her eyes wide with wonder, she scanned the group.

"Most definitely, my dear. Most definitely," replied the king who was the spitting image of the queen.

"I do believe she's the child whose cries have been heard throughout the kingdom, across the universe, and among the dimensions. It's none other than her, I say," the queen stated.

"Absolutely, absolutely, my darling," King Grimly replied emphatically.

"Take a seat and do tell us who you are and why you're here today," Queen Pittipotti said to Gwen.

Gwen sat in the only empty chair. Kendall positioned himself behind her chair a little to her left as if to protect her. Mistofisee remained in the center of the circle.

Through her tears, Gwen began to tell her story. "My name is Gwendolyn. I'm the Princess of Idlebury."

"The Princess of Idlebury?" Queen Pittipotti interrupted. "I dare say, your statement is a bit grandiose. Idlebury has no princess."

"Grandiose, most definitely grandiose," King Grimly replied.

Gwen blew her nose in a handkerchief offered to her by a mammoth woman sitting next to her. The woman's head was so gigantic that what appeared to be a teacup delicately perched upon it was actually a full-sized hat. Gwen thanked the woman for her kindness and continued. "I wasn't always a princess. One day, as I sat in front of the kitchen window playing with my magic coin box and waiting for the rain to stop—it had been raining for more than two weeks, which is very depressing—my mother was reading the latest *Universal Scandals* magazine. The front page headline read 'I GAVE MY BABY PRINCESS TO STRANGERS,' QUEEN DECLARES! Usually, the stories in my mother's favorite magazine are just stupid, but the picture of the queen caught my eye. She looked exactly like me. I begged my mother to read the article out loud but the phone called her away. So I grabbed the magazine and read it myself. It said the Queen of Idlebury had a baby girl ten years ago whom she placed for adoption. When I read the child could be living anywhere in the universe, I nearly passed out."

"Why would you pass out, my dear?" Queen Pittipotti asked with a look of concern.

Gwen rolled her eyes at Queen Pittipotti, indicating she thought the queen was an idiot. "Because I was born ten years ago and I'm adopted."

"Abandonment issues, wouldn't you say, Grimly?"

"Goes without saying, my dear," King Grimly said as he

judiciously jotted down every word Gwen and the queen said. "All adopted children have abandonment issues."

"I believe we're dealing with distorted thinking, magical thinking, and possibly a delusional disorder, and if my worst fears were to become reality, a full-blown, certifiable case of pathological narcissism. We have an extremely ill young girl before us," Queen Pittipotti said in a near whisper as she nodded regretfully to the king. "Do go on, my child," the queen said as she motioned for Gwen to continue.

"At the end of the article, there was an address to send your picture if you thought you were the long-lost Princess of Idlebury. I was so excited. So I showed the queen's picture to my mother and father. They were flabbergasted at how much I looked like the queen. So we all got dressed to go to Pretty Pictures and get my picture taken. My father and mother dressed up as a king and queen. I wore my princess outfit. Nigel, our dog, was dressed as the court jester. But Snickers, our cat, refused to dress up," Gwen said, then hesitated and blew her nose once again.

"Severe nerdism in family of origin. It's no wonder this child is ill," the queen said to the king.

"Agree… with the exception of the cat, of course," said the king.

"Please continue, my dear," Queen Pittipotti said.

"Then we went to the mall to get my picture taken at Pretty Pictures. The mall was packed with zillions of kids dressed in princess outfits—"

"Why are we listening to this? Some of us have *real* problems," Snibly Dourjoy, one of the younger group members said, interrupting Gwen's story. "Tell her to shut up and go back to Idleburg, Idlebury, *what-ev-va*."

"Miss Dourjoy, everyone's story is important. We spent much time on you yesterday. So please be respectful while we get to know our new group member," the queen firmly replied.

"But she's not from Anhedonia. Who is she to take up our precious time?" Snibly yelled in an arrogant, entitled manner.

"Miss Dourjoy, I will not tolerate another interruption from you. Please remain quiet."

Snibly Dourjoy became enraged. She stood and ranted as she pointed her unusually long index finger at the queen. "*You* are here to *serve me.* You are not serving me. How rude of you to put a new member before *me.* I've been here for two days and haven't had adequate time to explore my *unique* issues. I demand you serve me... now. What part of 'you are here to serve me' do you, Queen Pittipotti, not understand?"

The queen remained composed as she pressed a little red button hidden under her seat. Immediately, two guards entered the room.

"Gentlemen, please escort Miss Snibly Dourjoy to Bratsville where she belongs."

Miss Dourjoy exited the room with much commotion. After everyone settled down, the queen motioned for Gwen to continue.

Gwen sheepishly looked at the other group members.

"Do go on. We'd love to hear more about you," said an old man with a large lumpy head and the longest index fingers of anyone in the room.

"Thank you," Gwen said, not picking up on the old man's sarcasm. "A huge, scary man dressed in a black cape took me to Idlebury..."

The group tuned out. No one heard another word of Gwen's story until she said, "On the front door, there was a sign that said: WELCOME TO PERSONADONIA —"

A collective gasp from the group interrupted Gwen once again.

"No!" the huge stout woman sitting next to Gwen exclaimed. "Personadonia is a feared place for us. What did you do when you met your"—the woman gulped and took a deep breath as if to gather the courage to say the rest of her sentence—"other selves?"

"I'd rather die than meet my other selves," said a barefoot man with shaggy gray hair and long dirty fingernails and toenails.

"I thought it was fun," Gwen replied enthusiastically. "In fact, that's why I'm here. One of them is stuck inside me and I need to get her out. She's a whiny crybaby. Her name is Aislinn."

The group members scrambled to get away from Gwen as if she were contagious with a deadly virus. In a far corner of the room, they huddled and consoled each other.

Queen Pittipotti and King Grimly remained seated but looked uneasy.

"I fear psychosis as well. Poor girl," Queen Pittipotti whispered to her husband. In a voice tinged with fear she asked Gwen, "Is there anyone else here with you?"

"Yes. Kendall, my favorite self, is standing right here," Gwen said as she pointed to an empty space to her left. "And my dragon friend, Mistofisee, is standing in the middle of the circle. Can't you see him?"

The group members remained huddled in the corner. Some whimpered from fear. One complained aloud, "Please, not a dragon. I can't bear another trauma. I haven't recovered from breaking the heel of my shoe at my sister's wedding two years ago."

Queen Pittipotti rose and slowly walked toward the center of the circle.

King Grimly remained seated and continued to take copious notes.

The queen closed in on Mistofisee.

He didn't budge.

"Is he here?" Queen Pittipotti taunted Gwen.

Gwen shook her head no.

"How about here?" the queen asked.

"You're getting closer."

The Queen of Anhedonia hopped into the center of the circle, crinkled her nose, raised her brow, and said, "How about here?"

Gwen gasped when she saw the queen merge with Mistofisee.

The huddled mass of Anhedonians continued to whimper and whine.

Queen Pittipotti raised her hand to quiet the group. She turned to King Grimly and said, "Make a note that I've stepped into the center of the circle and there's most definitely, most definitely, someone here."

The group gasped again.

Many trembled.

Some wept.

The Queen of Anhedonia looked at Gwen and screeched, *"And it is I!"*

Gwen's face reddened. She felt devalued and dismissed by the queen's rude display. She didn't want to say anything she would later regret, so she contained her anger. As she continued to control herself, her anger reached a peak. When she could no longer maintain her composure, Aislinn miraculously popped out.

"I'm back," Gwen announced with glee. "Let's get out of here," she said as she motioned for Kendall, Mistofisee, and Aislinn to join her as she ran to the window, forcing the Anhedonians to move aside. "I don't have time to wallow on the pity potty. I have a universe to save."

Kendall made a gesture as if to tip an imaginary hat.

Mistofisee whirled his tail as if to take a swipe at the queen and king.

Aislinn reluctantly followed, seemingly sad to leave. "I feel so at home here. I wish I could stay," she said. Of course, the Anhedonians couldn't hear her.

Matilda snatched Gwen, Kendall, and Aislinn as they jumped out of the window. Mistofisee followed as they all headed for Idlebury.

Gwen glimpsed back at the castle and saw the entire group of Anhedonians peering out the window. But the group couldn't see Matilda or the others. What they saw was Gwen whizzing through the sky as if by magic.

Queen Pittipotti pushed her way to the window. She appeared panicked as she yelled to Gwen, "How did that make you feel?"

Gwen heard the queen's question but didn't bother to reply.

Queen Pittipotti sat next to her husband and put her hand on his pen to halt his note-taking. "Erase the last page of notes Grimly, my dear. Just say she was asked to leave because she wasn't appropriate for Anhedonia."

As Queen Pittipotti exited the room, she said, "Come Grimly, it's time to prepare for the Royal Assembly."

"Of course, my dear."

Chapter Seventeen
Wah Wah Wah Wah
Wah Wah Wah

Queen Filanthropi had no idea how long she'd been unconscious at the cellar door. Oddly, she felt revived as if she'd taken a much-needed nap. She stood, brushed off her gown, straightened her crown, took a deep breath, and then reached for the door handle.

"Wait. Are you sure you want to do that?" a man asked.

The queen looked around but saw no one. She thought she recognized the voice but wasn't sure. Determined to get to the cellar and find Matilda, she reached for the door handle again. As her fingers touched the cold brass handle, an icy, grayish blue hand grabbed hers. She looked up to see her darling Heroian looking like death himself.

"Heroian, my love. What has happened to you? Are you... are you... dead?"

"I'm not dead my dear, although I might as well be. The Soul Seeker has had my soul for a long time. So you might say I'm feeling a little out of sorts."

Queen Filanthropi looked into the eyes of the man she

believed to be her husband. An uneasy feeling tingled through her. Nonetheless, she stroked his face. His skin felt odd. When he didn't lovingly grasp her hand and kiss it, as was King Heroian's custom, she knew the being was not her husband.

"You are *not* my Heroian," the queen said as she moved away from the man. "How dare you pretend to be so?"

"Of course, I'm not your Heroian," a woman said, now recognizable as Wilameena, the enchantress.

"Wilameena, that was cruel," Queen Filanthropi said. "Why would you do such a thing?"

"Get over yourself. I'm here to help you. Are you going to accept my help this time? Or will you be your usual pompous royal pain in the butt?"

"That depends. Why do I need your help?" the queen asked indignantly. "I am about to find Matilda, as you requested, and now you are impeding my progress. Just how is that helpful?"

"Matilda isn't in the cellar," Wilameena said. "It's imperative you focus on the final touches for the Royal Assembly. The kings and queens from all the dimensions and kingdoms are on their way."

As Queen Filanthropi headed for the staircase, Wilameena added, "And as for Matilda, you needn't find her because she's about to find you." The enchantress let out a vicious laugh and disappeared.

"You nasty old hag," the queen said to herself as she climbed the stairs. "For the life of me, I do not know why you are called an enchantress because there is nothing enchanting about you."

Queen Filanthropi carefully closed the cellar door behind her. As she started to walk toward the Great Hall, the cellar door creaked as if it had opened. Queen Filanthropi stopped and listened, unsure if her ears were playing tricks on her. After a few moments of silence, she decided the dilapidated floors were the source of the squeak, just a reminder of the castle's desperate need of repair.

When sufficient time had passed, Fredia opened the cellar door. When she saw the queen, Oof, and a group of servants had gathered outside the Great Hall, she clutched Prudence firmly to her chest, and then she quietly and quickly headed for the stairs as if to go unnoticed. But a few servants broke their gaze and glanced at Fredia, causing the queen to look at what or who had snatched attention away from her.

"Fredia, you are just the person I am looking for," the queen said. "But I see you have your child with you. Cicely, please take care of the child so Fredia can attend to her *important* responsibilities."

As Fredia handed the baby to Cicely, little Prudence extended her arms toward the queen and said, "Momma."

Queen Filanthropi glanced at the child and smiled. *Why does the child look familiar?* she wondered. But when Prudence wailed and yelled, *"Momma!"* Queen Filanthropi took the child from Cicely. Once safely in the arms of the queen, the baby relaxed, stopped crying, sucked her thumb, and gazed into the queen's eyes.

The experience unsettled the queen, so she handed Prudence back to Cicely and commanded the servant take the child to Fredia's quarters. As Cicely exited, Prudence waved goodbye to the queen, but the queen didn't notice for she had already returned to the issue at hand.

"Preparations are in order for the most magnificent Royal Assembly ever to be held at Idlebury Castle," Queen Filanthropi announced, practically bursting with pride.

The Queen of Idlebury rushed into the Great Hall. Oof

motioned for the group of servants to quickly follow. As the queen dictated the chores to be done, she paced and anxiously wrung her hands. "The silver must be polished. All sleep chambers are to be appointed with the finest linens. The floors must be scoured. All wood is to be washed and waxed. Every fireplace is to be cleaned and stocked with wood. The horses are to be groomed. Carriages are to be cleaned and painted. All windows are to be cleaned. Every servant shall be dressed in new clothing. Musicians are to prepare an unforgettably fabulous performance. And a feast, yes, the finest foods are to be prepared and presented in the most magnificent manner."

"Yes, ma'am," Oof replied.

"One more thing, Oof. Wake the gardener. He must prune the bushes, pull the weeds, and for God's sake, have him plant some flowers. And have the stonemason repair the exterior of the castle. This must—no; this *will be* the most *glorious* day."

"Of course, ma'am," Oof replied as he snapped his fingers at the servants, indicating they needed to get busy.

"Wait. My jewels. They must be carefully cleaned and polished for they are to complement my gown made of the most glorious fabric," Queen Filanthropi exclaimed.

When she turned to leave the Great Hall, a pretentiously large painting of King Heroian's great, great, great, great grandmother, Queen Beggora, caught her eye. She studied the queen's ornate crown for which, due to its opulence, Queen Beggora had spent most of her life exiled to Opulencia. For generations, the Idleburians believed the crown had been declared a distasteful debauchery and rightfully discarded. But, in fact, the crown was stored in a deceptively simple wooden box in which it was cradled by the finest piece of purple velvet rumored to have been cut from Queen Beggora's wedding gown. And to this day, Oof secretly maintained it.

Queen Filanthropi pointed at the painting and declared, "And I will wear Queen Beggora's crown."

"Queen Beggora's crown?" a servant asked. "She's goin' ta wear Queen Beggora's crown?"

"But it don't exist," exclaimed another servant.

"It does and I shall wear it," Queen Filanthropi said in a snippy manner, indicating her decision was final.

"Excuse me, Yer Majesty," Fredia asked as she curtsied in reverence. "But what's da special occasion?"

"Dear me," the queen said, realizing she hadn't informed her staff as to the reason for the Royal Assembly. "The special occasion is for Gwendolyn of Idleburg, Pennsylvania in Dimension X, planet Earth. She is on her way home to take her rightful place as Princess of Idlebury."

The servants could hardly contain their joy. Several cried. Some jumped up and down as they hugged each other.

But Fredia did not join in the servants' happy display. She appeared lost in thought. Her hands shook. Her face turned pale.

"Come, come," Morgana's voice echoed through the Great hall. "Der's much work ta do. No time ta waste."

The servants giggled and chattered excitedly as they bounded out of the Great Hall and went their separate ways—some went upstairs to prepare the sleeping quarters, and others to the kitchen to plan a feast for the Royal Assembly. But Fredia, who appeared emotionally drained, could barely gather the strength to climb the stairs.

As Morgana watched the weary servant struggle up the stairs, she sneered and mumbled, "The queen took me Thane. I'll be damned if ya get ta keep Prudence."

For the next two weeks, Idlebury Castle was a hive of

activity. But many Idleburians who were asked to do grounds work refused to cooperate. Some staged protests to voice their right to idleness and demanded King Heroian and Queen Filanthropi do the work themselves.

To calm the people, the queen changed Gwilym's title from the Minister of Mindlessness to the Minister of Mindfulness. When he addressed the Idleburians about the importance of the upcoming event, many jeered and pelted him with rotten food. In despair, he gave up attempts to reform the angry people. Within several days, many Idleburians, who exerted more energy protesting than they would have if they had agreed to work, called for an all-out revolt.

Unaware of the mutiny of her people, Queen Filanthropi calmly stood on a pedestal as Morgana painstakingly measured and pinned heavy, gold-threaded fabric of what would soon be a glorious gown. As she admired herself in the mirror, an elderly man burst into the room.

"Yer Majesty. Please fergive me rudeness, but der's a matta of urgency of which ya must be aware," the man said.

"Do go on," the queen requested with curiosity.

"Da people refuse ta work. Many have protested against ya and the king, I'm ashamed ta say. And the princess's arrival is gettin' closer. I'd do da work meself, but as ya can see, well, I'm a very old man."

"What is your name, my man?" the queen asked.

"William, ma'am," the man said as he bowed before the queen.

"William, I proclaim you William the Brave for having the courage to inform me of the insolence of my people."

Queen Filanthropi stepped off the pedestal and put out her hand to William. He moved to kiss it.

"No, William, it is I who wish to kiss your hand, for loyalty such as yours has not been seen in Idlebury since the reign of King Wawchtphul more than fifteen hundred years ago," the queen said, then gently kissed the back of William's hand. "Do come with me."

Still wearing her partially sewn gown, Queen Filanthropi and the newly titled William the Brave walked out of the castle and into the square. Some of the people saw the queen approach and positioned themselves in front of the town crier's platform. As Queen Filanthropi and William neared, the crowd became increasingly rowdy. Some chanted, *"Work. Work. It's ours ta shirk. No work. No work. Dat is our perk."*

The queen took to the platform and addressed her people. "Ladies and gentlemen of Idlebury," she said in the most endearing voice she could conjure, hoping to calm the rowdy crowd.

As the crowd steadily grew in size and intensity, the queen again yelled, "Ladies and gentlemen," but her attempt to quiet her people failed. She became increasingly angry as she continued to yell at the crowd and motion for silence. But no one paid her the least bit of attention.

William disappeared and quickly returned with a ram's horn. He tugged on Queen Filanthropi's partially sewn gown and handed the horn to her. The queen yelled, "Ladies and gentlemen." The ram's horn carried her voice loud and clear far beyond the back of the crowd, yet the rambunctious Idleburians continued to ignore the queen as they chanted louder.

The queen's face reddened from rage. She raised the ram's horn to her lips again and screamed, "Wah wah wah wah wah wah wah."

To her surprise, the crowd fell silent.

"Well... I see I have your attention," Queen Filanthropi said.

"Don't da queen look pretty all red. I ain't neva seen her look so pretty," a man said, breaking the silence and drawing attention to the queen's red face.

In response, some people heckled the queen. The crowd was out of control again.

"Wah wah wah wah wah wah wah," Queen Filanthropi blared through the horn. "That is what your chants sound like to me. You are a bunch of crybabies. You are a whiny horde of human waste."

"Human waste?" a haggard woman yelled. "We're human waste?"

"Yes, you are leeches; undeserving, ungrateful leeches. For more than four thousand years, you and your ancestors have not lifted one finger to help yourselves. But you have opened your mouths to complain when life did not meet your expectations. You have never hesitated to demand that King Heroian and I take care of you and your broods of brats. We put food on your tables, clothes on your backs, roofs over your heads, and provide education for your children who undoubtedly will grow up to be demanding leeches such as the likes of you. Nonetheless, you are my people. And my purpose is to care for you. But I now see the errors of my ways. King Heroian and I have done you a great disservice."

"I knew she'd see da errors of her ways," said a woman in the front of the crowd.

"Yes, you are correct. I see the errors of my ways and the ways of the kings and queens before me. For we have done too much for you. We have deprived you of the opportunity to care for yourselves. We have robbed you of responsibility. We have protected you from yourselves. We have fought your battles. And in doing so, we have made you what you are today—a helpless, hopeless, lazy lot of losers who expect rewards for idleness. You are ingrates who demand their every need be catered to. And the more King Heroian and I do, the more you demand. You are an entitled bunch of ungrateful slugs."

"But ya made us poor. Ya wouldn't allow us ta have money," a young man yelled.

"You are right," the queen said. "Your ancestors demanded their every need be met. Hence, to uphold the wishes of their people, Queen Penniwize and King Powndphulish declared money useless. Therefore, they unwittingly declared their people useless. And anyone who had even a single coin was banished forever to the kingdom of Opulencia to spend the rest of their days mired in the muck of managing their money. But I come to you today with hope for a happy, prosperous future. For in a week's time, Princess Gwendolyn will return to Idlebury to save you and the universe."

"Save us from what?" a young man yelled.

"We like things da way day are," a woman yelled.

The crowd became rowdy and again chanted, *"Work. Work. It's ours ta shirk. No work. No work. Dat is our perk."*

William the Brave took to the platform. He graciously asked the queen to let him use the ram's horn. With a shaking, shriveled hand, he raised the horn to his parched lips and yelled, "Shut up!"

The crowd continued their chanting and chatter. William then drew a deep breath and screamed for all he was worth, *"Shut up!"*

The Idleburians fell silent.

"Who da ya think ya are old man?" a pudgy, middle-aged man asked.

"Why are ya protectin' da queen?" a woman standing next

to the man asked.

"Are ya her lover?" a voice echoed from the back of the crowd.

The last comment sent the crowd wild with laughter.

"*Quiet!*" William the Brave yelled. "I know some of ya have money. I've seen it with me own eyes, I have. I can name names ya know. Then it's off to Opulencia with ya. So I ask ya ta pay respect ta da queen and listen ta what she has ta say."

"Let's hear it den," a man from the middle of the crowd requested.

William handed the ram's horn back to Queen Filanthropi.

"Thank you, William," the queen said. "For those of you who do not know, I am pleased to announce that the title of William the Brave has been bestowed upon this courageous man for alerting me to the mutinous misbehaviors of the masses, which is the reason I stand before you today."

"Let's hear about da princess who's goin' ta save da universe and save our souls, mind ya," a woman in the back of the crowd said as she elbowed the woman next to her.

"How can da princess return when we ain't ever had a princess before?" asked a young woman.

"Good question, my dear woman," the queen said, then hesitated. She knew she had to tell the truth if she was to gain the trust of her people and motivate them to change their ways. So she took a deep breath and told her people about Gwendolyn. "Ten years ago, when I was the Princess of Seedonia and engaged to the Prince of Laborshire—"

"So it's true," a woman said, waving a copy of *Universal Scandals* magazine. "Da story in dis here silly magazine is true. The woman jumped up on the dais with the queen and grabbed the ram's horn. In a mocking voice, she started to read the article to the crowd. "'*I Gave My Baby Princess To Strangers.'* *Queen Declares!*"

"I'll tell the story myself if you don't mind," the *Universal Scandals* magazine said as it wiggled out of the woman's hands. Suspended in midair, the magazine relayed the story in a lively manner.

"*A reliable source has revealed that Queen Filanthropi of Idlebury, in Dimension XIII, gave birth to an eight-pound princess a little more than ten years ago...*"

Many of the Idleburians laughed and shook their heads as they remembered Queen Filanthropi's banishment to Cringley Castle for reasons unbeknownst to them.

"Our own queen, da picture of propriety, with child out of wedlock?" the woman who stood next to the queen declared. "How scandalous."

"Of course, it's scandalous, that's why it's between my covers," the *Universal Scandals* magazine said with a chuckle, then continued. When it got to the part about King Heroian fathering the child, the magazine was interrupted by a man who yelled, "Not our *one* and *only* respectable king," inciting his fellow Idleburians to boo and hiss their disapproval.

The *Universal Scandals* magazine raised its voice and continued. Nonetheless, the rowdy Idleburians carried on until the magazine reported. "*One Earth year after the birth and subsequent adoption of the child, Princess Filanthropi of Seedonia and Prince Heroian of Idlebury were wed and are now the King and Queen of Idlebury —*"

"How nice of dem ta make der union *legal*," a young man yelled as the magazine talked over him.

At the mention the queen was forced to give her child to commoners, the woman on the dais leaned in to the crowd and exclaimed, *"God forbid!* Her child is bein' raised by commoners. Fer shame, fer shame."

The crowd roared with laughter.

And when the magazine mentioned the deliberate destruction of all records pertaining to the child's birth and adoption, the woman chimed in again. "Deliberate destruction? How deceptive of our dear queen."

This time the magazine lost its patience. So it rolled up and whacked itself against the woman's head. Then it unfolded and continued, *"Rumor has it that the adoptive parents of the unknown princess are to be offered a king's ransom for the return of the child to Idlebury—"*

"King's ransom? Where's da money fer—" The woman interrupted again but stopped in midsentence when the magazine shook itself at her.

After the *Universal Scandals* magazine mentioned where to send photos for physical comparison with the queen, it burst into confetti-sized pieces of paper that sprinkled over the crowd.

"A photo?" a teenager in the front row asked. "What's a photo?"

Queen Filanthropi gently removed the photo of Gwendolyn from her dress pocket and held it up to the crowd. "This is a photo of Princess Gwendolyn," she announced.

The annoying woman snatched the photo from the queen and examined it. Without a word, she handed it to another person in the crowd.

The queen retrieved the ram's horn from the pesky woman and said, "Now you know the truth. So it is your choice whether or not you will help in the preparations for Gwendolyn's homecoming and investiture as Princess of

Idlebury. The kings, queens, lords, ladies, dukes, duchesses, marquesses, earls, viscounts, barons, and countless other nobility from throughout the universe will be here in two weeks. You can either allow them to see you as who you truly are... or as who you have become."

Queen Filanthropi didn't wait for a response from her people. She handed the ram's horn to William the Brave, descended the podium, and walked confidently back to the castle. But her thoughts nagged her. *Who leaked the story of the princess's adoption to Universal Scandals magazine? Did Oof read my letter to the Heroian? He could not. He would not. I would trust him with anything. I would trust him with everything, even my own life. So who did?*

As Queen Filanthropi walked up the staircase on her way to her chambers, she turned and looked at her servants who were busily at work. She saw Oof talking to a young woman whom she didn't recognize. The woman appeared to be taking notes. Oof glanced at the queen and then graciously bowed in honor of her presence.

"No, it is definitely not him. I know I can undeniably trust him," she mumbled to herself as she made her way to her chambers. *But who is that woman?* she wondered.

Chapter Eighteen
Mistofisee's Death Sentence

A HORRIFIC ODOR, like that of an immense, filthy zoo, filled the air as Queen Matilda escorted Gwen, Kendall, and Aislinn into Dimension I on their approach to the next kingdom. Gwen crinkled her nose in disgust. Aislinn gagged. Kendall did his level best to ignore the malodorous scent. Mistofisee, on the other hand, was overcome with joy. The stronger the stench became, the more he was sure of where they were headed—Beastonia. The excitement of seeing his ancestral home gave the pubescent dragon a surge of energy, allowing him to fly faster than ever before. Soon he joined his mother. She winked at him and soared ahead. He desperately tried to keep up, but he was still no match for the powerful dragon queen.

As the kingdom of Beastonia came into view, the Queen of Beastonia felt a pang of anxiety coupled with joy. She hadn't been home for more than two hundred years and didn't know what to expect. The familiar scent of her kingdom was comforting, although it was much stronger and rather more unpleasant than she'd remembered. Nonetheless, she flew with determination. After all, she was the queen. She hoped her subjects would greet her with open arms. But after what happened between her and her husband, King Anima, she was afraid they'd lost confidence in her ability to rule. Worse, two hundred years of Dragon's Sleep left her ignorant of the happenings in her kingdom.

Over the horizon, flashes of light appeared. Queen Matilda was uncertain as to their meaning. Suddenly, her elation turned to fear, for it looked as if Beastonia was on fire. The dragon queen increased her speed in hopes she'd reach her kingdom in time to save her subjects, the Innocents. Soon it became clear there was no fire, just bright lights illuminating the sky. As she got closer, she saw the lights formed words. When she closed in on her homeland, the words' message became clear. "Welcome to Beastonia—Land of the Innocents. Where we reign with no rules. And where the rule is no reins."

"No rules! No reins! What's become of my kingdom?" Queen Matilda roared and spewed fire.

The Beastonians, who represented every known animal found in the universe, happily went about their day, innocently unaware the return of their queen was about to shatter their world.

After the overthrow of Queen Matilda, following the questionable and violent death of her husband, King Anima, the Beastonians voted for a new form of government. Millennia of regimes with rigid rules of behavior and hygiene for each breed of animal left them longing to roam free and live according to the laws of nature.

Two hundred years later, anarchy ruled. Species upon species wars were pervasive. The intermingling of breeds resulted in thousands of new types of animals, many of which were cast aside as misfits, some used as slaves. Even worse, stories of cannibalism instilled fear and paranoia throughout the once joyous and playful kingdom. Despite this, some

Beastonians chose to raise their families in solitude and secretly instilled in their young the old rules of decorum as a reminder of their past greatness. This resulted in their blissful ignorance as to the decay of their homeland.

When Queen Matilda spotted Beastonia's Canny Castle, her heart raced with excitement. As she soared closer, she was relieved to see it appeared no worse for wear after her two-hundred-year absence. She lighted on one of the many castle towers and carefully unloaded Gwen, Aislinn, and Kendall. Below, she could see her subjects. After a few minutes of studying their behavior, the dragon queen realized she had gone unnoticed. So she slipped quietly behind the walls of Canny Castle and left Gwen and the others on the tower.

Mistofisee was nowhere in sight.

Queen Matilda wandered freely around the castle. With the exception of two centuries of gray fluffy dust, everything was as it had been on the day the Beastonians banished her to a dreary existence in the drab, boring kingdom of Idlebury. She walked over to a gargantuan painting of her husband, the last reigning King of Beastonia, and carefully blew away the dust. Seeing his picture again reminded her of what an enormously powerful dragon he had been. She smiled as memories of their glorious reign rushed back. But sad memories of how her husband's addiction to moat water reduced him to a lazy lump of lumbering flesh quickly replaced her happiness. She remembered how the king became totally unable to fulfill his duties. Worse, he put his kingdom and his subjects in danger.

Below the painting, an immense urn containing King Anima's ashes sat on a table. A bronze plaque nailed to the table read BORN A KING. SUCCUMBED TO THE ALLURE OF MOAT WATER. KILLED BY THE FIRE OF LOVE.

Matilda was stunned. "Killed by the fire of love?" she

whispered. "They know. They know why I had to do it."

Tears welled in her eyes at the thought the Beastonians understood what she had sacrificed to save them. A single tear of joy rolled down her face and dripped off her snout. She desperately tried to catch it, but she failed. "Oh no, what a dreadful mistake," Queen Matilda lamented. "An adult dragon tear is the most powerful substance in the universe. I've jeopardized everything."

The tear landed on the dusty floor. To the dragon queen's relief, nothing happened.

The clamor of a crowd outside distracted her. As she moved toward the window, her tail knocked over the table. The urn shattered on the floor, dumping its contents on top of her tear. But the deafening sound of animals roaring, barking, bleating, bellowing, growling, snarling, howling, yowling, whistling, chirping, twittering, mooing, cooing, and shrieking muted the sound of the fallen urn. The Queen of Beastonia studied the crowd, unsure as to the cause of their excitement. She wondered if the Innocents knew she had returned.

A moment later, an odd creature with the face of a frog, the mane of a lion, the body of a kangaroo, and the beautiful feathered fan of a peacock hopped over the moat and onto the drawbridge as if to block the crowd's entrance into the castle. Queen Matilda was horrified to see the beast wearing her crown, making her wonder who had the audacity to declare him the ruler of Beastonia in her absence. But her heart stood still when she saw some of the Beastonians carried Mistofisee atop their shoulders. She didn't know what to do. Her motherly instinct was to save him. But it didn't appear as if he was in danger. In fact, it seemed as if the crowd was celebrating his arrival.

Satisfied her son wasn't in harm's way, and angered by the

takeover of her kingdom, Queen Matilda decided her top priority was to find the members of her royal court. She'd left them in charge and it appeared they'd defaulted on their responsibilities. She had to get to the bottom of what happened to her subjects over the past two hundred years. From what she'd seen, they had some explaining to do. So she headed into the bowels of the castle where the secret room of the royal court was located.

Outside the castle, the Beastonians continued to celebrate Mistofisee's homecoming. As the crowd settled at the base of the drawbridge, the odd-looking creature, supported by its strong tail, rose to an extraordinary height. Its feathered fan expanded proportionately. To capture the crowd's attention, the creature roared like a lion. But when it spoke, its voice was peculiar and squeaky. "My fellow beasts," the creature said. "The dragon you bring forth to place on the throne of Beastonia is a fraud. Look at him. He's pudgy. His wings are stunted. He can barely breathe fire. He's the most pathetic dragon I've ever seen."

"When have you ever seen a dragon?" asked an elderly creature that resembled a goat.

The apparent ruler of the Innocents cleared its throat in an attempt to delay its response. "He's not worthy of your worship. I'm your king. And you're to worship *only* me," he demanded.

"That's not what Mr. Bleaty asked," exclaimed an elephant-like creature, delicately balanced on flamingo-like legs and covered in pink, fuzzy hair. "If my memory serves me, he asked: When have you ever seen a dragon?"

"I... I... I've never seen a dragon," the King of Beastonia said as he diminished in size and turned a bright red from embarrassment.

"I can't *hear* you," yelled a muscular rodentlike animal.

The crowd chanted, *"A dragon. A dragon. We all do see. Our king. Our king. We all agree."*

As the crowd of beastly creatures chanted and lifted Mistofisee for all to see, one of the birdlike creatures snatched the crown from the King of Beastonia. The crowd cheered as the eons-old crown, worn by every dragon king and queen since the beginning of Beastonia, was placed on Mistofisee's head.

"It's a perfect fit," a Beastonian yelled with joy.

"He looks kingly, I must say," declared another.

The crowd of Beastonians danced and cheered in celebration of the return of the rule of the dragons.

From atop the tower, Gwen, Kendall, and Aislinn watched.

"I have to do something," Gwen said. "I have to stop Mistofisee from becoming King of Beastonia."

"Are you out of your mind?" Kendall said.

"They could eat you alive," Aislinn whined.

"If Mistofisee is accepted as the new King of Beastonia, Queen Matilda will be shunned."

"So?" Kendall replied.

"If Queen Matilda doesn't regain power over Beastonia, the universe can't be saved."

Kendall wrinkled his brow. "How do you know?"

With no time or interest in debating her decision, Gwen ran down the tower stairs, through the castle, and out onto the drawbridge.

The apparent King of Beastonia desperately tried to hold his ground and convince his people he was the rightful king. But the sight of Gwen silenced the crowd. The king, who mistakenly thought he had regained control, took a deep breath as if to speak.

But Gwen spoke first. "Pardon me. I do believe you've got it all wrong. Mistofisee isn't the dragon king. It's Queen Matilda, his mother, who rules here."

The King of Beastonia stared at Gwen. He tilted his head inquisitively, because no Beastonian had referred to Queen Matilda by name for more than two hundred years. Worse, the most dreaded creature in all of Beastonia stood before him—a human.

"It's a human. Run for your life, or you'll be dinner tonight," a creature yelled, inciting a stampede of animals.

The King of Beastonia charged through the crowd, knocking down all in his path as he desperately tried to get away from the human child. But despite his desperation, he took the time to snatch the crown off the head of the young dragon.

In the rush, Mistofisee fell to the ground.

Gwen ran to him. "Mistofisee, are you all right?"

"I'm fine. For a moment I was almost the king. I must say I liked the thought. But maybe another time. Right now we need to find my mother."

Gwen and Mistofisee quietly headed up the drawbridge and entered Canny Castle where Kendall and Aislinn joined them.

"I feel as if I've been here before," Mistofisee said as he remembered the stories his mother told him in rare moments of wakefulness during the early days of her struggle with Dragon's Sleep. "And I think I know where to find my mother. Follow me."

Mistofisee and the others walked to the castle courtyard. The young dragon snooped around.

"What are you looking for?" Kendall asked.

"A secret entrance," the dragon replied.

"A secret entrance?" Aislinn said in her typically whiny voice. "A secret entrance to where?"

"I don't know where it'll take us. I just know it's here. I feel it," Mistofisee said, still preoccupied with his search.

"How could anything be a secret out here in the open?" Gwen asked.

"Some of the best-kept secrets are right under people's noses," Kendall replied in his typical know-it-all attitude.

Mistofisee stood before the castle well. "I know it's here."

"I'm thirsty," Aislinn said as she reached for the well's pump. When she started to pump the water she noticed a sign hanging from it that read BROKEN. DO NOT USE. "Just my luck, it's broken," she complained.

"That's it! The secret passage has something to do with this," Mistofisee said as he grabbed the pump. He pushed it down, but nothing happened. He pulled it up. Still, nothing happened. He cranked the pump repeatedly to no avail.

"Stop," Kendall demanded. "It's no use. It doesn't work. Can't you see it's broken?"

"It's not broken. The secret entrance is here. I *swear* it," Mistofisee answered impatiently.

A shadowy figure standing in a corner behind the young dragon grabbed Gwen's attention. Unafraid, she walked in the direction of the shadow.

When Kendall looked to see what Gwen was up to, he recognized the being. *"No!"* he screamed. "Gwen. No. Stop."

The Soul Seeker stepped out of the shadows and glided over to Mistofisee. The young dragon, paralyzed with fear, stared at the dark figure.

"For Pete's sake, turn it the other way," the Soul Seeker said in a booming, irritated voice as he raised his bony arm and forced the pump backward.

The old mechanisms creaked and moaned. The ground opened. Mistofisee, Gwen, Kendall, and Aislinn tumbled down a deep hole.

As the entrance slammed shut, the Soul Seeker said, "Idiots. I have to do everything for these moronic creatures. Then they hate me for it."

The foursome screamed and squealed as they slid down a narrow passageway. They landed in a heap on the floor in front of the castle's secret chamber.

"You nearly got us killed," Aislinn grumbled.

"Yeah, I knew you were supposed to pull the handle back," Kendall said with disgust as he dusted himself off. "You should've let me do it."

"Shh," Mistofisee demanded, ignoring Kendall's arrogant statement. Soon he saw light seeping under a door and heard muffled voices. "Someone's in there. They'll hear us," he said. "Be quiet and do as I do."

Kendall rolled his eyes at Gwen. Aislinn positioned herself next to the dragon. Together, they moved slowly toward the gargantuan door.

"That's the biggest door in the world," Aislinn whispered.

"No, it's the biggest door in the universe. And for good reason," Mistofisee replied. "My mother has to fit through it. No one but a full-grown dragon is strong enough to open that door. So it goes without saying, my mother is in there."

Mistofisee, Gwen, Kendall, and Aislinn put their ears to the door. They heard charged conversation.

"It's unheard of. I won't sacrifice my son for the misdeeds of his father," Queen Matilda said.

"If you want to sit on the throne of Beastonia, you will fulfill the wishes of the Innocents. You know the saying, 'as does the father, so does the son,'" said a male creature with an air of authority.

"Hogwash!" the dragon queen roared. "My son's just as much a part of me as he is a part of his father."

"It's simple, either your son dies or Beastonia has no queen," the male creature stated emphatically.

"My son won't die. I'll be queen and someday Mistofisee will be king of all Beastonia."

"And how will you pull that off? You think you can abandon your subjects for more than two hundred years and expect them to welcome you back?"

"Abandon? I didn't abandon my people. It was you, Justorum. You banished me to Idlebury, where I was held captive for two hundred years, and where my son was born."

"Idlebury? Does it have a moat?" a female creature asked in a snide manner.

"It does *not*. It's dark and dreary," a male creature said in a voice similar to that of a hyena. "A moat might do it and its dreadful people some good."

"So am I to assume your son has never partaken of moat water?" the same female creature asked.

"That's true, Piglona," Queen Matilda replied.

"And how old is he now?" an elderly male creature inquired.

"He's two hundred years old."

"A mere child," Piglona stated. "That means he is still innocent."

"And he can't be killed," the Queen of the Innocents declared.

"But he is still his father's son," Justorum firmly stated. "And his father, King Anima, destroyed this kingdom due to careless acts caused by intoxication from moat water."

"As I remember, he was given many RWIs, yet he appeared to care for nothing and no one more than he cared for moat water," a female creature known as Donki said as she gasped for air.

"RWIs?" a young male creature asked.

"Murkell, your ignorance is dumbfounding," Piglona brashly replied. "Everyone knows RWI stands for Ruling While Intoxicated."

"It's hard when one's responsibilities are mammoth and one's temptation colossal," Queen Matilda said in an attempt to defend her deceased husband.

"No, it is not hard. It is simply weakness and self-absorption," Justorum replied pompously. "Canny Castle has been protected by moat water for thousands of years and no one, I repeat, *no one* in the land of the Innocents ever succumbed to its temptation."

"I've sipped it myself. Nasty stuff," Donki said with an air of disgust. "You'd have to be crazy to give up your kingdom for it."

"How do you know no one has ever succumbed to it?" Murkell proudly said. "What about the mysterious draining of the moat four hundred and three years ago?"

"For sure. It was bone dry," said a young female creature named Tifoni. "And the Innocents of the time acted in not so innocent ways. Their behavior was despicable."

"I heard it on good authority that on a dark, moonless night, every Beastonian went to the moat and drank until not a drop of water was left," Murkell continued.

"I heard it was in protest of a tyrannical, abusive king," Tifoni added.

"Yes, King Fohrbidd. He disallowed all vices," Murkell said and snorted. "And that meant hard labor for all Beastonians and soft living for him."

"My son isn't responsible," Queen Matilda said, getting back on topic.

"Your son *is* responsible," Justorum stated angrily. "Your son's father, the King of Beastonia, should have thought about the ramifications of his affinity for moat water."

"Mistofisee will be sacrificed tomorrow at sunset," Piglona said.

"As the Queen of Beastonia, *I forbid it!*" Matilda roared.

"You are not the queen unless the people say so," Justorum declared. "Presently, I have the final say as to the future of your son. And I say he dies."

"You'll have to kill me first. My son is the most innocent of the Innocents. You're making a grave mistake by threatening his existence. You harm him and you'll destroy Beastonia. And if you destroy Beastonia, you'll annihilate the universe. So you may want to think about the ramifications of your affinity for power, prestige, and self-aggrandizement, Justorum."

Justorum pounded on the table. "Your son *dies* at sunset, tomorrow. Now open the door so we may exit."

"No," Queen Matilda replied.

"Then you're trapping yourself in here with us," Piglona said.

"Yes."

"It seems you have a death wish," Justorum stated.

On the other side of the door, Mistofisee shook from fear. "I can't help my mother. And I have no power over whether I live or die."

"How dare they sacrifice the universe?" Gwen said.

"I was kinda thinking how dare they sacrifice me?" Mistofisee replied anxiously.

"No one's going to sacrifice you," Kendall interjected. "The Beastonians wouldn't allow it. You saw how happy they were to see you."

"Yeah," Gwen agreed as she looked at Kendall with awe. "It's true. They don't know what's taken place in Beastonia. If we tell them, you'll surely be saved."

"But what about my mother? What if they kill her first?"

"No way," Kendall said. "Your mother is the largest, strongest, most ferocious creature in the universe. They're not going to mess with her."

"They're just messing with her mind," Gwen said as she smiled admiringly at Kendall.

Throughout the conversation, Aislinn remained silent for a good reason; she was engaged in a mind lock with Queen Matilda.

The dragon queen had powers of which no one, not even Mistofisee, knew. When needed, her vision could become so powerful she could see through the thickest solid object. And her hearing could be so acute she could hear a single particle of dust land on a surface, miles away. Therefore, she could see and hear Mistofisee and his friends on the other side of the door. But her most valued power, which she rarely used because it zapped her of energy and rattled her brain, was her ability to tap into the minds of others. It was this power with which she silenced Aislinn.

During the conversation with the royal court, Queen Matilda realized her strength and courage worked against her. So in a last-ditch attempt to save herself and her son, the dragon queen decided to tap into Aislinn's mind in order to understand how the mind of weakness and whining worked. Her mind lock with the wimpy girl gave her insight into her next move—one that would shock the creatures with whom she was negotiating for her son's life. They knew the dragon queen was strong-willed, emotionally controlled, and prone to quick yet logical decisions. So her tactic was to do the opposite.

Queen Matilda threw herself on the floor of the chamber as she blubbered and begged for Mistofisee's life to be spared. As dragon tears filled the chamber, the members of the royal court were frozen with fear. Within minutes, the pressure of thousands of gallons of tears shattered the large stained-glass window depicting King Anima and Queen Matilda's glorious reign. As the water rushed out the window, it swept the room's occupants and items into the now full moat. Queen Matilda swam to the chamber door and opened it, allowing a river of tears to sweep her, Mistofisee, Gwen, Kendall, and Aislinn out to the back of the Canny Castle.

The Queen of Beastonia picked up her son and his friends to save them from drowning. Then she addressed Aislinn. "Thank you, Aislinn, you've enlightened me."

"I did what?" Aislinn asked.

"You helped me see that I deny my emotional side. If I'm to save my son, I must appeal to my subjects on an emotional level, from the heart of a mother. For that, I thank you with all my heart."

"Oh, you're... welcome," Aislinn said. "No one's ever said anything so nice to me."

When the flood of dragon tears subsided, the dragon queen placed Mistofisee and his friends on the muddy ground.

"Mother, why didn't your tears harm us?" Mistofisee asked. "They're the most powerful substance in the universe and feared by nearly every living creature."

Queen Matilda grinned and said, "Because they were tears created by false emotions. Some call them crocodile tears, which have no power at all. Now, my son, you and I have something important we must do."

Chapter Nineteen
Questions, Answers, Gifts, & Misgivings

A FTER HER CONFRONTATION with the Idleburians, Queen Filanthropi was exhausted. Nonetheless, she was determined to continue with the preparations for the Royal Assembly. So she returned to her chambers where Morgana resumed the fitting for her gown. While her servant nipped and tucked and pinned and stitched, the queen stood quietly and patiently. But soon she tired. So she dismissed her servant and then took a short nap. When she awoke, she went to talk to Thane.

"He is only five years old, but I swear he has the wisdom of an old soul," she whispered to herself as she walked down the long, dreary corridor to Thane's quarters. To her surprise, she saw Morgana exit the boy's room and quickly head in the opposite direction.

The queen stood outside Thane's door and wondered why Morgana had been in his room. When she opened the door, she saw her son sitting on his bed playing with a toy dragon.

"Hello, Mother," Thane said with enthusiasm.

"Hello, my son."

"I guess you'd like to know why Morgana was in my room," the child stated as if he could read his mother's mind.

"Absolutely. I would like to know why Morgana was in your room."

"She came to tell me I'm the Prince of Idlebury. She also said she knows who the Princess of Idlebury is, and it's not Gwendolyn of Idleburg, Pennsylvania, as you believe," the boy said.

"And who does Morgana believe is the real Princess of Idlebury?"

"Prudence."

"Prudence? Who is Prudence?"

"Fredia's baby, Mother."

"And why would Fredia's baby be the Princess of Idlebury?"

"Because she was born right here in Idlebury Castle," Thane replied.

"Lots of the servants' children have been born in Idlebury Castle," Queen Filanthropi said with growing impatience. "That does not make them heirs to the throne."

"That's true, Mother. But Prudence was born of you."

"Me? Prudence was born of me? That was to be the name of the last baby I lost." Visions of Fredia's baby flashed through Queen Filanthropi's head. "Yes, Prudence is just the right age, and she has my black hair and Heroian's crystal-clear blue eyes," she said as she sat on Thane's bed. She took the boy in her arms, rocked him, and stroked his hair. "This is all too much," she said, her voice quavering. "Up until a few days ago, I was motherless. Now I am the mother of three."

Queen Filanthropi gently placed Thane on his bed. "Oh my, Morgana is right. Gwendolyn cannot be the rightful princess," she said as she rose and paced the boy's quarters. "Idlebury law clearly states the rightful heir to the throne *must* be born in Idlebury. Gwendolyn was born in Cringley Castle in Seedonia. She cannot save Idlebury. She cannot save the universe."

Queen Filanthropi rushed out of Thane's room as she yelled, "Gwendolyn must be stopped."

Thane watched his mother's hurried exit. With excitement, he said, "This is getting interesting."

Queen Filanthropi rushed to King Heroian's chambers in hopes he had returned. "Surely he must know of the plans for the Royal Assembly," she muttered as she entered her husband's chambers.

To her horror, the Soul Seeker awaited her. He spoke not a word but opened his cape to reveal the face of King Heroian.

"It is true, my love. Gwendolyn of Idleburg, Pennsylvania is not the rightful heir to the throne of Idlebury. Prudence is. Nevertheless, Gwendolyn is destined for greatness. Do not, I say, do not stop her. You must proceed with the Royal Assembly. For now, leave Prudence in the care of the servant woman. This is no time to create more chaos. I will join you and explain all," King Heroian said hauntingly, after which his image dissipated, revealing the faces of the many souls the Soul Seeker harbored.

Queen Filanthropi tried to respond, but the Soul Seeker stopped her. "Do not try to figure this out yourself. You have no power in these matters. For now, you are to follow, not lead. So go and prepare for the arrival of Gwendolyn." The Soul Seeker closed his cape and disappeared.

But the queen didn't notice the gigantic being's exit, for she was lost in thought, unsure of how to proceed. "I guess I have no choice. I must move on with the Royal Assembly," she said aloud as she headed for the door.

"Not so fast," Wilameena said.

"Where did you come from? And why do you seem to appear when the Soul Seeker is around?" the queen queried.

"Just a coincidence, my dear Filanthropi," the enchantress replied.

"I doubt it. I think you, of all people, are up to something. I dare say, I do not trust you."

"Whether you believe it or not, I'm here to help you."

"You keep saying you are here to help me. When have you ever helped me?" the queen said. "You are like a bad penny. You just will not go away."

"A bad penny, you say? Well, it's a penny that'll change your world. Mark my words."

"A penny?" the queen replied snidely. "A penny has no power here. It buys nothing. It means nothing. And no one has one."

"My dear Filanthropi, you're so naïve. Sometimes a penny can make all the difference in the world. And Gwendolyn will prove it. In fact, she'll prove you a fool."

"She will not prove me a fool. She is my child. Born of the innocent love my dear Heroian and I shared."

"And was it with innocent love that you discarded her?"

"Discarded her? Is that what you think I did? I did not discard her. I gave her to parents who would love and adore her. If I had raised her in Idlebury, she would have been the object of ridicule and cruelty. I gave her what any loving mother would give her child," the queen said.

"Like what?"

"I gave her life and then I gave her a life worth living."

"A life worth living? In Idleburg, Pennsylvania? Have you ever been there, Filanthropi?"

"No, of course not," the queen replied meekly.

"Well, I think it's time for you to see for yourself the life you gave your child when you gave her up," the enchantress said.

"Why are you so cruel?"

"Me? Cruel? You declare to love your child, yet you gave her to commoners in Dimension X. They've raised her without the knowledge of who she really is and without the knowledge of her true potential. You gave her away due to shame and selfishness. You were afraid of what your subjects would think of you for bearing a child out of wedlock—a child you say was conceived in love."

"I did what I thought was best for my child."

"You did what you thought was best for you."

"It was not my choice. I would have kept Gwendolyn, but..." The queen turned away from Wilameena.

"But what?"

"Heroian did not want her. There, I have said it." The queen wept.

"You poor tortured soul. Let's see what you've done to your child," the enchantress said as she snapped her fingers. Instantly, Wilameena and Queen Filanthropi found themselves transported to Idleburg, Pennsylvania ten Earth years in the past.

The two women stood in a darkened bedroom where Evaline Fanny lay on a bed, staring at the ceiling. She wasn't crying, yet tears rolled down the sides of her face, wetting her pillow. While her husband, Arston, was at work, she'd often spend her days watching the neighborhood children play.

Usually, it filled her with happiness, but some days it caused debilitating depression, making her take to her bed. This was one of those days.

Soon a ringing phone broke the silence and startled Evaline from her imaginary world. She halfheartedly picked up the phone and managed a meek *hello*. An excited voice greeted her.

"Evaline, this is Hilda Jones from the adoption agency. I have exciting news."

Evaline held her breath and waited for the next sentence.

"We have a baby for you. You and Arston must come to my office and sign the papers immediately. Otherwise, the adoption will proceed with another couple."

Evaline gasped. "You have a baby for us?"

"Yes, indeed. And she's healthy and beautiful."

"It's a girl?"

"Yes, can you come now?" Hilda asked.

"Of course," Evaline said as she wiped tears and tried to catch her breath.

"Good. See you in a little while."

Evaline anxiously dialed Arston's work number. He answered.

"Maintenance, Arston Fanny speaking."

"Arston, it's Evaline."

"What's wrong, darling?"

"Nothing. Everything's wonderful. We have a baby! You have to come home now and pick me up. Then we need to go to the agency and sign the papers."

"I'm on my way." As Arston rushed out of the building, he yelled to his coworkers, *"I'm a father!"*

"They love her already and they have not yet seen her,"

Queen Filanthropi said to Wilameena.

"A mother and father don't have to see their child to feel love for it," Wilameena said.

"But Gwendolyn did not grow inside her. How can she feel so much love for this unknown child?"

"You've mistaken biology for love. Love is a spiritual connection. Evaline and Arston knew before they'd set eyes on Gwendolyn that she was meant to be their child."

Queen Filanthropi was baffled. "Proceed," she commanded.

The enchantress rolled her eyes and continued. Scene after scene of a happy, loving family played before them. Queen Filanthropi watched as Evaline and Arston brought their daughter home. She marveled at how family and friends lovingly welcomed Gwen. She saw every day of Gwen's ten-year life: the birthdays; the holidays; Sunday dinners at her grandparents' house; how her parents soothed her when she was upset; how they comforted her when she was ill; how they celebrated her first word and first step; how they protected her on her first day of school; how they kissed her boo-boos; dressed her in beautiful clothes beyond their financial means; allowed her to explore the world on her terms; and encouraged her curiosities and budding talents.

Finally, Gwen was ten years old, perched at the bay window in the kitchen of the Fannys' modest home. Evaline was dressed in a robe and faux animal fur slippers, with her head adorned with pink sponge rollers. She appeared lost in a copy of *Universal Scandals* magazine.

Queen Filanthropi watched as the circumstances leading to Gwen's arrival in Idlebury unfolded before her. Suddenly, grief overcame her.

"What's wrong?" Wilameena asked.

"I feel her mother and father's sadness and desperation. They do not know what has happened to their child. Gwendolyn is their child. She is in their hearts. She is part of them. I do not know how to ease their pain," Queen Filanthropi lamented. "But she is my child too. I want her just as much."

"Do you? Why?"

The queen didn't answer. After a few moments of silence, she turned to Wilameena and said, "If you are truly here to help me, you will transport Evaline and Arston Fanny to Idlebury for the Royal Assembly. They must see their child for who she really is. For due to them and their unselfish love, Gwendolyn will achieve prominence."

The enchantress smiled. "As you wish."

Soon Queen Filanthropi found herself back in King Heroian's chambers, unsure of the reality of what she'd experienced. She opened the door to summon Oof. To her surprise, he was waiting on the other side.

"Bring the Knight in Shining Armor to me at once," the queen demanded.

"Yes, Your Majesty," Oof replied.

Queen Filanthropi hardly had enough time to walk to the other side of the room before there was a knock on the door. When she opened it, she was amazed to see Oof accompanied by the Knight in Shining Armor.

"Thank you, Oof. That is all," she said as she motioned for the knight to enter the king's chambers.

"Your Majesty. How may I be of service?" the knight asked as he bowed.

"I have an assignment for you to perform during the Royal Assembly."

"Of course, ma'am. It would be my pleasure."

"May I assume you can tell when someone truly loves another?"

"Yes, ma'am. It's one of my specialties."

"Excellent. Princess Gwendolyn's adoptive parents will be attending the Royal Assembly. It is of the utmost importance you determine their true feelings for her. This is a big job. The future of the universe is at stake. Are you up to it?"

"Without a doubt, ma'am. You can count on me," the knight said as he once again bowed before the queen.

"Very well. You are dismissed."

As the knight clinked and clanked and respectfully backed out of the king's chamber, he bumped into a table and crashed into the door, startling the queen who stared out the window, once again lost in thought.

When the queen looked to find out what the racket was about, she noticed the tarnished state of the knight's armor. "By the way, do polish your armor for the occasion. I am sure Morgana will lend you a hand."

"Yes, thank you, ma'am. I will do so immediately."

The knight reached behind him for the door handle. He firmly grasped it and pulled, but the door wouldn't open. Once again, he yanked the handle and pulled with all his might, causing the door to open with such force that it banged into the wall. He made an ungraceful exit, after which the heavy wooden door slammed in his face.

The queen shook her head, wondering if she should trust such an important task to a man who couldn't effectively leave a room. However, she felt a sense of peace. For the first time in her life, she knew her purpose.

"It all makes perfect sense," Queen Filanthropi said as she looked out the window again. "Gwendolyn is destined for greatness. And Matilda will return. I feel it."

Exhausted from the day's events, the queen returned to her chamber where Anna, a plump, morose servant greeted her with a basket of letters.

"Please, Yer Majesty," Anna said as she curtsied. "Dees must be attended ta immediately."

"Why so, Anna?" the queen asked.

"Dees are letters from da kings and queens of all of da dimensions throughout da universe. I don't know what der about, but der all stamped URGENT."

"Thank you, Anna. Please leave them and I will attend to them momentarily."

"Pardon me, ma'am, I mean no disrespect, but I have strict instructions fer ya ta attend ta dem immediately. Den I'm ta take yer instructions ta Morgana."

The queen eyed Anna with suspicion but decided to indulge the servant's request. "Very well," she said as she sat on her bed and opened the first envelope. To her surprise, a live-action photo of King Kokoa of Chocolatonia appeared.

"I thought you'd never open my letter. I'm to leave in three days for the Royal Assembly and I absolutely must honor the new princess with the best of my chocolates. So how many milk and dark chocolate truffles will delight your guests?"

"That is most generous of you. I think two hundred dozen dark chocolate truffles and one hundred dozen milk chocolate truffles would be greatly appreciated."

"I'll happily double your request. Ta."

Queen Filanthropi opened the next envelope. It was from Queen Garbini of Dresstoria who chattered madly about the time constraints on the design and production of Gwen's gown she was all too excited to provide. An illustration of the glorious gown was enclosed.

"My, my, Queen Garbini, the gown is the most magnificent ever made in the entire universe. Thank you."

"Then I guess it's a go," the Queen of Dresstoria said as she snapped her fingers at the seamstresses behind her. "Can't wait to see you. Bye-bye."

Queen Imelda of Cobblerstonia sent a live image of the beautiful velvet and gemmed shoes she'd chosen for Gwen. They purred in response to her gentle strokes.

"They are perfect, most exquisite. I cannot believe your generosity," Queen Filanthropi exclaimed.

"Only the best for you, my dear Filanthropi. You and your princess do so deserve it," Queen Imelda replied before signing off.

King Carnivorian of Butcherdonia requested confirmation as to the type and number of meats to supply for the feast.

"I graciously accept your offer. Enough to feed five thousand would do."

"Excellent," said the king. "Love to you and my cousin, Heroian. See you in a few days."

The next envelope was from King Phlurtateous and Queen Sentuoss of Loverpool. The image showed the royal couple positioned on a beautifully appointed bed, sipping champagne, and eating the most luscious strawberries. Queen Sentuoss giggled as King Phlurtateous whispered in her ear.

"Excuse us Filanthropi, my dear. We ask your permission to provide luxurious bedding and romantic candles for your guests' quarters," Queen Sentuoss stated.

"Lovely," Queen Filanthropi replied. "I am overwhelmed with your offering. There will be twelve hundred guests staying over. I hope it is not too much to ask."

"It's piddly. Hugs and kisses to you until we meet," the Queen of Loverpool replied.

Queen Leitus of Vegetonia offered to supply vegetables of all varieties, and stated, "Of course, they are fit for kings and queens."

"Wonderful. We would be happy to partake of any and all of your universally renowned vegetables," Queen Filanthropi replied enthusiastically.

In their massive wine cellar, King Merlo and Queen Shardonei of Sommelierdonia enjoyed the official royal tasting of the year's finest wines. Queen Shardonei sipped a cabernet while King Merlo carefully examined a glass of the same. "Umm, there you are my dear, dear cousin," the queen said in an intoxicated manner as she smiled, revealing wine-stained teeth and lips. "I was concerned that if you did not open our letter soon, I would have partaken of too much wine and forgotten why we wrote. But there you are, and we," Queen Shardonei said as she pointed her glass at King Merlo, sloshing wine on his fine garments, "would like to provide the best wine from our extensive collection for the sole purpose of celebrating the homecoming of Princess Gwendolyn. We understand she is expected momentarily and the festivities are to commence— "

"That would be marvelous," Queen Filanthropi interrupted, knowing in this state her cousin could yammer endlessly.

"Okeydokey. Cheers," the King and Queen of Sommelierdonia replied as they toasted Queen Filanthropi.

The most beautiful music filled the air as Queen Filanthropi opened a large letter from the King and Queen of Melodonia who offered their finest musicians to honor the great event. "Filanthropi, my great-niece, I hope this melody is to your liking," King Klef inquired.

"Most magnificent, my dear uncle. I cannot wait to see you both," Queen Filanthropi said as she blew a kiss.

The queen's heart filled with joy as she responded to each letter offering the finest from the many kingdoms to celebrate the investiture of the Princess of Idlebury. But despite the generosity and well wishes of her counterparts from the many kingdoms, Queen Filanthropi felt anxious. The Royal Assembly was only days away. There was much work yet to do, and most of her people were not cooperating.

Overcome with mixed emotions, the queen decided she'd had enough for one day. "Enough, Anna. Please thank all the kings and queens for their munificent offerings. Tell them King Heroian and I are honored by their presence at the Royal Assembly. And notify the chef as to the culinary offerings so he can plan accordingly."

"Yes, ma'am," Anna said.

As the servant curtsied and exited the room, an envelope fell to the floor and slid under the queen's bed.

Neither queen nor the servant noticed.

Chapter Twenty
Reclaimed Innocence

QUEEN MATILDA AND Mistofisee glided over Beastonia. Their view of the kingdom revealed utter devastation. The transformation of the once beautiful land into a depository of animal waste along with the resulting stench was a sensory and emotional overload.

When mother and son swooped over the castle, something caught the dragon queen's eye. Nearly buried at the west edge of Beastonia, she saw what appeared to be a beautiful, peaceful village. She signaled for Mistofisee to follow as she sped in for a closer look. What she saw filled her heart with hope, because protected by the dense, lush forest stood a replica of Beastonia of the past, complete with Canny Castle and its infamous moat.

As Queen Matilda and Mistofisee neared the magnificent structure for an up-close look, a single tear escaped from the dragon queen's eye, dripped down her snout, and splashed into the moat. When the tear merged with the moat water, an intense light shot skyward and formed a brilliant rainbow that engulfed the village. Within seconds, the village inhabitants emerged from their homes; some shielded their eyes against the bright light.

The Queen of the Innocents recognized some of her subjects and could hardly believe they were still alive after nearly two hundred years. Then she saw hundreds, possibly thousands, of young purebred Innocents, many of whom cheered and waved flags; but for what, she didn't know.

Queen Matilda and Mistofisee landed on the castle drawbridge. Soon many Innocents rushed to the edge of the moat and bowed before them.

"What are they doing?" Queen Matilda said.

"They're waiting for your arrival, you moron," someone replied.

The dragon queen swung her massive head toward the voice behind her but no one was there.

"Go ahead, you sorry excuse for a dragon. More than two hundred years ago, you left your subjects to fend for themselves. Now you're surprised to see they've run amok?"

"Is that you, Wilameena, you nasty creature?" Queen Matilda asked.

"Now you're touched a few Beastonians preserved the old ways and saved the last of the pure Innocents? They did your job while you wallowed in Dragon's Sleep," the being replied, ignoring Queen Matilda's question.

"I asked, is that you, Wilameena, you nasty creature?"

"Why don't you look at me and find out?"

Queen Matilda jerked her cumbersome body toward the voice but saw no one. She swung her powerful head in all directions but still saw no one. Suddenly, total darkness surrounded her and Mistofisee.

"Mother—"

"Be quiet," Matilda commanded.

"But I know where we are," Mistofisee said.

"Quiet. I know where we are as well."

"Where?"

"We're in the cape of the Soul Seeker, but he can't hurt us."

"Why not?"

"Because we're Innocents."

"Innocents?" the Soul Seeker roared. "You are not innocent."

"I am, Matilda, Queen of the Innocents."

"You are the queen of a bunch of vile cretins, overbred beasts, and self-absorbed filthy fools. All in all, poor excuses for what you call Innocents."

Queen Matilda roared and blew fire into the darkness. The flames illuminated the inside of the Soul Seeker's cape and revealed the faces of the thousands of souls he harbored. One of which she recognized as her deceased husband.

"What's he doing here?" she asked the Soul Seeker.

"Who?"

"My husband, King Anima." Queen Matilda's voice quavered when she said, "He's dead."

"He is not dead. He is still alive in my world. He is only dead to those who believe in death."

"But... I killed him."

"You incinerated his body. You did nothing to harm his soul."

"But he's dead. I swear it," the dragon queen said, hardly believing the whininess in her voice.

"I say he is not. And if you want him back, you will return to your people and take back your power."

"Take back my power? I never gave it up."

"You did as much when you allowed yourself to be exiled to Idlebury, of all places," the Soul Seeker said in a disgusted manner.

"I had no choice."

"You always had a choice. Your problem was you had a secret."

"I have no secrets," Queen Matilda replied defensively.

"So you would call me a liar?"

"I don't understand. I have no secrets."

"Your family has been harboring a secret for millennia. It is why your exile was in a land of humans, not Innocents."

"Secret? I remember no family secrets, just myths."

"Then how did the Idleburians see you fly over their kingdom."

"I didn't know they saw me."

"Oh… but they did."

"How?"

"Let us see. Humans cannot see Innocents, but the Idleburians saw you for one of two reasons: either they are part Innocent or you are part human. Which is it?"

"But it was so long ago."

"Which is it?" the Soul Seeker yelled, nearly terrifying the largest beast in the universe. "Are they part Innocent or are you part human?"

"I… I… I am part human," Matilda muttered. "But it… it… it's been bred out of me. I have no human blood running through my veins."

"You are wrong and right," the Soul Seeker said. "You are wrong about being part human. Therefore, you are right that not a drop of human blood flows through your veins."

"So if the Idleburians saw me, they must be part Innocent," Queen Matilda said.

"Right again. And for this reason, the kings and queens of Idlebury protected their people. They did everything for them. The shame of being part Innocent was too much to bear. And obviously mixed breeds such as Queen Merry of Hedonia were expelled from Idlebury altogether. The kings and queens of Idlebury created a monster. They created a kingdom of lazy do-nothings. Worse, they spread their mixed breeds throughout the universe. With the exception of Beastonia, there are no thoroughbreds… anywhere," the Soul Seeker said.

"Does Filanthropi know?"

"No, she does not. Neither do her people. But it no longer matters. What does matter is for the people of Idlebury to regain their power. Their future depends on it. The opposite is true for Beastonia. That means you must take back your power from your subjects. But to do so, you will have to start over—from the beginning."

"From the beginning of what?"

"From the birth of your kingdom."

"Why?" Queen Matilda squinted, suspicious of the Soul Seeker's purpose.

"Because there is no way to undo the calamity that has occurred in Beastonia. The Innocents are no longer innocent. This has unbalanced the universe. And balance must be restored or the universe will be destroyed."

"But how?" Queen Matilda begged as she began to realize the magnitude of her mission. "How do I start over?"

"If you are the powerful being you believe yourself to be, you will figure it out. Remember, rigid rules resulted in the ruin of your kingdom. On the positive side, your exile was for human reasons, not Innocent reasons. Now go. Show your people who rules Beastonia."

With a snap of his cape, the Soul Seeker vanished, leaving Queen Matilda and Mistofisee on the drawbridge of Beastonia of the past.

The Soul Seekers words, "Your exile was for human reasons, not Innocent reasons," ran through Matilda's head. *Is it possible the Beastonians have forgiven me for killing my husband, their king? Why did humans intervene?*

"Where's everyone?" Mistofisee asked, bringing his mother back to reality.

"I don't know. But I have a feeling we're not in Beastonia."

"It looks like Beastonia to me."

"Take a closer look. Look at the trees. Look at the castle. Look at the roads and paths," Queen Matilda said in a curiously monotone voice as her giant yellow eyes scanned the area.

"So?"

"The trees are barely taller than you. The castle is brand-spanking new. The roads are narrow and fresh, and the paths lead nowhere. There are no homes. And the air is as fresh as the first air to ever breeze through this kingdom. This is the Beastonia of pure possibility. This is Beastonia of yore."

"Of what?"

"Of yore. You uneducated, ignoramus, indolent…" Matilda stopped herself. She looked at her son and noticed he looked unnerved by her outburst. "I'm sorry, I have no right to talk to you that way. I get upset and forget you're still young."

Mistofisee lowered his head as he fought back tears. "It's okay, Mother."

"No, it's not. So I'll answer your question. This is Beastonia of yore, Y-O-R-E. Meaning this is our kingdom in ancient times. It's a time from which our myths, fables, beliefs, and laws emerged. And you and I are about to witness the creation of the land of the Innocents. The Soul Seeker has transported us here for a reason, so we'll have to wait and see what transpires."

"Okeydokey," Mistofisee said

Matilda sniffed the air. Mistofisee did the same in an attempt to discover what his mother already knew.

"They're coming," the dragon queen declared.

"Who?"

"The first of the Innocents. I can smell their lovely stench."

A cloud of dust emerged over the horizon. Queen Matilda and Mistofisee heard the distant thunder of a racing herd of beasts. The sound became louder and louder as the dust cloud grew larger and larger. Mesmerized by the approaching mass of creatures, Queen Matilda stared straight ahead. She now knew the Soul Seeker brought her here so she could change Beastonia from its inception in order to change its future.

As the mass of motley creatures made their final approach to the castle, the Queen of the Innocents could finally make out the words to their continuous chant: *"We will not be beaten, prodded, or eaten. We claim this castle and land as our Eden."*

The dragon queen allowed the beasts to approach. As they reached the moat, they pushed and shoved their way for a drink of water. The first to drink knew something was terribly wrong.

"Don't drink the water," an ugly, hairless, smelly, rotten-toothed giant of a creature commanded. "It's tainted. It's poisoned."

The crowd pulled back, but the creature kept drinking. They

seemed unaware of Queen Matilda's and Mistofisee's presence. A few of the beasts joined the giant creature as he drank from the moat. A few minutes later, the creature turned to the crowd, attempted a smile, belched, and passed out. Others rushed to the moat but most kept their distance.

When Queen Matilda realized the ugly creature was their leader, and they apparently were now leaderless, she stepped forward, and in a regal manner, addressed the crowd. "Hello. Welcome to Beastonia. I've eagerly awaited your arrival."

No one responded.

"Hello," Queen Matilda repeated. "I'm the Queen of Beastonia and you're my subjects."

Still, the horde of Innocents didn't respond.

"Mother, it's as if we're invisible."

"It appears that way. But my guess would be they can't see us because they have no concept of a dragon," Matilda replied while keeping a close eye on the creature and his followers who were quickly becoming drunk from moat water.

"I don't get it. We're standing right here. You're the biggest creature in the universe, and they can't see you?"

"Exactly. Creatures of all kinds throughout the universe perceive only what conforms to their collective understanding of their worlds."

"Does that mean we only see what we want to see? Are there beings and things around us right now we can't see because we have no concept of them?" Mistofisee looked around as if to check if something or someone he couldn't see lurked behind him.

"Yes, that's what it means," Queen Matilda said as she kept a watchful eye on the crowd of drunken beasts.

"So what do we do about it?" Mistofisee asked.

"We have to figure out what they can conceptualize."

"We'd better figure it out fast. They're getting drunk and some of them are heading right for us."

Queen Matilda took a deep breath to contemplate her dilemma. As she exhaled, a burst of fire escaped from her mouth. She noticed many of the creatures looked toward the flame. "*Yes!*" the great dragon said excitedly. Knowing fire was the one thing animals feared most, she rose on her massive hind legs and spewed a flame so brilliant it lit the far reaches of space.

The horde of sober and inebriated beasts gazed at the flame. The outline of a creature, the likes of which none had ever seen, appeared. As the image of the dragon queen took shape, instinct told them they were in the presence of greatness, for the beast had the power to elicit their most dreaded fear and then take it away in an instant. To show their respect, they knelt before Queen Matilda.

The dragon queen seized the moment and addressed the crowd, "My subjects. I'm Matilda, Queen of Beastonia."

Captivated by the presence of the great dragon, the creatures listened intently to her every word.

"I stand before you at the most critical time in our existence. For from this moment on, we'll define ourselves according to our natural laws. We're pure of heart. We have no sins before our creator. Possibility and innocence resonate from our being. Collectively, we'll have an immeasurable impact on the universe. Because we're the only creatures who give and receive love without expectation or obligation, we've been chosen for a purpose beyond our comprehension. From this day forward, we will be known as the Innocents. And as the queen of our kingdom of Beastonia, I bestow upon you the following inalienable rights:

"One: *Equality*—All breeds are equal. No beast, including me, will control or inhibit the natural instincts of another.

"Two: *Unbridled Freedom*—All Innocents are free from harnesses, holsters, leashes, ropes, saddles, and all other contraptions that limit movement or break one's spirit.

"Three: *Choice*—All Innocents are granted the freedom to exercise personal options in order to care for themselves and their offspring in a manner best suited to their individual breed.

"Four: *Free Will*—No Innocent shall endure the torment of being a beast of burden for any other creature in the universe.

"Five: *Free Assembly*—All Innocents, regardless of age or gender, have the right to hold council and participate in the establishment of the laws by which they shall be governed.

"Six: *Freedom of Speech*—All Innocents have the right to speak their minds in verbal and/or written form and in the animal language of their choice.

"Seven: *Integrity*—All Innocents have the right to refuse to entertain any living creature, anywhere in the universe, by the wearing of clothes unnatural to their breed and/or temperament.

"Eight: *Dignity*—All Innocents are to be provided with designated areas in which to answer the call of nature in private.

"Nine: *Wanderlust*—All Innocents are free to roam the vast ranges of the universe until their heart's content.

"Ten: *Right to Life*—All Innocents have the right to never be the dinner entrée for any creature."

The Innocents of Beastonia rose, cheered, and chanted, "*We will not be beaten, prodded, or eaten. We claim this castle and land as our Eden. Hail Matilda, our queen.*"

165

The Innocents celebrated the birth of Beastonia. Some danced. Some sang in their individual breed voices. Matilda was enthralled with the Innocents' acceptance of her as queen. Mistofisee, bursting with pride, barely managed to hold back his smoke burps.

Suddenly, Beastonia burst into the present day and the Beastonians reverted to their modern selves.

"Why are we back in the present?" Queen Matilda mumbled. "The Soul Seeker said there was only one way to undo the calamity of what Beastonia had become. The only way to save the Innocents was to start from the beginning. Now we're back to where we don't want to be."

"What's that?" asked a ratlike creature with bulging eyes, bucked teeth, and antlers.

"I say, it's hairless," said a rabbit-like creature with long curly red hair. "I beg your forgiveness, but it's quite ugly."

Matilda turned to look at what the Innocents were talking about only to see Gwen standing next to her.

"It's a human I've heard tell about," exclaimed a beautiful catlike creature that barely looked up as it licked its paw.

"I thought it was a mythical creature," blurted a hairy rhinoceros-like animal. "If I didn't see it with my own eyes, I wouldn't believe it."

When the others noticed the presence of the human standing before them, they started to back away. Some turned and ran.

"*Wait!*" a large marsupial creature yelled. "I've heard that before a certain age, humans are as innocent as we are. So do give her the respect she's due."

"Yes, I've heard the same," a female gazellelike creature nursing her young said. "Listen to what the human has to say."

Gwen stepped forward and addressed the crowd. "I'm

166

Princess Gwendolyn of Idlebury. And I've come to you in innocence to ask for your help."

The crowd of Innocents became restless. Some bleated, barked, and bellowed.

A raccoonlike creature that stood nearly five-feet-tall and displayed threatening fangs asked in a gruff, snarling voice, "You're who? You're what? And why?"

"I said I'm Gwendolyn, Princess of Idlebury. And this is Kendall and Aislinn," Gwen said, pointing to the twosome who had joined her.

"There's no one there. She's delusional," declared a young, fluffy creature.

"Wacky," said a creature that resembled a four-legged fish.

"A real nutter," said a minuscule mouse.

"And they say I'm loony," a loon-type bird said and then snorted at its own joke.

"We can't trust her. She's trying to pull the wool over our eyes," a purple-and-yellow spotted lamb said.

"Of course we can't, we can't even trust ourselves," said a creature from the back of the crowd.

"Exactly," Queen Matilda said. "You can't trust yourselves because you're not empowered. You've stifled your natural curiosity in exchange for false security. You've thwarted your most cherished desires in order to satisfy the insatiable greed of others. You're no more than wild beasts or worse, slaves to others. In other words, you've lost your innocence."

The Beastonians protested their queen's claims.

When their complaints became unbearable, Queen Matilda took charge. *"Silence!"* she roared as she spewed fire at her subjects. "None of this is new to you. For generations, you've known your lives were out of control. You're not here by chance. You're here because each and every one of you thirsts for freedom—you long to exercise your free will; you hanker for reconnection with your true selves; you hunger to know life as it was meant to be—these are the reasons you stand before me. You're at the crossroads of greatness. This young human has come to help you. And by doing so, she'll save the universe."

"Why do we need the help of a human?" the lamblike creature asked.

Queen Matilda took a deep breath and then she said, "Because all life forms in the universe are connected. Right now, the common themes of freedom, free will, self-awareness, and the exploration of individual and collective greatness are playing out throughout the thirteen dimensions of the universe. Thanks to the innocence of the Innocents, the universe is joyful, playful, and loving. Without our continued freedom to express our innocence, the universe would emanate negativity. With a buildup of negativity, it will implode into nonexistence."

The Innocents didn't utter a sound. Then a fluffy small creature, innocent by its mere youth, chanted, *"We will not be beaten, prodded, or eaten. We claim this castle and land as our Eden. Hail Matilda, our queen."*

The self-proclaimed King of Beastonia emerged from the back of the crowd. The sea of creatures parted to make way for him as he approached the huge dragon. Some bowed in respect. Others looked on with suspicion. When he reached the foot of the drawbridge, he placed the crown of Beastonia over his heart and bowed before the great dragon. A few seconds later, he rose on his tail, displayed his beautiful feathered fan, and motioned for the great dragon to lower her head. She did what the creature asked, thus allowing it to gently place the crown on her head. In his odd, squeaky voice, he said, "I declare you Queen of Beastonia."

The crowd cheered, "Hail, hail, Matilda. Queen of Beastonia."

With Gwen, Kendall, Aislinn, Mistofisee, and her subjects following behind, Queen Matilda entered Canny Castle. To her surprise, the castle looked restored. On the wall next to the entrance she noticed a framed scroll titled INNOCENTS' BILL OF RIGHTS. She scanned it and saw the ten rights she had proclaimed before her fellow Beastonians were listed.

Queen Matilda smiled, knowing that Mistofisee's life had been spared, and once again, Beastonia was the land of the Innocents.

Chapter Twenty-One
Evaline's R&R in Restoria

Safe under a cozy blanket, Evaline Fanny cuddled on the living room couch surrounded by empty tissue boxes, half-eaten boxes of chocolates, and dozens of flowers given to her by friends and family in an attempt to console her over the disappearance of her daughter. Crunched up tissues and brown candy cups peppered the floor.

Unbearable grief took its toll on the Fanny family. To ease his emotional pain, Arston buried himself in work. Gwen's paternal grandmother drowned her fears in alcohol, making her useless as a support to Evaline and Arston. At the opposite extreme, Gwen's maternal grandparents started a *Welcome Home Gwen* fund by selling magic coin boxes to children throughout the community. In the weeks since Gwen's disappearance, they'd raised more than two thousand dollars. No one had a clue as to what to do with the money. Nonetheless, Gwen's grandparents continued to rally support for their missing granddaughter.

As Evaline rested on the couch, she fought a powerful urge to go into Gwen's bedroom. Finally, she gave in and dragged herself down the hall. Gwen's bedroom door creaked as she pushed it open. A musty smell emanated from the room. A feeling of doom swept through her, causing her to slam the door. Evaline, too weak to act on her impulse to run, leaned her back against Gwen's bedroom door in an attempt to keep from fainting. She then slid ever so slowly to the floor. Suddenly, she heard voices. She put her right ear against the door and listened intently. There was no doubt; the voices were coming from inside Gwen's room.

"Gwen, is that you? Please tell me it's you," Evaline pleaded.

Evaline pulled herself up, turned the knob, and yanked open the door. The room was pitch-black which she thought was unusual considering the brilliant noonday sun normally bathed Gwen's room with warm light.

"Don't be afraid," a man with a raspy voice said. "I've come with information about your daughter. She's well. She's destined to save the universe. The Queen of Idlebury requests that you and your husband attend the Royal Assembly in three days. You must prepare. You must come with positive energy. You have seventy-two hours to overcome your grief and present yourselves before Queen Filanthropi. You have no choice in this matter. You must attend or Gwen will die and the universe and all its dimensions will be destroyed."

Evaline shook from fear, yet at the same time, she was elated to hear her precious daughter was well. She stared into the darkness, attempting to see the form of the creature before her. "Who are you?" she asked.

"Never mind who I am. Just know I'll return for you and your husband in exactly seventy-two Earth hours."

The being moved just enough to let sunlight seep into the room. Gwen's mother could see the outline of an immense being. With a whoosh, the being was gone and the room burst with light, blinding Evaline.

Evaline stumbled back to the kitchen, grabbed the phone, and called Arston. In her excitement, she misdialed several times. When she finally dialed correctly, the phone rang, and rang, and rang, but Arston didn't answer. Frustrated, Evaline slammed the phone in its cradle, snatched her purse, and then made a mad dash for the garage. "I hope Arston got that hunk of junk working," she mumbled, referring to the old car Arston spent every free moment repairing for her.

As she rummaged through her purse in search of the car keys, she realized she'd left her wallet on the living room table. Still mumbling to herself, she stormed back into the house. "Where is Arston? And what does one wear to a Royal Assembly?"

Evaline hurried into the living room. As she searched for her misplaced wallet, she fussed over the mess. While she quickly picked up the tissues and candy wrappers from the floor, she was surprised to see a pair of men's shoes in front of her. She looked up to see Arston standing before her.

"Arston, thank God you're here. A scary creature just paid me a little visit. He told me Gwen's fine and she's to save the universe. Can you imagine, my love, our little girl is, in fact, the Princess of Idlebury? The creature is coming back for us in seventy-two hours to take us to the Royal Assembly in Idlebury, Dimension XIII. And there's so much to do. New clothes. Hairdo. Nails. Not to mention new shoes and a handbag. And you'll need new clothes too, my dear. By the way, we absolutely must attend the Royal Assembly as the world and all its dimensions will be destroyed or something if we don't show. Intriguing, isn't it?"

Arston stared straight ahead. He didn't move. In fact, he didn't blink his eyes.

Evaline inquisitively stared back at her mute and motionless husband. "Arston? What's wrong with you? Talk to me," she begged.

When she got no response, she reached to tug on his jacket, but her hand passed through him as if he were a ghost. Frightened by the image of her husband, Evaline stepped back. On wobbling legs, she managed to take refuge in a wingback chair.

"Oh, Arston. You're dead and you've come to say goodbye. No, it can't be. Our daughter is about the save the entire universe. You must be there. You absolutely must. I refuse to go without you."

Arston extended his ghostly arm toward Evaline. His hand appeared real. Evaline reached out to her husband. When their hands touched, Arston pulled Evaline into Dimension III, where he happily greeted her.

"There you are, my love. So sorry about the eerie show, but it's nearly impossible to break out of this dimension. I knew you wouldn't give up on me though," Arston said as he hugged and kissed his confused wife.

"That wasn't funny Mr. Fanny. But I'm happy to see you're okay. Where are we?"

"We're in the kingdom of Restoria in Dimension III. I think you'll like it here. As the parents of Gwendolyn, Princess of Idlebury, we're to be mollycoddled, indulged, and pleasured into a state of pure repose," Arston said with an air of excited anticipation.

"But we have only seventy-two hours to get back home," Evaline protested.

"Not to worry, my dear. Everything's taken care of."

An incredibly handsome man, carrying soft, fluffy, monogrammed robes approached the Fannys. The back of each robe displayed a stunning gold-embroidered Idlebury coat of arms surrounded by the inscription Proud Parent of Gwendolyn, Princess of Idlebury. The man handed a robe to each of Gwen's parents. With a wave of his hand, they were minus their clothes and dressed in the robes.

Soon a beautiful woman approached the Fannys. She was followed by an entourage that included a masseuse, a hair stylist, a manicurist, a personal trainer, a nutritionist, a meditation instructor, and others. One person carried a sign. It read Welcome to Restoria. Where Recreation is Re-creation and Re-creation is Recreation.

Evaline waved goodbye to Arston as her personal masseuse escorted her to a private room. But something was amiss. She noticed Arston appeared stiff. As she entered her privately appointed massage room, she glanced back at him. A chill ran down her spine when she saw two men carrying what appeared to be a manikin that looked like her husband.

The matronly masseuse closed the door. "My name is Wilameena," she said.

Evaline plastered herself against the wall, afraid of what she'd just seen.

"Mrs. Fanny, if you please," Wilameena said, gesturing toward the massage table.

"I will not," Evaline said as she grabbed the doorknob.

"But you must. The Soul Seeker has demanded you be treated royally before he takes you to the Royal Assembly."

"The Soul Seeker?"

"Yes, ma'am. I believe he paid you a visit in your daughter's room earlier today. He means no harm despite his menacing appearance."

"What about my husband? What have you done to my

Arston?"

"Nothing. He's not here. He's with the Soul Seeker. As are the King of Idlebury, the King of Hedonia, the supposedly dead King of Beastonia, and countless others. But no need to worry. He and the others will be at the Royal Assembly. Everything's going as planned. Now, please relax and enjoy the fine art of massage as only I can provide. I'm the best masseuse in the universe. If you disagree, feel free to inform the Soul Seeker and he'll relieve me of my duties."

"I'm sure you'll do fine," Evaline said as she hopped up on the massage table, shamelessly dropped her robe and then rolled over on her stomach for the massage to proceed.

Wilameena gently placed a towel over Evaline's buttocks, lit incense, and dimmed the lights. When she pressed a button on the wall, beautiful music filled the air and Wilameena began to perform her magic. Within minutes, Evaline entered an altered state of consciousness.

As if in a dream, she found herself floating in space with everyone she'd ever known—her mother and father, her grandmothers and grandfathers, her siblings, aunts, uncles, cousins, friends, and acquaintances. As Arston floated toward her, she reached out to him, but he drifted away. When she saw Gwen, her heart raced as she tried in vain to connect with her. "Gwen," she whispered. Gwen looked at her, but instead of rushing toward her as Evaline expected, the child put up her hand as if to warn her mother to not come any closer.

"Mother, don't proceed. The man whom you joined in Restoria isn't Father. The Soul Seeker duped you. It's imperative you return home at once. Your presence here is a detriment. I'll see you soon. I promise. Go back now."

When Evaline awoke, the masseuse was gone. She was alone in the room. So she grabbed her robe and quickly put it on. As she sat on the edge of the massage table, she reviewed Gwen's warning. Something was awry. "Imperative? Detriment? Duped? Mother? Father?" she whispered. "These aren't words Gwen would use. Someone doesn't want me to attend the Royal Assembly."

Evaline quickly left the room to search for Arston. As she made her way down the corridor, she got an ill feeling.

The hallway was stark.

No doors.

No people.

"Where am I?" she asked of no one. She feared she was no longer in Restoria. *Where am I? And where is Arston?* she wondered. To her horror, twenty-four hours had passed. "Oh no, there are only forty-eight hours left until the Royal Assembly. How could I have lost an entire day? Who's trying to thwart me? I must get home. I must find Arston."

Evaline charged down the endless corridor until she came upon a door bearing a plaque engraved with her name. It read Evaline Fanny, Earth Mother of Gwendolyn, Princess of Idlebury. Without hesitation, she opened the door and found herself back in Restoria, where she was greeted with fanfare.

"For heaven's sake Evaline, where have you been?" Arston asked. "The masseuse ran out of the room screaming you had evaporated into thin air right before her eyes. You nearly scared the poor woman to death."

"Arston, we must go now. There are only forty-eight hours until we leave for the Royal Assembly and I'm not ready. The Soul Seeker said we must return within seventy-two Earth hours, which appears to be twenty-four hours ago. We must go home now."

With the mention of the Soul Seeker, the Restorians fell

silent. The Queen of Restoria, who had been watching Evaline's transformation as if it were a spectator sport, floated down to the center of the room from her viewing area.

"Mrs. Fanny, I am Queen Taaketeezee."

Evaline curtsied before the queen.

"I must inform you that my people and I do not have an affinity for the being to which you refer. In fact, the mention of his name is forbidden. Nonetheless, we do not deny his existence and power. In my experience, it is of the utmost importance to honor his demands. So you must go at once."

"Thank you, Your Majesty," Evaline said as she curtsied once more. "Come Arston, you heard Queen Taaketeezee. We must leave right now."

"I am sorry Mrs. Fanny, but your husband is not here. What you see is a lifelike representation of him. I conjured it to help you relax and restore your spirit. I believe your husband is already in the presence of he whose name is forbidden."

Evaline nearly fainted. She tried but couldn't speak.

"Do not despair. No harm will befall your husband. Now you must go."

Queen Taaketeezee clapped her hands to the beat of *Shave and a Haircut.*

Instantly, Evaline found herself back on her couch surrounded by her mess and safely snuggled under her blanket. It took a few minutes for her to get her bearings and determine if her experience was a dream or reality. Her gut told her to get moving.

Once again, she grabbed her purse and car keys. She ran to the garage, jumped into her car, and prayed it would start. As it sputtered to life and filled the garage with black smoke, she yanked the stick shift into reverse and floored the gas pedal.

The car sped backward out of the driveway and into the street. The tires screeched as Evaline raced toward the shopping mall. After all, she had little time left to find an outfit fit for the mother of a princess.

As Evaline sped through the neighborhood on her way to her shopping spree, masses of people lined the road. She thought she heard someone yelling her name. She slowed down to avoid running over anyone. Many cheered. Some waved a magazine at her. Through squinted eyes, she saw it was the latest edition of *Universal Scandals* magazine. Much to her surprise, the cover photo was of her smiling and showing off the back of her robe on which words embroidered in gold read PROUD PARENT OF GWENDOLYN, PRINCESS OF IDLEBURY.

"It did happen," she muttered to herself. "I did go to Restoria."

Without warning, she and her car rose into the air as darkness engulfed her.

Chapter Twenty-Two
Lessons Learned

GWEN, AISLINN, AND Kendall rested in Canny Castle's massive courtyard while they waited for Queen Matilda and Mistofisee to reacquaint themselves with their kingdom and their subjects. Aislinn and Kendall fell asleep, but Gwen remained wide awake, envisioning the pomp and pageantry of what she knew would be the most extraordinary day of her life—her investiture as Princess of Idlebury. Visions of kings and queens who bowed and curtsied before her to kiss her huge ring that bore Idlebury's coat of arms thrilled her. Normally, her imaginary world filled her with energy, but today the blazing, hot sun zapped her. Still, she struggled to stay alert, but after a few minutes she surrendered and closed her eyes. Shortly, she slipped into an altered state of consciousness in which vivid, scary images haunted her. Aware she was in a vulnerable situation, she tried to fight her fatigue. But despite her best efforts, she couldn't open her eyes. Finally, she relaxed and committed to the unknown journey.

Nonsensical images flashed before her eyes. She thought she saw her mother floating in space and reaching out toward her. Jumbled visions of friends and family raced in front of her.

Suddenly, the images stopped. Gwen found herself immersed in water, floating in a cramped yet peaceful space. She strained her ears to hear muffled voices nearly drowned out by what sounded like a beating heart. Soon silence surrounded her and she heard a woman crying and begging to keep her baby.

"Please, do not take my child. She is love's creation. There is no shame in that. Please let me keep her."

"Keep her? It appears you've failed to consider the consequences of your romantic alliance with Heroian. Your hapless indulgence resulted in the creation of a child. Now you beg to keep it? It's so unbecoming of royalty."

"I do not care about royalty. It is nothing more than a burden on my heart and soul. I would give up the world to raise my child with the man I love."

"The man you love? Is this the same man who hasn't visited you since your exile to Cringley Castle? My, my, love acts in unusual ways."

"You are wicked. You know nothing of love, Wilameena. I dare say you have never been loved."

"You cut me to the quick, Filanthropi. But you're mistaken. I've known love more true and enduring than anyone who's ever lived."

"Liar. You know not love. And you know neither my love for Heroian nor his love for me."

"You're naïve. The man who's vowed his love to me will test your love. Mark my words. At birth, your child will be ripped from your arms and given to commoners in a far-off dimension, dooming the child to a boring, ordinary life. As punishment, you and Heroian will marry, yet you'll remain childless until my loved one determines the time is right for you to mend your ways."

"Who is this man you describe? This man who you say professes his love for you and controls the love of others. Who is he? I demand an answer."

"Answers aren't freely given. But I can tell you the child you carry is destined for greatness. But first, you must forfeit her so she can come back to you."

"Why should I trust you? You banished Matilda to the bowels of Idlebury Castle. She was my dearest friend."

"Matilda will also return to you. Don't question your life's purpose. Time will reveal all. Trust me. You must give up your child if you want your child back."

A gargantuan creature dressed in a hooded cape entered the room. "It is time," the creature declared in a booming voice.

The vibration of the powerful voice caused the yet-to-be-born Gwen to open her eyes. The walls of her birth mother's uterus contracted and convulsed, alerting her to her impending birth. Soon the power of an unimaginable force expelled her from her mother's body. Within seconds, warm sheets swaddled her newborn body. As a servant sneaked her out of the castle and into the cold darkness, a crack of thunder followed by a bolt of lightning and the scream of a woman preceded the newborn princess's arrival in Dimension X, Planet Earth, Idleburg, Pennsylvania. In seconds, cradled in the arms of her adoptive parents, love surrounded her. She was at peace knowing these were the parents with whom she was destined to share her life.

The next ten years of Gwen's life raced before her eyes. A sense of safety and security engulfed her.

Suddenly, Gwen's mother appeared before her with outstretched arms. "My dear child. Your father and I will see you soon," she said. "Go into life with peace and the conviction you were born to change the universe."

Gwen's eyes popped open. Dazed, she tried to come to her senses. Kendall and Aislinn were still next to her and appeared dazed as well.

"That was amazing," Kendall said.

"Amazing? That was freaking scary," Aislinn said. "In case you didn't notice, the Soul Seeker was there the entire time. He was in your birth mother's belly with us. I don't like it. I don't like it at all."

"Aislinn, you get more bizarre each day," Gwen said as she stood. She looked skyward and said, "Watch out world, I mean universe, because here I come. I'm Gwendolyn, Princess of Idlebury."

"Not so fast, you impudent child," the Soul Seeker interrupted. "You are not qualified to fulfill the role for which you are to be entrusted."

"Yes, I am. It's my destiny," Gwen declared.

"It may be your destiny, but you have the audacity to declare your greatness without being duly tested. How brazen? How arrogant? You draw too much energy from Kendall. Therefore, your bravado will not go untested. In order to stand before the Royal Assembly, you shall be tested in ways unknown to those born into positions of power—those who refer to themselves as blue bloods. You are nothing. You are ordinary. You are despicable. You reek of mediocrity. You ooze the inexperience of a sheltered, pampered child. You must prove me wrong, or the universe will be destroyed."

Kendall rolled his eyes.

"Do not mock me, you insolent boy," the Soul Seeker said as he turned to confront Kendall. "You perceive me as powerless because your concept of power is misguided. You think anger is power, but you are wrong. Anger is weakness in its most primitive form."

The Soul Seeker faced Gwen. "When I am through with you, then and only then will you be ready for the universe. Until then, you are nobody. You are nameless. You are nothing more than a worthless, vile concoction of organs, flesh, and bones. You *disgust* me, Gwendolyn Beatrice Villroy Hilda Wainwright Morgan Madison Katrina Dimwitty Francine Patrice Fanny."

The Soul Seeker's cruelty startled Gwen, but she was more shocked to hear her full name. Even she wasn't sure of the order of the many names given to her so as not to insult any family members.

"Now, your lessons begin," the Soul Seeker announced as he flung open his cape to reveal the entire universe of stars, galaxies, asteroids, comets, planets, and moons. A star exploded and created a spectacular display. The thirteen dimensions were visible.

In each dimension, Gwen observed the preparations for her investiture as Princess of Idlebury. In Chocolatonia, King Kokoa monitored the production of his highly prized chocolates. In Dresstoria, Queen Garbini supervised the sewing of what would become her gorgeous gown. In Cobblerstonia, Queen Imelda sat in her huge shoe closet, caressing the shoes that would adorn Gwen's feet. And servants in Loverpool, Sommelierdonia, Vegetonia, Butcherdonia, and all the other kingdoms busily gathered and wrapped the goods promised to Queen Filanthropi for the Royal Assembly.

But when Gwen caught a glimpse of Idlebury, she saw something disturbing. While the queen and her servants engaged in activities necessary for the success of the Royal

Assembly, a group of Idleburians gathered in a back room in one Idleburian's home. Gwen studied the group and noticed one man appeared out of place. He was better dressed. In fact, he wore a crown. Gwen gasped when she realized it was none other than King Heroian, her own flesh and blood. She instinctively knew his intentions were less than honorable.

"I must go to Idlebury. Please, I must go at once," Gwen pleaded as she tried to push past the Soul Seeker.

"You will do no such thing. The vision you see may not be true. Plus, you know not the ways of the people of Idlebury. They are extraordinarily clever at getting the most for the least amount of work. You are no match for their laziness," the Soul Seeker said with a defiant chuckle. "Let us begin."

With a snap of his cape, the Soul Seeker transported Gwen, Kendall, and Aislinn to an open field surrounded by a dense forest.

"This looks and smells familiar," Kendall said.

"It makes me nauseous," Aislinn whined.

"Yes, but we've gotten used to you," Kendall replied with a laugh.

"What?" Aislinn said. "I don't get it."

"He thinks he's funny," Gwen replied.

"Silence," a woman demanded.

"Who goes there?" Kendall asked with the boldness of a medieval knight.

"No one," the woman replied. "Although I am very much alive, I am not human. "And no one of any substance has honored me with their presence for several millennia."

"I know where we are," Gwen whispered.

"Where?" Aislinn whispered.

"We're in the Field of Wisdom."

"For goodness' sakes. There is no need to whisper. I can hear you loud and clear. In fact, I can hear your thoughts. And you, Mr. Kendall, are afraid you will no longer be needed when Gwen assimilates you, or worse, rids herself of you once and for all."

"That's silly," Kendall replied. "I'm a part of Gwen. I'll always be with her."

"As I recall, you are the part of Gwen she likes most. It does not mean she will always like you the most. Nor does it mean you will always be with her. Although your arrogance, insolence, vanity, and bravado are of great service to her now, she will, in fact, outgrow the need for your boyish charm. As for you, Miss Scaredy Pants Aislinn, you think you are the part of Gwen she hates the most. This is true, for it is you who presents her with the biggest challenges. Therefore, you have and will have the most powerful influence on her life. Not you Mr. Kendall. You are nothing more than a useless braggart. Therefore, you will be a detriment to Gwen's development."

Kendall started to rebuff his accuser, but the Field of Wisdom cut him off before he had a chance to utter a word.

"It would be wise of you to realize your days are numbered, Kendall. Now, let's do proceed."

A beam of light engulfed Gwen as Kendall and Aislinn watched helplessly. The word *compassion* illuminated the sky. A vision of a diseased old woman who begged for food appeared before her. Passersby yelled obscenities at the woman. A few spat at her.

As Gwen approached the old woman, the woman's stench repulsed her. When she saw the woman's yellow, scaly skin, her dirty, twisted fingers, and her tattered clothing, she wanted to gag and walk away. Instead, she stared at the woman.

185

Instantly, Gwen felt unbearable hunger pangs. Weak, shaky, and faint, she knew she was experiencing the woman's pain.

Next, Gwen noticed a canvas bag on the ground and picked it up. Inside was enough food for one person. She fought the urge to gobble it all at once. Through milky eyes, the old woman looked at her. Gwen contemplated the possibility the woman couldn't see the bag of food.

"No," Gwen said as she handed the bag of food to the old woman. "I can't turn a blind eye to the need of another person. The food is for you."

The old woman smiled, revealing a mouthful of rotten teeth. When she touched the bag, a flash of light transported Gwen to her next lesson.

The word *forgiveness* lit up the sky. Gwen saw herself window-shopping along a bustling city street. Christmas, her favorite time of year, was only a week away. Although the excitement of shopping for the perfect gifts for her family and friends kept her awake the previous night, she burst with energy and wonder. Snowflakes floated through the air, adding to her delight. Thanks to the darkness of the drab winter day, the holiday lights shone their brilliance early.

Decked out in her favorite purple wool coat with a black velvet collar, a stunning black velvet hat, and luxurious purple mittens, Gwen was the picture of sophistication. Her coordinated purple and black handbag contained two hundred dollars she'd earned from doing extra chores around the house and from saving every penny of her birthday money.

The stores' stunningly imaginative holiday window displays mesmerized Gwen. As she peered through one store window, she momentarily lost herself in the magical world of Santa and his elves. But a tug on her handbag yanked her out of her make-believe world and into a nightmare.

Out of nowhere, a man tackled her. The force threw her into traffic where a car hit her and threw her back on the sidewalk. The last thing she remembered was looking up at a giant poinsettia wreath hanging from a lamppost.

For a moment, Gwen experienced a state of nothingness. Suddenly, she found herself sitting at a table in a courtroom. The perpetrator of the assault and theft of her money looked straight at her as an attorney interrogated him. Rage tingled through her body as she listened to the man lie to the judge and jury. He denied the commission of the crime. He denied being in the city on the day in question. Worse, he blamed Gwen for her false accusations against him. The thief told the court he was a hardworking, loving husband and father who would never dream of harming another person, particularly not a child.

The man, who was exceptionally handsome, used the power of his good looks to manipulate the judge and jury. Some of the women jurors appeared hopelessly in love with him. Men jurors shook their heads in agreement to every lie the man told. The judge, so taken by the defendant's convincing story, declared the man not guilty. The courtroom exploded in applause. Women cried. Men cheered. Gwen tried to jump out of her seat to protest the decision, but her confinement to a wheelchair halted her. Her body, paralyzed from the waist down, was completely useless. She cried for help but no one, not even her lawyer, paid her any attention.

As the man left the courtroom, Gwen screamed, "This is a travesty. You'll pay for what you've done to me. You stole my hard-earned money and crippled me for life. I can't forgive you and I don't know how you can forgive yourself."

A female police officer quickly wheeled Gwen out of the courtroom. As they made their way down the long corridor,

Gwen spotted the man standing with his family. His wife rested her head on her husband's shoulder as a little girl, probably no more than three years old, clung to the man's leg. Three older children, a boy and two girls looked at Gwen with what she interpreted to be shame and fear. She knew they needed their father more than she needed justice. She understood she had to forgive her perpetrator. She knew she'd never forget the horror of that day, but she had to forgive him for the sake of his family and for the sake of her sanity.

Once outside, a large, specially equipped van awaited Gwen. She looked up and saw huge wreaths hanging from the lampposts. A snowflake gently landed on her eyelash. The door to the van opened and her mother greeted her with open arms.

"Let's go shopping, Mother," Gwen said with renewed enthusiasm. "I see it's nearly Christmas and you know how I love to shop for the perfect gifts."

An electronic lift eased Gwen into the van. As the door closed, another flash of light transported her to her next lesson.

Gwen's lessons continued for what seemed like forever. She managed them all with ease except for patience which after three tries, she failed.

Kendall stomped his feet and griped, "This is nonsense. She needs me. I'm the best thing that's ever happened to her. How dare she take on the universe without me? She'll fail. I just know it. She'll fail. I'll make sure she does. I'll show her."

On the other hand, Aislinn nearly burst with pride as she witnessed Gwen's successes. "I wish I had her strength and courage. Oddly, I have patience. Maybe I can help her with that," she said to Kendall. But due to his ongoing hissy fit, he didn't hear her.

The beam dissipated. Gwen appeared before Kendall and

Aislinn looking unchanged from her experience.

"Thank goodness, I thought for sure you would have changed in some way after what you'd experienced," Kendall declared. "But I see you're still the same."

"You know Kendall, you're wrong. I've changed in ways you'll never understand. I've changed from within my core. Everything's about appearances for you, isn't it? I'm through with you, Kendall." Gwen huffed as she walked away. "Come on Aislinn, we have a universe to save."

Kendall tried to dispute Gwen's words, but as soon as she turned her back to him, his entire body, with the exception of his mouth, became as stiff as stone. Silenced by his rage-filled hardened body, he watched Gwen and Aislinn head into the Slothful Forest on their way to Idlebury.

"Not to worry. She'll be back for me," Kendall said as he winced and tried to wiggle free. "She can't live without me just as she couldn't live without Aislinn."

Laughter rang out and the Field of Wisdom spoke. "My dear boy, of what are you most afraid? Is it that Gwen cannot live without you? Or is it that *you* cannot live without Gwen?"

Chapter Twenty-Three
Thane's Misuse of Powers

STILL SEQUESTERED IN his quarters, Thane peered out the window which overlooked the ceremonial court and tried to imagine the pageantry of Gwen's upcoming investiture as Princess of Idlebury. But he was simply too bored to feel excited. Worse, it had been hours since anyone had checked on him, making him wonder if, in the midst of the servants' hustle and bustle, he'd been forgotten. He sighed as he daydreamed about the whereabouts of his father and speculated as to why the King of Idlebury had been excluded from an event as important as the investiture of the princess.

As darkness veiled Idlebury, Thane stared at the lit huts of the Idleburians and fantasized about happy children sitting down to supper, chatting and laughing about the day's activities, playing games, then being lovingly tucked in bed with kisses all around.

But one particular hut caught his attention and jolted him with energy. The illumination from candles cast eerie shadows in a small room where nearly twenty-five men gathered. One man stood, pounded his fist on the table, and then angrily shoved the table, which would have toppled over if there had been room for it to do so.

Thane's imagination ran wild. "This is the most fun I've had all day," he said out loud as he studied the scene in the hut. He smashed his face against the glass in hopes of getting a closer look. "There's something weird about that man," he muttered. "He's different. Too well dressed."

The man in question took something off his head and waved it at the room's occupants.

"Is he waving a crown? It's the king," Thane declared. "He's up to something, and something tells me it's not good. I've got to find out."

Thane tried in vain to open the window. Even if he could, the drop from the window to the ground would surely harm him. So he plopped on his bed and thought real hard about how to get out of his room.

"Help… help," he screamed, but no one responded.

He banged on the door and yelled, but once again he got no response.

"I know I'm not supposed to use my special skills, but I think I'm going to have to," Thane mumbled as he moved to the center of the room. He stood as straight as he could; so straight it nearly hurt. His arms were rigid at his sides; his eyes closed; his head tilted back. At first, he appeared to be in pain. Soon his body relaxed and his head dropped toward his chest. Fairy dust sparkled around him.

"I want to go to my father," he said, but nothing happened.

"I want to go to the king," he said, but still nothing happened.

"I want to go to the hut… *now!*" he shouted.

The room shook as the fairy dust flew around, setting off a light show. The lights bounced around the room faster and faster until they created a tornado which engulfed the child.

Thane vanished.

Morgana had just left the queen's quarters when she felt a vibration and saw light and fairy dust seep under Thane's door. "Oh no," she muttered. "Why did me Thane use magic?" She shivered as goose bumps covered her arms, for she knew if Thane misused his gifts for his own pleasure or gain, he would suffer dire consequences, possibly even death. "What a ridiculous power ta give ta a child. It's as if he's doomed. Be safe me child, fer although I'm not yer mother anymore, yer still in me heart," Morgana said as she kissed her hand and touched the door to Thane's room. Lost in worried thoughts, she headed toward the stairs.

In her inattentive state, she stumbled into the Knight in Shining Armor, who had just reached the top of the stairs. He clanged and banged as he tumbled down the long staircase.

Morgana rushed to his aid. "Are ya okay? I didn't see ya. I can't imagine dat I couldn't hear ya creakin' yer way up da stairs. I must have lost me senses," she said as she helped the knight to his feet.

"My dear woman. Thank you for your concern, but I am fine. I have taken much more disastrous falls during my long, and I must say, notable career as a knight. I remember as if it were yesterday, the time I bravely went into battle alone and single-handedly defeated—"

"I'm sure der are many triumphs ya could recall," Morgana interrupted, knowing the knight was about to recap a long-winded tale of glory. "But do ya remember why ya were headed upstairs?"

"Certainly, I was headed to your quarters, my fair lady," the knight said as he bowed.

"Ain't ya a bit presumptuous? What makes ya think I'd receive ya in me quarters?" Morgana said with disgust as she moved away from the knight. "I'm floored at yer arrogance."

"My apologies, my dear woman. But I approach you upon the request of the queen."

"Da queen requested ya come ta me quarters? Now I've heard everythin.' Go away."

"I can't defy the queen's request. You're to polish me into a state of perfection for my presence at the Royal Assembly."

"I'm ta what?"

"Polish me. It's requested by the queen," the knight replied.

"Absolutely not. Ya'll have ta find some other fool ta polish ya fer da Royal Assembly."

The knight didn't know what to make of Morgana's rejection. He was about to restate his argument when one of the other servants walked down the hall toward them.

"Well, here's a fool ta spit shine ya," Morgana said. "Maddie, me dear, see if ya can polish dis old knight so he's presentable fer da Royal Assembly. Da queen has requested his presence. Do da best ya can as it's probably an impossible task."

"Yes, Morgana," the servant giggled. "Me pleasure," she said as she took the knight by the hand and escorted him down the hallway.

"Fool," Morgana said as she wrinkled her face in disgust.

Once again, Morgana's thoughts went back to Thane. What she didn't know was he had already reached the edge of the castle grounds and was about to step into the unknown world of the Idleburians.

Chapter Twenty-Four
Queen Matilda's Deepest Desire

As day turned to dusk, Queen Matilda paced Canny Castle and contemplated why she felt so happy yet so scared. As she reviewed the day's events, she questioned the Beastonians' quick acceptance of her. Even more, she wondered if the ability to travel into the past was a trick.

"Mother," Mistofisee interrupted. "If this is a brand-new start, does it mean Father will come back?"

"That's an interesting thought, my son, and quite profound, considering you're only two hundred years old."

"I'm serious, Mother. If we've started over, wouldn't it make sense for Father to come back?"

"Yes and no. If Beastonia has truly started over, you wouldn't be born, yet here you are. You haven't changed, and neither have I."

"So?"

"Something's not right," the dragon queen said in an annoyed manner. "The Beastonians have reverted to their former selves, but we haven't."

"Maybe we don't have any reason to."

"Maybe," Queen Matilda said. "And maybe all this is just an illusion."

"A what?" Mistofisee asked.

"An illusion. We're seeing what we want to see, not what's really there."

"Why?"

"Another good question, my son, but I don't have an answer."

The dragon queen stopped pacing and peered out a window that overlooked her kingdom. Everything appeared normal, too normal, she thought.

"Mistofisee, come here," the dragon queen requested with urgency.

"I'm busy. Do I have to come now?" Mistofisee whined as he played with some mice by the light of the fireplace.

"Yes, I said *now*. If you're to rule Beastonia someday, you need to hone your observation skills."

"Okay," Mistofisee unenthusiastically said as he dropped the mice then moved his increasingly cumbersome body across the room. When he joined his mother at the window, she appeared startled by his presence. "What's wrong? You asked me to come over here."

"Nothing. It's just for a second I thought you were your father. I believe you're beginning to look more like him every day. Anyway, what do you see?" Queen Matilda asked, pointing at the Beastonians.

"I see a bunch of beasts wandering around the courtyard looking pretty normal," Mistofisee said.

"Yep, they're wandering around, looking normal, but are

they doing anything in particular?" Queen Matilda asked.

"No."

"Right again."

"Your point would be?"

"Don't take that tone with me."

"I'm sorry, Mother, it's just a phrase," Mistofisee said sheepishly. "No disrespect intended."

"If you're going to be king one day, you need to be mindful of your words. Words are the most powerful instigators of positive and negative behaviors in the universe."

"Yes, Mother. They look normal to me."

"I challenge you to take note of something else, my son."

Mistofisee studied the Beastonians' behaviors, but for the life of him, he couldn't see anything other than a bunch of beasts acting normal. As darkness took over the evening light, he became increasingly frustrated as he examined the crowd in the courtyard. "Mother, I see it! They're doing the same thing over and over. They're walking in the same patterns, talking to the same beasts, stopping and starting over and over. They're not real."

"Yes, my son. You're right. But who would play a trick like this on us? It's a diversion. And what a lovely diversion it is. For a moment, I was happy in the belief I had the acceptance of my people, all was forgiven, and once again, I was the all-powerful Queen of Beastonia. There's something going on that someone doesn't want us to know." The dragon queen paused as she continued to stare out the window. "Where are Gwen, Kendall, and Aislinn? Weren't they with you?"

"No, they were with you," Mistofisee replied.

"Obviously not. Come, we must find them."

As the two dragons headed for the castle's front door, the Queen of Beastonia took one more glance out the window. She wasn't surprised to see the courtyard empty. Not a single Beastonian remained.

"As I suspected," she muttered.

"Mother?" Mistofisee said. "Who is that?"

Queen Matilda turned to see her husband, King Anima, standing in the doorway as if to block her exit.

"Father, is that you?" Mistofisee asked, half scared and half excited.

"Mistofisee, get away from him. He's not your father. He's another illusion."

"But I'm sure he's Father. I'm sure."

"You didn't know your father. I knew him extraordinarily well, and that's not him. Now do as I say and back away."

As Mistofisee carefully stepped back, King Anima transformed into the Soul Seeker.

"You are wise, Matilda, Queen of Beastonia. But you are not wise enough to trust me," the Soul Seeker said.

"And why should I trust you?"

"Because I have something you want."

"Don't play mind games and make me believe you'll return my dear Anima to me. I'm not that green."

"Your dear Anima has already returned. But he is not what you want. Admit it. You want what I have."

The dragon queen's heart skipped at the thought Anima had returned, but she refused to allow the Soul Seeker to see her excitement for fear he would use it against her. Besides, without evidence, she had no reason to trust him. "What is it you have that I would want?" she said.

"Power. You want my *power*," the Soul Seeker spat.

Queen Matilda took a deep breath, knowing her deepest desire had been revealed.

"But it too is an illusion," the Soul Seeker continued. "I have no power other than what others give me. If they stopped fearing me, they would see I am powerless."

"Liar. If I believed you had no power, then I'd be powerless in your presence. My belief in your power gives me the strength to fight against you and keep you from sucking me into your wicked world."

"It is sad you can be so wrong. Those who know I have no power do not fear me. An Innocent should detect my true motives. I am afraid you have been among humans for far too long. It appears their pomposity has infected you. Until you regain your innocence, you will not be Queen of Beastonia. That will be to the detriment of your kingdom and ultimately, the universe. Remember, without you as Queen of the Innocents, Gwendolyn cannot save Idlebury or protect the universe."

"I don't trust you," Queen Matilda said. "I've heard many stories about your evildoing; how you collect the souls of beings throughout the universe and use them for your own deranged purposes."

"Pure conjecture. Probably something made up by the writers of *Universal Scandals* magazine. I am not what I appear. It is my burden in life to have others misunderstand, reject, and despise me. It causes me great suffering, but I endure, longing for the day when I can reveal my true self."

"Oh please. Are you asking for my pity?"

"No. Never."

"Then prove yourself to me."

The Soul Seeker hesitated; happy Queen Matilda finally took the bait.

"How?"

"Bring my husband, King Anima of Beastonia, back to me."

"I cannot."

"Charlatan!"

"No, I am not a charlatan. You think I am here to grant your wishes. What about your husband's wishes? What makes you think he wants to return to you… after what you did to him?"

The Soul Seeker's words stung, causing the dragon queen to pause to gather her thoughts.

"How dare you speak to my mother like that?" Mistofisee said, taking advantage of his mother's silence. "Who do you think you are? All wrapped up in a big black cape… hiding from everyone… pretending you're so high and mighty. I'm not afraid of you."

Queen Matilda grabbed her son as he started to challenge the Soul Seeker. The Soul Seeker laughed, but it wasn't a mocking laugh, it was a full-body, joyous laugh. A second later, he vanished.

"Let's get him, Mother. He has some nerve to scare you."

"Hold on, my son. He didn't scare—"

The castle shook from the thud of heavy footsteps. It sounded as if a huge monster approached. Mistofisee huddled close to his mother. The giant beast stopped and pushed on the massive front door. It didn't budge. So the beast pounded on the door. Matilda and Mistofisee didn't move. In fact, they hardly breathed.

The unknown creature on the other side of the door said, "Matilda, I know you're in there. Open the door."

Chapter Twenty-Five
The Knight's Dilemma

IDLEBURY WAS LESS idle than usual. Although Queen Filanthropi was happy some of her people participated in the preparations for the Royal Assembly, she worried the majority of her people held fast to their right to idleness. Worse, King Heroian was nowhere to be found.

"Where is Heroian?" Queen Filanthropi said aloud as she sat at her desk and reviewed the list of things yet to be done for the Royal Assembly. "I cannot believe he is ignorant of what is going on in his kingdom. It is the talk of the universe." She groaned.

Memories of the many times her husband was not by her side when something of importance occurred disturbed her concentration. She placed the list on the desk and put her head in her hands. As she continued to review King Heroian's inconvenient absences, she became queasy. For the first time, she doubted her husband's love for her.

Queen Filanthropi slowly walked over to the wall on the other side of the room and pulled the cord to summon Oof. He appeared as if by magic.

"Oof, if only King Heroian were more like you."

"Thank you, Your Majesty." Oof smirked. "How may I be of service?"

"Please bring the Knight in Shining Armor to me at once."

"Yes, ma'am. As you wish." Oof bowed and backed gracefully out of the room.

In her heart, the queen knew something was wrong, but mostly she feared Wilameena was right. *Am I a fool to believe Heroian loves me? Is it possible his love for me was the creation of my imagination?*

As Queen Filanthropi recalled the countless times Heroian had let her down, she also remembered the few times he visited her bedchamber. The thought he could be unfaithful was too much for her to consider. She nearly fainted as she tried to get this thought out of her mind. As she moved toward her bed, fearing she would faint, there was a knock on the door.

"Enter," the queen said, barely audible.

"The Knight in Shining Armor, Your Majesty," Oof said as he bowed and exited, leaving the knight, who looked a bit disheveled, kneeling awkwardly before the queen.

"My dear man," the queen said. "I am weary. And with weariness comes silly thoughts. But no matter how silly my thoughts, they cause me great displeasure. I was hoping you— a man whose heart rules his life—would be able to entertain my worries, in the strictest confidence, of course."

"Of course, Your Majesty," the knight replied as he maintained his bow and tried desperately to make himself presentable. "Please excuse my unkempt appearance, but I was in the middle of getting polished for the Royal Assembly, as you requested."

Overwrought with the thought Heroian didn't love her, Queen Filanthropi was completely unaware of the knight's appearance and comment. Quite unexpectedly, she flung herself at his feet. The knight lifted his visor to ensure what he saw was real. When the queen grasped his leg, the knight stumbled backward. Nonetheless, the queen clung to the knight who managed to remain upright while the queen cried and begged for answers. A few hours later, Queen Filanthropi regained her composure and thanked the Knight in Shining Armor for his help.

"My pleasure, ma'am," the knight replied.

To his dismay, the queen didn't excuse him. Instead, from her position on the floor, she looked at him like a lost little girl, and asked, "Does Heroian love me?"

"With all due respect, ma'am, I would have no knowledge of such matters," the knight replied.

"It is a simple *yes* or *no*. Does Heroian love me or not?"

"It depends, ma'am."

"*It depends?*" the queen yelled. "I want an answer. Yes or no?"

"Well… I must say, I've never heard anyone suggest the king isn't totally committed to his relationship with you," the knight responded as he nervously shuffled his feet.

"Why would anyone *ever* suggest to you *anything* about my relationship with the king? Who are the snoops, the liars, and the vindictive louts who would suggest such a thing?" the queen screamed, nearly out of control.

"I can't imagine there's an ounce of evidence in the entire universe to indicate anything other than the king's undying love for you. What evidence do you have to suggest the king doesn't love you?"

"Now that you mention it, there is quite a long list of evidence," the queen sobbed.

The knight sighed, grabbed a chair, and sat. "I fear this will be a long night," he muttered. Then he waited patiently for the queen to wipe her tears and begin.

"For starters, he did not attend our engagement party. He attended our wedding because he had to or there would be no wedding. He insisted on separate honeymoons. He was not present at the birth of our children. He was away on business when the plague of all plagues struck Idlebury, killing many poor souls. He has not attended even one of my birthday parties. Matter of fact, he has never celebrated our anniversary either. He did not attend my grandmother's funeral. He was not in town when the Idleburians revolted due to a shortage of flour. He has never been present for any holidays. He did not answer my letters requesting advice regarding the disputes between Hedonia and Anhedonia..."

While Queen Filanthropi went on and on about how Heroian was never there for her, she failed to notice the knight had fallen asleep.

Sometime later, the knight's own snoring jolted him awake. To his surprise and dismay, the queen still rambled on.

"Excuse me, ma'am," the Knight in Shining Armor interrupted. When it was clear he had the queen's attention, he proceeded. "Maybe I should have asked you to tell me about the times King Heroian was there for you."

"What?" the queen asked, wiping tears from her cheeks with the sleeve of her gown.

"Tell me about the times King Heroian was there for you," the knight requested.

"Oh, let me see." The queen struggled to answer. "Hmm, I cannot recall... this is embarrassing... most discouraging... most depressing. I cannot recall a single time when my Heroian was there for me when I needed him most. What do you make of this?" the queen asked the knight as she stared at him with pleading eyes.

"Well," the knight said as he cleared his throat. "May I be blunt?"

"Please do."

"With all my heart, I believe if someone truly loves you, they are with you for the most important events of your life, be the events happy or sad."

"Go on," the queen commanded as she held her breath in anticipation of what she knew the knight was about to conclude.

"So, ma'am, I must say… I've given this much thought… I'm drawing on my vast experience… as a man who—"

"Just say it, my man," the queen interrupted in a most impatient tone.

In a rapid manner, the knight said, "King Heroian doesn't exhibit the qualities of a man who honors his convictions."

"Meaning what?" the queen queried as she made an awkward and unsuccessful attempt to stand, at one point, ungracefully aiming her rear end at the knight.

The knight was so nervous about what he was about to say he didn't notice the queen's struggle to get up from the floor. "Meaning, ma'am, with all due respect, King Heroian doesn't love you in the manner *you wish*."

"And you believe this with all your heart?" Queen Filanthropi asked.

"With all my heart and soul, ma'am."

"You are a brave and honest man. For your honesty, I am forever in your debt. Therefore, I promise a great future for you," the queen said looking up at the knight.

"Thank you, ma'am. My pleasure, ma'am." The knight bowed as he extended his hand in an offer to help the queen get up.

"Be off with you," Queen Filanthropi said as she refused the knight's helpful gesture. "You must look absolutely radiant for the Royal Assembly, for you will be in a special place of honor."

The knight backed his way to the door, knocking over a chair in the process. When he reached the door, he bowed and tried to exit, but he couldn't turn the knob with his back to the door.

The queen bounced up from the floor and rushed to the knight's side. She gently laid her right hand on his forearm. With her left hand, she opened the door for his exit. The knight bowed again as he stepped back through the doorway. The queen closed the door, kissed her hand, and ran it down the door's worn, rough wooden panels. As she slid to the floor, she whispered, "I love you."

Chapter Twenty-Six
The Kingdom of the
Dead Awakens

HAND IN HAND, Gwen and Aislinn skipped into the Slothful Forest. Despite the filth and stench of the grotesque woodland, Gwen felt lighter, almost happy to be free of Kendall. She didn't share this with Aislinn for fear her weaker self would talk her into going back to the Field of Wisdom to get him. The twosome entered the dark forest and slowed their pace to a walk.

"This is a horrible place," Aislinn said as she pinched her nose and fought back a gag. "But don't worry. We'll be fine without Kendall."

"Are you reading my mind?" Gwen asked.

"I don't have to read your mind. I put the thought in your head."

For the first time, Gwen was suspicious of Aislinn. The thought her weaker self could deceive her was unnerving. "Why aren't you scared that Kendall isn't here?" she asked.

"I figure it this way. You must've taken on some of his strengths to have the courage to leave him behind. Therefore, I feel a little more at ease. Besides, I don't like him. I don't like him at all."

"What do you mean you don't like him? He's part of me and you're part of me. That's like saying you don't like yourself."

"So? What's wrong with not liking every part of yourself? I don't think you like him either."

"Well, just between us girls, I love him, but I don't like him," Gwen said. "He's full of himself. And sometimes he's downright embarrassing."

Gwen and Aislinn laughed as Gwen recounted some of Kendall's embarrassing behaviors.

"Stop," Aislinn pleaded. "I think I'm going to wet my pants."

But Gwen was in a silly mood and went on and on about Kendall. Eventually, the girls laughed so hard they fell to the ground, unaware of the fact that they rolled in the stinky muck.

"I bet he's still standing in the middle of the Field of Wisdom as hard as a rock," Gwen said, still laughing.

"Yeah, and he probably has no idea we're glad he's gone," Aislinn replied.

Suddenly, Gwen's mood changed. "What have I done?" she cried. "I've left the part of me I love the most behind and now I'm venturing on the journey of a lifetime with you, the part of me I like the least. How stupid could I be?"

"That hurts my feelings," Aislinn replied. "For a minute, I thought we were friends."

Gwen and Aislinn wept uncontrollably. If they'd had the wherewithal to look up, they would've seen a celestial event never before witnessed. For above them, Dimension IX vibrated and gyrated. Thanks to the cries of the two young girls, the dimension of the dead was awakening. And everyone in the other dimensions didn't like it at all. Their complaints echoed throughout the universe.

"There she goes again. I told you if she didn't stop, she'd wake the dead. Now it looks like she's gone and done it."

"What does she have to cry about? She's slated to save the universe."

"Not if she doesn't hush."

"Someone must stop her or we're all goners."

"I demand you stop her at once!"

"I didn't hear the magic word," someone said.

"The magic word?"

"What magic word?"

"Please! The magic word is *please*."

"Pleeease," every being from every dimension requested in unison.

"*Shut up!*" someone near Gwen and Aislinn said.

"Excuse me?" Gwen responded.

"I'm sorry, shut up *please*," the unknown person or being said in a much gentler and kinder manner.

"Who said that?" Aislinn asked nervously.

"I did," the being replied.

"Who are you?" Gwen demanded. "Show yourself."

"I'm Lightening, the Queen of Idlebury's horse," a majestic white steed said as he walked out from behind a tall bush.

"Why did you tell us to shut up?" Gwen asked.

"Because your cries were about to wake the dead in Dimension IX. That would be ever so disastrous for you and the rest of the universe."

"Oh no, not the dead. We nearly woke the dead," Aislinn whined. "I don't like this. I don't like this at all."

"The dead? How can you wake the dead?" Gwen asked. "Wouldn't that imply they weren't dead at all?"

"Yes, you're correct. In fact, there's no such thing as spiritual death, only physical death. But because some believe pure death does exist, they're allowed to experience the state of what they believe to be death."

Aislinn shook her head and made noises remarkably like that of a horse. "That makes no kind of sense to me."

"It makes perfect sense to me," Gwen said. "And I believe if we woke them from their self-imposed death, they'd be horribly confused and angry and might just try to take revenge on the living."

"Exactly," Lightening replied. "Only the Soul Seeker and Matilda, the Queen of Beastonia, have the power to stop the King of the Dead. And right now they're both preoccupied with helping you get to Idlebury."

"The Soul Seeker is helping her?" Aislinn said as she pointed at Gwen.

"I told you he wasn't here to harm us," Gwen said. "But no one believed me."

"Never mind. We could argue the point for another millennium. We've got to go. Hop on and I'll take you to Idlebury," Lightening said as he kneeled to allow Gwen and Aislinn to mount.

Gwen eagerly jumped on Lightening's back, but Aislinn was hesitant.

"Wait a minute," Aislinn said. "Don't you think it's just a little weird a talking horse has agreed to take you to your final destination?"

"Who said anything about taking her to her final destination?" Lightening sniped. "I said I would take her to

Idlebury."

"You're wasting time, Aislinn. Just get on so we can get going," Gwen demanded.

"I will not. I don't like this one bit."

"Fine, I'll go without you."

"No, you won't," Aislinn said in a snippy manner.

"And why not?"

"Because you can't live without me, remember?"

"I seem to be doing just fine without Kendall, so I'll take my chances with leaving you behind. Besides, I've changed since we first met, remember?"

"I'm still not going," Aislinn declared with uncharacteristic courage.

"Onward Lightening. I've got a universe to save."

With Gwen holding his beautiful white, silky mane, Lightening bolted toward Idlebury, leaving Aislinn dumfounded and alone in the Slothful Forest.

"What am I to do now? I can't believe I'm alone again in this god-awful place," Aislinn said as she rested against a towering tree. "Last time, a giant snake tried to devour me. Now what?"

Aislinn looked skyward, hoping for an answer to her question. Instead, she saw a hideous face peering at her. Instinctively, she knew it was the face of the King of the Dead. She tried to get up and run, but the tree reached down its branches and held her in place.

"Do not move. He cannot see you if you are still," the tree said.

"Okay," Aislinn said, shaking like a leaf.

"Be still. I will protect you."

"Okay," she mumbled as she took several deep breaths in an

attempt to calm herself.

The hideous face came toward Aislinn as it searched the forest for evidence of human life. Then it came face-to-face with the terrified girl. Its breath smelled like rotting flesh, but Aislinn didn't move.

Blowing blood and saliva on the child with every word, the creature spoke. "You've awakened my people. You'll pay for this. The universe will pay. Nothing and no one will be spared."

The horrific being searched the forest one last time before it withdrew to the sky. As the King of the Dead retreated into Dimension IX and the kingdom of Deadonia, he repeated his threat, "Nothing and no one will be spared."

"Yikes, that was disgusting," Aislinn said as she wiped off the King of the Dead's saliva from her face.

"Gwendolyn is in danger. Kendall and you must go to her at once."

Aislinn looked at what she believed to be the tree only to see the caped figure of the Soul Seeker. "Why are you helping me?" she asked.

"Do not waste time with foolish questions, you silly girl. I do not have time for the likes of you. *Now go!*" the Soul Seeker yelled as he flew after the King of the Dead.

On her way back to the Field of Wisdom, Aislinn stopped to wash in a brook. The warmth of the water surprised her. "This is wonderful. I think a little rest and relaxation is called for," she said as she eased into the water.

As the waters soothed her, she thought she heard voices. She listened intently, but the voices were inaudible. Disgusted, she sat up. "I knew it was too good to be true. Nothing ever goes right for me. Now something or someone is after me again."

"No. It's just me," said a high-pitched, babyish voice.

"Who's me?"

"Me... I'm a babbling brook."

"What are you babbling about?"

"This and that. Nothing in particular."

"If you have nothing in particular to say, why do you keep jabbering?" Aislinn asked.

"It's what I do. It's my purpose. Lots of people babble on and on about nothing in particular. Besides, every once in a while I say something profound. Usually, there's no one to hear me."

"Thank you for allowing me to enjoy your warm waters."

"You're welcome. Now you must go. Gwen needs Kendall and you. The King of the Dead will return. Go now. Be safe," the babbling brook said as it dried up and left Aislinn sitting on its rocky bed.

"A babbling brook?" Aislinn said to herself as she dusted off. "I think I'm losing my mind."

A bright light shone through the trees. Aislinn walked toward it, believing it emanated from the Field of Wisdom.

She was wrong.

Chapter Twenty-Seven
The Deception

THANE CREPT TO the hut where from his bedroom window he'd seen King Heroian and a group of men engaged in angry conversation. As he focused on the activity inside the hut, he didn't see the stars form words of warning—*Stop. Danger. Turn back.* Nor did he hear rustling from a nearby bush. Thus, he was unaware a bony hand tried to grab his leg, but missed.

Suddenly, Thane ran toward the hut. Fairy dust, glistening by the light of the moon and swirling through the air as if it were snow gently cascading from the sky, caught the king's attention. When Thane saw the king look out the window directly at him, his heart raced with fear and excitement. Instinctively, he dove for cover and rolled beneath the window to hide from view.

Among the loud chatter of the men, he thought he heard King Heroian say, "Stop. We have an intruder."

As Thane sat on the ground under the window, trying to catch his breath and avoid discovery, he noticed a trail of sparkling fairy dust led from Idlebury Castle straight to him. "Oh no, they're going to find me now," he said in a quavering voice. His body shook. His heart raced. He looked up as if to ask for heavenly advice, but he saw only blackness. The trail of fairy dust had disappeared along with the stars and the moon as if something blocked them from view. But he didn't realize anything was wrong. In fact, he was relieved the twinkling trail that marked his location was gone.

"I'm sorry. I thought I saw someone outside," King Heroian said as he peered out the window and no longer saw the fairy dust or anything else; not even Idlebury Castle was in view. "My eyes must be playing tricks on me."

Relieved he had gone undetected, Thane mustered the courage to crawl to the front door of the hut. When he knocked on the door, the men inside discontinued their heated conversation. But no one opened the door. So Thane knocked again.

"Well, answer it," a short, stout man said to a tall, skinny man standing next to the door.

The tall man partially opened the door and looked outside; unwittingly allowing Thane to slip into the room unnoticed and quickly hide behind a couch.

"Ain't no one der," the tall man said.

"Den close da stupid door, ya moron," said the stout man.

"Okay, ya needn't get testy. 'Twas yer idea ta open it."

"Gentlemen, let's do proceed," the king requested. "As I was saying, according to my knowledge of the situation, the child known as Gwendolyn isn't entitled to the title or position of Princess of Idlebury."

"But da entire universe is preparin' fer her investiture," said a man who stood next to the king.

"Yes, that's true. But the queen's been harboring a secret—a secret so dire it undermines the identity of the true Princess of Idlebury."

"Prudence," Thane whispered.

"Who said that?" the king demanded.

"Said what?" asked the stout man.

"I didn't hear nothin,'" a bearded, middle-aged man said as he looked at the couch behind which Thane had taken refuge.

"Never mind. As I was saying," the king continued, "the child called Gwendolyn isn't entitled to become the Princess of Idlebury. I admit Gwendolyn of Idleburg, Pennsylvania in Dimension X is the queen's child, but the child wasn't born in Idlebury, which is a requirement if one is to inherit the throne. And to make matters most reprehensible, the child was born when the queen was still the Princess of Seedonia. The queen has kept the existence of her child a secret for many years."

"Meanin' what?" asked the tall man.

"Meanin,' ya idiot, dat da child was born out of wedlock," the stout man said. "Da child is illegitimate, which means our ever innocent Queen Filanthropi is… well, she's a promiscuous woman," he said and then sighed as he looked down in shame.

"A what?" asked the tall man.

"She's a woman of ill repute," another man replied.

"A what?" the tall man asked again.

"A slut. A whore. Dat's what she is," blurted an angry, old man from the back of the room.

"Oh, me own mother was one of dem, she was," said the tall man as he grinned from ear to ear, obviously happy to understand the others' descriptions of the queen's moral standing.

Thane, still hidden behind the couch, stirred, barely able to control his anger and his urge to defend his mother. Although he didn't understand the words the men used to describe her, he knew they were degrading, cruel, and incorrect. "It's not true. It's simply not true," he whispered.

The king heard Thane's whispered remark and saw the bearded man glance at the couch. He was about to ask the man if he'd heard the couch speak when another man interrupted.

"Why would she keep such an important secret from her people? Making us think da wrong princess was da right princess," asked a young man dressed in filthy clothes, obviously due to his work cleaning the castle grounds in preparation for the Royal Assembly.

"Yeah, what other secrets has our dear, innocent queen been keepin' from us?" asked another man in a sarcastic manner.

"The queen's full of secrets," replied the king. "And one involves the exile of the Queen of Beastonia, who lived in Idlebury Castle for two hundred years."

"A dragon? Here?" the tall, skinny man asked.

"I knew it," Gwilym, the Minster of Mindfulness, blurted. "I knew I'd seen a dragon fly over Idlebury."

"You didn't see no dragon. Ya lunatic," the stout man said. "There's no such thin's as dragons."

"Gentlemen." The king interrupted as he waved his hand to hush the men and moved to the center of the room in an attempt to regain control. "Whether or not dragons exist could be debated until the end of time. But there's no denying Queen Filanthropi's been keeping secrets. The fact she's called for a Royal Assembly should raise your suspicions, particularly when she knows Gwendolyn of Idleburg, Pennsylvania in Dimension X isn't the rightful heir to the throne. Therefore, I *command* you to stop Gwendolyn via any means possible. Are you with me or against me?"

"*Stop!*" Thane yelled as he emerged from behind the couch. "Don't trust that man. He isn't the king."

"Excuse me, young man," the king said in a charming manner as he approached Thane. "Whatever possessed you to say such a thing? I'm King Heroian of Idlebury," the king said as he looked to the other men for confirmation as to his royal position.

"I know ya," said Gwilym. "Yer da boy who also saw da dragon fly over Idlebury. I believe ya said her name is Matilda."

The collective gasps of the men filled the room.

"I must confess, I saw it too," the stout man declared.

"Me too. I saw da dragon," the tall, skinny man said and then nervously giggled.

"Me wife and children did too," another man chimed in. "And me mother, who never told a lie in her long-lived life, saw it just before she died. I didn't believe her... bless her soul."

The king stomped his feet in an attempt to quiet the men and regain control from the five-year-old boy. "What makes you think I'm not the king?" he asked Thane.

"The real king wouldn't allow these men to say bad things about his queen," Thane replied. "The real king would defend the queen's honor."

"You're a mere child. You know nothing of being king. I must defend my people against the immoral misdeeds of every person in Idlebury, including those of my beloved queen."

Thane bravely refused to back down from the king. "But weren't you the Prince of Idlebury when Gwendolyn's was born?" the boy respectfully asked.

"I was," the king replied with a quizzical look.

"And wasn't the queen engaged to the Prince of Laborshire when the child was born?"

"No, she wasn't," the king abruptly replied.

"Why not?" Thane continued.

"I don't answer to you. I'm the King of Idlebury. Not only are you a child, but you're also my subject. You answer to me."

"Answer him," said a woman in a stern manner. The men looked at the door and were surprised to see Queen Filanthropi.

"Mother!" Thane exclaimed as he rushed to the queen.

"Do you not recognize your own son, Heroian?" the queen asked.

"I have no son," the king replied.

"You do, and you owe him an explanation as to why I was not engaged to the Prince of Laborshire at the time of Gwendolyn's birth."

"I don't know."

"Liar!" Queen Filanthropi exclaimed. "If you do not answer, then you will confirm what I already know."

"And what's that?"

"That you are *not* the king."

"I told him that, Mother," Thane said.

"I won't stand for an inquisition as to whether or not I'm King Heroian."

"He's not the king." Thane faced the group of men and said, "I beg you, don't believe him."

"If you were King Heroian, you would know who fathered Gwendolyn," Queen Filanthropi stated as she ignored Thane.

"I do know."

"Who?"

"It was none other than I. Princess Gwendolyn is my child," the king said as he raised his crown and waved it at the group of men, hoping to restore their faith in him.

"Da king has a secret too," the tall, skinny man said.

"I don't trust him. I don't," said the angry, old man who sat in the back of the room.

Queen Filanthropi raised her hand to silence the men. She looked intently at the king and spoke with firmness indicative of a real queen. "Wilameena, give up this charade. I have already told my people that Gwendolyn is Heroian's and my child."

"How come we didn't know?" the tall, skinny man whispered to his friend.

"Musta been sleepin,'" the short, stout man replied.

"Yeah, musta been."

The king didn't answer. Before the unbelieving eyes of all in the room, he slowly morphed into a fat, dumpy, middle-aged woman.

"You have been duped," the queen said. "Wilameena, who claims to be loved by the most powerful being in the universe, obviously does not understand love. She has fooled you. King Heroian would never undermine those he loves. And that includes you, his people."

"Yer Majesty," Fergus, the elderly man said. "How da we know dat yer not foolin' us right now?"

"You do not, my dear man," the queen replied. "It is a matter of faith, which I would suspect you have not experienced for many years, for you appear bitter and arrogant."

"Bitter and arrogant? It's bitter and arrogant of ya ta make such a comment," Fergus defensively replied.

"What is it you want from me, my man?" the queen asked with genuine concern.

"From you? Nothin.' What I want is a new Idlebury. I want ta live da life I choose, not a life chosen fer me. I want ta determine me own future, develop me talents, experience da joy of bein' fully human, gain da respect of me family and friends, and... have self-respect."

Queen Filanthropi was at a loss for words, for this bitter old man had expressed her heart's desire as well. "My dear man," the queen said to Fergus. "Your wish is my command, but you must trust King Heroian and me to have your best interests at heart."

"Here, here," said the tall man.

"Here, here," said the others.

Queen Filanthropi smiled and said, "Now, if you trust in King Heroian and me, you will return to your homes and get a good night's rest, for tomorrow as one united kingdom, we will continue our preparations for the Royal Assembly."

The men exited the room and respectfully bowed as they passed the Queen of Idlebury.

After the men had departed, the queen took Thane by the hand and said, "As for you, my son, you have misused your powers. This is an egregious violation. We will discuss the issue tomorrow. Now it is your bedtime."

"But Mother—"

"Be silent," the queen said as she and Thane walked briskly back to Idlebury Castle. Neither spoke, but the queen was lost in memories of the many times she fought off urges to use her powers; powers she obviously passed on to her son. *How might things be different if I had used my gifts, as Father called them?* she wondered.

Halfway through their silent walk, Thane noticed his mother appeared to have gained unusual strength. The moon no longer appeared in the sky, but oddly the castle remained fully illuminated as if the stars and the moon still cast their light upon it. The queen's steps became labored as if she was of massive weight. Her gait became much longer. Thane looked at his mother and noticed she was much taller than usual. Trancelike, she stared straight ahead. When he felt bony fingers clutch his tiny hand, he looked up only to see darkness.

A man with a powerful voice said, "Do not be afraid. This is meant to be."

As the Soul Seeker disappeared with Thane, the queen's anguished cries rang out in the night.

Chapter Twenty-Eight
Mistofisee's Reality Check

QUEEN MATILDA DIDN'T recognize the voice of the person or creature on the other side of the castle door. So the dragon queen and her son stared at the massive barrier to what or who lurked on the other side, unsure if it was safe to open.

The being called out a second time. "Matilda, it's me. I know you're in there. Open up."

"Who's that?" Mistofisee asked.

"I don't know, but the voice is familiar," the Queen of Beastonia whispered.

"So let's look at what we do know," Mistofisee said in a bossy manner, reminiscent of his father. "We know it's a woman, so obviously it's not a man. It sounds distinctly human, but one can't be so sure. It doesn't sound big or intimidating, so if we had to, we could probably defend ourselves. It sounds a little desperate, so more than likely its intention is not to harm us. It's not banging on the door, so it's not aggressive. It's waiting in silence, so it must be a patient creature. It's not—"

"Enough," Queen Matilda said as she blew fire at Mistofisee and singed his snout. She yanked open the door and revealed a coiffed, beautifully dressed, young woman.

"See, I told you it was a woman," the young dragon had the nerve to say as he rubbed his charred skin.

"Hush, Mistofisee," his mother sniped.

"May I come in, Matilda?"

Distrustful of the woman's intentions, the dragon queen moved her massive body just enough to allow the woman to enter the room.

"Don't you remember me?" the woman queried.

"No, I certainly don't," Queen Matilda replied.

"Then why did you let me in?"

"Because you asked to be let in," the dragon said.

"And you sounded rather harmless," Mistofisee interjected.

"Harmless, you say? Pish posh. All isn't what it seems," the woman mocked Mistofisee's naiveté.

"Oh, it's you, Wilameena, you horrible excuse for an enchantress. Disguising yourself as Queen Prudea, one of my dearest childhood friends. You're undeniably the most despicable person I've ever had the displeasure to know."

Wilameena couldn't contain her laughter as she transformed into her true self. "You still think you can outsmart me, don't you, Matilda?"

"No. But I believe you take great pleasure in trying to outsmart others, which only proves you're not as smart as you think."

"Well, let this be a warning to you and your pint-sized, pudgy, poor-excuse-for-a-dragon son: Prudea and Filanthropi have both publicly denied your existence. Therefore, your presence at the Royal Assembly will only serve to frighten everyone and ruin one of the most-awaited days in the entire universe. For that, they'll kill you and your son. And that, I must say, would be most harmful to the future of Beastonia. Just imagine your subjects once again running amok with no ruler, no rules, and no reins."

"You're disconnected from reality, Wilameena. You know nothing of the power of friendship. You're shamefully devoid of love. And you mistakenly believe others don't see the true motives of your conniving actions. I pity you. You're a sad soul." The dragon queen paused as if contemplating her next comment. "Now leave."

"Very well, I'll leave. But before I do, let me remind you that I was once your friend too." Wilameena waited for a response from the dragon. When none was forthcoming, she vanished.

"Mother, why is the enchantress so nasty?" Mistofisee asked.

"I believe the word witch is more appropriate."

"Why do people call her an enchantress?"

"It's just a more polite word for witch," Queen Matilda said with a chuckle.

Mistofisee was about to comment when there was another knock on the door.

"Matilda, I know you are in there. Open the door."

"Not again," Mistofisee said as he rolled his eyes.

"Shh," Queen Matilda silenced her son. "Who is it?"

"Matilda, it is I, your long-lost friend, Prudea."

"How do I know you're Prudea and not Wilameena?"

"Why would I be Wilameena, that vile, tubby, perfidious person?"

"You didn't answer my question. How do I know you're Prudea and not Wilameena?"

"You do not. You have to trust I am who I say I am and that I would not say I am someone who I am not."

Queen Matilda instantly remembered the word games she, Filanthropi, and Prudea used to play. Energized with joy, the dragon opened the door.

Queen Prudea, who had imagined she would hug her old friend, stood in disbelief at the size of Queen Matilda. "Dear me, you have grown."

"So have you, my dear friend."

"How did you know it was her, Mother?" Mistofisee asked.

"How rude of me. Mistofisee, this is Queen Prudea of East Wisdomere."

"Pleased to meet you," Mistofisee said in a grown-up manner as he respectfully bowed to honor the queen.

"My, my, what a fine young dragon you have become. Nice to meet you again, Mistofisee. I do believe you look like your father."

"You knew my father?" Mistofisee asked as he rubbed his still scorched snout.

"Unfortunately, no. Since you do not look like your mother, I naturally assume you look like your father."

"Please, sit down. We have so much to catch up on," the Queen of Beastonia said, offering Queen Prudea a tiny chair the dragon queen kept for the comfort of her much smaller friends.

"Matilda, I wish I could stay and reminisce, but I cannot," Queen Prudea said as she politely refused the offer to sit. "I have come to ask for your help."

"My help?"

"Yes. I believe Filanthropi is in danger."

"From whom or what?"

"Wilameena."

"Yes, that horrible woman was just here pretending to be you."

"Pretending to be me?"

"And she warned me that you and Filanthropi have publicly denied my existence. Those were her exact words."

"She is a fool. She does not understand the bond of old friends."

"So how may I help?" the dragon asked.

Queen Prudea pulled a note from a deep pocket in her dress and handed it to Queen Matilda. "Take this note to the King of the Dead in Dimension IX."

"Why me?"

"Because you are the only being in the entire universe that instills fear in King Morrebidd's coal-black heart."

"Who gave you the note?" Queen Matilda asked, suspicious as to who had penned the message.

"No one. It came to me and demanded I give it to you."

"Why didn't it come directly to me?"

"I don't know. I don't ask questions. I do only what I'm asked."

"What does it say?" Queen Matilda asked.

"I do not know. Ask it."

"Prudea, this is no time to engage in our childhood games."

"Go ahead. Ask me," the note said as it squirmed out of Queen Prudea's hand. "Put me on the table, please," it requested as it took the shape of an arrow and pointed at a table near the window.

Queen Prudea grabbed the note, dragged the human-sized chair to the dragon-sized table, and flung the note in the air.

She and the others watched as it landed on the table and struggled to open.

"Oh, don't help me," the note said. "Just stand there and watch me struggle."

Queen Matilda reached toward the note in an attempt to lend a hand.

"No! Don't touch me," the note demanded. "You might smudge my words."

Without asking, Mistofisee blew warm breath on the note.

"Dragon breath, great. You nearly set me on fire," the note said as it opened.

"It's blank," Mistofisee said as he leaned in closer to examine the note.

"No, it isn't," Queen Matilda replied as she hunched over the note. "You can't see the message because it's not for you to see."

"Hurry up," the note begged. "I feel so exposed."

With great effort, Queen Prudea climbed on the table and quickly scanned the note. "I do not believe it. Why would Filanthropi slight the King of the Dead? Why did she not respond to his letter offering his services for the Royal Assembly?"

"Filanthropi and Gwendolyn are in grave danger," the dragon queen said as she paced the room. "I must leave at once for the kingdom of the Dead. I must talk to Morrebidd. I must restore Filanthropi's honor."

"And I must save Gwen," Mistofisee blurted. "If she dies, the universe is doomed."

"You won't and can't come to the kingdom of the Dead with me."

"I'm going, Mother," Mistofisee stated emphatically.

"No, you are not. You'll have to save your friend another way. If you follow me, I'll be forced to kill you in order to save the universe. This conversation is over."

Queen Matilda grabbed the note and flew out the window on her way to the kingdom of the Dead.

Mistofisee headed for the window but had second thoughts about following his mother. He turned to Queen Prudea and asked, "Do you see me?"

"Obviously. Why do you ask?"

"Because in order to see a dragon, you have to be innocent. Yet you're fully grown. Therefore, by the nature of your physical, mental, and emotional maturity, you're not innocent."

"What are you saying?" Queen Prudea asked.

"I'm saying you're something other than what you appear to be."

"I am who I am and I am not who I am not," Queen Prudea defensively said.

Mistofisee stared at Queen Prudea while he mulled over the information and the thoughts that swirled through his head. "I believe you're telling the truth, but I also believe there is a truth of which you're unaware," he said.

"Of what truth do you speak? You are a young dragon. How would you know of such things?"

"What things?"

"For starters, it is not only the innocent who can see dragons." Queen Prudea paused and stared at the young dragon. "I don't know if you are mature enough to know the truth," she said.

"Go on. Please," Mistofisee requested.

"Let me see if I can explain this." Queen Prudea wrung her hands and paced as she tried to determine the appropriate manner in which to explain her thoughts. "Forget it. I'll just say it. The so-called innocent see dragons because they believe in dragons. On the other hand, older children and adults do not see dragons because they do not believe in them, at least not any longer."

"That means those who are not innocents can see dragons," Mistofisee said with excitement.

"Yes, but they deny what they see. They deny their own perceptions of their world in other ways as well."

"Why?"

"Because they were taught to not trust their observations. It is a form of control to which most people succumb. For example"—Queen Prudea sat, indicating a long conversation was ahead—"let's say you are a small child. You fall and scrape your knee. When your mother hears your cries, she comes over, inspects your wound, determines it is not serious, and tells you, 'do not cry, it does not hurt.' Because you are only a child, you believe the pain you are experiencing cannot be real. After all, your mother, the person your life depends on, said so.

"On another occasion, you run home and excitedly tell your mother and father about your amazing new friend. They listen attentively until you say, 'Her name is Matilda, and she is a dragon.' You watch your parents' faces change from enthusiasm to disgust. Your father screams, *'There are no such things as dragons!'* But you know your new friend is real so you challenge your father's comment. You say, 'Father, I know Matilda is real. I played with her. I talked to her. I touched her. She is very real.' Still, your father does not believe you and says, 'You are forbidden from this day forward to ever talk about dragons again.' So you ask others about the existence of dragons and you get the same response: 'There are no such things as dragons!'

"Now, you begin to doubt your own observations. So their tactics worked, just as they have worked on previous generations. And once you doubt your own perceptions, your reality changes forever. But if you are strong-willed, you refuse to deny your reality.

"So, to confirm your reality, you take a friend—one who you believe is still innocent—to meet your new dragon friend. Of course, in case your friend has already learned to deny her perceptions, you do not tell her she is going to meet a dragon.

"The two of you go off to play as usual and you pretend to accidentally stumble upon a secret place. Your heart races with excitement; you can hardly breathe. Your friend catches your excitement. She tries in vain to open the door to where your dragon friend awaits while you light a lantern to brighten what you already know is a dark stairway which leads to a damp, musty cellar. The unusually large door makes an eerie creaking noise as it resists your tugs, but you persist until the door gives up the fight and opens. Then you let your friend go down the stairs in front of you as you pretend you are scared of what lurks in the cellar. You get to the bottom of the stairs and place your small foot on the soggy dirt floor. The stench is wretched but you ignore it because you are too excited to care. You swing the lantern around the room, casting shadows in shapes so scary you wonder if monsters lurk where your dragon friend lives. When the light falls on the spot where the dragon had lain, you see she's gone. In her place, an adorable purple creature lays perfectly still. Because of its color, you know it is a newborn dragon that has not yet suckled. Nonetheless, once again, you doubt your own perceptions. You say to yourself, 'the others are right, there are no such things as dragons; my mind is just playing tricks on me. There is no huge dragon here, just this poor baby creature that appears alone and motherless.'

"When your friend shrieks, 'She is gone! Matilda is gone!' You can hardly believe your ears. Your friend knows the name of your dragon friend. You ask, 'Who is Matilda?' Your friend feigns ignorance and says, 'Matilda, well, I do not know. Did I say Matilda?' You question your friend, hoping to get her to admit what you already know—Matilda is a dragon. You say, 'I know Matilda. She is a dragon, and that is her baby.' Your friend stares at you in disbelief and says, 'But there are no such things as dragons.' You say, 'Yes, there are because Matilda is my friend and she is a dragon.'

"The two of you dance and celebrate your regained sense of reality. You pick up Matilda's baby and hold it. You notice it smells sweet like a newborn human baby. It does not budge because it is fast asleep, exhausted from its recent birth. You both pet it and kiss it before laying it back down. As you both scurry up the stairs, your friend stops you halfway up and says, 'We can never tell anyone about Matilda. She is our secret.' You agree and continue up the stairs. You and your friend return to her castle, hide out in her chambers and talk about your mutual dragon friend; glad to have a shared secret.

"For a while, the two of you spend many happy days playing with the dragon and her precious baby. One day, you go to the cellar to check on Matilda and her baby. To your horror, you find the door cemented shut. Your friend and you are horrified and saddened. You know someone else knows about Matilda and is trying to force you into their denial. Your friend and you pledge to never give up trying to be friends with Matilda. You find other ways to get into the cellar, but you can only watch from afar as Matilda lovingly cares for her baby.

"When you next check on your dragon friend, you notice the door's cement seal is gone. You open the door ever so carefully and quietly descend the stairs into the cellar. You see your dragon friend. Your heart momentarily jumps with joy until you realize she is still, as if she is dead, and she is purple rather than green. Instead of helping her, you do the unthinkable—you ignore her situation, shut the door, and never see her again. To handle your guilt for what you have done, you try to deny your dragon friend's existence as you whisper to yourself, 'There are no such things as dragons.' But you do not believe yourself."

Queen Prudea stopped in anticipation of Mistofisee's questions, but it appeared she was to be sadly disappointed.

"Thank you for the story," Mistofisee said. "It made me realize I can't deny my responsibility to save my friend Gwen. If I have to face the King of the Dead to save her, so be it."

The young dragon charged to the open window and took off for Deadonia.

"He does not get it," Queen Prudea said as she watched Mistofisee disappear into the sky. "He does not need to save Gwendolyn. He needs to save himself."

Chapter Twenty-Nine
A Great and Mighty Clash

WITH UNFLAPPABLE DETERMINATION, Mistofisee soared through several dimensions on his mission to save Gwen from the King of Deadonia. But when he realized he didn't know the location of the kingdom of the dead his confidence began to wane. Nonetheless, he flew on. Soon a disturbing thought haunted him. From what or whom was he to save Gwen? Since the Soul Seeker was protecting her, maybe she didn't need him to save her after all. If not, whom was he supposed to save?

As Mistofisee contemplated his dilemma, he became aware of a sense of peace and enjoyment such as he'd never experienced. He felt grown-up—confident, independent, and powerful. The young dragon envisioned himself as the King of Beastonia as he reminisced about the adulation the Beastonians bestowed upon him when they mistakenly thought he was their king.

Lost in his make-believe world of power, prestige, and popularity, Mistofisee was unaware of his passage into Dimension XIII. Hence, he didn't notice the spectacular aerial view of the Slothful Forest, the Field of Wisdom, and Idlebury, as well as East and West Wisdomere. Plus, due to his break with reality, he didn't see Gwen racing toward Idlebury on the back of Queen Filanthropi's steed, or Aislinn walking into a bright light of unknown origin, or the statuesque Kendall in the middle of the Field of Wisdom.

While entertaining his fantasies, Mistofisee soared a great distance, leaving his friends far behind, each to the perils of his or her own predicament. As he unknowingly slipped into Dimension IX, the appearance of the horrific face of the King of the Dead jolted him back to reality.

"You're trespassing into a dimension and a kingdom where you don't belong. Leave or you'll be destroyed."

"Okay," Mistofisee said as he quickly retreated in fear.

But something caught his eye—a small flying creature headed for the forbidden kingdom. *That creature is either incredibly brave or unimaginably stupid,* he thought. He turned to leave but the sight of the creature grabbed his attention again. It looked familiar.

The horrific face reappeared.

"Go. Now. Or I will destroy you."

"If you don't mind, I'd like to take a closer look at the flying thingy headed for your kingdom," Mistofisee asked in a cheeky manner.

"It's no concern of yours. *Now go!*" the grotesque creature screamed.

"You don't scare me," Mistofisee said defiantly. "If you wanted to harm me, you would already have done so."

"Your defiance will cost you dearly. See for yourself what creature has the audacity to enter the kingdom of the dead."

Magically, Mistofisee's vision became telescopic. As he focused on the unknown creature, it became larger and larger until it was recognizable.

"Mother," the young dragon blurted.

"You may call her Mother, but I call her a dead dragon. Care to join her?" the King of the Dead said as he cackled and disappeared.

Mistofisee fought the urge to rescue his mother. He knew he was no match for the King of the Dead. Plus, his mother's words of warning echoed in his head, "If you're to save your friend, you must do it another way. Follow me and I'll be forced to kill you in order to save the universe."

So Mistofisee flew off, passing through Dimensions X, XI, and XII before he reentered Dimension XIII and headed back to Idlebury. This time he clearly saw the Slothful Forest and a person standing in the Field of Wisdom.

"That's odd," he said out loud. "There's a person standing in the Field of Wisdom yet no light surrounds them. They're just standing there not learning anything. Maybe this is the person I'm supposed to help," he said with excitement as he made an ungraceful landing in the field.

"It's about time," Kendall said, obviously annoyed.

"What are you doing standing there like some statue?" Mistofisee asked.

"Gwen did this to me. How could she? I'm her favorite self."

"I think you've got it wrong. I believe you're the part of her she likes or, in your case, liked the most. You're not her favorite self, remember?"

"Shut up. She can't and won't be the princess without me. I'm the one who'll rule. She'll be my puppet."

"It's nice to see you haven't changed," Mistofisee said facetiously.

"Of course, I haven't changed. I'm perfect," Kendall blurted.

"I always was and always will be perfect just the way I am. I'm special. I'm unique. And I don't have to prove it to anyone."

"You certainly can't prove it by me." Mistofisee chuckled.

"I'm not joking. If you can't accept my perfection and superiority, it's your problem. Unfortunately, only special people can understand me, and I haven't met anyone as special as I am."

"The sad fact is you're not joking," Mistofisee said. "You're so full of yourself that you make a mockery of yourself. You think you're smarter, cleverer, more handsome, and more cultured than others when in fact you're a conceited, insecure, lazy, annoying, good-for-nothing braggart others make fun of. So it would seem your imaginary perfection and superiority *are* your problems."

"I won't listen to this. No one can tell me what to do or how to be. I'm me, and me is perfect."

"Don't you mean, I'm perfect?" Mistofisee said, correcting Kendall's grammar.

"What? You aren't perfect. You're the least perfect being in the entire universe. When I rule, you'll be caged in a zoo for all to ogle and scorn."

"Luckily for me, you'll never rule anything until you learn to rule your thoughts, emotions, and attitude. And despite the fact you're a universal pain in the butt, I feel sorry for you just a teensy bit. So if you're willing to stop being your narcissistic self for just a few minutes, I might be willing to help you get out of your marble straightjacket."

"I don't need your help. I'm perfectly capable of helping myself."

"Oh, I forgot to add know-it-all and stubborn to your list of virtues. So be it. Help yourself. I'll just watch. Maybe I'll learn something from you, Mr. Perfect," Mistofisee said sarcastically.

Kendall strained as he tried to escape his marble prison. He spewed affirmations to help him endure his plight. "I'm all powerful. I am what I think I am and I think I'm great. I have the strength and courage to overcome all obstacles. I'm smarter and better than others. I believe in me. I'm unique and special. I can do and be anything. I create my own reality. I can manifest anything I want." Hard as he tried, he remained encased in marble.

For a while, Mistofisee feigned boredom. When he could no longer stand Kendall's gross grandiosity, the dragon rolled with laughter.

"What are you laughing at?" Kendall asked angrily.

"You. You're hysterical. You think all that mumbo jumbo is going to turn you back to flesh and bones. You're daft."

"You don't know anything. I've always done things my way. It's worked well for me." Kendall sneered and then repeated his affirmations.

Mistofisee watched with increasing disgust and impatience. "It doesn't look like your way is working. Let's try my way." He took a deep breath. When he exhaled, an enormous flame engulfed Kendall. Its tremendous heat cracked the marble just enough so Kendall was able to fight his way free.

"What are you trying to do, kill me?" Kendall said.

"A thank you would be nice."

"Thank you for what? I got out by myself."

"If I hadn't blasted you with fire, you'd still be reciting those silly sayings and waiting for a miracle."

"Now look who's full of himself."

"Stop it. This isn't getting us anywhere. Gwen is lost out there."

"Worse, she's with Aislinn, that whiny, dowdy downer."

"Okay, give it up. We've got to find Gwen."

"Why would I bother with her when she doesn't want or need me?"

"I don't know. All I know is we're wasting precious time talking and not doing. I'm going to look for Gwen. Are you with me or not?"

"Not!" Kendall screeched. "If she wants me, she can come find me."

"Fine. I'm off then. See ya around." As Mistofisee departed, the ground shook. "What's that?" he asked as he looked at Kendall, hoping his know-it-all friend actually did know it all.

"I believe it was you. You've gotten huge. I can't believe you could be so fat and still walk. You should—"

Another vibration interrupted Kendall.

"I don't believe it was me, Mr. Know-it-all."

Kendall moved toward Mistofisee as if he expected the dragon to protect him from some great harm.

The ground shook. The sky turned violent as black clouds billowed and lightning ripped through the air. Frightened, Kendall quickly hid in the gap between Mistofisee's butt and tail.

Suddenly, the face of the King of the Dead appeared. But this time, he seemed to be looking for someone other than Mistofisee or Kendall. In fact, he didn't seem to notice them at all. Nonetheless, Mistofisee watched the King of the Dead for fear he'd make good on his threat to destroy him.

When Kendall peeped around the dragon's tail, he saw the Soul Seeker lumbering in their direction. But something was different. The Soul Seeker was more massive than usual. In fact, he was nearly ten times his normal size. It was he who shook the ground with his every step. Frightened, Kendall was unable to utter a word of warning to his dragon protector. So he slapped and kicked Mistofisee's tail, but got no response. *How can he not see or hear the Soul Seeker coming?* Kendall wondered. He looked at the sky and saw the image of the King of the Dead, but Mistofisee wasn't looking at him either. His dragon friend was fixated on another massive being heading at them from the other direction. Kendall recognized Mistofisee's mother instantly. "Thank goodness. She's come to save us," he said with relief.

Queen Matilda spotted her son standing in the middle of the Field of Wisdom. "What's he doing? He's too young to be exposed to wisdom. He hasn't learned from his mistakes yet. This mistake could scar him for life." The dragon queen soared in and grabbed her son with her massive claws.

Unaware Kendall had taken refuge under Mistofisee's tail, Queen Matilda left him in the Field of Wisdom, alone and unprotected.

As she tossed Mistofisee into the Slothful Forest she yelled, "What's about to take place isn't for you to see. Now go. Find Gwen. The end is near."

"But Mother," Mistofisee pleaded as he tried to get the great dragon's attention. But he was too late, for the dragon queen had already headed back to the Field of Wisdom to face a potential cataclysm.

Mistofisee paced. He was torn. *Should I save Gwen as my mother demanded, or should I protect my mother from the King of the Dead?* he wondered.

"Go find Gwendolyn," a meek voice said.

"Who said that?" Mistofisee asked.

"I did," a tall tree said. "Now go. I will watch over you and

Gwendolyn. She is already in Idlebury. She needs your help. But you mustn't fly because if the Idleburians see you, all is lost."

Mistofisee fought his desire to fly as he hurried in the direction of Idlebury. He didn't look back at the Field of Wisdom. If he had, he would've seen his mother, the Soul Seeker, and the King of the Dead prepared for a battle: the outcome of which could change the lives of all creatures throughout the universe.

The three great beasts silently gathered in the field. Queen Matilda and King Morrebidd eyed the Soul Seeker. "Why has he chosen to exhibit such force with his drastically increased size?" King Morrebidd asked.

Queen Matilda shrugged.

The Field of Wisdom spoke. "Matilda, Queen of Beastonia, are you ready to see the truth and fight to the death for your beliefs?"

"I am," Queen Matilda responded.

"Morrebidd, King of the Dead, are you ready to see the truth and fight to the death for your beliefs?"

"I am," King Morrebidd said in a strong yet whispery voice.

"And he who has no name but is known as the Soul Seeker, are you ready to see the truth and fight to the death for your beliefs?"

"I am," the Soul Seeker roared.

"King Morrebidd, enter the center," the Field of Wisdom commanded.

"I will not," the King of the Dead stated emphatically.

"You will do as I say or forfeit your kingdom."

King Morrebidd entered the center of the field. The Field of

Wisdom's magnificent light revealed his ghastly figure. His body was a mangled mass. His flesh dripped off his bones. He looked more pathetic than powerful.

"I'm ready!" he howled.

"Queen Matilda, step into the center," the Field of Wisdom demanded.

Without reservation, the Queen of Beastonia moved her massive body into the center of the Field of Wisdom. She basked in the warmth of its light as it revealed a heart made of solid gold shackled by chains leading from her mind; a mind obsessed with duty.

"Now for you," the Field of Wisdom said as it shone its light on the Soul Seeker. "I have saved you for last, for you are the most difficult of all. Your resistance to the light of knowledge has stunted your wisdom. Step forward so I can see if you can redeem yourself."

The Soul Seeker didn't move.

"I said step forward," the Field of Wisdom demanded.

"It's not that I won't, it's that I can't."

"Why?"

"Because I'm not the Soul Seeker."

"Then who are you?"

"I can't—"

A powerful force pushed the gigantic caped creature into the center of the Field of Wisdom. It shriveled, revealing its true form.

"Well, it is none other than you, Wilameena," the Field of Wisdom said. "Take your leave as I will not grant wisdom to one so despicable."

"Do not blame her," the real Soul Seeker said as he entered

the Field of Wisdom. "She is merely a pitiable soul. She understands not what she does."

"Very well. Be off with you, Wilameena," the Field of Wisdom said as a flash of light threw the wretched enchantress into the Slothful Forest.

The Soul Seeker savored the wonder of the Field of Wisdom. The souls he harbored cried out in joy as they learned their true purposes. But the Soul Seeker's physical being remained hidden by his cape and hood, thus prohibiting the revelation of his true self.

"You are resisting my powers," the Field of Wisdom said.

"I am not resistant to the light of knowledge. But I am resistant to others seeing my truth as it is not mine alone. It is the truth of all the universe's creatures. It is a truth for which few, if any, are ready."

"Enough. It is time," the Field of Wisdom said.

Gwen appeared before them.

"What's she doing here?" the King of the Dead asked.

"She is what each of you truly wants," the Field of Wisdom said. "You have all vowed to fight to the death for her. So get on with it."

The Queen of Beastonia, the King of the Dead, and the Soul Seeker remained silent and still for some time as Gwen patiently stood before them. Suddenly, King Morrebidd snatched the child and attempted to escape. Queen Matilda glanced at the Soul Seeker to assess his intentions, but he didn't move. The Queen of Beastonia reached into the sky just in time to retrieve the grotesque king. She grabbed Gwen and held her close.

Unexpectedly, the Soul Seeker removed his hood, revealing he was a handsome man with an effeminate softness to his otherwise bony features. "Please, give her to me, Matilda. She is the last soul I seek. Then my job is complete."

"No, I won't give her to you. She's innocent. And her innocence will save the universe."

"Her innocence will save all souls," the Soul Seeker said.

"But you'll imprison her soul and doom her purpose," the dragon queen said.

"I need her soul in order to free the souls I now hold."

"All souls are meant to be free. The freedom of her soul will save us all."

"Come, come, Matilda. Act from your heart, not your head."

"I saw what you are," the dragon queen replied. "You're nothing without the souls you've taken. Gwen is just one more."

"But she will complete me. I need her."

"No, she's not yours. She's not mine. She belongs to the universe."

"I want her dead so the universe will continue on its current course of glorious destruction," the King of the Dead interrupted as he snatched Gwen from the mighty dragon queen.

Queen Matilda roared and spewed fire, momentarily stopping King Morrebidd's departure. The Soul Seeker grabbed the child, but she slipped through his bony fingers. Queen Matilda lunged at King Morrebidd. The Queen of Beastonia and the King of the Dead tumbled to the ground, causing the earth to crack. Gwen was knocked aside, allowing the Soul Seeker to sweep her up in his arms. As he tried to engulf her in his cape, the dragon queen seized Gwen. With the child firmly gripped by her strong talons, the mighty dragon lifted her and began to speak. "As the Queen of the Innocents, I declare…"

The Queen of Beastonia noticed something alarming, causing her to pause. The child she held wasn't Gwen. In fact, the child wasn't real. It was a doll. In an instant, she knew the fight wasn't about Gwen. It was about the integrity of the three most powerful creatures in the universe—the King of the Dead, the Soul Seeker, and her.

Queen Matilda cleared her throat and started over. "As the Queen of the Innocents, I declare this child liberated to exercise her free will. She and she alone shall choose her destiny," she said as she placed Gwen on the ground.

As expected, the King of the Dead and the Soul Seeker clamored for possession of the child. Queen Matilda watched the duo fight their way skyward, creating a storm so fierce, its memory would haunt every creature in every dimension throughout the entire universe.

The Queen of the Innocents remained in the center of the Field of Wisdom. As she soaked in its magical light, she experienced a powerful revelation. Her beliefs about her subjects were wrong. They didn't need to accept her; she needed to accept herself. It was now all so clear. Lack of self-compassion had hardened her heart and false beliefs had imprisoned her mind. Her greatness was within her control, but only if she surrendered to that over which she had no control. For the first time in her life, she felt truly free and powerful. So, in full command of her faculties, she flew to Idlebury where she would face her deepest fear and in doing so unleash her greatness.

Kendall stood dumbfounded. He had gone unnoticed and totally unscathed. Instead of relief, he was angry the three most powerful creatures in the universe had ignored him. "I'll show them. They'll *never* ignore *me* again," he mumbled as he walked into the Slothful Forest on a trek that would end at Idlebury.

Chapter Thirty
The Power of
Thought Control

T HE SLOTHFUL FOREST seemed eerier than usual as Gwen rode Lightening on their journey to Idlebury Castle. Even more unsettling was the speed with which the queen's steed raced through the cluttered forest. Gwen listened for the sound of the racing horse, but it was unusually quiet. She was positive Lightening's hooves didn't touch the ground. Plus, her hair and clothes didn't billow in the wind.

"Don't ask questions. You must keep an open mind," Lightening said as if he could read Gwen's thoughts.

Gwen was about to respond when Idlebury Castle came into view. *Home sweet home,* she thought as she envisioned herself as the all-powerful Princess of Idlebury.

"And don't make assumptions either," Lightening said.

"Are you reading my mind?" Gwen asked.

"No."

"Then how do you know what I'm thinking?"

"Because thoughts are extremely powerful. Once you

release them to the universe, they're available to anyone who's sensitive enough to receive their energy, which most humans aren't. But because I'm an Innocent, I'm extra sensitive to the energy of thoughts. So I'm not reading your mind, you're literally talking out loud."

"I guess you've been listening in for some time," Gwen said nervously.

"Yes, but most of what you say is nonsense," Lightening said with disgust. "Just the ramblings of one who has much to learn."

"Sorry I disturbed you, but I can't control my thoughts," Gwen said, feeling annoyed an animal had the gall to pass judgment on her.

"See, you just proved my point that you have much to learn. The truth is you can and must control your thoughts, for they are the most creative force in the universe. Remember, what you think about, you attract into your life. It's a universal law," Lightening said.

"Okay, but I don't get it."

"No, you don't want to get it. You want the conversation to end," Lightening said. "And as you wish, I'll desist."

As the twosome continued toward Idlebury Castle, Gwen thought about what Lightening had said. "If my thoughts are so powerful, and what I think about is what I attract into my life, then why haven't I gotten everything I've ever wanted?" Gwen asked in a flippant and dismissive manner.

"For example?" Lightening asked.

"Well, last semester I desperately wanted straight As, but I didn't get them. I didn't get close."

"Why did you want straight As?"

"So my parents would buy me a princess bed I saw in a

catalog."

"And did you get the bed?"

"Yes, my grandmother bought it for me for my birthday. And I got the sheets and comforter too."

"So what you really wanted was the bed, not the As. The grades were just a way to manipulate your parents into buying you something they couldn't afford."

"I guess so," Gwen replied meekly.

"Do you remember the thoughts you had regarding your acquisition of the bed?"

"Yes, I told myself I would get it somehow. And one way was to tell my grandmother I wanted it for my birthday. I put pictures of it on my bedroom wall. And every night, I would imagine I was sleeping in a beautiful bed fit for a princess."

"So the universe did conspire to give you your heart's desire. But you also said you wanted straight As. When you say you want something, you create the state of wanting. So the universe also gave you what you wanted in that situation. It gave you the experience of wanting As. If you'd stated your thoughts in a more action-oriented manner, such as 'I'm a straight-A student,' or 'I'm working hard to get all As,' the universe would've helped you get high grades. But that wasn't what you asked. The lesson is; your thoughts are extremely powerful. So be careful what you wish for because the universe will conspire to give it to you."

Gwen's head was spinning from confusion. *I wish he'd shut up,* she thought.

"I heard that," Lightening said. "You want me to shut up, so I will. But remember what I just told you."

Shortly, Lightening and Gwen exited the Slothful Forest and entered Idlebury. The moment the steed set foot on the soil of the kingdom of the lazy, Gwen sensed a profound change in the animal's energy. He emanated powerlessness. When Gwen realized Lightening had responded to the collective thoughts of the Idleburians, she knew her task as Princess of Idlebury wouldn't be easy for she would have to change their negative, hopeless thoughts if she were to save them.

Lightening motioned for Gwen to dismount. As she alighted, a weatherworn sign arose before her. It read WELCOME TO IDLEBURY. WHERE EVERYONE GOES TO DO NOTHING AND NO ONE GOES TO DO SOMETHING.

Gwen groaned as she remembered uttering these very words at the gates to Hedonia in response to King Funzy's question, "Who goes there?" "I guess I wished for this," she said out loud.

Lightening acknowledged Gwen's statement with a disapproving snort.

Soon Gwen was lost in fantasies of being a beautiful, powerful princess. A few moments later, another thought popped into her head. *What if I was much more than just a princess? What if I could be greater than any princess could dream to be?*

Lightening's words played in her head, "The lesson is your thoughts are extremely powerful. So be careful what you wish for because the universe will conspire to give it to you." Gwen smiled to herself as she thought, *I'm destined for greatness, and I think the universe knows it.*

"I believe I'm supposed to take on this challenge," Gwen said. "After all, I'm Gwendolyn, Princess of Idlebury."

Lightening snorted again and started to walk toward the castle. Gwen followed humbly.

The walk took longer than Gwen had expected. When she

was getting too tired to continue, she spotted Idlebury Castle's drawbridge. "Finally, we're here," she mumbled as she continued to walk toward the castle.

"Yo! You're headed the wrong way," Lightening said as he veered to the left and followed a wall around to the side of the castle.

Halfway around, the steed paused and stared at the wall. He walked a little farther, stared at the wall again, stomped his right front leg four times, snorted three times, rose on his hind legs, and whinnied twice. Nothing happened.

Lightening then moved a little farther down the wall and repeated his seemingly odd behavior. This time the wall bubbled as if it were made of boiling purple goo. He entered the goo without comment to Gwen. Not sure of what to do, Gwen followed the horse. Once through the goo, she noticed a huge double-paneled door. Excited voices were heard from the other side. A horrible stench filled the air.

"Smells like a filthy barn," she mumbled.

"Shh," Lightening silenced the child as he gently kicked the door.

"Who goes there?" someone asked in a strange, harsh voice.

"It is none other than the carrier of the innocent," the horse responded.

"What's the password," the same being asked.

"Blabber, dabble, snabble, and snoo. Crittle, brittle, prittle, and droo. Wally, winkle, stinkle, and croo. Mumbo, jumbo, crumbo, and zoo."

The wall opened like a stage curtain. A menagerie of Beastonia's most exotic animals clapped as Lightening and Gwen entered the room. Gwen was completely confused as to the animals' enthusiastic reception. But Lightening bayed and

249

stomped with excitement.

"You've done it, my dear man," said a kangaroo-like creature.

"Well done," said a zebralike creature whose coat of gold and silver stripes shone with such luster that Gwen could see her image reflected in the animal's fine hairs.

The animals bowed. Gwen didn't know how to respond, but for the first time in her life, she felt like a real princess.

"Please stand up. I don't deserve such worship," Gwen said as modestly as possible, hoping she could disguise the fact her heart nearly burst with pride.

"My, my, conceited, aren't we," someone said from the back of the room.

The animals parted to make way for an elderly creature. With the support of two younger creatures and a cane, it hobbled to the front of the room. Gwen wasn't sure what type of animal it was or how old it was, but its sagging skin was covered by sparse, coarse gray hair. Its eyes were milky. Its teeth rotten. It appeared to be wearing the remnants of red lipstick. It was disgusting. The decrepit creature came face-to-face with the child. Its breath reeked.

"Are you scared of me, my child?" the old creature asked.

"No, I'm not scared of anyone," Gwen arrogantly replied as she tried to not breathe the creature's awful breath. *Where's Kendall when I need him?* she wondered.

"Liar!" the creature screamed. "You're scared out of your wits and you're too impudent to admit it. You expect us to believe a human creature can come into our cozy little lair and not feel the least bit uncomfortable?"

Gwen fought the urge to back away.

"Worse, you thought the Innocents bowed before you. Silly

girl. They bowed before the royal steed of Queen Filanthropi, who, by the way, is also the father of Queen Merry of Hedonia. He has done much for our world. You, on the other hand, have done nothing."

"That's yet to be seen," Gwen said, holding her ground against the bullying creature.

"Touché. Right you are," the old creature said as it banged its cane at Gwen's feet. "But before you take the title Princess of Idlebury, you must first earn it. Therefore, tomorrow morning you shall embark on the most important and quite possibly the most dangerous journey of your life."

Gwen controlled her fear, but her red face revealed her anger.

"I see you're angry, my dear," the old creature continued. "But don't worry your pretty little head just yet. For tonight, we party."

The other creatures cheered. Tables were quickly set up. Massive amounts of food appeared as if by magic. And hundreds of pitchers of moat water passed through the crowd.

Lightening leaned down and spoke in Gwen's ear. "Relax. She was just trying to scare you. Have fun tonight. The secret to your successful passage into the new you depends on one specific creature in this room."

"Who?" Gwen pleaded.

"It's for me to know and for you to find out," Lightening said with a wink.

"But I can't stand being here," Gwen protested. "I won't eat that foul food. And I can't possibly get close enough to one of those smelly creatures to talk to it."

"Hold your judgment. These creatures may seem a bit unsavory, but if you're open to the experience, you'll find they're quite nice beings. And one of them has the information you need to become what you've always imagined. Lastly, remember your thoughts are powerful and they can hear them."

Lightening moved away from Gwen and disappeared into the crowd.

Gwen fought back tears as she mumbled, "What am I doing here? Am I in a nightmare? I'm taking advice from a talking horse. I've befriended a dragon. I hang out with two people who are just parts of me. I've been kidnapped by the Soul Seeker. I've been tested by a field. I've been to other dimensions. I've even been back in my birth mother's belly. I think I'm certifiably nuts."

"No, you're not. Knutthyder's the name," a large, well-groomed squirrel said, extending his paw to Gwen. "I've seen many nuts and you're not one. But I must say, I'm quite partial to nuts."

"You're the first creature, other than Lightening, that we have back home in Idleburg, Pennsylvania. But that I know of, our squirrels don't have names and don't talk."

"Certainly they do. All Innocents..." Mr. Knutthyder hesitated. "Did you say, Idleburg, Pennsylvania? I have family there."

"Squirrels can travel to different dimensions?"

"Of course. What a silly question. Maybe you are nuts. Ooh, I like you already."

"Can you help me learn who in this room has the information I need to pass my test tomorrow and be proclaimed Princess of Idlebury?"

"My pleasure. I would be happy to. It's none other than..." The squirrel motioned for Gwen to lean toward him. She stooped down and put her ear to the squirrel's mouth. "It's none other than Ms. Crabbina Walleybird."

"Who's that?" Gwen asked impatiently.

"You've just spoken with her, you have."

Gwen's heart sank. "That crabby old thing has the information I need to save the universe. Her name sure is fitting," she whispered.

"Shh. Don't think and talk like that or you'll never get to speak with her."

"Okay, okay. So what do I do? Just walk over and talk to her?"

"Are you nuts? Oh, I already asked you that and the answer is no." Mr. Knutthyder chuckled. "You must work your way through the crowd and find the right Innocent to introduce you to Crabbina Walleybird, who, by the way, is the eldest of the Sullywobbles, a tribe believed to be the first Innocents to inhabit the area now known as Beastonia. They are noble protectors of the kings and queens. Some believe they're solely responsible for the survival of Beastonia. That means Crabbina is the eldest Innocent of the oldest Innocents in Beastonia. Even the queen bows to her."

"Queen Matilda bows to her?"

"Yes, now go and work the crowd. Follow me. I'll help you."

Gwen wandered behind Mr. Knutthyder as he made introductions to his fellow Innocents. But try as he might, Gwen was ignored. A few bowed. Fewer politely listened to her questions about how she could get the information she needed to achieve her life's desire. Most just walked away.

A creature that appeared to be a small ball of white fur hopped on a table and jumped up and down furiously. It made such a racket that the room's occupants were quickly silenced—all except Mr. Knutthyder who continued to jabber to a short, burly, hairless, yellow creature with oozing green boils and no ears with which to hear the squirrel's endless chatter.

The ball of fluff, known as Mr. Fluphinekel, rose on wire-thin legs that had been well hidden under his fur. With surprisingly long, skinny arms he reached out and whacked the squirrel on top of its head, and in a powerful, deep voice said, "Mr. Knutthyder, please shut your trap. The most respected Ms. Crabbina Walleybird is about to speak."

"So sorry, so sorry, so sorry. Ms. Walleybird, please do forgive me. I didn't hear Mr. Fluphinekel call the Innocents to attention."

Crabbina, who sat on a throne to the left of the table, motioned for the squirrel to zip his lips. "Squirrels are such a nuisance," she said. "Real nutters, some say. Nonetheless, they are Innocents and we are to accept them as they are."

The crowd cheered as a few of the Innocents patted Mr. Knutthyder on the back in a show of support.

Crabbina waited a few seconds for the Innocents to settle down. When it took longer than she felt necessary, she banged her cane on the table, knocking Mr. Fluphinekel to the floor. He scurried back on top of the table, cleared his throat, and yelled, "*Quiet!* The distinguished Crabbina is ready to speak."

Crabbina rose slowly from her seat as she refused help from two of the younger creatures. In an attempt to steady herself on her weak legs, she braced herself against the table. The room's creatures, now so quiet you could have heard a feather drop, looked at her with awe. With the eloquence of a much younger Sullywobble, Crabbina said, "Ladies and gentlemen, my most dear Innocent friends, I have it on good authority that our queen, Matilda, will return to Idlebury within the next two days."

The Innocents rustled and whispered excitedly to each other. A few cried tears of joy.

Crabbina ignored the chatter as she continued, "So for those of you who thought our job here was done, I happily announce, you're wrong. Our beloved queen is to return."

The Beastonians cheered again. Some hugged. Others jumped up and down while making wild animal noises.

Crabbina raised her wrinkled hand to quiet the Innocents. "In the past, our presence in Idlebury was a well-kept secret. Our queen didn't know we were here to protect her during her exile from our homeland. This kept our existence and her existence a secret from the Idleburians. But this time, things will be different. It's time we make ourselves known to our queen and to the people of Idlebury."

The room filled with silence. The creatures glanced at one and other in hopes someone would have the courage to question the revered Crabbina. But no one did, except a child who had entered the room unnoticed.

"How do you know that Queen Matilda and the people of Idlebury don't already know you're here?" said the small child.

Every Innocent turned to the entrance where a young boy with curly black hair and crystal-clear blue eyes stood. Fairy dust fluttered around him. *I've never seen him before, yet I know him,* Gwen thought, forgetting the Innocents could hear her. But they didn't because the beauty of the human child captivated them all.

"That's the most beautiful human I've ever seen," said a female Innocent.

"I just want to pick him up and cuddle him," said another female.

"He's so cute. I love him," said yet another.

"Can we keep him for a pet?" asked a young female Innocent.

"What?" Crabbina screamed as she fought her own urges to pet and snuggle the child. "No Innocent is to ever entertain the idea of having a human for a pet. Don't ever ask that question in my presence again."

"Are you going to answer my question?" asked the small child.

"What is your name, child?" Crabbina asked.

"My name is Thane. I'm the son of King Heroian and Queen Filanthropi of Idlebury."

"You're the Prince of Idlebury?" Gwen asked, fearing her right to the throne of Idlebury was about to slip away.

"Yes, and you are?" Thane asked flippantly.

"I'm Gwendolyn, Princess of Idlebury," Gwen said, sounding like Kendall.

"So you're who everyone's waiting for," Thane said.

"My dear boy, we have much to do, and Gwen has a journey to embark on in the morning. I declare this party over. Clean up and go to bed," Crabbina abruptly commanded, causing many Innocents to guzzle as much moat water as possible before it was put away.

"Gwen and Thane, you'll sleep over here with me," Crabbina said, motioning for the children to join her in the corner on a bed of disheveled matting. Gwen took Thane by the hand and obeyed the old Sullywobble.

As Crabbina tenderly tucked Gwen in bed, the child looked up at the old creature and respectfully asked, "Ms. Walleybird, may I ask you a question?"

"Of course, my dear."

Gwen gulped, fearing Crabbina would yell at her if she asked the question that had been eating at her all evening. But she knew if she didn't ask she'd never learn the secret to realizing her desire. So she took a deep breath and said, "How do I achieve my dreams?"

"That's a personal question, young lady, for only you have the answer," Crabbina said calmly. "But I do have some words of advice I hope will help."

The old Sullywobble closed her eyes and took a deep, relaxing breath. When she looked at Gwen, her eyes, no longer milky, sparkled with youthful enthusiasm. Her voice was soft and soothing as she said, "Remember, you get what you focus on. Negative thoughts beget negative outcomes. Positive thoughts beget positive outcomes. And only positive thoughts allow you to overcome obstacles, of which there will be many during your life journey. Don't give up in the face of difficulties. They're necessary in order for you to achieve your greatness. Now sleep. Tomorrow, you'll face one of your greatest obstacles."

Gwen wanted to ask another question, but she fell asleep as if she'd been drugged.

Crabbina grabbed Thane and said, "Wilameena, you louse, present yourself."

The child transformed into Wilameena. "How did you know it was me?"

"I didn't. But you didn't fall asleep when I cast my spell on Gwen and you. No innocent human can resist its power. So I knew you weren't innocent. And there's only one being in the universe that thrives on making fools of others. You," Crabbina said through clenched teeth.

"Well, Crabbina, for your information, I'm here to warn you about a little problem regarding Queen Matilda's return to Idlebury," Wilameena said.

"What problem?" Crabbina asked.

"It appears she is bringing someone, or I should say *something* with her."

"Who or what is she bringing?"

"Morrebidd. Remember him? He's all grown up. And he's the King of the Dead." Wilameena's wicked laugh echoed through the room as she disappeared.

"Morrebidd? The King of the Dead?" Crabbina stroked Gwen's hair and said, "My dear, you have more to overcome than I thought."

Chapter Thirty-One
King Heroian's Warning

Q UEEN FILANTHROPI WAS in a tizzy. Only two days remained until the investiture of the Princess of Idlebury, and the castle was in complete disarray.

Morgana tried to assure the overwhelmed queen everything would be done in time, but with the arrival of the goods and services promised by the kings and queens of the many dimensions, the queen became increasingly anxious.

Vegetables, meats, baked goods, linens, flowers, candles, candies, desserts, wine, musical instruments and more were piled everywhere. Musicians, chefs, cooks, and servants sent from other kingdoms wandered aimlessly while offering help that went unaccepted.

The queen rushed through the castle issuing commands and making changes to almost everything, which only added to the servants' frustration.

"If she tells me ta change one more thin' in da guest rooms, I'll bop her one, I will," one of the servants said.

"I'll help ya," said another.

"Oh, Yer Majesty," said the servant as she offered a partial curtsy. "I didn't see ya der."

Queen Filanthropi overlooked and overheard the activity from the balcony. She was about to admonish the servants for their disrespect when someone pounded on the castle door. Instantly, all activity came to a halt.

Oof appeared out of nowhere and opened the door. Two distinguished men, dressed in the finest clothes, stood silently. One held a small bejeweled box. The other held a large, beautifully wrapped box.

"From where do you hail?" Oof asked.

"I've come from Cobblerstonia to present Queen Filanthropi with the princess's shoes. It is a most splendid gift from Queen Imelda."

"And you?" Oof asked the other man.

"I, my dear man, have traveled through no less than six dimensions in just under three days. In my care is the gown that will adorn Princess Gwendolyn two days hence," the second man said. "Queen Garbini of Dresstoria has lovingly provided this magnificent garment. If you please, I ask that the queen receive this gift in person. I have explicit instructions to hand it to no one other than the queen herself."

"As do I," the first man from Cobblerstonia said.

"Very well. I shall fetch her," Oof replied in his typically haughty manner.

The Queen of Idlebury was about to go downstairs and investigate the loud knock on the door when Oof suddenly appeared beside her. "Oof, you are forever scaring the willies out of me," she said as she wrung her hands. "What is it this time?"

"Two gentlemen are at the door, Your Majesty. One is here to present you with the royal shoes from Queen Imelda of Cobblerstonia. The other is from Dresstoria—"

Be Careful What
You Wish For

Queen Filanthropi pushed Oof aside and charged down the stairs with the enthusiasm of a school girl. *"They are here! The princess's dress and shoes are here!"* she screamed with delight. She ran to the door, grabbed the boxes from the two men, slammed the door, and then ran back up the stairs.

Soon there was another knock on the door. Oof opened the door to find the two men still there. They appeared stunned by the queen's behavior.

"With all due respect, was that frenzied woman the queen?" the man from Dresstoria asked.

"I am afraid so. She is a little stressed," Oof replied with as much dignity as possible.

"I see. My best to you," the man from Dresstoria said as he and the man from Cobblerstonia took their leave.

Queen Filanthropi holed up in her chambers to admire the princess's gown and shoes in privacy. But her excitement turned to despair when she thought about her other children. She shivered as she remembered the night when the Soul Seeker took Thane. Nonetheless, in her heart, she knew Thane would return to her unharmed. But when the queen thought about her sweet baby, Prudence, she knew she'd have to gather the courage to take her daughter from Fredia at the Royal Assembly.

"I hope it does not turn into a horrible spectacle," she muttered to herself. "But I am afraid if I try to take her back now, Fredia will run away with her. Besides, Heroian told me to leave Prudence in the care of the servant woman. He said he would explain everything. That is, of course, if he was, in fact, Heroian and not Wilameena playing tricks on me. Oh, I do not have time for all this worry. In less than two days, for better or worse, all the pomp and circumstance will be over."

The queen delicately removed the jeweled shoes from the

box and held them up to the window. The sunlight, captured by the spectacular jewels, caused tiny yet brilliant prisms of color to leap across the room's walls and ceiling. Enthralled by the beauty of the shoes, Queen Filanthropi decided to try them on.

"I do believe these could fit," she said as she arched her right foot and not so delicately tried to force it into the undersized shoe.

"Ouch!" the shoe said. "Do you think your mammoth foot will fit in my dainty form?"

The queen looked around the room to see if someone had slipped in unnoticed. "Who said that?" she asked.

"I did," the shoe said as it jumped out of the queen's hand and onto the bed next to her. "And if you try that with the other one of me, I'll run home to Cobblerstonia and file an *Abuse of Royal Footwear* report to none other than Queen Imelda herself. She doesn't take kindly to mistreatment of her shoes, you know."

"Well, excuse me. You are just so beautiful that I had to see if you fit," the queen replied.

"Oh, thank you," the shoe replied humbly. Then in an angry tone, it said, "But if you try that again, I will follow through with my threat. Consider yourself warned."

Queen Filanthropi threw the shoes into their box and slammed the lid shut.

"You didn't have to do that," the shoe said in a muffled voice.

The queen then untied the box that contained the princess's gown. Its elegance overwhelmed her. She held it up to herself and sashayed in front of the mirror. "This is the most wonderful gown I have ever seen," she said. "Oh, how I wish it were mine."

"Don't *even* think about trying to slip into me," the gown shrieked. "You're liable to pop my pearl buttons."

"Now a talking gown. Is there no end to this weirdness?" the queen said.

"Who are you calling weird?" the gown asked.

"Never mind," the queen said in a dismissive manner as she threw the gown back in its box. "I have more important matters to contend with."

"La-di-da," the gown complained.

Queen Filanthropi sat at her desk and reviewed the list of things done—and the longer list of things yet to be done—for the Royal Assembly. She looked up and glanced out the window. The sky looked ominous. When she heard screams coming from the courtyard, she ran to the window to see what was happening. People huddled. Some hid their faces while others looked skyward. The queen looked up to see a huge dragon flying straight at her.

"Matilda?" the queen whispered.

Suddenly, a hideous face appeared in the sky. "No, it is Morrebidd, the King of the Dead. I was so hoping not to have to deal with him during the celebrations," the queen said as she reached for the cord to summon Oof.

"There is no need to call your trusted servant. He will not be coming," a powerful voice declared.

Queen Filanthropi turned to see King Heroian standing on the other side of the room.

"Heroian? Is that you?" The Queen of Idlebury started to rush toward her husband but then hesitated. "Or are you Wilameena, playing games with me again?"

"It is me, my love. But do not come near me just yet," King

Heroian said as he motioned for the queen to keep her distance. "I've come to warn you about the King of the Dead. He will try to terrorize Idlebury during the investiture of the princess. Remember, Morrebidd is a tease. He is harmless. Your task will be to convince the Idleburians of this truth."

"But why has he shown up now?" the queen asked. "It has been so long."

"Because you ignored his offer for the Royal Assembly."

"I got no such offer," the queen said as she searched her memory.

"Yes, you did. But you dropped his letter on the floor. It slid under your bed. I believe you will find it there."

Queen Filanthropi fell to her knees and searched under the bed. To her horror, there was a black envelope from the kingdom of the Dead. The blood-red seal that bore the likeness of King Morrebidd had been broken.

"It has been opened," the queen said, confused as to who would have opened a letter addressed to her and stamped with a royal seal.

"Yes, and I believe there was another time when you found a sealed envelope opened," the king stated.

"Yes. It was my letter to you. I found it on your desk already opened. But who would be so brazen to open a royal letter?"

"Perhaps someone in whom you have placed too much trust," King Heroian replied.

"Who?" the queen said as she furled her brow. "I trust no one that much."

"I believe you do," the king replied.

"Who?"

"Oof."

"Oof? Yes, I trust him completely. He would never betray me. He could not. He is practically family."

"Sometimes we trust the untrustworthy. Now I must go, my love. I will return for the Royal Assembly. That you can trust," the king said as he blew a kiss. As he disappeared, his voice trailed off as he said, "And do not put your trust in the Knight in Shining Armor. He knows not my heart."

"Heroian, I am sorry I questioned your love for me," the queen said as she watched her husband vanish.

Queen Filanthropi rushed back to her desk and opened the letter from the King of the Dead. As she read, her faint giggles turned into roaring laughter. "Morrebidd, you have always been one of my favorite friends," the queen said as she carefully returned the letter to its envelope and laid it on the desk.

Suddenly, the room darkened as if someone had turned off the sun. The queen looked up to see what appeared to be a snout at her window.

"Matilda! I nearly forgot," Queen Filanthropi said as she rushed across the room to open the window.

"My dear Filanthropi. It's so good to see you," the dragon queen said with unusual exuberance. "All is falling into place. Gwendolyn is in Idlebury."

"Gwendolyn? Here? But where?"

"I don't know. But I do know she has yet to complete one final test. The hardest test of all."

"Yes, I know it well, for I have failed it many times. No one has ever passed it," Queen Filanthropi said in a dejected manner, momentarily lost in the unhappy memories of her many failed attempts at greatness.

"Don't worry. She'll pass, for her heart's still innocent," the

Queen of Beastonia said. "I must go. My son's out there somewhere probably creating havoc. And your people are terrified of me. See you in two days."

Queen Filanthropi watched Matilda fly into the distant sky.

"Gwendolyn is here," she said in an excited whisper as she shut the window with such force it banged and shook the room.

She paced and flung her arms as she excitedly spewed her thoughts aloud, "My child, who will save Idlebury and change the universe, is here. My wildest dreams are about to come true. And Matilda, my beloved friend has returned. And Heroian will be here, and he does love me. I could not wish for more."

The queen stopped pacing and dramatically plopped on her bed. She remained silent for several minutes.

"I will wish for more. Why not?" she said as sprung up and sat on the edge of the bed. "I wish my other children, my darling Thane, and Prudence, the rightful heir to Idlebury's throne, are returned to me. And I wish—"

Rocks pelting the window interrupted the queen's wish. She went to the window and looked out to see an empty courtyard.

"I must be imagining things," she said as she went to her desk, forgetting about asking for her wishes to be granted.

While the Queen of Idlebury reviewed the details for the Royal Assembly, another stone hit the window, but the queen, preoccupied with writing instructions for the servants in hopes of expediting the preparations, didn't hear it. Another stone hit the window. Still, the queen didn't notice. A few moments later, another stone hit the window, then another and another, until a shower of stones bombarded the window. The queen ran to the window and looked out at an empty courtyard.

"What in the world is going on?" she asked.

"I thought you'd never ask," said a discarnate woman.

Queen Filanthropi scanned the room but saw no one. She looked out the window and still saw no one. She opened the door to her chamber and glanced down the long hall. No one was there. A sense of unease swept over her as she realized she was alone in the great big castle. "Where did everyone go?"

"I thought you'd never ask that either," the same person replied.

"Who are you? Why are you here?" the queen asked as she tried to disguise her fear.

"No need to be afraid of me," the woman said.

"I am not," said the queen.

"You can't fool me. You're afraid. I can't say I blame you. I'd be afraid if I were hearing voices."

"What do you want?"

"I've come to warn you."

"About what?"

"Not what, whom," the woman whispered.

"Okay, then about *whooom?*" the queen said impatiently.

"About you."

"Me?" the queen responded indignantly.

"Yes, you."

"I am the Queen of Idlebury. Who are you to say such a thing to me?"

"I'm the part of you that weighs your thoughts and feelings against your expressed words and actions. Many times your words and actions contradict your true thoughts and feelings. I'm that nagging voice in your head that alerts you to these discrepancies. Usually, you listen. But lately, you've tuned me out and proceeded with your every whim. Your fantasies about Gwendolyn's ability to save your kingdom have blinded your ambitions. Your deliberate secrecy about the motives of the many past kings and queens of Idlebury has overshadowed your sincerity. You almost blurted the secret to your people in your speech, but you bit your tongue. You must reveal the truth to them before the Royal Assembly. If not, the results will be disastrous. And Gwendolyn will be annihilated. This truth you know. Now act upon it."

The queen stared out the window.

Numb.

Speechless.

Resistant to what she knew she had to do.

Chapter Thirty-Two
Kendall's Conceit

D ARKNESS FELL AS Kendall approached the Slothful Forest on his way to Idlebury.

"It's getting dark," he mumbled. "Good, I'll sneak up on them. I'll show them who the mightiest person in the universe is. It's me, Kendall of Peasporagehot. My name will go down in history. Gwen will never leave me behind again."

As Kendall wandered through the forest, he became frustrated with the debris and disorganization. He kicked twigs and rocks out of his path. He lifted fallen branches and tossed them aside. The disgusting odor of rotten food and animal waste wafted in the air, nearly causing him to gag. Plus, he became furious at his inability to avoid stepping in the waste of the forest's many creatures. When he came upon a dead animal, he stopped to look at it. "What kind of thing is that?" he uttered. "Thank God it's dead. It's the ugliest thing I've ever seen," he said as he stepped over the creature's carcass and moved on.

For the next half hour, Kendall trekked through the forest. He felt fortunate the bright moonlight lit his way. He realized he was enjoying the journey when he noticed something disturbing. More and more leaves littered the ground, making it difficult to follow the path. Still, he trudged on. The farther he walked the deeper the leaf cover became. It wasn't long before he was waist deep in leaves. "This is utterly ridiculous. What a mess," he complained.

Up ahead, he saw a huge mound of leaves blocking his path. He stared at it as he tried to figure out how to get around it. "I can't go around the left side. One misstep and I'll fall over the edge into the stinking creek. I can't go around the right side because the stupid trees are so dense I can't walk between them. I guess I'll have to go through it. But I better do it fast so I don't suffocate before I get to the other side."

Kendall pushed aside the leaves and knelt down as if he were behind the starting line for a race, waiting for the starter gun to signal him into action. He took deep breaths as he rocked back and forth to stretch his muscles. He looked at the mound of leaves to make sure he didn't underestimate the speed needed to run through it safely. As he charged the mound, he let out a loud scream. He'd barely entered the mound when he hit something with such force it threw him backward. He landed on the leaf-covered forest floor. When he sat up, only his head peeped out of the leaves.

"What was that?" Kendall and someone else said in unison.

Kendall sat still, unsure if his voice echoed in the woods or if someone else had said the same thing at the same time. The mound stirred. He ducked under the leaves to hide. He heard the ground vibrate as if something heavy had taken a step. He that worried a gigantic beast would squash him, but he was too afraid to move.

Next thing Kendall knew, something swept away the leaves in front of him, leaving a clear path. He peered out of the leaves and saw a huge creature, but clouds blocked the moonlight, obscuring the creature's features. Fortunately, the huge beast looked in the opposite direction from where Kendall remained hidden.

Kendall studied the situation and weighed his options. He was confident he could take down the beast and escape relatively unscathed with just a few cuts and bruises to serve as battle scars and bragging rights.

"My first challenge is to slay the beast," he said as he reached for a large branch to use as a weapon.

Kendall snuck up on the creature and gave it a hard whack on the back. The beast didn't respond. He hit it again, harder. Still, no response. He hit it again even harder. This time the creature reached back and scratched the area where Kendall had whacked it. As it turned to look behind it, the clouds parted, allowing bright moonlight to illuminate the forest. The creature looked directly at Kendall and without warning, spewed fire at him.

"Mistofisee. It's me, Kendall."

The creature emitted another spray of fire. The leaves went up in flames and rapidly burned a path through the forest in the direction of the Field of Wisdom. With the light from the fire, Mistofisee could now see Kendall.

"What are you doing here?" Mistofisee said in a weak voice.

"What were you doing hiding in a mound of leaves?" Kendall retorted.

Mistofisee's behavior was odd. He appeared drunk and stumbled as he approached Kendall.

"What's wrong with you? Why are you purple?"

"Dragon's Sleep," Mistofisee said as he fell to the ground with a thud. "You have to help me," he pleaded

"How?" Kendall said hesitantly, not knowing whether it

was to his benefit to help the dragon or take advantage of his friend's weakened state.

"Keep me warm. That's why I was under the leaves. If I get much colder, I'll go into Dragon's Sleep. I can't. I must save Gwen."

Kendall smirked at the dragon. "No, I'll save her. You stay right here and rest," he said as he ran toward Idlebury, not giving Mistofisee a second thought.

Left alone, the young dragon was at the mercy of the elements. He struggled to get up but he was too weak. Worse, he was almost completely purple.

As Mistofisee drifted into dreaded Dragon's Sleep, he heard his mother's voice. "Son, you must help yourself. Try. Time is running out."

"Mother, help me," Mistofisee whimpered.

"Try, my son. Try."

The young dragon looked to see if the forest was still ablaze, but the density and dampness of the debris had choked out the fire. *Just my luck,* he thought. Soon Dragon's Sleep defeated him.

If he could've cracked an eyelid, Mistofisee would've seen a beam of light transport Aislinn to the spot where he lay.

"Thank you. I had a wonderful time," Aislinn said as the beam gently placed her on the ground.

"Our pleasure. See you at the Royal Assembly," someone inside said as the beam dissipated.

Energized from her adventure in Foolsville, Aislinn skipped through the Slothful Forest. But her positive mood quickly waned when she saw Mistofisee asleep on the ground. "Mistofisee, wake up. You're all purple. Wake up," she said as she slapped the dragon on his snout.

The dragon struggled to open his eyes. His excitement at seeing Aislinn gave him a slight burst of energy. "Help me," he said.

"How?" Aislinn asked.

"Keep me warm."

"How?"

"Fire," Mistofisee said as he fell back into Dragon's Sleep.

"Fire?" Aislinn asked. "How do I make a fire?"

Aislinn scurried through the forest, gathered twigs, and laid them in a pile near Mistofisee.

"Now what?" she said.

"Excuse us," two rocks said. "If you rub us together, we'll make a magnificent spark that just might light your fire."

"Yes," Aislinn said. She grabbed the rocks, gently rubbed them together and said, "Light my fire." But no sparks ignited.

"Excuse us again," the rocks said in unison. "We do believe you've got it wrong. Whack us together. Yes, that should do the trick."

The rocks sparked with each whack. Aislinn grew increasingly inspired and whacked them harder and harder. Sparks flew everywhere except on the pile of twigs. Nonetheless, she continued her effort. A few minutes later, several flying sparks united, creating a small flame. The flame landed in the leaves surrounding Mistofisee, setting off a massive fire. The rocks jumped out of Aislinn's hands and danced for joy at her feet. But she was horrified to see the flames engulf her dragon friend. Worse, the fire was spreading. "I don't like this. I don't like this at all," she said as she watched the inferno.

Mistofisee stirred and sat up. Part of him was green again. When the warmth of the fire had brought him back to life, he stood, stretched, and yawned.

"Come on, Aislinn. We have to save Gwen," he said as he lumbered out of the fire and headed toward Idlebury.

"Hey, don't I get a thank-you?" Aislinn yelled as she ran after Mistofisee. When she looked back at the forest to see it completely engulfed in flames, she said, "Never mind."

The closer Mistofisee and Aislinn got to Idlebury Castle, the brighter the night sky became, revealing a new and improved Idlebury Castle. But Mistofisee's increasing size caused the ground to shake, throwing Aislinn off balance.

"Walk a little lighter," Aislinn said. "You're shaking the ground."

"I can't help it. I seem to be growing very fast lately."

"I see that," Aislinn replied. "Do you see a man kneeling in front of the moat?"

"Where?"

"Up there. Straight ahead."

"Yep, I see him."

"Who is it?"

"Guess."

"The king?" Aislinn asked.

"No."

"How do you know?"

"I know. Guess again."

"Oh no, what's *he* doing there?" Aislinn said with disgust.

"I guess we'll find out."

Despite the trembling ground due to the weight of the dragon, the person at the moat didn't notice Mistofisee and Aislinn approaching.

Aislinn ran ahead and was the first to arrive at the moat. She patiently watched as Kendall admired his moonlit reflection. The dragon soon joined his friends.

"What are you doing?" Mistofisee asked Kendall.

"I had no idea I was this good-looking," Kendall responded, trancelike. "I just can't get enough of myself. With a face like this, I could rule the universe."

Mistofisee moved closer to look at Kendall's reflection in the moat water. "I guess in your case beauty is only skin deep. You're the most loathsome person I know. Now get over yourself. We have to save Gwen."

"No, I won't save her, because I am Kendall the Great, Ruler of the Universe," Kendall said without looking up.

"Let's go without him then," Mistofisee urged Aislinn.

"Okay. Let's."

"Stop. You can't go without me. I'm as much a part of Gwen as our whiny little friend there," Kendall said to Mistofisee as he pointed at Aislinn. "Gwen needs both of us. But only one of us will prevail," he said with a smirk. "So anyone got any ideas how we get into the castle?"

"Follow me," Mistofisee said in a dejected manner.

The reunited trio made their way around the side of the castle. Mistofisee stopped in front of the castle wall. He stomped his right front leg four times causing the wall to crack. He snorted three times expelling a large amount of smoke. Finally, he rose on his hind legs and roared twice. The wall became a mass of bubbling, boiling purple goo. He motioned for Aislinn and Kendall to follow him, which they did without uttering a word. The three friends now stood before the same door Lightening and Gwen had entered earlier that day. An odor seeped through the door, making the air nearly unbreathable.

"This place smells more horrid than the Slothful Forest if that's possible," Kendall complained as he and Aislinn gagged.

"Who goes there?" a man asked in a raspy voice.

"It is I, the son of the Queen of the Innocents," the dragon responded.

"What's the password?" the man asked.

"Blabber, dabble, snabble, and snoo. Crittle, brittle, prittle, and droo. Wally, winkle, stinkle, and croo. Mumbo, jumbo, crumbo, and zoo."

The door opened. Crabbina approached Mistofisee as the other Beastonians looked on. Mistofisee bowed before the eldest elder of his kingdom.

"Mistofisee," Crabbina said with her eyes ablaze with delight. "You have grown into a fine young dragon. Welcome. I see you've brought your friends."

"Yes," the dragon said as he motioned for Kendall and Aislinn to bow before Crabbina.

"Pleasure," Aislinn said as she curtsied.

"I would think your pleasure is meeting me," Kendall said as he stood irreverently before Crabbina.

"We shall see. Shan't we?" Crabbina said with a smile, revealing her crooked, discolored teeth.

As Crabbina guided Mistofisee and his friends into the room, Mr. Knutthyder made a flying leap and landed on Mistofisee's snout.

"Mistofisee, I'm so happy to see you. Things have been nuts here without you. So sorry you were sent to Personadonia, in Dimension XII. But now you're back, and that's all that matters. How's your mother? Fine, I do suppose. You've gotten awfully big, but I guess that's a good thing. It means you're—"

"Mr. Knutthyder, I'm happy to see you haven't changed," Mistofisee interrupted as the squirrel stared into the dragon's right eye. "We certainly had some great times together. And don't feel bad about my banishment to Personadonia."

"All righty then," Crabbina interjected. "Your banishment to Personadonia was necessary to create the events that led to the revival of your mother, our queen, as well as the arrival of Gwendolyn the Great, Princess of Idlebury."

"You mean Kendall the Great," Kendall muttered.

"Excuse me?" Crabbina said to Kendall in a scornful manner.

"Nothing, please continue," Kendall replied arrogantly.

"Don't mind if I do," Crabbina said. "At first sunlight, Gwendolyn will be awakened for her final journey before attending the Royal Assembly. I suggest you take a much-needed refreshment and rest before tomorrow, which will arrive in approximately six hours."

Crabbina ushered Mistofisee, Aislinn, and Kendall to an elegantly set table on which the finest of foods were displayed—breads, hot vegetables, salads, bean dishes, potato casseroles, cakes, cookies, and more. It was clear nothing to be eaten could claim a mother or father.

"This looks wonderful. Thank you," said Aislinn.

"Where's the meat?" queried Kendall. "I must have my meat."

Mistofisee had enough of Kendall's rudeness and let him know by smacking him on the back of the head, which Kendall ignored. While the dragon and Aislinn enjoyed their meal, Kendall watched Gwen sleep.

"She won't go on her final journey without me," Kendall

whispered.

"Don't be so sure," Mistofisee replied. "She's not the same person. She's grown. I don't think she'll have much use for your big-headedness."

After eating their fill, Mistofisee, Aislinn, and all the creatures settled in for a good night's sleep. But Kendall, angry and restless, stared at the sleeping Gwen and muttered to himself. Snoring, snorting, and other sounds muffled Kendall's whispered comments, making it impossible for anyone to hear him tell Gwen, "I must have you to myself, so I can destroy you."

Chapter Thirty-Three
The Fire Within

MIDNIGHT BROUGHT WELCOMED sleep to every Idleburian, except one—Queen Filanthropi. She paced her moonlit bedchamber as she practiced the speech she knew she must give to her subjects at daybreak.

"My most valued—no, that is not right," she said as she walked to her desk and began to write down her words.

"My precious subjects, I—no, that is not right," she said as she scribbled out the words.

The queen slowly paced as she practiced what she hoped would be a transformational speech.

"My fellow Idleburians. As your queen, I stand before you to speak of a matter long secreted from you, your parents, your grandparents, and many generations before. It is a secret the kings and queens of Idlebury, past and present, vowed to hold, never to speak of, not even to each other. If it were not for King Heroian's absence, he would deliver this important message to you himself—oh, that is not right either," she said as she looked out the window at the darkened huts of her people.

She wondered if what she was about to tell her people would matter. *Do they harbor an ounce of hope? Are they as helpless as they seem? Will they revolt at the thought of their personal freedom? Fergus and some of the other men in the hut seemed supportive. But was it just a ruse? If my people don't accept their freedom, Heroian and I will remain their slaves? If they embrace their freedom, will Heroian and I be cast aside? Why am I so afraid to find out? Why has the burden of truth fallen on my shoulders?*

"Heroian, this is *your* job, not mine," the queen said as she walked to her bed. "You are the king, the ruler of Idlebury. You have forsaken your responsibilities. How convenient for you to return to your kingdom after the work is done," she said as she plopped on the bed and clutched a pillow.

"Speak from your heart, not your head," an elderly woman said, hidden in the shadows of the poorly lit room.

"Speak from my heart? I was speaking from my heart."

"No, you weren't."

"How do you know?"

"When you speak from your head, your thoughts are jumbled. Therefore, your message is stifled, and your words fall on deaf ears," the woman said. "But when you speak from your heart, your thoughts and feelings flow freely. Your genuineness and sincerity touch the hearts of all who hear your words."

"I know not my heart in this situation."

"But you do. Your feelings on the matter have never been a secret to you. Now is the time to speak your piece and free your people."

"I cannot. I will not betray my king and all who came before us," Queen Filanthropi said with a lump in her throat. "I feel them watching me. They are warning me to hold my tongue. I must keep the secret. It is to the benefit of all."

"You've been chosen to change your people. You're to free

them from the bondage of idleness and self-hate. And you choose the easy way out? You choose to keep the secret? Coward."

"It is Gwendolyn's destiny to save my people. I cannot interfere with destiny."

"You poor, deluded creature. You know in your heart what you must do. If you don't do it, you'll undermine Gwendolyn's power to save Idlebury and protect the universe. You'll stand in the way of her greatness, just as you've stood in the way of your own greatness."

"What do you mean by that?" Queen Filanthropi asked as she stared at the shadowy figure.

"The things you could've done. The friendships you could've had. The places you could've seen. The dreams you buried. The joy you refused to experience. The happiness you denied yourself," the woman said. "And in so doing, you stole your subjects' dignity, integrity, and hope. And you hate them for their laziness, despondency, and dependency. You have one more day before the investiture of the Princess of Idlebury. We both know it isn't Gwendolyn. She has a greater purpose. Your people must be released from their mental and emotional shackles if they're to ensure Idlebury's readiness for this event—an event with universal consequences."

"Who are you?" the queen asked.

"It would be of no benefit to you to see me."

"I want to know who knows my heart so well."

A haggard old woman stepped out of the darkness. Light streamed through the windows and cast a silvery light upon her.

"Who are you?" Queen Filanthropi asked.

"It's me, my dear friend Filanthropi," the old woman said.

"Look at me. Do you mean to tell me you don't recognize one of your oldest, and I hope, dearest friends?"

"Your voice is familiar, but I cannot place your face," the queen said as she squinted in an attempt to see the old woman more clearly.

There was a long silence between the two women before the old woman transformed into a rotund, middle-aged woman.

"Wilameena! I am *disgusted* with you and your antics."

"No, Filanthropi. I've just revealed my true self to you. I'm a pathetic old woman. For I've done to myself what I just accused you of doing. You thought the words I spoke pertained to you, but in fact, I was talking about myself. Misery has taken its toll on my mind, body, and spirit. I wanted to give my soul to the Soul Seeker, but he wouldn't take it, as my energy is too negative. Yet he honored me by being my friend. It's why I'm with him so often. He gave me the power to change myself into anyone and anything I want."

"So why did you choose the form of a pudgy, matronly woman?" Queen Filanthropi asked as she continued to distrust the motives of her old friend.

"Because it's the persona with which I'm most comfortable. Believe it or not, it's freeing not being young and attractive anymore. People lower their expectations when you're a plump, older woman with yellow teeth and gray hair."

"But I do not understand. You are an enchantress."

"I'm no enchantress." Wilameena chuckled. "It's a title given to me by people who are too scared to see the real me—a miserable person."

"I am sorry for your misery."

"Don't pity me. I did this to myself. I was nasty, conniving, selfish, and manipulative. I abused my body with food and

282

drink. I abused my mind with anger and jealousy. And I neglected my spirit. Now it's too tired to provide me much energy. But I've gained wisdom. I'm sorry my words hurt your feelings, but I was sincerely trying to help you."

"I may be a fool, but I believe you."

"Thank you for your trust, my old friend. Now, please do what you know you must do. Talk to your people. Tell them about the deception imposed on them. And by all means, tell them about Matilda. Your people deserve freedom, joy, and self-respect. It's your faith in them that'll free them. In turn, they'll honor you with the dedication and determination needed to put on the most magnificent Royal Assembly in the universe." Wilameena looked out the window to see the sun rising over the horizon. "And need I remind you that you have only a little more than twenty-four hours?"

"I will talk to my people," Queen Filanthropi said as she took her friend's hands in a gesture of gratitude.

Wilameena took a moment to absorb her friend's energy before she disappeared.

Queen Filanthropi rushed to summon Oof. She had barely pulled the cord when he appeared at her side.

"Oof, bring William the Brave and Gwilym Innaine to my chambers immediately."

"As you request, Your Majesty," Oof said as he bowed and backed out of the room. Just before he exited the queen's chambers, he asked, "If I may, ma'am, shall I bring Lightening as well?"

"Yes, please do," the queen said, startled by the thought Oof was reading her mind again.

As Oof left the room, the queen mumbled to herself, "I must find out the truth about that man."

For expediency, the queen dressed herself for her appearance before her people. As she placed her crown upon her head, there was a knock at the door.

"Enter," the queen commanded.

Oof entered the room and announced the arrival of William the Brave, Gwilym Innaine, and Lightening.

The queen nodded to acknowledge the presence of her honored subjects and her trusty steed. William the Brave and Lightening appeared relaxed and self-confident, but Gwilym, the Minister of Mindfulness, perspired profusely as he wrung his hat and giggled nervously.

"My dear man," the queen said to Gwilym. "There is no need to be so nervous. You are in no trouble. Please, relax."

"Thank you, Yer Majesty. I will," Gwilym said as he took several deep breaths in an attempt to calm his nerves.

"Gentlemen, I guess you are wondering why I have requested your presence. It is because I need your support for something I am about to do. At precisely 6:45 this morning, I will address my people and present the most important speech of my life. Gwilym, I need you to arouse everyone—every man, woman, and child—and gather them in the courtyard. William the Brave, I need you by my side to represent the type of person all Idleburians should aspire to become. And Lightening, I need you to dispel my people's fear of dragons and all other Innocents. Is that clear, gentlemen?"

"Yes, Your Majesty," the two men and Lightening said in unison.

Upon hearing the queen's steed speak with a human voice, Gwilym stared at Lightening and giggled nervously. William the Brave patted Lightening in a show of support and said, "You have the hardest job of all."

"Gwilym, please go and direct the Idleburians to the courtyard, for less than an hour remains before I am to speak to my people. Then return to my chamber."

"Yes, ma'am," Gwilym nervously yet respectably replied as he bowed and left the queen's chambers.

"Gentlemen, pardon me as I prepare my speech," Queen Filanthropi said as she gestured for the old man and the horse to exit her chambers. "Please, wait outside. I will come and get you at exactly 6:35 a.m."

"Yes, ma'am," William the Brave and Lightening said as they bowed and departed.

"Speak from your heart. Speak from your heart. Speak from your heart," Queen Filanthropi repeated as she looked out the window over the courtyard where a few Idleburians had already gathered. She bowed her head and prayed for strength, clarity of thought, and purity of heart. As she prayed, more and more Idleburians filled the courtyard. The queen was jolted out of her prayers by the chanting of her people, "We're here, we're here, and full of fear. Now speak, we say, and make our day. Our eyes are open. Our ears do hear. So speak, our queen, and have your say."

The Queen of Idlebury saw her people had brought sticks, shovels, hoes, rakes, and brooms with them. A few carried flags bearing Idlebury's insignia which represented their right to idleness. Her heart skipped at the thought they had come prepared to work—prepared for change.

The clock chimed, alerting Queen Filanthropi to the fact it was exactly 6:35 a.m. She opened the door and summoned William the Brave, Gwilym, and Lightening. "It is time," she said.

"So I hear," said Lightening in response to the Idleburians' chants.

Queen Filanthropi, William the Brave, the Minister of Mindfulness, and Lightening walked through the long corridor and down the winding staircase as servants, chambermaids, and other staff clapped in a show of respect. But when the queen and her entourage proceeded to the courtyard where a platform had been set up, they were greeted by an angry mob of Idleburians. Some chanted and pounded their tools on the ground. Some booed and hissed. Others threw garbage at the queen.

The disrespectful behavior of her people changed the queen's mood from enthusiasm to disappointment. She raised her hand to silence the crowd, but her people continued their rowdiness. William the Brave handed the ram's horn to the queen. She thanked him and then began to address her people, but to no avail.

William the Brave took the ram's horn from the queen in an attempt to silence the crowd himself. He was about to speak when Lightening rose on his hind legs and yelled, "On behalf of the Queen of Idlebury; William the Brave; Gwilym Innaine, our Minister of Mindfulness; and myself, I respectfully request that you *shut up!*"

The crowd, in a state of disbelief, fell silent.

Then a small child said, "Horsey talk."

Laughter filtered through the crowd. People chatted about the ridiculousness of a talking horse. Although the queen feared she would not gain control of her people, she maintained her regal presence.

"Yes, my child, Lightening talks, as do… dragons," the queen said, eliciting gasps from the crowd.

"Dragons? Der are no such thin's as dragons," a man yelled.

"If she believes in dragons, why should we believe anythin'

she has ta say?" another man said.

"Quiet," Gwilym's wife said. "Me wants to hear what she has ta say."

The queen bent down to speak to the child's mother. "May I hold your child?" she asked.

The mother of the child appeared hesitant as she handed her child to the queen.

Queen Filanthropi held up the child for all to see and addressed her people. "Look at this child. He does not deny reality. He heard my steed talk and he innocently said so. Some of you saw a dragon, yet you continue to deny the undeniable—dragons do exist. The dragon you saw was Matilda, the Queen of Beastonia. She was banished here and lived in the castle cellar for two hundred years. I suspect some of you knew about her, but you chose to believe the kings and queens who told you there are no such things as dragons. You doubted your own reality and believed what you thought you were supposed to believe.

"Well, dragons do exist. And they, as well as other Innocents, are not to be feared. They are our allies. Matilda, the Queen of Beastonia, will play a vital role in the advancement and success of the new Idlebury—the Idlebury in which this child will grow up.

"So take a good look at this child. He represents pure possibility. He knows no limitations. He is incapable of manipulation and harm, yet he is vulnerable to their forces. He is innocent. Just as all of you once were. But the kings and queens who ruled Idlebury for nearly four millennia robbed you of your innocence and potential. They stole your free will and dreams. They enslaved you under the pretense of compassion. They made you believe you were too incompetent to take care of yourselves. They created you as lazy, hopeless, helpless people to satisfy their own distorted need for control.

"When I spoke to you before, I told you I had seen the fault of their ways, and it is true. But I spoke to you with disrespect. I called you a lazy lot of losers. I called you ungrateful slugs. I called you crybabies and a whiny horde of human waste. I apologize for my arrogance. For my heart tells me it is not your fault as to who you have become. You were condemned to live up to the expectations of the kings and queens of the past and present. I am ashamed I followed misguided beliefs I knew in my heart were wrong. In reality, I believe no man, woman, or child should be denied the ability to explore his or her true self and reach the heights of his or her human potential. I believe you have the innate right to dream and make those dreams come true. I believe at birth, *every* person is entitled to freedom. I believe you are not truly free until you are free to succeed and free to fail. For if you have not failed, you have not tried to succeed.

"For some of you, a flicker of freedom burns deep in your hearts; a flicker that could become a flame and ignite your burning desires. I know, because the same flame flickers in my heart. By upholding the perverse rules of my predecessors, I have not only denied you your greatness, I have denied myself my greatness.

"Tomorrow, Gwendolyn, my child, will return to Idlebury. At that time, you will be emancipated. It will be written that starting tomorrow all Idleburians are free. This means you can create your own lives, live your dreams, and develop your talents. You can experience integrity and self-respect. Further, you will be free to reap the financial rewards of your labors. As of tomorrow, each of you will be free to walk into the Field of Wisdom and experience the ecstasy of discovering yourselves in all your glory. From tomorrow forth, the kingdom of

Idlebury is no longer idle."

The queen waited for cheers of acceptance from her people, but they remained mum. The silence of her people was nearly unbearable. She cleared her throat and proceeded in a much louder voice.

"That brings me to my next point. Much work remains to be done before the Royal Assembly. But your first act as free people is to choose whether or not to participate."

"But we don't want ta be free," a woman yelled from the back of the crowd.

"We like thin's da way day are," a young man said. "We like bein' taken care of."

"I think ya need ta get off yer high horse," said another, instigating laughter from the crowd.

"So be it," the queen replied complacently. "Your fate is *not* in my hands; it is in yours. Tomorrow, an opportunity for profound change will be presented to you. It is up to each of you whether or not to accept it. It is up to you to ignite the flame of freedom and restore your right to live according to your desires—to gain self-respect, honor, and integrity. It is unquestionably your choice to experience yourself in all your glory, or not."

Queen Filanthropi was about to walk away when Matilda appeared in the sky. The great dragon hovered over the crowd, casting a shadow so dark it appeared as if night had fallen over Idlebury.

The Queen of Beastonia blew fire, roared, and said, "Gwendolyn's ready for her final test. You best get to work."

A great number of Idleburians—those still in denial of the existence of dragons—ran for the shelter of their homes. But others remained.

Fergus, accompanied by his daughter and grandson, walked up to the platform where the queen stood and said, "Me, me daughter Liridona, and me grandson Aden want self-respect. I, fer one, believe hard work is da only way ta earn it. So we're here ta work."

"Thank you," Queen Filanthropi said to Fergus. She turned to the boy and said, "I do believe your name, Aden, means little fire."

"Yes, Yer Majesty. And me mother's name means longin' fer freedom. So I guess it's our destiny ta be here today."

"Does anyone else care to join Fergus, Liridona, and Aden in their quest for freedom and self-respect?" Lightening asked the rapidly thinning crowd.

"I do," the mother of the boy the queen still held said with conviction.

"Me as well," a young man replied.

"And me," an older woman chimed in.

"Me too," the small boy said as he looked to the queen for approval.

"Let's go," a man demanded.

As the man walked proudly through the small crowd of remaining Idleburians to the platform, he chanted, "Work. Work. We do not shirk. Work. Work. Where freedom lurks."

Others joined him as they chanted and followed Queen Filanthropi into the castle. Once inside, the servants, chambermaids, and others took up the chant. The queen stood on the stairs and motioned for the crowd to quiet.

"Your enthusiasm fills my heart with joy. But time is running out. In less than twenty-four hours, Gwendolyn will stand before you as your savior and protector. I know as a new kingdom united by the fire of freedom, we will host the most

290

spectacular Royal Assembly ever."

As Queen Filanthropi climbed the stairs to return to her chambers, the crowd cheered, clapped, and stomped in approval of her sentiments. Once the queen was out of sight, Morgana issued commands. With fervor, the Idleburians pitched in to help.

Queen Filanthropi stood at her chamber window and looked out over Idlebury. In her heart, she knew there was a long road ahead before her people understood the power of independence and freedom of choice, for she couldn't deny the fact that most of her people had chosen another day of idleness.

CHAPTER THIRTY-FOUR
THE FORCE OF FRIENDSHIP

"GWEN, IT'S TIME," Crabbina said as she gently shook the child. But Gwen didn't awaken. Crabbina shook Gwen again, but the girl didn't open her eyes.

As the old Innocent continued to try to wake the child, she noticed a small bottle lying at the foot of the bed. She picked it up and blinked her milky eyes. "Darn eyes," she said as she struggled to bring the words on the label into focus. "No... can't be," she said as she glanced at Gwen then glanced back to the bottle. "She'll die," Crabbina said aloud, waking Aislinn.

"She's what? She's dead?" Aislinn said.

As the Innocents began to stir, Mr. Knutthyder scurried over to Crabbina, grabbed the bottle from the old creature's hand, and read the label. *"No, not that!"* he screamed as he dramatically fell to the floor.

Ms. Eegal, a majestic birdlike creature, flew over to Crabbina and asked permission to read the label. "If you would permit, I'd like to view the label. They don't call me Ms. Eegal Eye for nothing, you know."

Crabbina handed the bottle to Ms. Eegal, who examined the label, gasped, and fanned a wing over her eyes in disbelief.

"Well, what is it?" Crabbina asked impatiently.

"It's the most feared substance of all," Ms. Eegal said.

"It's" —Ms. Elliefant gulped—"rotteroot."

"Rotteroot?" Mistofisee asked in disbelief.

"Not rotteroot. Not here," Ms. Elliefant cried.

"What's rotteroot?" Aislinn asked.

"It's the most dangerous and feared substance in the entire universe. Even the King of the Dead fears it," Crabbina replied.

"Where does it come from?"

"There's only one place it can be found."

"Where?" Aislinn demanded with unusual confidence.

"The Slothful Forest," Crabbina said as she sat on the bed next to Gwen.

"How long does it take to wear off," Mistofisee asked.

"It doesn't," Mr. Knutthyder replied.

"You rot to death," Crabbina said as she tenderly stroked Gwen's hair.

"It does that to Innocents, but are we sure it affects humans in the same way?" Mistofisee asked.

"No living creature has ever escaped its wrath," Ms. Elliefant said.

"That's not totally true," Crabbina said with authority. "There's one who has survived rotteroot. It's said only the most determined of souls can survive. And the one who did is known as"—she paused and took a deep breath—"known as"—she paused again, gulped, and said—"the Soul Seeker."

"Don't speak his name. He has the soul of our king," Ms. Eegal said in a nervous voice.

"Why is the King of the Dead afraid of rotteroot?" Aislinn asked.

"Because in the Kingdom of the Dead there's no such thing as death," Gwen whispered. "So rotteroot makes King Morrebidd's people rot for eternity, making them of no use to him," she said as she fell back into a deep sleep.

"Where's Kendall?" Aislinn asked.

"He left during the night," said a large raccoonlike creature known as Mr. Masquedwan.

"How did he get out?" Crabbina demanded. "No one gets in or out without the password. Who gave him the password?"

"It may be my fault," Mr. Knutthyder said. "He said he felt claustrophobic and needed some fresh air, so I opened the door for him. But I swear I didn't see him leave. I swear."

The Innocents looked to Crabbina to respond, but she was speechless as to Mr. Knutthyder's extraordinary lack of judgment. After a few moments of silence, she said, "I'm sure Mr. Knutthyder meant well."

"Meant well? That nutter of a squirrel let a murderer escape," Mistofisee blurted.

"Just a minute. We don't know Kendall administered the deadly substance to Gwen," Crabbina said.

"Yes, we do," Mistofisee and Aislinn said in unison.

"No, you don't. If he handled rotteroot, he would die as well. So, if Kendall was the suspect, he would be lying here near death or worse, dead."

"Well… that may not be such a bad thing," Mistofisee said as Aislinn nodded in agreement.

"Mistofisee, this is no time for immature humor," Crabbina scolded the young dragon. "So," she said addressing all in the room, "that means there's only one creature in the universe who could've done this." Crabbina paused, barely able to say the name again.

"Whoo?" Mr. Aul asked.

"The Soul Seeker," Crabbina said with concern.

"I knew it. I knew it. I knew it," Mr. Knutthyder said with excitement. "I knew it was him I saw last night."

"You saw him and didn't wake us?" Ms. Eegal shouted.

"I didn't want to wake Gwen."

"It doesn't matter. The Soul Seeker comes and goes and does or doesn't do as he pleases. We have no say and no control over his behaviors," Crabbina explained.

"We have to stop Kendall," Mistofisee said.

"No, that wouldn't matter either. He can do no harm. He only thinks he can. Our only hope is Gwen has the fortitude to fight the effects of the rotteroot; thereby, ensuring she'll pass her final test and deserve to be crowned Gwendolyn, Princess of Idlebury. This was meant to be," Crabbina said with delight. "Now, we wait."

"I can't wait," Gwen whispered. "Help me up."

Crabbina cupped Gwen in her arms and helped her sit up. Aislinn offered her a cup of tea, which Gwen accepted gratefully.

After Gwen had regained awareness and strength, she said, "Kendall didn't do this to me. In fact, he merged with me to save my life."

"What? That no good, arrogant idiot is inside of you?" Mistofisee angrily asked.

"Yes, I need him to survive. I draw strength from his confidence. And right now, I need all the confidence I can get."

"What about me? Don't you need me? I'm the one who balances Mister Smarty Pants," Aislinn said as she straddled Gwen. "You need me. I know you do," she continued as she merged with the soon-to-be Princess of Idlebury.

Gwen shook her head as she regained total awareness. "My strength is back. It's time for me to embark on my final journey. I must present myself to the Idleburians today." Gwen rose from the bed and said, "They can't wait any longer. They must be saved now. And I've got Kendall and Aislinn, the two best parts of me, to help me succeed."

Mistofisee begrudgingly allowed Gwen to pass as she headed for the door.

"Wait just a minute, young lady," Crabbina yelled. "You're about to step out into a world for which you're not prepared. Don't let your apparent fame deter you from your purpose. There are many on the other side of the door who wish to prosper from your trials and tribulations. They appear to want you to succeed. Be leery of them, because they seek fortune from your fame. You have been warned. Now go."

Gwen didn't know what to make of the old creature's warning. With mixed emotions—excitement about becoming the most popular person in the universe and fear of failing her final test and returning to the nobody she was before—she put on a brave face and reached for the doorknob. She pulled, but the door didn't open. She pulled with more force, but the door didn't budge.

"Good luck," Crabbina said.

"Yes, most definitely, the best of luck to you," Mr. Knutthyder said.

As the other Innocents wished Gwen much success, Mistofisee reached over and opened the door. The light of countless camera flashbulbs blinded Gwen. She maintained her composure despite her impulse to run back into the room, slam the door, and hide. Unexpectedly, someone grabbed her and pulled her before a camera.

"Mike Muckraker here from *UST* better known a *Universal Scandals Tonight,* a subsidiary of *Universal Scandals* magazine. I'm here with Gwendolyn Fanny of Idleburg, Pennsylvania in Dimension X who read about Queen Filanthropi's desperate search for her princess in our own universally popular publication. Gwen is about to become Princess Gwendolyn of Idlebury." The obnoxious Mr. Muckraker thrust a huge microphone in Gwen's face as he smiled for the camera. "Is there anything you would like to say to the people back home and across the universe?"

"No."

"No? Did she say no?" Mr. Muckraker said to his staff.

"Yes, I said no," Gwen replied in a tone reminiscent of Kendall. "I'm not here to become fodder for a *UST* special report. I have something important to do. Something that'll change the future of the universe," Gwen said as she pulled away from Mr. Muckraker and walked around to the back of Idlebury Castle.

Throngs of reporters and photographers chased her. Mistofisee proudly protected Gwen and held the reporters and paparazzi at a safe distance.

"Is that a real dragon?" a reporter from the *New Universe Times* newspaper asked.

"Of course not, everyone knows there are no such things as dragons," said a bizarrely dressed woman reporter from *Galaxy Fashion* magazine.

"I wouldn't be so sure," replied a camera operator from the *Universe Today* morning show.

Gwen stopped.

"Why are you stopping?" Mistofisee whispered to Gwen. "What are we doing at the back of the castle?"

"I don't know. I have a feeling this is where my journey will begin."

"Okay, then let the journey begin."

The words were barely out of Mistofisee's mouth when the Soul Seeker appeared. Gwen and the young dragon were surprised the reporters and photographers didn't react to the presence of the massive, menacing being.

"Do not worry. They cannot see me, for they have no souls. I am here to help you with your final test. The fact you have overcome the effects of the rotteroot is a testament to your determination and strength. I am the only other being to ever survive a dose of this deadly poison. So you have joined a minute yet powerful alliance. From here on, you are completely on your own. No one can help you now. You must prove worth, fortitude, purity, and innocence. In a few seconds, an opening in the wall will appear. You are to step through. If your heart is impure, you will be annihilated instantaneously. Any effect your life had on other people, places, and events will be erased. It will be as if you never existed. This, of course, will affect the entire universe. On the other hand, if you succeed, you will emerge as one of the purest souls ever created. You will go on to greatness. You will have a profound positive effect on all living things throughout the vast universe. You will live forever in the souls of all others. Do you have any questions?"

Gwen gulped and whispered, "No."

The Soul Seeker waved his bony hand in front of the wall. Nothing happened. He waved his hand again. Still, nothing happened. "We have missed it. We are too late. The universe is in peril. It cannot be saved now," he complained angrily.

Just then, Queen Matilda appeared in the sky. She soared over Idlebury. Photographers rushed to capture pictures of the great beast. Reporters took up their microphones and began transmitting news too remarkable to believe.

Mr. Muckraker was the first to break the amazing story. Motioning to his camera operator to take a close-up of his face, he began his broadcast. "We're here at the back of Idlebury Castle in Dimension XIII where we're awaiting Gwendolyn Fanny's transformation into the Princess of Idlebury. For nearly five minutes, she's stood before the castle wall mysteriously silent."

The camera panned to a shot of Gwen and Mistofisee.

"As you can see, she's accompanied by a rather odd-looking creature," Mr. Muckraker continued. The camera operator swung the enormous camera skyward. "We now have a visual on the sky above Idlebury," Mr. Muckraker announced with heightened enthusiasm. "If you look at the left-hand corner of your viewing screen, you'll see a flying creature approaching. We have no idea what this creature is. We don't know whether it intends peace or harm. Do you have a fix on the creature?" he asked his camera operator.

"Yes, there it is," the camera operator said as he pointed at the sky, carefully balancing his heavy camera on his shoulder.

Mike Muckraker paused as his assistant approached and handed him a note.

"I've just been handed this information. The creature in the sky above appears to be Matilda, Queen of Beastonia. It says she is a—" He stopped in midsentence, crumpled the note, and tossed it at his assistant. "I can't report this rubbish. This is impossible," he remarked as he cupped his hands over the microphone to mute his complaints.

When he heard another reporter announce that Matilda, Queen of Beastonia was believed to be a full-grown dragon, Mike Muckraker angrily snapped at his assistant, "What? Is she scooping *my* story? Nobody will ruin my reputation," he mumbled as he grabbed the crumpled note, quickly read it, and then said, "The creature, which is rapidly approaching, is Matilda, the Queen of Beastonia. She's said to be a dragon." He rolled his eyes and muttered, "I can't believe my distinguished career has come to this."

The crowd of media people panicked as Matilda flew closer. Her enormity became more apparent, scaring many into retreat. A few brave reporters, photographers, camera people, and others remained.

"It's a dragon. It really is a dragon," a camera operator yelled while he desperately tried to control his shaking body in order to get clear footage of the mythological creature.

"*Mother... Mother. Over here,*" Mistofisee yelled.

A young, female reporter heard Mistofisee's plea. Smelling an exclusive story, she waved for her crew to follow her to the young dragon. She approached the dragon as a camera operator pushed his way past her and pointed his huge camera in Mistofisee's face.

"Did I just hear you call that flying creature Mother?" the female reporter asked as she shoved the microphone toward Mistofisee.

"Did I say Mother? I don't believe I said Mother," Mistofisee said nervously. How could she be my mother if she's a dragon and I'm not? I don't see the possibility of that, do you?"

Gwen turned to the reporter and said, "I think you should leave before that thing swoops down and eats you for breakfast."

Queen Matilda was just about to land when the reporter and her crew ran for cover.

"Mother, what are you doing here?" Mistofisee asked.

"I'm here to do the job he can't," the dragon queen replied, pointing at the Soul Seeker.

"What job is that?" Gwen asked as her voice quavered.

"Don't be nervous my child. The Soul Seeker doesn't have the power, or the authority, to create a passage through which you'll enter for your final test."

"Why do you say that I do not have the power or authority to create the passage, Matilda?" the Soul Seeker asked.

"Because you're not the Queen of the Innocents."

"Apparently, neither are you," the Soul Seeker said.

"Oh, but I am. And only I, or a creature of my designation, can allow Gwen to pass through this wall."

The Soul Seeker didn't comment. He knew if Gwen didn't complete her test soon, his purpose would go unfulfilled. The souls he carried were getting more and more disgruntled. They longed to return to their kingdoms, their people, and their loved ones, as he had promised. And keeping the young soul of Thane in check was more exhausting each day. So without challenge, he moved aside and allowed Matilda to get closer to the wall. But she didn't move.

"Mistofisee, if you're to be King of Beastonia someday, you must also prove your honor today. Therefore, I choose you to open the passage."

"What if I fail?" Mistofisee said.

"Then she dies, as the Soul Seeker has already told you. But on a more positive note, you won't suffer at all. The memory of Gwen's existence will be erased so you and everyone else, including her family, won't recall what transpired on this day."

"Then he has nothing to lose by not trying," Gwen said.

"Yes, I do. I'd lose your friendship," Mistofisee said.

"But you won't remember. No one will remember, not even

me. It won't be your fault and you won't be punished. So why does it matter?"

"Because it matters to me *right now,* in this moment. And right now is all that matters. I can't stand the thought of losing you. You're my best friend. I'll never have another friend like you. And if I don't try, you'll never express your greatness. And if you don't express your greatness, neither will anyone else, including me. You've been chosen to save Idlebury and the universe. Only you can do it. And only I can help you."

"Then let's do it," Gwen said with a renewed sense of confidence.

"Okay, but how?"

"Use your natural talents, my son. You'll figure it out," Queen Matilda said as she took to the sky, leaving Mistofisee, Gwen, and the Soul Seeker staring at the wall.

"Time is running out. *Do it now,*" the Soul Seeker roared.

Mistofisee walked up to the wall. He touched it. He blew hot air on it. He roared. He blew fire at it. He stomped and flapped his underdeveloped wings. But nothing happened.

"I don't know what to do. I don't know what my natural talents are." Mistofisee looked at Gwen as if to plead for guidance.

"Don't look at me, I don't know what they are either."

Mistofisee wanted to laugh at Gwen's comment, but sadness at the thought of her demise consumed him. As he continued to stare at her, tears filled his eyes. A single tear dripped from his cheek and landed on Gwen's chest right over her heart.

Instantaneously, she disappeared.

"Let's hope that worked," the Soul Seeker said.

Mistofisee didn't reply. He was too afraid he had failed.

Chapter Thirty-Five
Gwen's Final Passage

"WELL... WELL... WELL. I see you made it," a woman said in a voice indicative of someone who had just awakened from a much-deserved nap.

Gwen, still discombobulated from the effects of the rotteroot, her encounter with fame, and her instant transportation from the blinding light into total darkness didn't respond.

"I dare say, you best be getting on with the task at hand. Everyone is waiting for you."

"Who are you?" Gwen groaned.

A dim light appeared in front of the child. She was surprised to see she was still outside the castle wall. She looked around but saw nothing and no one.

"Who I am does not matter. What you are about to do is what matters. You are standing before the Wall of Passages. In a few moments, it will open to allow you to cross its threshold. It does not take kindly to those who do not know their purpose. Therefore, I suggest you contemplate your reason for entering. And remember, you enter at your own risk. No one can help you once you are inside. Those who lied about their heart's desire were never seen or heard from again. The survival of the universe depends on your success. Therefore, you must draw on your every ounce of courage, fortitude, and determination. I wish you well."

"Thank you," Gwen replied meekly.

Gwen waited for the wall to open. When it didn't, she ran her hands over the bricks and mumbled, "How do I get through the wall? There's nothing here. I've been tricked. I don't like this. I don't like this at all." In despair, she slumped to the ground and pouted.

"Get up. Your behavior is not becoming of someone who is destined for greatness," the wall said as huge hunks of brick smashed to the ground.

Gwen rose and faced the wall. A magnificent gold-etched door appeared. Soft light radiated from the space between the door and the wall. The door opened slowly. Angelic music filled the air. Gwen felt completely at peace.

"You are the first to enter through this door. Others have attempted to enter through the wall inside the castle. I regretfully inform you that no one was successful in his or her quest. They were not pure of heart. They did not know their purpose. They sought easy passage by working their way downward rather than upward. Success requires an upward climb; therefore, you must ascend to greatness. Once you cross my threshold, you must put forth a great effort. You are to face situations that will try your patience, challenge your intelligence, dispute your integrity, test your honesty, and confront your loyalty. Your innocence will be on trial. The essence of who you are shall be revealed. If your spirit emerges broken from this test, your soul will be lost—forever."

"I've already been tested in the Field of Wisdom and passed with flying colors," Gwen said. "So this should be a piece of cake."

"Hmm. Youthful exuberance? Or just outright stupidity? The Field of Wisdom tested you via scenarios from your world. You were in your situational and emotional comfort zones. Now you will be tested via otherworld scenarios for which you have no point of reference. You will battle great beasts, defend creatures of all kinds, fight temptations, tolerate frustrations, work through heartaches, toil through exhaustion, and fight for your life and your soul. Once you enter, there is no turning back. Are you ready?"

"Yes," Gwen said a little less confidently.

"Enter, Gwendolyn," the Wall of Passages announced with much pomp.

Gwen stuck her head through the door to see what she was about to get herself into. A part of her wanted to turn back and forget about being the Princess of Idlebury. Another part egged her on and reminded her of her glorious destiny. She smiled and felt reassured that Aislinn and Kendall were still with her.

"Okay, Kendall, you win," Gwen said as she stepped over the threshold.

She heard the gold door slam behind her, but she didn't look back because the most majestic sight she'd ever seen or imagined held her spellbound. She looked around at the interior of the most spectacular palace with countless gilded passageways. Her eyes, wide with wonder, felt as if they would pop out of her head. She could barely take in its grandeur. She imagined herself dressed in exquisite clothes walking through the hallways and gliding down the great staircases. Then she noticed gold- and diamond-studded placards hanging from the ceiling above each passageway. A word was etched on each.

Gwen ran from placard to placard as she read each word

aloud—"love, wonder, compassion, curiosity, gratitude, forgiveness, union, peace, joy, purpose, generosity, empathy, serenity, respect, patience, determination, honesty, redemption, unity, and truth. Where do I begin?" she asked.

"It does not matter which you choose first. Just choose wisely. There is only one, if chosen first, that will start you on the wrong path. Nonetheless, you will complete them all before the day is done."

Gwen pondered her choices before she announced, "I choose patience."

"Good choice. But for what purpose?"

"Because I have so little of it. I figure I'll need to learn patience in order to succeed at the rest."

"Excellent. You have chosen wisely. Proceed."

Gwen stood before the passageway labeled PATIENCE and watched in awe as the other passages rearranged themselves in ascending order based on her choice. She was now aware of the lessons to be learned on her path to greatness.

"Now what?" she asked.

"Every journey begins with one step."

Gwen nodded and stepped into the passageway. Immediately, she was sucked down the long narrow hallway as she began the journey from which, if successful, she would emerge victorious.

***

In the main part of the castle, a host of servants and others rushed to put the final touches on the preparations for the Royal Assembly. Morgana looked crazed as she yelled at anyone in her way.

A servant named William Dawgs appeared on the staircase and screamed at the top of his lungs, *"The guests are coming! The guests are coming!"*

Queen Filanthropi couldn't believe her ears. "The guests are coming?" she said as she ran from her chambers, down the staircase, and out the front door. She stood on the drawbridge and fixed her gaze on the distant road. Sure enough, the dust stirred up from the many approaching carriages signaled the arrival of her guests. Now she was a complete and utter wreck. She raced back to the castle and screamed for her servants to get her dressed at once. Chaos broke out as everyone sped up his or her activities.

"I don't know who's more mental, the queen or Morgana," a servant groaned.

"Don't matter much, I suppose. Work still has ta be done," replied another.

Suddenly, the castle shook. Pictures fell off the wall. Vases of flowers crashed to the floor. The sound of plates and glasses shattering echoed throughout the castle. Servants scurried to clean up the mess as they grumbled and cursed their bad luck.

The queen had almost reached the door of her chambers when the strong vibrations knocked her to the floor. As she raised herself up, the massive Dimension Clock in the Great Hall chimed. She looked around, uncertain if she heard what she thought she heard, for until now, the clock only rang to warn of possible invasion from another dimension. It hadn't rung in more than six hundred years.

It chimed again.

The queen darted down the stairs and raced to see the clock. A group of servants, including Morgana, followed her. Dust and rust coated the queen as she stood beneath the grand clock. The hands of the clock creaked as they moved to new positions. The little hand pointed to XIII. The big hand was a blur as it furiously swirled past the dimension markers I through XIII.

The queen knew exactly what this meant.

"Someone has entered the Wall of Passages," she whispered. "But who? And why? No one has ever gotten through. Not even I."

Finally, the clock's hands moaned to a stop. The big hand pointed to the X and the little hand pointed to the XIII.

"It's someone from Dimension X," Morgana said.

"Who do we know from Dimension X?" a servant asked.

Queen Filanthropi smiled. In a deep, airy voice she said, "Gwendolyn." As she darted from the Great Hall, she snapped her fingers to alert her chambermaids, servants, and Morgana to follow her. Once her chamber doors closed, she could no longer contain her excitement. She paced, muttered, and chuckled to herself. She appeared to have lost her mind. But no one had the nerve to question the queen's odd behavior.

"Get me dressed… immediately," the queen requested of her servants. "Morgana, you, and only you are to go to Gwendolyn's chambers and lay out her gown and accessories. And be careful with her shoes, they are quite sassy."

"Yes, ma'am," Morgana said as she made a quick exit.

Queen Filanthropi could hardly stand still long enough for her servants to dress her as she kept running to and from the window to check on the progress of her arriving guests. A knock on the door diverted her attention. The servants stopped dressing the queen and looked to her for direction.

"I will get it," she said as she romped to the door in a state of partial undress.

She opened the door ajar, fearing whom or what was on the other side may not have the best intentions. Her concerns were validated when Mike Muckraker from *Universal Scandals Today* burst into the queen's chambers followed by his camera crew and a reporter from *Universal Scandals* magazine.

"How *dare* you burst in on me, sir?"

Mike Muckraker ignored the queen as he began to broadcast.

"I'm here in Idlebury Castle with none other than Queen Filanthropi, birth mother of Gwendolyn Fanny from Dimension X who is soon to be crowned Gwendolyn, Princess of Idlebury. How do you feel about the undeniable magnitude of what will take place here today?"

"Out! Get out of my chambers, now!" the queen screamed.

"I understand, but if you would just answer this one question, I'll be off," Mike Muckraker continued, obviously oblivious to his rudeness and insubordination.

"I command you to leave, *now!*" Queen Filanthropi screeched as she grabbed Mike Muckraker and dragged him out the door. His camera crew followed behind, capturing every moment for posterity.

"Ms. Syvil Gossep, you may stay," the queen said to the reporter from *Universal Scandals* magazine. "I want to have a few words with you."

"Yes, Your Majesty," Syvil replied, her eyes wide with fear.

"Sit," the queen said as she sat and motioned for the reporter to do so as well.

"Thank you, ma'am."

"I have asked you to stay for a reason. Although I must acknowledge the vile tittle-tattle of your publication sickens me, I am well aware of the power of *Universal Scandals* magazine to reach the masses throughout the universe. Hence, I wish to honor you with a request," the queen said.

"Yes, ma'am. I'm flattered."

Queen Filanthropi nodded and said, "Here is my request. I

will allow you to gain exclusive access to Idlebury Castle, me, my people, my servants, my guests, and Gwendolyn if you promise me one thing."

"Yes, of course," Syvil said.

"I want you to tell the truth and nothing but the truth," the queen said as she tilted her head and raised an eyebrow, anticipating Ms. Gossep's answer.

"But… but ma'am," Syvil stuttered.

"No ifs, ands, or buts. You will promise to tell the truth or I will choose Fulla Bulship from *Star Gazer* magazine instead." Queen Filanthropi paused to gauge Syvil's reaction. "I believe deep down you are a woman of great integrity who will go far if, and only if, you choose a more reputable career path. Therefore, you are my first choice. What is your choice?"

"May I ask a question?"

"No, not until I have a firm answer from you."

"My answer is, well, it's…"

Syvil's hesitation made the queen wonder if her offer was going to be refused. "I'm pleading with you woman to woman to woman, not royalty to commoner," the queen said.

"It's yes. I choose to tell the truth," Syvil said with conviction.

Queen Filanthropi closed her eyes and sighed with relief. "Thank you. Now, what was your question?"

"Why did you choose me over Fulla Bulship? She's obviously more experienced and more admired than I am."

"Actually, it is quite simple. Ms. Bulship is the most renowned liar in the universe. People love her not because she is believable but because her stories are exquisitely entertaining. Unfortunately, her lies hurt many. If I chose her, assuming she would tell the truth, no one would believe her stories. They would think they were just more of her amusing tales. Hence, the truth would go unrecognized. On the other hand, although you write for a magazine that thrives on gossip and innuendo, your reputation for fact-finding and truth-seeking makes your work more believable, though there have been times when you have stretched the truth. Therefore, your reputation is less dishonorable than Ms. Bulship's. So when you tell the truth about what is to transpire here today, some may discount it as entertainment, but many will see it for what it is—something quite rare, a solid piece of fact-based journalism. But although your story may be written off as mere entertainment, at least the truth will have been told. So, as you can see, the value of the message is determined by the reputation of the messenger."

"I see. I feel somewhat ashamed."

"How so?"

"Well, since I have promised to tell the truth, I have something to confess."

"Go on, then."

"I wrote the *Universal Scandals* magazine story about Gwendolyn's adoption."

"Where did you get such information?"

"From Oof, ma'am."

"Oof?" Queen Filanthropi flinched upon hearing Oof had divulged private information. "Well, I guess the truth needed to be told. Now you can redeem yourself."

"Thank you, ma'am. Where do I start?"

"Acclimate yourself to the castle and the grounds. I will inform the Idleburians and my staff it is my wish that they speak openly with you. Now go. You have much work to do. As you can see, my guests are nearly here."

Syvil Gossep curtsied and exited the room. She looked down the hall that led to the staircase. *Hmm! Dingy. Does she want me to report how dingy the castle is?* she wondered. "I promised to report the truth," she muttered as she jotted notes on a notepad.

Back in the queen's chambers, the servants worked hurriedly. Morgana had returned from setting out Gwendolyn's clothing and once again issued orders. Oof appeared next to the queen, who admired herself in a large mirror. No one noticed he'd appeared out of nowhere.

"Your Majesty, you called?" Oof asked.

"Yes, Oof. Please inform all staff that Ms. Gossep from *Universal Scandals* magazine is to have full access throughout the castle. Also, inform all Idleburians that they are free to answer her questions honestly. There is no need to conceal the truth from her. She and they have my blessing."

"Yes, ma'am. As you wish, ma'am."

Chapter Thirty-Six
The King's Confession

MORGANA CAREFULLY PLACED Queen Beggora's crown upon Queen Filanthropi's head and admired the queen's beauty. "I do believe ya look unusually beau-ti-ful taday, Yer Majesty," she said.

"Thank you, Morgana. I feel radiant as if this day will be the most glorious ever."

Suddenly, the room went black, nearly dashing the queen's hopes. Two beams of light shot into the room, after which, everything returned to normal.

"Mother, you look beautiful."

The queen turned toward the voice to see Thane standing near her bed. "Thane, you have returned. I knew you would," the queen said as she hugged the boy. "Are you all right? Did the Soul Seeker harm you?"

"No. It was fantastic. I learned everything about life. I now understand why men do what they do."

"Well, I would love for you to share that with me." The queen chuckled. "But not today. The Royal Assembly is about to start."

"I could explain it to you," a man said from the other side of the room.

"Heroian," the queen squealed as she rushed into the waiting arms of her husband. "Are you back or is this just another tease?"

"No, I am back this time, hopefully for good," King Heroian said as he took his wife's hand and gently kissed it.

Queen Filanthropi smiled, knowing the man was truly her husband. Still holding his hand, she replied, "I am so happy you and Thane have returned to me. But you both must hurry and get cleaned up for the Royal Assembly."

"Yes, but before I do, I need to talk to you, in private, about—" King Heroian paused as a knock on the door interrupted him.

The queen took a deep breath and rolled her eyes.

"Please answer it, Morgana, and if it is Mr. Muckraker again, have him beheaded."

"Me pleasure," Morgana said as she opened the door.

"What are ya doing here with her?" Morgana asked the person at the door.

"Please Morgana, don't make dis harder fer me dan it already is," a young woman responded.

"Who is there?" the queen asked apprehensively.

Morgana didn't answer.

"Morgana, step aside and let me see who is at the door."

Morgana moved to the side to reveal Fredia holding Prudence.

"Come in, Fredia," the queen said, somewhat surprised at her excitement to see the servant. "Morgana, please take Thane to his quarters to get dressed."

"Yes, ma'am," Morgana said as she grabbed Thane by the hand and angrily led him out of the room.

"What brings you to my chamber at this hectic time?" Queen Filanthropi asked Fredia.

"Momma," Prudence said as she reached out for the queen.

"Prudence is da reason I'm here, Yer Majesty," Fredia said with downcast eyes as she curtsied before the king and queen. "I do believe dat she is da rightful heir ta da throne."

"And?" the queen said barely able to breathe at the thought her child was about to be returned to her.

"And I want ta give her back ta ya. I'm sorry fer any sorrow me act caused," Fredia said as tears streamed down her cheeks. "But I do love Prudence as much as any mother would love her child."

"Are you saying the child you hold is our child?" King Heroian asked.

"Yes, Yer Majesty. Prudence is most definitely yer child."

"How come I was not informed of the birth of this child who is the rightful heir to Idlebury's throne?"

Queen Filanthropi held up her hand to silence her husband. "I will explain, but now is not the time."

As much as the queen wanted Prudence, she felt it wasn't the best time to take her from Fredia. So she stifled her own eagerness to hold her child. "Fredia, I would like you to present Princess Prudence to King Heroian and me at the Royal Assembly," the queen said before she retrieved a box from under her bed, and handed it to Fredia. "All I ask is that you dress Prudence in this gown. It is the gown I wore when my parents presented me before the people of Seedonia as their princess. It has been in my family for generations. I have saved it in hopes that one day my child would wear it when I presented him or her before the people of Idlebury. I see that day has come."

"Yes, ma'am. Thank ya, ma'am," Fredia said as she accepted the box from Queen Filanthropi. "Yer most kind, ma'am. I misjudged ya."

"Then you are a courageous woman to come before the king and me to return our child when you thought I would be less than understanding," the queen said.

"Yes, ma'am. I love Prudence with all me heart, but I couldn't go on livin' a lie. I had ta do what was best fer me child, I mean, yer child. And I know it's best fer her ta be with ya and King Heroian and take her place as da Princess of Idlebury. After what ya said da other day, I couldn't deny Prudence her greatness. No lovin' mother could," Fredia said in all earnestness.

"Fredia, I do believe you love Prudence as a mother would. Therefore, I want you to be her governess, to watch over her and protect her when she is not under the watchful eye of the king or me. Now go. The Royal Assembly is about to begin."

"Yes, ma'am. Thank ya, ma'am. I'm forever grateful," Fredia said as she curtsied and backed out of the queen's chambers in reverence to the king and queen.

"Bye-bye," Prudence said as the door closed.

Lost in thought, Queen Filanthropi stared at the door for a few moments. "Now Heroian, do you have something you want to explain?"

"Yes, my love," King Heroian said as he took the queen's hands in his and moved her toward the bed. "I believe I told you I would explain everything to you about my disappearance and the arrival of Gwendolyn. But first, I want you to know how much I love you. While I was with the Soul

Seeker, I was privy to your thoughts and deeds. I know you have felt lonely and betrayed. I know the depth of your love for me, and your desperation regarding your doubts about my love for you. You were right. I was not present many times when you needed me most. For this, I apologize. But I was not present for what I believed to be good reasons. I thought I did not deserve you, so I was on endless quests to prove my manhood in hopes you would love and admire me. What I did not know was I already had what I hoped for. And in my efforts to prove my manhood, I almost lost you."

"You could never lose me, my love," the queen said.

"That is not true. Any man or woman who does not attend to their loved one's needs risks losing that person to someone who will. For a moment I thought I had lost you to the Knight in Shining Armor."

"Oh please, Heroian. The man is nothing more than a melancholy mess contained in a can."

"Nonetheless, he was able to give you something in your time of need that I could not. He listened. He did not ridicule your thoughts or feelings as I have in the past, which I did only because I was envious of your intelligence and intuition. This is something of which some men are guilty when it comes to their wives. Many men try hard to please their wives and provide for their families, and in trying, they sometimes push them away. I was desperate to prove to you that I was an extraordinary man. The protection of you and our people was my highest ambition. My fear of giving up my old ways that I thought worked in the past resulted in unabashed bravery.

"On the morning Prudence was born, I left for Seedonia to meet with your father. Shortly after leaving the castle, I accidentally rode into the Field of Wisdom. My instinct was to get out quickly, but it was too late. The Field of Wisdom captured me in its dazzling light. I saw the person I could be. I saw a life in which I was happy, free, loving, clever, productive, talented, and joyous. It was the most wondrous experience. I rode off feeling as if I could take on the world.

"When I realized I had forgotten the list of goods I needed to collect on my trip to Seedonia, I rode back to Idlebury. I was shocked to see the decay of our kingdom and the crumbling walls of our castle. I saw our people idling about. For the first time, their misery deeply saddened me. I was appalled to discover many of them had lost all desire for life. I was now fully aware our people had become lazy and hopeless. Yes, I saw the physical decay of our kingdom. But worse, I saw the decay of human spirit. I realized I had lost my soul along with the souls of our people. And I realized I was not a king. I was merely a servant to people who have no hopes, no ambitions, and no visions of a better life. And being their servant was doing them more harm than good. In that moment, I knew I could no longer be a part of the disempowerment of my people under the guise of compassion. But I did not know what to do or how to change.

"So I prayed for my soul. I consulted with other kings and found they, too, were lost. They were pained about their sometimes reprehensible behaviors toward their loved ones, particularly their wives. In our hearts, we knew women are powerful, dynamic, and capable of achieving anything they wanted. But our denial of this caused us to put aside our emotional lives and lose our souls.

"We begged the Soul Seeker to heal our souls, but he did not want to take on so many kings at once. So we pleaded relentlessly until he consented. While in his care, we watched what our queens would do without us. We discovered our wives could do the work without us, but their hearts were broken. They longed for us, not for the things we did for them, but for companionship, understanding, affection, and partnership. Over time, our souls' sorrow drained the Soul Seeker's energy. So he sought an energetic pure soul."

"Thane," the Queen whispered, shaking her head in acknowledgment.

"Yes, he took Thane," the king said with a smile. "That boy was almost more than the Soul Seeker could handle. But thanks to Thane's innocence, purity, determination, and love, we were restored. That is the positive side. The Soul Seeker is after Gwendolyn. For as pure as Thane's soul is, Gwendolyn's soul is the most coveted of all. He does not intend to harm her. He merely wants to preserve her soul forever, just as he has preserved the souls of other great beings."

"Has she no say in the destiny of her own soul?" the queen asked with concern.

"Of course, she does. It will be her life's quest to hold the Soul Seeker at bay until she is ready to offer him her soul."

"And if she does not?"

"Then he will chase her soul until the end of time."

"Oh, my," the queen said as she took a deep breath and exhaled. "It appears Gwendolyn is destined for greatness. I wonder what the future will bring for Thane and Prudence."

"Their stories are yet to be written, for they are much too young. Now we must go. Gwendolyn is nearly ready. I cannot wait to meet our daughter."

"Yes, our daughter," Queen Filanthropi said with quickly fading joy, as she remembered the Fannys' presence at the Royal Assembly and the task she'd assigned to the Knight in Shining Armor.

For the first time, she hoped the Fannys' love for Gwen was

false. For if their love was genuine, Gwen would return with them to Idleburg, Pennsylvania.

"What is wrong, my love?" King Heroian said, noticing the queen's pallor.

"Nothing, I could not be better. Now go. Get ready. I will call the Royal Assembly to session," the queen said as she walked to the door. The king cupped her face in his hands and gently kissed her on the lips. He then opened the door to discover Morgana weeping.

"Morgana, what is the matter?" the queen asked as she helped the servant woman into her chamber and sat her on a chair.

"Gwendolyn's gown and shoes are gone. Der gone," Morgana cried.

"No, they're not. I saw them walking down the staircase," Thane chimed in. "They were headed to the Wall of Passages."

"Thane, how did you get in this room?" the queen admonished the child.

"I willed myself here," Thane replied with enthusiasm.

"I told you he was a handful," King Heroian said.

"If the Soul Seeker could not handle him, I do not know what we are going to do," the queen said to the king.

When she turned to look at the child, she discovered he had vanished, leaving behind a scattering of glistening fairy dust.

King Heroian chuckled as he left the queen's chambers.

The queen pulled the cord to summon Oof, who, of course, instantly appeared.

"Your Majesty. How may I be of service?" Oof asked.

"Tell William the Brave that at exactly 11:06 a.m., he is to blow the royal horn and start the procession of carriages. King

Heroian and I shall sit on our thrones at exactly 11:08 a.m. We will begin receiving guests at exactly 11:11 a.m. and eleven seconds. I strongly suspect Gwendolyn will arrive at the stroke of noon. Therefore, all guests are to be announced and seated before that time. It is imperative that my parents, the King and Queen of Seedonia, are announced first. Gwendolyn's parents, Evaline and Arston Fanny, who will be escorted by the Knight in Shining Armor, will be announced second. I know this break with protocol could be scandalous, but so be it. Afterward, continue with the traditional announcement of the remaining guests."

"Yes, ma'am. What about Queen Matilda of Beastonia?" Oof asked without emotion.

"What is your concern, my dear man?"

"Considering there are no such things as dragons, I am not sure of the type of reception she will receive," Oof said in a haughty manner.

"Not to worry. I will handle it if need be," the queen said.

"There is one more thing, ma'am."

"Do tell."

"The king and queen who are feared and despised throughout the universe are the last to be announced."

"Oh, for joy," Queen Filanthropi said with obvious delight, knowing exactly to whom Oof referred. "This will indeed be the most glorious day."

Oof watched the queen lift her gown and run to the window. "Go on, man. You have work to do," she said as she waved for Oof to leave while she eyed the long line of carriages. "It is a glorious day. A glorious day, indeed."

Chapter Thirty-Seven
The Royal Assembly

A LONG THE DIRT road that led to Idlebury Castle, hundreds of carriages of all makes and marvels awaited the official horn to announce the commencement of the day's festivities. Unfortunately, the extremely long line forced a few guests to wait in the charred, filthy, smelly Slothful Forest.

Some of the carriages were wooden with intricate carvings. Some were gilded and bore gemmed royal seals. Others were large enough to carry a horde of people. And a few were cozy for just two. But one carriage, which transported the King and Queen of Imaginoria, was invisible.

The carriage at the head of the line belonged to Queen Filanthropi's parents, King Harvestor and Queen Plantiana of Seedonia.

Lord and Lady Flatbottom from Reclineshire appeared to be the most comfortable in their plush, posh pram complete with reclining seats.

The carriage carrying King Phlurtateous and Queen Sentuoss of Loverpool—adorned with red hearts on its white enameled cab and pulled by a dozen cherubs, each holding a red rose—rocked back and forth as the unmistakable giggle of

Queen Sentuoss filled the air.

King Kokoa from Chocolatonia roamed from carriage to carriage, offering everyone a sample of his fine chocolates.

Queen Imelda of Cobblerstonia and Queen Garbini of Dresstoria chatted and exchanged a hug upon discovering Princess Gwendolyn would be dressed in their finery.

Queen Merry of Hedonia lamented to Queen Nunnora of Abbeyville about the absence of King Funzy. Queen Nunnora asked Queen Merry how King Funzy could've vanished when he was standing right next to her at the time of his disappearance.

Out of sight in the Slothful Forest at the rear of the line, a black hearse-shaped carriage, emblazoned with a skull and crossbones and pulled by a team of the living dead, harbored King Morrebidd and Queen DeMysora of Deadonia.

But just in front of the King and Queen of the Dead was the most massive carriage of all, for it was carrying Queen Matilda of Beastonia.

It appeared everyone—especially those representing Foolsville—was having a good time, with the exception of Queen Pittipotti and King Grimly of Anhedonia, who pointed their long index fingers out of their carriage window as they whined and blamed Queen Filanthropi for the wait.

Suddenly, the Soul Seeker was spotted approaching from Idlebury Castle. Soon complete darkness blocked out the sky and snuffed out the excitement of the guests. One by one, flashes of light brightened the area as the missing kings were deposited in their appropriate carriages.

King Funzy jumped out of his carriage, kissed Queen Merry, and requested from this moment forth, a good time be had by all. The crowd cheered, with the exception of Queen Pittipotti and King Grimly, of course.

"It's eleven o'clock. When are they getting this show on the road?" Queen Pittipotti complained. "We've been here for nearly five hours."

"Yes, we most certainly have, my dear. Most unacceptable," King Grimly responded as he jotted down the details of the couple's every painful moment in his *Journal of Grumbles and Grievances.*

As the new arrivals enjoyed warm welcomes from their queens and attempted to explain their disappearance, the royal horn sounded.

"Finally," Queen Pittipotti exclaimed. "I wonder why the Soul Seeker didn't take you Grimly, my dear."

King Grimly shrugged his shoulders as the carriage lurched forward and began its final approach to Idlebury Castle.

Back in the Slothful Forest, things were a bit quieter. No one dared to get out of their carriage for fear the stories about the disgusting forest were true. So no one noticed a pair of eyes peering out of a large bush. If they had and cared to investigate who or what was hiding there, they would have found the giant sloth staring at Queen Matilda's carriage, wondering why he was not invited to the Royal Assembly. "I don't understand it," the giant sloth lamented. "Why does she get to go and I don't?"

King Morrebidd slithered out of his carriage and sneaked over to the carriage bearing the royal seal of Beastonia. He looked around to make sure he'd gone unnoticed before he jumped inside to surprise Queen Matilda.

"Morrebidd, my dear friend, you nearly scared me to death."

"They don't call me the King of the Dead for nothing," King

Morrebidd said as he and Queen Matilda exchanged hugs.

"Does Filanthropi know you're here?" Queen Matilda asked.

"I'm not sure, but she will soon."

"Don't you find it amusing that we're at the back of the line?" the dragon queen queried.

"We are the two things people fear most—death and dragons," the King of the Dead declared with a snicker.

"Don't forget responsibility, accountability, and success," Queen Matilda replied snidely.

"Well, by day's end, they'll no longer fear death or dragons."

"Yeah, we'll show them."

"By the way, where's Anima?"

"Now Morrebidd, that's cruel. You know he's dead," Queen Matilda said with a sudden change of mood, remembering her conversation with the Soul Seeker about her husband's death.

"I know he's not, or he'd be in my kingdom now, wouldn't he?"

Suddenly, Queen Matilda's carriage rolled forward.

"Got to go. Ta," said King Morrebidd as he hurried back to his carriage.

Once inside his morose carriage, he nuzzled up to Queen DeMysora and whispered, "She doesn't know."

"About what?"

"Anima."

"Then I guess she is in for a surprise." Queen DeMysora giggled as she kissed her husband on the forehead.

The thunder of the rolling carriages awoke the Idleburians, who, despite the late hour, were still asleep. Many rushed to their windows and front doors to see what was happening.

Gwilym, the Minister of Mindfulness, yawned and scratched his head as he stumbled to his bedroom window to see what the commotion was about. His eyes nearly popped out of his head upon seeing the first carriage, bearing Queen Filanthropi's parents, cross the drawbridge.

"We've overslept. It's startin,'" Gwilym shouted. He shook his sleeping wife, Boreena. "*Hurry,*" he shrieked. "It's started. The Royal Assembly has started."

Gwilym and his wife grabbed the clothes they'd so carefully laid out the night before and rushed to get dressed.

"Der's no time. Come on," Gwilym yelled as he yanked his wife out of the bedroom, through the house, and then out the front door.

The other Idleburians watched as the Minister of Mindfulness and his wife darted toward Idlebury Castle while they desperately tried to finish dressing.

"I think his original title was more fittin,' don't ya dear?" said a woman standing on her front porch with her husband and kids.

"Yes, Minister of Mindlessness is certainly more fittin' fer Gwilym Innaine," the man said as he went back inside to catch up on his lost sleep.

But Fergus, Liridona, and Aden, already dressed in their finest clothes, walked with pride toward the castle.

Soon other Idleburians, dressed in their finest yet tattered clothes, headed to the castle as well.

⋙◈◈◈⋘

King Heroian and Queen Filanthropi sat in silence while they waited for the announcement of their guests. Syvil Gossep sat discreetly in a corner of the room while she spoke into her handheld tape recorder. Hordes of photographers and film crews were placed strategically throughout the room. The queen noted that even Mike Muckraker was behaving appropriately.

At precisely 11:11 a.m. and eleven seconds, the door to the Great Hall opened. The herald blew his horn after which he announced the first guests.

"King Harvestor and Queen Plantiana of Seedonia in Dimension IV," he said as Queen Filanthropi's parents entered amidst the flash of lights from the paparazzi's high-powered cameras.

The Knight in Shining Armor and Gwen's parents were next.

"Mr. and Mrs. Arston Fanny of Idleburg, Pennsylvania in Dimension X, planet Earth; escorted by the Knight in Shining Armor."

The queen examined the knight's behavior, searching for an indication as to his decision regarding Gwen's parents' love for their child. The knight faced the queen, bowed, and then handed a single red rose to Evaline Fanny. Mixed emotions flooded the queen—happiness, jealousy, and sadness. She was happy the Fannys genuinely loved Gwen, but she wanted her too. After all, Gwen was her flesh and blood, not theirs. The Fannys' love meant the child would return home with them and not remain in Idlebury.

Lost in a world of emotion, Queen Filanthropi was completely unaware of the announcement of the other guests. King Heroian glanced at the clock and noticed it was nearly noon. He put his hand on the queen's hand and motioned with his head for her to note the time. Queen Filanthropi's heart skipped with excitement. Only five minutes remained until Gwen's expected arrival.

When the herald stopped, everyone looked toward the door to see what had suddenly halted his announcements. What they saw was a massive green creature blocking the entrance.

Queen Filanthropi screamed, *"Matilda!"* as she broke with protocol and ran to the door. The herald jumped out of the way, barely escaping a collision with the frenzied queen. In a voice that expressed complete and utter joy, Queen Filanthropi turned to her already seated guests and said, "Queen Matilda of Beastonia."

Queen Matilda bent down, pushed her head through the door, and with great effort, squeezed herself into the room.

Cameras flashed. Film crews fought their way for a closer shot of the great beast. Mike Muckraker excitedly reported the arrival of the dragon queen. A few guests gasped, but what was most surprising was the roomful of royals stood and clapped for the Queen of the Innocents.

"Thank you. I'm completely overwhelmed with your warm reception," the Queen of Beastonia said as her eyes filled with tears. But she dare not shed a single one for fear of destroying everything and everyone in the room. "Now, my dear, dear friend Filanthropi, Queen of Idlebury, I have another surprise for you." The dragon queen stepped away from the door and said, "King Morrebidd and Queen DeMysora of Deadonia."

The room became deathly quiet. Despite the thrill of seeing King Morrebidd, her childhood friend, Queen Filanthropi remained still and silent. After a few moments, she said, "Do you hear that?"

"Hear what?" Queen Matilda queried.

"That," Queen Filanthropi said as the wall at the rear of the room blasted open.

A cloud of sparkling dust followed the roar of escaping air. The Dimension Clock chimed and played the most beautiful music. After the dust cleared, Gwen appeared—disheveled, dirty, and still dressed in her own clothes. She marveled at the magnitude of the crowd. When she saw her parents, waving and blowing kisses, she was overcome with happiness.

Suddenly, the Wall of Passages spoke. "Let it be known that no one in the history of the universe has ventured through my passages and emerged through this exit. This means this child has achieved at an unprecedented level—one never attempted by another living creature. Therefore, this child has earned the most prestigious title in all creation. I am proud to present to you"—the Wall of Passages took a deep breath—"Gwendolyn the Great, Savior of Idlebury, Protector of the Universe."

Everyone cheered.

Music played.

Evaline and Arston Fanny hugged each other and wept with pride at their daughter's success.

Queen Filanthropi and King Heroian joined Gwen, who, still dazed, didn't hear the Wall of Passages' proclamation as to her greatness.

"I am so happy to meet you, my child," King Heroian said as he kissed Gwen on the top of her head.

"Wait," Gwen shouted, apparently ignoring the king as she scanned the room for her friends. "Something's not right. Not everyone's here. Queen Matilda, where's Mistofisee? Where are the Beastonians?"

"I don't know," the dragon queen said with sadness. "I think Mistofisee went off in search of his father."

"King Heroian and Queen Filanthropi, where are your people?"

"They have obviously chosen not to come," Queen Filanthropi muttered.

"Then we'll wait," Gwen said.

Queen Pittipotti jumped up and yelled, *"Wait?* We've put up with your self-centeredness long enough." She glanced at her husband and in a low voice said, "Don't you agree, Grimly, my dear?" King Grimly shook his head in agreement and wrote in his journal.

"But they're coming. I know it."

The words were barely out of Gwen's mouth when the Idleburians marched into the Great Hall chanting, "Der are such thin's as dragons. Dragons we do see. And now we take fer ourselves respon-si-bil-ity."

Gwen's eyes twinkled with delight. As if on cue, Mistofisee entered the castle followed by a parade of Beastonians—Crabbina, Lightening, Mr. Knutthyder, Ms. Aul, Ms. Elliefant, Ms. Eegal, Mr. Fluphinekel, and all the others, including the former self-proclaimed King of Beastonia.

As the room filled to capacity, Mistofisee asked, "Do we have room for just one more?"

"I certainly hope so," King Anima said as he squeezed through the door and joined his wife.

This time, Queen Matilda couldn't control her tears. As she desperately tried to keep them from dripping on the floor and ruining the magnificent event, King Anima said, "Don't worry dear. Tears of joy never hurt anyone. Look what they did for me. They brought me back to life."

"Quiet!" King Heroian shouted. "I do believe it is time to begin. Morgana, please escort Thane and Prudence into the room."

Thane, looking handsome and mature in his extravagant prince's uniform, ran into the room, and took his place next to his father. Fairy dust glimmered in his path. Enthusiasm lit his face. Fredia entered holding Prudence and positioned herself next to the king as well.

"My dear guests, Beastonians, and of course, my beloved Idleburians. I now have the honor of introducing you to our children," the king proudly announced.

"Children?" someone asked.

"Yes, our children," the King of Idlebury said as he took Gwen's hand. "This is Gwendolyn Fanny. She is the child Queen Filanthropi and I placed for adoption due to circumstances beyond our control. Her parents, Evaline and Arston Fanny from Idleburg, Pennsylvania, Dimension X, Planet Earth, are here with us today to share in this momentous event. This beautiful boy is Prince Thane," the king continued as he placed a hand on the Thane's shoulder. "Some of you may recognize him. He is the son we thought we'd lost at birth. We are thrilled he has been returned to us." The king turned to Fredia and gently stroked Prudence's arm. "And this adorable baby is also our child, Princess Prudence." Fredia handed the child to Queen Filanthropi. A servant, holding a pillow on which the princess's crown nestled, moved next to the king.

"Did he say Princess Prudence?" King Funzy asked Queen Merry.

"I thought we were here for the investiture of Princess Gwendolyn," Queen Imelda whispered to Queen Garbini.

"Today is the day for which we have waited with much anticipation. For on this day, I crown Prudence, Princess of Idlebury," King Heroian said as he placed the crown on the baby's head.

"I thought I was the princess," Gwen interrupted. "Daddy, tell them I'm the Princess of Idlebury. I know I am," she said, pleading with her father, Arston Fanny.

"No, my child," King Heroian said with genuine

331

compassion. "Prudence is the rightful Princess of Idlebury. You, on the other hand, are much more than just a princess. By passing the most grueling test of personal fortitude, you have proven you will go on to greatness unsurpassed by any living being. You, my child…" The king paused as he withdrew an ornate gold sword crafted with magnificent etchings and enhanced with sparkling gems. He knelt before Gwen, gently tapped his sword on each of her shoulders, and declared, "You are Gwendolyn the Great, Savior of Idlebury, Protector of the Universe."

Immediately, the magnificent gown and shoes provided by Queen Garbini and Queen Imelda materialized on the child. Gwen looked radiant. She couldn't believe the feelings coursing through her.

With an air of sophistication, she addressed King Heroian and Queen Filanthropi. "I'm proud to know you're my biological mother and father. I'm thankful for my new family, including my brother, Prince Thane, and my sister, Princess Prudence. I'm honored to have been befriended by Mistofisee and all of the Innocents of Beastonia. I'm extraordinarily grateful for the lessons I've learned from Lightening and the Field of Wisdom. I'm forever indebted to Queen Matilda and the Soul Seeker for the protection they provided to ensure my safe arrival in Idlebury. But I must make one thing *absolutely* clear. My heart *always* has been, and *always* will be, with my *real* parents…" Gwen paused.

Queen Filanthropi crossed her hands over her heart as if to prepare herself for a joyous moment.

"Evaline and Arston Fanny," Gwen said, and then rushed to join her parents.

The Fanny family hugged.

The queen held back tears of disappointment.

Music played.

All was well until Fergus stopped the celebrations.

"What about us?" he asked. "I believe Queen Filanthropi promised us somethin' taday."

"Thank you for reminding me, Fergus," King Heroian said. He took a deep breath and in the most kingly of voices pronounced, "Let it be written that on this day, you, the people of Idlebury, are granted the freedom to create your own lives, live your dreams, and develop your talents. You are free to experience integrity and self-respect. Further, you are free to reap the financial rewards of your labors. And you are free to walk into the Field of Wisdom and experience the ecstasy of discovering yourselves in all your glory. I now declare the kingdom of Idlebury no longer idle. From this day forth, every twenty-third day of June will be a day of celebration known as Rebirth Day."

To King Heroian's and Queen Filanthropi's disappointment, the Idleburians remained silent.

Fergus broke the silence. "Exactly how are we ta be emancipated when we have no means by which ta earn a livin'?" he asked.

"I don't know," the king responded.

"Hot air. The king is nothin' more dan hot air," another Idleburian shouted.

"Wait," Gwen demanded as she pulled her magic coin box from a hidden pocket in her dress. Queen Garbini winked at the child, indicating she knew about the coin box. Gwen opened the box to reveal an empty coin slot. The Idleburians moaned with disappointment.

"Figures. She's Gwendolyn da Great, Savior of Idlebury, and she can't save nothin,' not even a stupid penny," a young woman declared, inciting jeers from her fellow Idleburians.

Gwen smiled mischievously as she raised the magic coin box in the air. She rapidly closed it. When she yanked it open, a shiny new coin that depicted the new royal seal of Idlebury—a man and woman working in a field—flew into the air and landed in the palm of Fergus's right hand.

Immediately, the room burst into brilliant color. Every Idleburian was now dressed in brand-new clothes. Some rushed outside to see Idlebury Castle restored to its original grandeur. Flowers, in full bloom, refreshed the usually foul air. Even the skeptical Idleburians, who'd remained in their homes, were transformed.

In the Great Hall, celebrations broke out again. But the merriment was short-lived as the room went black, signaling the arrival of none other than the Soul Seeker. Royals and commoners alike ran for cover. To everyone's horror, the Soul Seeker grabbed Gwen and flew off.

King Heroian and Queen Filanthropi were miffed at the arrogance of the Soul Seeker. Plus, they feared for the well-being of their child.

Queen Filanthropi smiled, turned to King Heroian, and said, "I dare say, it is Wilameena. Even the Soul Seeker would not have the audacity to ruin such a spectacular day."

King Heroian shook his head in disgust and said, "I do believe Wilameena will be more of a challenge for Gwendolyn than the Soul Seeker could ever be."

Queen Filanthropi looked at Queen Matilda and the two friends laughed wholeheartedly.

The celebrations continued into the wee hours of the morning.

CHAPTER THIRTY-EIGHT
WISH FULFILLMENT

G WEN PEERED OUT the kitchen bay window lost in a daydream.

Evaline sat at the kitchen table dressed in the robe presented to her in Restoria, but the words on the back now read PROUD PARENT OF GWENDOLYN THE GREAT, SAVIOR OF IDLEBURY, PROTECTOR OF THE UNIVERSE.

Arston, dressed in a matching robe, busily prepared a fancy breakfast to celebrate Gwen's return home from her first mission to protect the universe.

"Here, my princess, have some breakfast. You must be tired after your episode with the Soul Seeker," Arston said as he put a plate of food on the table at Gwen's usual place.

"I told you, Daddy, it was Wilameena, not the Soul Seeker. Besides, the Soul Seeker can't take my soul unless I want him to. So I guess I'll be tangling with him and Wilameena for a long time," Gwen said as she pulled out the kitchen chair and sat to eat.

"I guess so, my dear. I guess so," Evaline said as she sipped tea and picked up the latest edition of *Universal Scandals* magazine. "I do so love the articles by Syvil Gossep," she said as she flipped through the magazine's pages.

Suddenly, fairy dust swept through the room. Thane, looking much older, appeared in the Fannys' kitchen.

"Thane? Is that you?" Gwen asked.

"Yes, it's me."

"You look nearly as old as me."

"That's because I am. Time isn't the same in Dimension X. You age much more slowly. I'm nearly eleven now," Thane said, obviously not thrilled with what he perceived to be idle chitchat. "I'm here to take you back to Idlebury. You must return at once. Everything's out of control. Some of the people have fallen back into their bad habits. Father has disappeared again. Mother is distraught. And Prudence has become a total brat."

"Why do I have to go back?" Gwen asked, perturbed to be made responsible for problems that to her obviously belonged to the king and queen.

"Because you're the Savior of Idlebury, remember? Let's go," Thane said as he grabbed Gwen's hand, and they both disappeared in a cloud of fairy dust.

Arston smiled at his wife and kissed her on the forehead as he leaned over to pick up the book he had started reading several days ago. He returned to the kitchen table and took a few bites of food from Gwen's plate as he muttered, "Be careful what you wish for."

"Because it might come true," Evaline said without looking up from her magazine.

Arston chuckled and wondered what adventures his daughter would embark on next. He looked over at the bay window, half hoping he would see her there daydreaming and dressed in her princess wannabe outfit. Part of him wished she was still just his little girl and not Gwendolyn the Great, Savior of Idlebury, Protector of the Universe.

He looked out the window, sighed, and then began to read a book titled, *Idlebury: The True Story of the Kingdom of Hope*, by Syvil Gossep.

About the Author

JM Hughson grew up in the Washington, D.C. area where her lifelong love of reading and writing began early. She wrote her first story, *The Whimsical Lion,* at the age of eight. As a child, her favorite book was *Jane Eyre* by Charlotte Bronte. She credits her mother's passion for reading and weekly trips to the library as a child for her love of books. She had a successful career as an advertising copywriter/creative director followed by a career as a mental health therapist. She hopes her readers have as much fun reading her books as she had writing them.